Sizzling NIGHTS

USA TODAY BESTSELLING AUTHOR
PJ FIALA

To the lovely women of my reader group, PJ Fiala's Road Queens, who help me out with names of characters, places, and businesses, thank you. I appreciate and adore you.

Characters
The Road Queens who named Characters:

Amy Burkhart - *Devin Karason - Marco's brother*

Lyne Carroll - *Perry Henry - Attorney in Blossom Springs*

Angela M Carter - *Effie Karason - Marco's sister*

Angela M Carter - *Blossom Springs Tribune - Newspaper in Blossom Springs*

Karen Cranford LeBeau - *Keely Benson - Wife of Celtics member who helped Theresa*

Karen Cranford LeBeau - *Gavin - Server at the Sandbar*

Gene Fiala - *Celtics Crime Syndicate*

Linda Gurath - *The Daily Reporter - Newspaper in Maine*

Belinda Jackson Hercule - *Carolyn Sutton - Theresa's Editor*

Belinda Jackson Hercule - *Wesley Charles - Owns the cabin*

Carol Jones Karason - *Marco Karason - Hero*

Jodi Krill - *Gabby - Mitch's employee*

Jodi Krill - *Devin Krill - Counselor*

Terra Oenning - *Bradford Bennett LLC - Future Business*

Nicky Ortiz - *Paradise Gardens - Event Venue in Blossom Springs*

Denise Scott - *Kelsey - Waitress at the Sandbar*
Michelle Terry - *Torin Terry - Chairman of the Benefit for Childhood Leukemia*
Monique Mousseau Westwood - *Brock Karason - Marco's older brother*

To my family, my greatest blessing and unwavering support system. Your love, encouragement, and sacrifices have made this dream possible.
And to my husband and best friend, Gene—thank you for standing beside me every step of the way. Your belief in me, your patience, and your love are the foundation of everything I do. Words will never be enough to express how much you mean to me, but I will spend my life showing you.

***

To our veterans and all those currently serving in the armed forces, police, fire departments, and as EMTs—your courage, dedication, and sacrifices do not go unnoticed. Thank you for your unwavering commitment to protecting and serving. It is with heartfelt gratitude and deep respect that I honor you here. You are the true heroes, and your contributions inspire every word on these pages.

Map of
Blossom Springs
Drawn by PJ Fiala

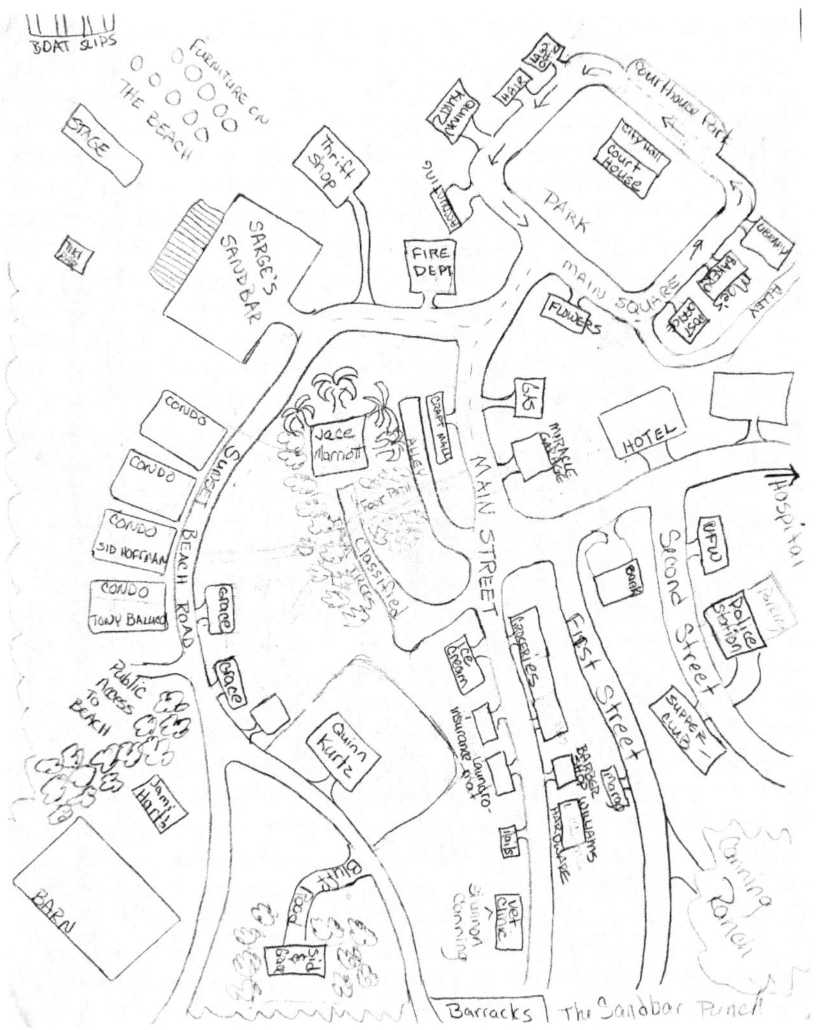

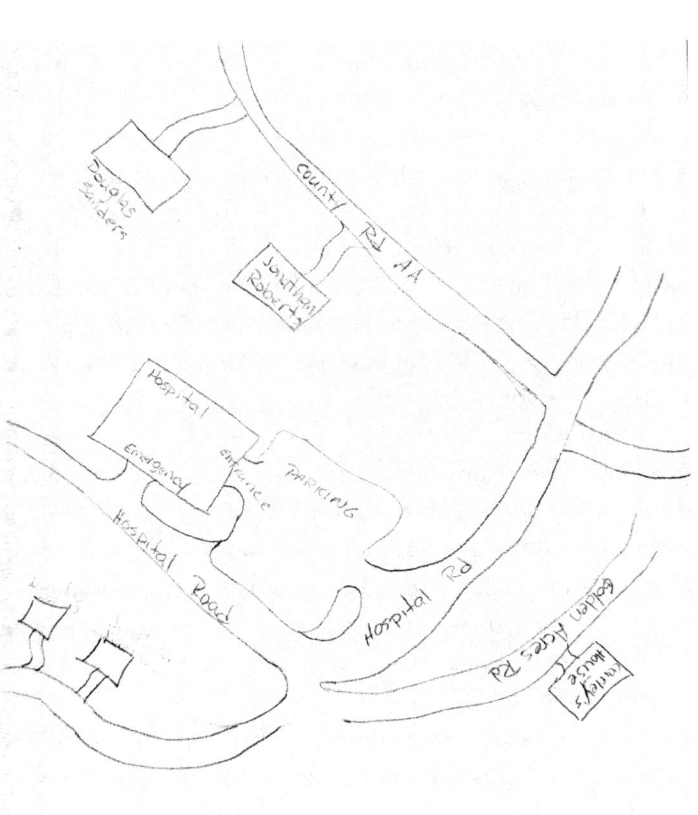

County Rd AA
Douglas Sanders
Jonathan Roberts
Hospital
Emergency
entrance
PARKING
Hospital Road
Hospital Rd
Golden Acres Rd
Family's House

DESCRIPTION

Love may be the only thing strong enough to save them from the flames of the past.

When danger ignites, only love can douse the flames.

Former Navy SEAL Marco Karason has traded the battlefield for the kitchen, seeking solace as the head chef at Sarge's Sandbar in the quiet town of Blossom Springs. But peace is fleeting when his protective instincts are triggered by Theresa Miklovic, the fiery server with a past as mysterious as her captivating smile.

Theresa isn't just rebuilding her life; she's hiding from it. A former investigative journalist, she exposed a dangerous criminal syndicate, only to become their next target. Strange events including threatening notes, vandalism, and suspicious shadows, prove her enemies haven't forgotten her. Now, she must trust the one man who seems capable of protecting her, even as their undeniable chemistry threatens to complicate everything.

As danger closes in, and danger threatens to destroy the restaurant and possibly their lives, Marco is forced to step out of the kitchen and back into combat mode. Together, he and Theresa must uncover the truth, outsmart their enemies, and confront the sparks that fly between them.

Can they extinguish the danger before it consumes them both?

Sizzling Nights is a steamy, small-town romantic suspense that blends passion, danger, and redemption. USA

Today bestselling author PJ Fiala delivers a heart-pounding story of love that burns as bright as the flames threatening to destroy it all.

1

M arco stepped from the shower, toweled off, and dressed. He swiped a brush through his hair, trying to ignore the grays that seemed to reach for the light and shine bright. His hair was getting long again. He often let it grow longer than he should between cuts. When he'd been a SEAL, he had to keep his hair short, so this was his rebellion now. He didn't have to do shit with his hair. But he did. He kept it neat, clean, and in some sort of style. But he didn't have to. That was the bonus.

He stepped from his bathroom into the bedroom of his new home. The condo he'd purchased in the Barrack's Condominiums. The old Army barracks had been abandoned years ago, and Quinn, a local contractor, had a vision. It was a good vision. Marco loved his place here. The decorating was simple but somewhat elegant and clean. His condo was on the second floor, and he had a perfect view looking down Main Street of Blossom Springs. It was what drew him to this condo. He loved this spectacular view. Now that it was December, the local businesses were beginning to decorate for Christmas, which was exciting. It reminded him of home. Small town. Charming. Quaint. His hometown in Wisconsin was cold. Here it was warm 11 months out of the year. He especially loved that. Plus, his siblings were spread out over the US. His older brother, Brock, was in Colorado. His younger brother, Devon, was in Houston. His sister, Effie, the youngest of their family, lived in West Virginia. Their parents were gone. So, for him, home was anywhere he wanted it to be, and that was here in Blossom Springs.

Dressing for work, he donned a white t-shirt and a pair of black cargo pants. He slipped on his comfortable tennis shoes and headed toward the door.

His drive was short, as he lived only a few blocks from the Sandbar, but he grinned most of the way. As he passed the grocery store, he noted the large ornament that surrounded the front entrance requiring customers to walk under it to enter the store. It was nice. He made a note to himself to remember to look at it when he came home tonight to see if it was lit up.

He parked alongside the Sandbar, near the pantry door for employees, and whistled as he entered the building. As he rounded the corner the first person he saw was Theresa Miklovic, the hot-as-heck waitress and front-end manager. She wore black shorts that showed off her gorgeous legs and a white tank top that showed off her...other assets wonderfully. She donned the little black apron around her waist and wore black high-top tennis shoes which only Theresa could pull off. The entire outfit made him lay awake at night thinking about her assets. All of them.

"Hey, Marco. How's it going?"

How's it going? Trying to sound casual as shit "Good. How's it going with you?"

She grinned and cocked her hip to the right. "It's all good, I guess. Expecting a large crowd tonight."

He liked her silhouette with her hip cocked. She looked sassy and ready to take on the world. "That's a fact. The Christmas parties are beginning."

"Wait till you see what Margo did with the decorations. It's beautiful."

He nodded slightly but looked into Theresa's dark brown eyes. She was a beautiful woman. And she had an air about her that called to him. She was confident and sure of herself. But she also seemed as though she was hiding something. Maybe that's what intrigued him about her. "She's very good at all that."

"Yeah." Theresa pulled a new container of salt from the shelf in the pantry. He stared at her body as she stretched up, the swell of her breast from the side slid smoothly into her thin torso. The curvy lines were perfect and if he were an artist he'd beg to paint her. She turned, and their eyes met. She smiled sweetly, then sauntered out without another word.

He swallowed to remove the dryness from his throat, then inhaled deeply before moving himself forward into the kitchen.

Pulling his white jacket on, he stepped to the stove and lit the gas burners. As they warmed, he turned to the stainless-steel table behind him and inventoried the stacks of vegetables being peeled and cut up by the staff.

"Everyone ready for tonight?"

"Yes, Chef."

"Good. It's going to be busy. We're beginning the season of Christmas parties and merriment. Let's do our best to leave everyone excited about the meals they eat here."

"Yes, Chef."

He made eye contact with each of his three workers, then grinned. He turned and pulled his first fry pan toward him and drizzled oil in the pan before stacking cut carrot pennies into the pan. He set the pan on the stove and began pulling his spices and utensils out. This was exciting. This beginning where everything was fresh and clean and none of his staff had the dark circles under their eyes from working a hard day in a hot kitchen. That would come later.

The chart that hung near the stove with the foods listed he'd need for tonight caught his attention, and he glanced at it once more. He'd carefully perused it all week, ensuring he wasn't forgetting anything. He didn't. He was good at this. This was his arena now and he excelled in it. It's what kept his PTSD at bay. Enjoying the activity of making delicious meals for customers and the praise he always received from Jace, Margo, and the staff as they tried his food. Yeah, this was where he felt alive. His blood sizzled through his veins as the aromas of the cooking vegetables reached his nostrils. The staff chattered and communicated behind him. He listened partially to make sure communication was on point, but his mind was now on the delicious meals he'd prepare.

The first order came in as the waitress, Kelsey, slid it up on the order reel. "Order up." She called out before disappearing in a whoosh of black and white. Everyone here wore black slacks, shorts, skirts, and white tops. During the evening, shorts needed to be less casual and dressier. But, these servers worked hard, so shorts were still allowed, they just needed to be more like khakis, no denim. No one wore them like Theresa though.

He shook his head to get it back in the game. But almost as if she were summoned, Theresa entered the kitchen.

"Marco, we have a party of eighteen coming in at six-thirty. What do you need set up ahead of time?"

He turned his head and grinned at her. "Have them order as they enter and before they sit."

"Will do." She smiled before she stepped out of the kitchen.

He grinned and shook his head. She smiled at him. He continued dropping steaks on the grill and checking his orders. But this time he felt a little lighter.

A few minutes later, Marco pulled the steak off his grill and set it on the plate. He arranged it just the way he liked. He was particular about how he displayed his food. He hadn't made head chef by being sloppy.

He called out, "Vegetables."

"Yes, Chef," one of the kitchen workers yelled. They came over, grabbed the plate, and began adding the vegetables to it.

Marco turned back to his grill and inspected the next steak. He plated it, then called out, "Kelsey, order up."

"Got it, Marco," she called back.

He turned his head to see Theresa watching him from the doorway. He nodded and received a smile again. If he didn't know any better, he'd think she was beginning to warm to him. He liked her. She was smart, always on the ball, never a problem. She showed up on time and got the job done. She was what you'd call a dream employee. Yeah, he liked her. Plus, it didn't hurt that she was a looker.

He pulled the slip from the spring above him and glanced at the next order. Three more steaks and a lobster. He quickly grabbed the food from the cooler next to his grill, placed the steaks on the fire, and double-checked their doneness. Then he looked at the next order in line.

It was a good night.

He glanced over his left shoulder as Theresa sauntered into the kitchen to grab the plates. She caught his eye and grinned. Yeah, she liked him. He'd almost place money on it.

Marco kept cooking, calling out orders, not really barking, just clear and steady. Before he knew it, the end of the night was near.

As the kitchen staff cleaned up, Marco worked on his grill. He was particular about how it was cleaned, so he performed this task rather than leave it to someone else. From the corner of his eye, he watched Theresa hustling back and forth. She brought in condiments, refilled jars, and wiped everything down. She was meticulous. Always meticulous.

Her phone rang, and she reached into her apron. When she glanced at the screen, her brows furrowed. She tucked the phone back into her apron and took a deep breath. Marco found it curious, but he didn't know much about her life. A little, maybe. They talked some, but she was always secretive about the details. He wondered about that. She didn't wear a wedding ring. She never mentioned a man—or a woman—at home. She didn't talk about her life much at all. Come to think of it, he probably didn't share much about his own life either. He didn't want to bore anyone with his life's issues.

Her phone rang again. This time, Marco turned to watch as she pulled it out. Her lips tightened, and her shoulders straightened.

"You okay, Theresa?" he asked.

She looked startled and quickly tucked the phone back into her apron. She nodded. "Yeah, I'm okay."

"You don't look okay. Are you sure?"

"Yeah, it's okay. I'm okay."

He nodded, but he didn't believe her. He felt again that she was hiding something.

The kitchen cleared out, leaving just him and Theresa. Marco looked around and then walked to the end of the counter where she was filling ketchup bottles for the next day. He leaned against the table; arms crossed.

"Hey, if you need anything, you let me know, okay?" he said.

She tried to smile, but it didn't reach her eyes. It barely creased her lips. "Okay, I will."

She was lying again.

When she finished her task, Marco busied himself with his own work. He was planning to follow her out to her car to make sure she was okay. But following her home? That was probably off-limits.

Right?

Maybe he should follow her home. He'd do that.

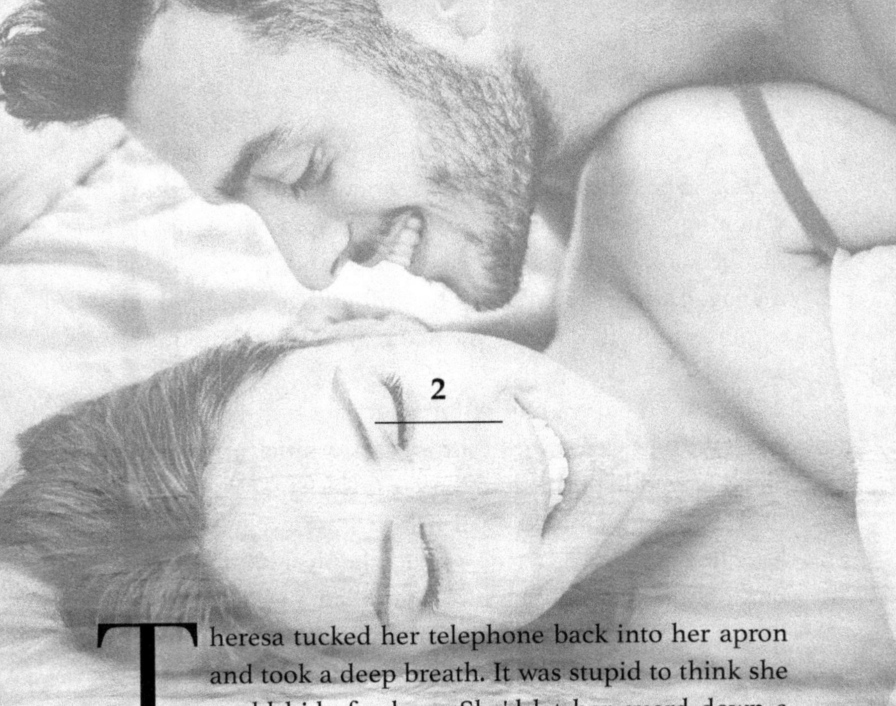

2

Theresa tucked her telephone back into her apron and took a deep breath. It was stupid to think she could hide for long. She'd let her guard down a little bit. She'd been here six months, and she felt pretty safe, but things were starting to fall in on her.

She looked up and saw Marco watching her. She tried to smile. She knew it didn't reach her eyes, but right now, she was trying to process it all. Was she scared? Fuck yeah, she was scared. Did she know how bad this was? Well, possibly. They'd threatened her. She should have made sure she had better protection before she released that exposé. Now it was out there, so it was too late. And now she was having to worry about protection on the fly.

Maybe she'd ask Jace for a couple of days off, kind of lay low. And she'd probably have to get a new phone since they seemed to have found her number. Fuck. Just when she thought things were going all right.

She picked up the tray of ketchup containers and put them into the walk-in cooler. As she stepped out, Marco stood leaning against the table, his arms crossed, which was a nice sight. He had beefy, big arms. He was built, and strong. She always knew that about him. She enjoyed watching him work at the stove. For a bigger man, he made his job look effortless. He was nimble and quick. He could manage thirty-six steaks on the grill and get them all done to perfection. It was like he had a weird sense about him with that.

But she'd enjoyed him from afar. And sadly, that's where it would have to stay. She brought too much trouble with her. She couldn't bring it to Marco. It wasn't fair to him.

Her phone chimed again. This time it signaled a text. Her fingers rubbed her brow, and she decided to ignore it. But it chimed again. She lifted her head and let out a deep breath and saw Marco watching her.

"Are you sure you're all right?" he asked her.

"Uh, yeah. Yeah, it's okay. It's just some shit at home."

"Anything that I can help with?"

He had a nice smile. His eyes were sincere. Beautiful brown eyes. His hair had a slight wave to it. She wondered if he knew how many women were jealous of that beautiful wavy hair he had. He probably didn't. Men seemed to effort-lessly get long eyelashes and beautiful hair. What the hell? Women paid thousands of dollars for stuff like that.

"Yeah, it's okay. It's okay. I'll be all right."

He came closer to her, and she held her breath. Up close, he was bigger, more imposing. Damn it, more attractive.

"You seem like you're trying to talk yourself into thinking that you're all right, not that you're actually all right. So, I'll just leave you with this. I'm here. I'm perfectly capable of helping you with anything that you need help with. All you need to do is let me in."

She took a deep breath and pressed her lips together. "Thank you, Marco. I'll let you know if I need anything. This is just a... well, I don't know what it is right now, so I guess there's really no need in us getting worked up over it."

"Okay, just letting you know. I'm here."

"Thank you."

She skirted around him and went out to the restaurant area. She had already pulled the mustard containers off the tables. She had put them on a tray. She picked up the tray and carried it into the kitchen. The condiment station was directly behind where Marco cooked, and she began refilling the mustard bottles and wiping them all down. They'd be all fresh and clean tomorrow. She liked starting out the day with everything fresh and clean, not having to clean up from last night's mess. Plus, Jace and Margo insisted everything be cleaned up at the end of the day.

She could hear Marco behind her. He always did an inventory at night before he left what was in the cooler and what he'd need for the next day. He looked over his menu and wrote Jace a note with needed food items.

Jace walked in. "There you two are. Glad I caught you before you left. Great job tonight. Great job. Everybody raved about the food, Marco. Once again, as always, you've knocked it out of the park. Margo and I are thrilled to have you here on board with us."

Margo entered the kitchen just as Jace had mentioned her name. She grinned. She simply nodded at Marco and smiled.

Margo turned her head and smiled at Theresa. "Theresa, great job. You managed to get those tables turned quickly. The way you handled the staff is amazing. We completely appreciate everything that you do. Thank you so much. It looks like you've got Kelsey all up to speed. She was doing a good job tonight. Thank you for training her. We appreciate you two very much."

Theresa smiled. "Thank you. I appreciate knowing that. I thought tonight went really well. And Kelsey's doing a great job. Ashley and Krystal are doing well also. And Kacen's coming along too. So, I think we've got a good staff here. Are you still looking for one more?"

Jace nodded. "Yeah. Margo's got some interviews tomorrow, don't you, hon?"

"I do. And I think a couple of them are promising, so we should have some help for the season. Unfortunately, it's a busy time to train someone, but I guess there's nothing like a baptism by fire, right?"

Theresa chuckled. "That's right. Baptism by fire. I love that."

Jace put his arm around Margo and squeezed her. "All right. Well, we're about to head out. How about you guys? You ready to go?"

Theresa nodded. "I'm ready to go."

Marco replied, "Yep. Just heading out myself. I have my note to you here, but nothing earth-shattering, so you can read it tomorrow. I'll lock up the back door here."

She watched him saunter to the back door and twist the lock. He tried the handle to make sure the lock caught. It was amazing how much she enjoyed watching him. For a big man, he seemed almost like a ballerina, which would probably piss him off to hear. A former SEAL probably didn't care to be likened to a ballerina. But his movements were fluid.

He turned to look at the three of them watching him and nodded. "I'll catch the lights here."

She turned and followed Jace and Margo out of the kitchen and into the dining room. The dining room had already been locked up, which she did before she began cleaning and organizing. The lights were off, the only ones illuminating the room were the night lights and bar lights. She glanced around it one last time before she left for the night. When she got back here tomorrow, it would already be messed up from the early lunch crowd. It gave her a sense of accomplishment seeing that she'd been instrumental in reorganizing and cleaning up the mess from the huge crowds they'd had here tonight. She usually let the other wait staff go home after they'd cleaned up their assigned areas. She enjoyed spending time alone here, working on her own after having so much to do during her shift. It was a bit of downtime before going home and climbing into bed.

She could feel Marco approach from behind her. She just knew he was there. He was quiet as a mouse, but she could sense him. The four of them strode to the pantry area behind the office and out the employee exit. Jace had his keys handy. He turned and locked the doors, as they all walked to their respective vehicles parked close by.

She got into her car with a quick glance at Marco. Tonight, she was glad to not walk to her car alone. If the texts were accurate, they may have found her here, and she'd have to leave soon. That weighed her heart down. She liked it here. She enjoyed her job, even though it wasn't the job she'd trained for. It was a good job with good people.

She noticed Marco watching her. She nodded slightly as he asked. "You sure you're okay?"

Her eyes glistened and her nose tingled. When had anybody cared for her like this?

She sniffed, "Ah, yes, I'm good. Thank you, though. Thank you."

She hurried to get into her car before she actually broke down in tears. Letting out a huff of breath she whispered to herself. "I'm just tired. That's all it is."

She started her car. Marco got into his vehicle, which was parked right next to hers, and Jace and Margo got into theirs. She backed away from her parking space first and noticed that Marco followed behind her.

She left the Sandbar parking lot and headed left on Sunset Beach Road. She turned right on Main Street and left on Hospital Drive and noticed that Marco was still behind her. Her brows furrowed together. She thought he had purchased a condo over at the barracks. He should have gone straight on Main Street. So why was he following her home?

She increased her speed a little bit but thought better of it. She didn't want to get a ticket, so she slowed once more and navigated Hospital Road carefully. It was dark out. There were deer, dogs, and other creatures outside. She didn't want to hit an animal, or God forbid, a human. At Hospital Road, she made a sharp right to turn onto End of Town Road. She rented a little house at the end of it. She had liked it until now. Now she second-guessed her decision to move out here. It seemed desolate. Not enough neighbors around. And it was dark out here. They didn't even have streetlights on the road. Maybe tomorrow she'd look for something in town. Maybe it wouldn't be long, and she'd have to leave town. Or maybe she needed to begin making plans to leave soon.

That made her heart feel heavy once more and tears threatened again.

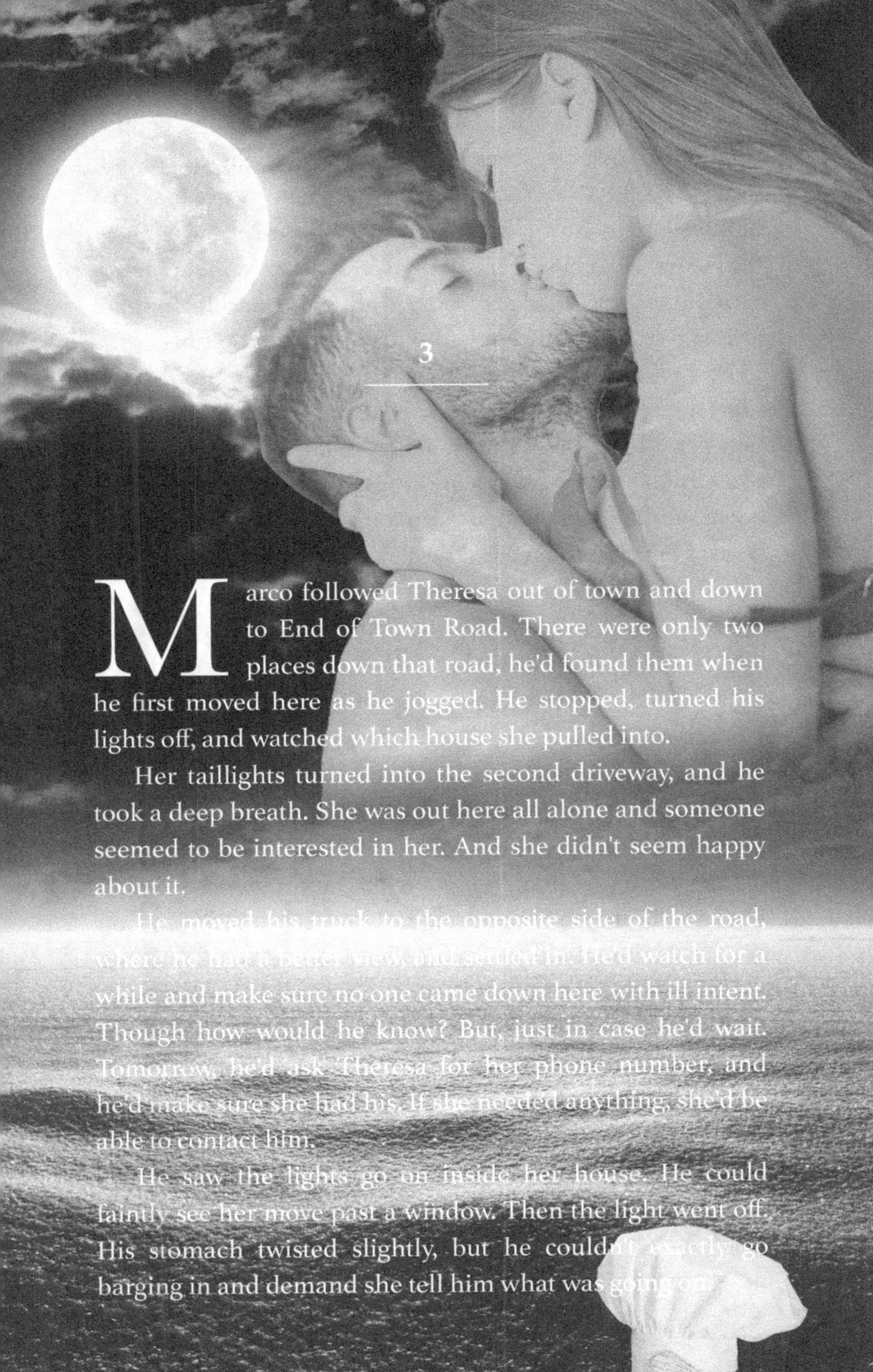

3

Marco followed Theresa out of town and down to End of Town Road. There were only two places down that road, he'd found them when he first moved here as he jogged. He stopped, turned his lights off, and watched which house she pulled into.

Her taillights turned into the second driveway, and he took a deep breath. She was out here all alone and someone seemed to be interested in her. And she didn't seem happy about it.

He moved his truck to the opposite side of the road, where he had a better view, and settled in. He'd watch for a while and make sure no one came down here with ill intent. Though how would he know? But, just in case he'd wait. Tomorrow, he'd ask Theresa for her phone number, and he'd make sure she had his. If she needed anything, she'd be able to contact him.

He saw the lights go on inside her house. He could faintly see her move past a window. Then the light went off. His stomach twisted slightly, but he couldn't exactly go barging in and demand she tell him what was going on.

He'd always had good sense, and he could read people. That was one of his strengths. When he'd fought in the military, he could almost sense someone's next move. It served him well. He wasn't going to ignore that sense now.

He watched her house and saw a little movement inside, he assumed she'd gone to bed. He allowed himself a minute to imagine being in that bed with her, but when his pants tightened, he decided to think of other things. She'd given him no reason to think there'd ever be anything more between them, though he sensed she liked him. There was something holding her back. Almost as if she'd let her guard down and then she pulled it back up before anything could be said or acted upon. He'd respect that for a while, but he'd be damned if he'd let her get hurt.

Glancing at his watch, he noted the time was now two in the morning. He'd been here three hours. He could stay here all night if he needed to, but it seemed quiet enough. Huffing out a deep breath, he started his truck and eased away from the road and out onto Hospital Road before turning his lights on. He didn't want to spook her or her neighbors.

He paid attention to the various decorations on Main Street as he neared home. There were some new ones up tonight. It brought a grin to his face as he let the Christmas spirit, and the pretty lights lift the burden on his heart.

As he entered his condo, he let the rest of the stress slip away. It was true when they said, "Home Sweet Home." He'd never felt that until he'd purchased this place. Now he finally felt like he had a home. A real home. A place he wouldn't have to leave unless he wanted to. No new orders telling him to pack up and go. When would that feeling finally go away?

He started the water warming in his shower while he

gathered clean underwear and a t-shirt. After showering he fell into his bed, exhaustion taking over. But as he closed his eyes, pictures of Theresa working in those shorts and white top danced in his head. Her legs were sexy. She was sexy. She was appealing in so many ways. But she was secretive, and she was also an unknown. He let himself drift off to sleep letting that thought seep into his brain. Did he even want to get involved with someone who kept secrets as well as Theresa did?

The next morning, Marco woke feeling rested and refreshed, except there was a heaviness in his heart that he couldn't explain. He rolled out of bed and grabbed a pair of running shorts, his running shoes, and socks. He'd take a nice jog out by Theresa's place and make sure everything was alright. Once he confirmed her safety, he'd feel better. He set out at a slow pace until he warmed up his muscles, then he increased his speed until he was at a full run. He easily jogged down Main Street and out to Hospital Road. Once out of town, the smells of the grasses warming in the morning sun reached his nostrils, and the sun warmed his skin. That's when he felt the most alive. He was healthy, happy and he could do things like run. He worked hard at the Sandbar, and he was making friends. A horn honked and brought him around to his surroundings. He grinned as Mason drove past on his way to the hospital and waved. He waved in return and grinned. Yeah, he had friends here. He'd set down some roots and he liked it. He wanted to grow here. Flourish, like his siblings were doing in their respective homes.

He neared End of Town Road and turned right. He'd jog past Theresa's place and make sure it looked peaceful. As he drew closer though, his heart fell hard in his chest. Theresa was carrying boxes out to her car. A suitcase and several totes sat on the driveway next to the car as if she were moving. He slowed as he neared.

"Good morning. Are you moving?" he called out from the end of the driveway.

She turned and stared at him. Her eyes burned a path down his entire body and he recognized the signs of appreciation. If he didn't know better, he'd say she liked what she saw, but she never made a move to indicate such a thing.

"Ahh, I'm...going...well...I'm not sure."

He moved closer to her and kept his voice even and steady, though he didn't feel even and steady right now.

"You either know if you're moving or not. It's not a *sort of* thing."

That brought a smile to her face, but she stared into his eyes and didn't respond. He stepped even closer until they were an arm's length apart. His voice softened as he said, "Let me help you, Theresa."

Tears instantly fell from her eyes. She angrily swiped them from her cheeks and wiped her fingers on her shorts.

"I don't want to be trouble."

He swallowed. "You're no trouble. Let me help you."

"It's just that...I'm a danger to you. And to anyone who would help me."

"Let me be the judge."

She swiped at the tears again on her cheeks and sniffed. He watched her throat constrict as she swallowed, and her breathing came in shorter bursts. He stood steady, waiting for her to trust him. Because that was it, she needed to trust him.

Another tear trickled down her cheek and he reached up with the back of his fingers and brushed it away for her.

Her lips quivered as she said, "Marco."

It was soft, almost like a plea. He watched as her tongue

slowly swiped across her bottom lip. It was mesmerizing. She was enchanting him.

Finally, she pulled a small slip of paper from her front pocket and handed it to him. Written in perfect printed English were the words, "Found you."

He stared at the words then looked into her eyes. "Who found you?"

4

Theresa watched the changes on Marco's face as he read the cryptic note. She took a deep breath and swallowed the fear in her throat.

"It's a crime syndicate I exposed."

Marco's eyebrows shot up. She noticed the perspiration beaded up on his chest, and his forehead and realized he'd been jogging. Her heart constricted slightly as the world came more into focus. She'd been thinking only of herself this morning as she took the note from her windshield. They'd been close last night, which meant, they knew where she was.

"Exposed how?"

She swallowed. "Should we go inside and get out of the sun?"

Marco nodded. "Let's get your things in the car first."

He immediately picked up the totes and set them in the back of her SUV. She picked up her suitcase and put it in the backseat.

He closed the hatch on her SUV and she closed and locked the door. She moved toward the house and felt

Marco follow her. Inside she pulled a pitcher of water from the refrigerator and poured them each a glass. She turned to see Marco watching her. He looked incredible. As always. But she'd have to imprint his image in her head because she'd have to go soon.

She carried their waters to the table and nodded for him to sit. She put the water pitcher back into the refrigerator and glanced out of the window above the sink.

Moving to the table, she looked into Marco's eyes. He was watching her closely and a sizzle ran down her spine, but it wasn't a good sizzle. It was a warning. What if he was sent here to get to her? He was also fairly new in town.

A knot grew in her throat, and she stood frozen trying to decide if she should run.

"I'm not going to hurt you."

Her eyes widened and her fingers shook slightly. "How do..."

He shook his head. "I have the ability to sense things. It's served me well over the years."

She nodded slightly but still remained where she'd been standing.

He nodded to her. "Sit. Tell me what's going on."

Her eyes darted to her chair at the table. Taking a deep breath, she moved woodenly to the chair and sat at the very edge of it in case she had to run. She didn't think he was here to harm her. He would have done it by now. But shaking that initial fear was getting harder to do the closer they got to her.

He was patient. He sat still, waiting for her to tell him what was going on. The longer he sat, the more nervous she became. She reached forward to pick up her glass of water, but her hand shook, and she fisted it instead.

"You followed me home last night." She stated.

She'd watched in her mirror and saw him turn off his headlights and sit in his truck.

"I thought you might be in danger. Or at least some trouble since you didn't seem happy about the texts."

"You were out there for hours."

He merely nodded.

She swallowed to wet her throat. It didn't work, so she picked up her glass. She took a long drink of the cold water and set her half-empty glass on the table. She glanced at Marco's glass. The perspiration on the outside beaded up and slowly dripped to the table. She stared at it for a while then took a deep breath.

His voice was low when he finally responded. "Yes."

"Did you see..."

She felt for the note she'd had in her pocket and realized she hadn't gotten it back from Marco. He dropped it on the table in between them. "No. And I'm mad at myself for not waiting around a bit longer. I may have seen who did it."

Her heart beat faster. "They're dangerous."

"Who are they?"

She swallowed again and took a deep breath. "The Celtic Crime Family. I wrote an exposé on them last year. I'd spent an entire year gathering data and intel. I followed employees. I found some of the wives and followed them. I knew they were laundering money for government agencies that had gone to the dark side. I get so mad when the government won't help people who actually need it, because of corruption. My tax dollars...your tax dollars...that's not supposed to be used for their personal gain. But they were doing it. Celtic was instrumental in getting several congressmen installed in their positions. I followed the money trail. I traced some of it back to the President of the United States. Money was moved and laundered through shell companies. They used laundromats, restaurants, bars, commercial real estate and apartment buildings. I followed some of the residents of the apartments. On the books, the apartments are rented for three thousand a month. One of the residents worked at a fast-food restaurant. No way he made that kind of money. I watched him. Chatted him up. Got his trust. He told me he only paid five hundred dollars a month for the great apartment."

Marco's jaw twitched. But he waited. Apparently waiting was his forte.

"I asked if they had any openings and he said he'd ask. Then he stopped working at that place. When I went to his apartment, I found he'd moved out."

Her fingers shook again. "I don't know what happened to him. I've worried about it since then."

"It wasn't your fault, whatever happened to him."

"But I was a fake. I pretended to need an apartment and to be his friend."

"That's what investigative reporting is sometimes."

She took a deep breath. "I know. I've just felt terrible, because he didn't deserve for anything bad to happen to him."

"You don't know that it did."

She swallowed. "Yeah. So, anyway. I wrote my story, and it exposed a lot of dirt in the government, but it also exposed the Celtic Crime Syndicate. I named names. Within hours of the story breaking, I was threatened. My apartment was broken into while I was at work. My car was keyed. My boss told me to get out of town and lay low until she felt it was safe to come back. She helped me get out of the building and she sent someone to my place with me to help pack my things."

"How would you decide it was safe?"

"No threats. No phone calls."

Marco nodded. "Now the peace you've found here is shattered."

"They've found me."

"But haven't tried to harm you."

"Not yet. Which is strange. But I think they know I have more dirt on them and they want it before they harm me."

Marco leaned forward. "Do you?"

She swallowed the lump in her throat. Her fingers shook again. She tried to speak but her voice wouldn't come. She merely nodded.

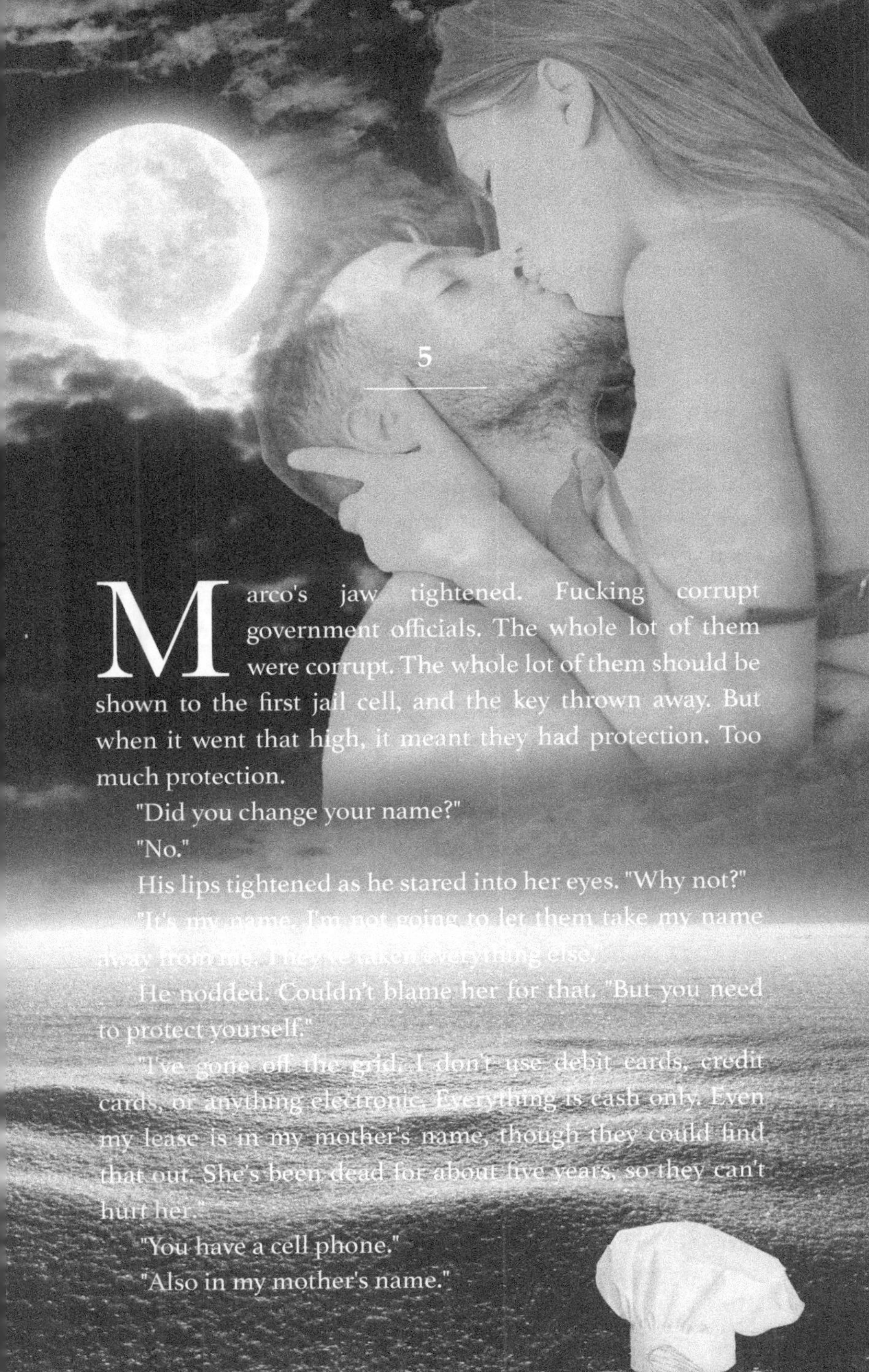

5

———

Marco's jaw tightened. Fucking corrupt government officials. The whole lot of them were corrupt. The whole lot of them should be shown to the first jail cell, and the key thrown away. But when it went that high, it meant they had protection. Too much protection.

"Did you change your name?"

"No."

His lips tightened as he stared into her eyes. "Why not?"

"It's my name. I'm not going to let them take my name away from me. They've taken everything else."

He nodded. Couldn't blame her for that. "But you need to protect yourself."

"I've gone off the grid. I don't use debit cards, credit cards, or anything electronic. Everything is cash only. Even my lease is in my mother's name, though they could find that out. She's been dead for about five years, so they can't hurt her."

"You have a cell phone."

"Also in my mother's name."

"So now they know you're here. They know what kind of car you have. And since they found your cell phone number, they've connected the dots to your mom. It's no longer safe for you."

She bit her bottom lip. "Right."

He didn't hesitate. "Come to my place."

Her eyes grew round, and she abruptly stood. "Marco, I can't..."

He stood but didn't move toward her. "I have two bedrooms. I have security. The building has additional security. My friend, Mitch DeMario is in the security business, I'll have him take your car and get you another one. I can keep you safe."

"Why?"

"You need it. It's part of who I am." He shrugged. "And I like you."

He watched her throat constrict as she swallowed. "You have to go somewhere. It's not safe out there on your own. I can keep you safe."

She took a deep breath. "I don't know. It's not..."

"It's not safe for you in the wild alone. Here you have friends. You have me. I have the means to keep you safe and help you with this. What else are you going to do?"

They stood staring at each other for what felt like an hour. But he was willing to wait her out. Then the window above the sink shattered and a rock skittered across the floor and stopped near her feet. She turned and ran across the room, he ran to the window to see if he could see someone. A man with reddish hair darted across the lawn and into the woods. Marco ran to the door and darted out after him. He chased him for a while, but the man had too much of a head start. Plus, he could be leading him into a trap.

He ran back to the house to find Theresa rushing toward

her car. He met her in the driveway and held his hand out for her keys. "My place is safe."

She swallowed again and nodded. He held his hand to the small of her back and led her to the passenger side of the SUV. After seeing her inside, he hurried around the front of the vehicle, but his eyes were watching the horizon. Especially in the direction the man ran.

He hopped in the driver's side of the vehicle and backed out of the driveway. He pulled his cell phone from his armband and found the notes app he used. He handed it to Theresa.

"Write in here, your cell phone number. Your mother's name, your landlord's name, and anything else we need to secure for you."

She took the phone from his hand and began typing into the app. He focused on the road and watched for anyone who might be following. He thought he saw someone duck behind a building as they neared, but didn't see anything else that seemed out of place. Driving past the hospital, he scanned the parking lot. As he turned down Main Street he didn't make his usual appreciative perusal, he was in duty mode. He was watching for danger. Sometimes the man can leave the military, but the military doesn't leave the man.

Driving into the parking area in front of his building, he parked at the space directly below his unit. Theresa looked out her window, then twisted in the seat and looked out the back window. Then she turned her head toward him. "Can you park in the back?"

"This won't be here long. Mitch will take care of it. And..." He pointed to the two cameras on the building focused on the parking lot. "See those? We'll be able to see anyone nosing around here."

"Oh."

"As soon as we get inside, I'm calling Mitch to come and get your car. He'll find a place to store it until things are safe for you. He'll get you another one and he can make sure it's titled in his name. Harder to trace to you."

He saw her swallow and her chest heaved as she inhaled deeply. "I don't know how I'll be able to thank you."

"Don't worry about it. For right now, let's get things taken care of with Mitch. Then let's get you settled. We'll ride to and from work together so you're safe. I'll mention to Jace that someone is bothering you and I'm helping you."

Her fingers shook as she tucked a lock of dark hair behind her ear. He couldn't look away as her silky hair wrapped around her ear. Her fingers shaking made him feel bad for her. She was scared. And she was a tough cookie, so her being scared said a lot.

"Let's get you and your things inside."

He opened his door and stepped out of her SUV. He immediately opened the hatch and pulled the totes from inside. Theresa pulled her suitcase from the back seat, and he led her inside the building. Once they'd entered, he relaxed. "This is the common area. Pool tables, ping pong table, microwave, sink, and refrigerator. Once in a while, the guy down the hall shoots pool with me in the morning. We both work nights. And bonus, Mitch DeMario lives at the end of the hall."

She nodded. "That's cool."

He grinned and started up the staircase to the upstairs. Once upstairs he stepped down the hall to the last door on the right. He set the totes on the floor and unlocked his door. He stepped back and let her enter first, then he brought the totes inside and closed the door.

"So, obviously this is the living room. He nodded to his right, "The kitchen is over there."

Moving toward the spare bedroom he set her totes on the floor. "This is your room. You have your own bathroom right outside the door. I have one in my room, so we don't have to share."

She looked around the room and a small grin appeared on her face. "It's very nice. Did you decorate this yourself?"

He shook his head. "No. I hired someone to help me. It's honestly the first home I've ever owned, and I wanted it to be amazing."

Theresa nodded. "It is."

He smiled as he watched her eyes roam around the room. "I'll leave you to settle in. I'm going to call Mitch and get things in the works for you."

He hurried from the room and pulled his phone from his pocket. Tapping Mitch's number, he leaned against the wall next to the large window that offered him a spectacular view of Main Street.

Mitch answered on the second ring. "Hey, there. What's up?"

"I need some help."

"You got it."

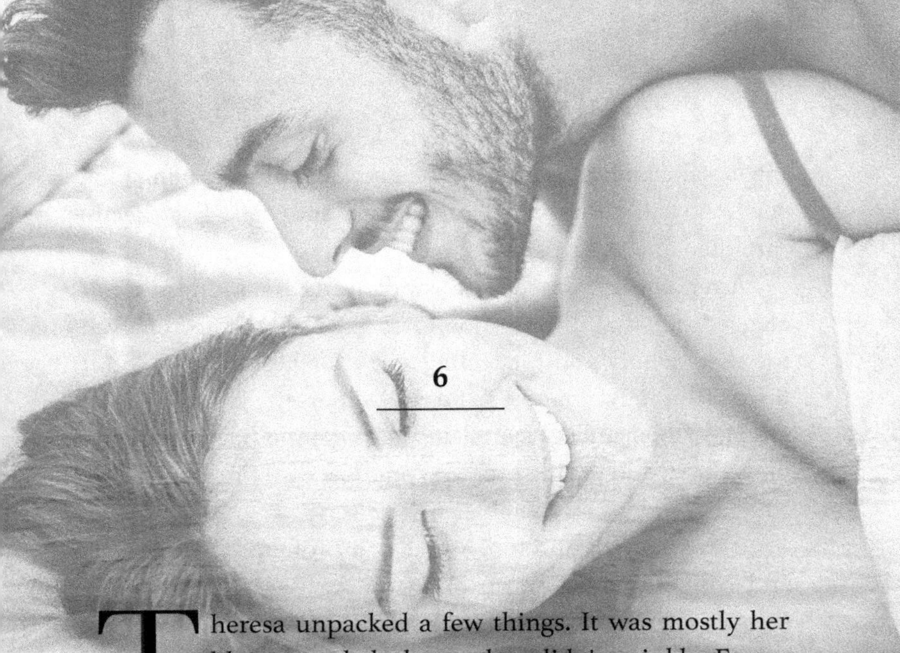

6

Theresa unpacked a few things. It was mostly her blouses and slacks, so they didn't wrinkle. Everything else she left in her suitcase and tucked it in the closet. She wasn't sure if she'd be here long. She may just need to leave right away. If the Celtics came for her, she'd leave before Marco got hurt. She should probably leave right now, before she lost access to her vehicle.

Her heart began beating rapidly. She was in a position right now to be stuck. No vehicle, no way to get away. She inhaled slowly and deeply to keep the panic at bay. She needed to think.

After a few deep breaths, she felt calmer. She glanced around the room. The designer had done a nice job. It definitely felt like a home and not a rental or temporary home. She understood Marco's desire to make this his home. She had been in the military a few years before getting out. Then she'd gotten her job at the paper back in Maine.

She huffed out a breath thinking about all she'd lost. She hadn't been in touch with her boss, or anyone from Maine. She didn't have family anymore. Her parents were gone, and she was an only child. No one to leave behind. Except for the life she knew, the friends she had, and a well-paying job she enjoyed. In essence, everything she had. Her head throbbed and she closed her eyes and rubbed her temples.

After she'd calmed, she swallowed the sadness that clogged her throat. She shook her head sternly to remove the melancholy and for feeling sorry for herself. "Get your head on straight, Theresa," she chided herself.

She stood and gathered up her shampoo, conditioner, blow dryer, and styling products and placed them where she wanted them in the cabinets and shower.

It was a nice bathroom. Muted colors of tans and browns and coppers. It felt warm and homey. She sniffed at the thought of not having a home. Even in Maine, she'd only had an apartment. There hadn't been time to lay down roots.

She stepped from the bathroom and made her way to the living room where Marco sat perched on the edge of the sofa, his phone to his ear, and he was making notes in a notebook on the coffee table. She waited quietly as he finished his conversation. He glanced at her a couple of times and nodded. Each time her tummy tingled. He was a handsome man. Strong, confident, and sure of himself. He was her kryptonite. Everything she loved in a man. Everything.

His deep rich voice filled the air as he spoke. "Thanks, Mitch. I'll let her know."

He tapped his phone and set it on the coffee table next to his notebook. When he looked at her, she couldn't look away from him. His deep brown eyes were magnetic. She saw fine lines at the corners that she'd never noticed before. On him, they looked sexy. It made him more worldly to her. As if he'd had life experiences, which she knew he had.

He'd been a SEAL in the past. Did they still consider themselves SEALs when they were out? Marines did. *Once a Marine, always a Marine.* She'd heard it over and over on base.

Marco smiled. "Mitch will be here in fifteen minutes to take your car. If you give me your keys and also the key to your apartment, he'll go over and replace the window to secure the place, so you don't get in trouble with your landlord. He'll also take a look around. I asked him to set up some cameras and put a couple of timers on the lamps, so it looks like you're there. We'll watch and see if someone comes back."

She swallowed. "Okay."

She hesitated though. Her lips quivered slightly and she immediately became irritated with herself for feeling weak and vulnerable. He cocked his head slightly but didn't say anything. He was apparently willing to wait her out. She'd noticed that about him.

She filled her lungs, "I don't like being this vulnerable."

His lips pursed briefly. Even that was sexy.

"I understand."

"I don't think you do. I can't imagine you've ever been vulnerable."

He chuckled. "You have no idea. I've had to go into situations where I didn't know if I'd come out alive. I trusted my brothers-in-arms. I trusted every single one of them. But the enemy can be unpredictable, and shit can happen. I've been more vulnerable than you can ever believe."

She swallowed. "I'm sorry. I guess I'm feeling sorry for myself. I knew the chance of them finding me was possible, but I let myself believe it was safe here."

"The best way to not feel vulnerable is to set yourself up for the win. Have everything in place to defend yourself and keep yourself safe to the best of your ability. That's what we're doing for you."

She nodded slowly, then moved to the bedroom and pulled her keys from her purse. She pulled the Sandbar keys from her keyring and handed the rest to Marco. "The key fob works for the car." She pointed to three keys. "This is for the glove box, this is for the doors if you don't have the fob, and this is my apartment key."

"Got it. If you're ready, I'll show you where everything is in the kitchen. You should feel free to make yourself at home."

She swallowed to wet her throat. This felt so weird. Her head spun from all that was happening. She hadn't even gotten sufficiently scared, other than to pack some things and start to leave. In her mind, that was more a resolute circumstance, than fear. She'd always told herself when they found her, she'd move on. It seemed natural.

"I don't think I'll stay long Marco. If they find me..."

"I'll be here to protect you."

"It's not your job to protect me."

"It is now."

"Why?"

He stood and moved close to her. She tilted her head up to look into his eyes, he bent his head down to meet her gaze.

"I've already told you. It's natural for me to protect. And I like you, so it adds a bit more to it for me."

"You can't like me enough to put your life at risk."

"I did it for millions of Americans I've never met when I was in the military. And over the past six months, I've gotten to know you a bit better than most. So, yes, I do know you enough to put my life at risk to protect you. And I think you're worth protecting."

Her nose tingled, signaling the threat of tears. A knock on the door made her jump. Marco put his hand on her shoulder and said softly, "It's okay. It's Mitch."

"How do you know?"

"Knock, space, knock, knock."

His hand on her shoulder was more comforting than she wanted to admit. He made her feel things. Sometimes her tummy felt like there were thousands of butterflies trying to get out. Sometimes she felt...comfortable. Sometimes she felt admiration for such a man. Right now, she felt grateful in so many ways. But she was also afraid. She could never repay him if he got hurt.

arco opened the door to let Mitch in.

"Mitch, this is Theresa Miklovic. Theresa, Mitch De Mario."

Mitch stepped forward with his hand out and Theresa met him halfway with hers. They shook hands and Mitch got right to it.

"I brought one of my cars for you to use. It's in the name of my security firm, MitchCo."

"I hate to take one of your cars. You may need it."

Mitch chuckled. "I've got a few of them. Don't worry about it. I also have a secure garage on the edge of town where I keep them. Your car will go in there and be safe from tampering and them finding it."

"Thank you so much."

Marco watched Theresa's face as she processed all of this. He could see her bouncing between relief and fear. Mitch handed her keys to the car.

"If you come to the window, I'll show you your new ride."

She grinned and it was cute. Everything she did was cute.

He followed Mitch and Theresa to the window and viewed the car from above.

"It's the champagne-colored Buick. It's comfortable, new, and it'll get you everywhere you need to go. I have insurance papers in the glove compartment should you get stopped and need to show them, and I've put a letter in there with all of my contact information if the police need to confirm that you have my permission to drive it."

Theresa looked up at Mitch and smiled. "Thank you. I don't know how I can repay you."

Mitch grinned, then looked at Marco.

"This guy right here has your back. And, he's had mine a time or two, so we're all good. We help each other out and that will always be the case."

Her voice was soft when she repeated. "Thank you."

Theresa turned to Marco and smiled. "Thank you. I do appreciate all you've done and are doing for me."

He smiled in return because it was hard not to. "You're welcome. We've got you."

She nodded and smiled.

Mitch turned toward the door. "I'll let you know once we've installed the cameras at the house. Oh, and one more thing, I need your cell phone. They've obviously gotten this number, so I have a new one for you."

He pulled a new cell phone from his pocket and turned it on. He waited for it to boot up, then handed it to her.

Theresa handed her phone to him, and the swallow she made didn't escape him.

Mitch shook his head, "I won't get rid of this. I'm going to monitor any calls or texts coming in from them though."

He did some button pushing, then connected the two phones with a cord. "This will transfer your phone numbers and texts to this phone."

"I appreciate that. I don't have many on there."

Mitch nodded. "Then it won't take long."

The information transferred, and Mitch handed her the new phone.

"There you go. Are you two working tonight?"

Theresa gasped and looked at her watch. Her shoulders relaxed when she saw the time. "Yes. I have to be there at eleven to set up for lunch."

Marco nodded. "I go in at the same time."

"Okay." Mitch opened the door. "I'll text you, so I don't interrupt you at work."

Theresa stepped closer to the door. "Thank you again, Mitch. I do appreciate it."

He grinned at her and then nodded to Marco. "See you later."

He disappeared from the doorway and Marco turned to Theresa. "Are you hungry?"

Her hand pressed against her tummy. "A little. Now that I'm settling in."

"Good. Let me whip something up, then we can get ready for work."

"Thank you. May I help?"

He chuckled. "I appreciate that, but the kitchen is my domain. Now that doesn't mean you can't cook when you want, but I'm sort of a solo chef."

"Okay." She smiled softly. "Maybe I'll go and take a shower, so I'm not tempted to help you."

He nodded. "Good idea. Breakfast will be ready in thirty minutes."

She nodded and headed to the spare bedroom, which was now her bedroom. He turned and sauntered to the kitchen. Opening the refrigerator door, he looked inside and began pulling out eggs, bacon, fresh fruit, and milk. He'd had his kitchen custom-built when he had this place designed. His mixer was in a lower cabinet, on a shelf. All he had to do was open the cupboard door, lift up the shelf the mixer sat on, and raise it to counter height. It was his favorite detail in this kitchen.

He busied himself making breakfast, excited to have someone to cook for in his home. He had planned to have his friends over for dinner, as a sort of housewarming party, but he worked most evenings and on the nights he didn't work, he liked playing pickleball, running, or reading. So, he'd not found the time to entertain. And now that he thought about it, entertaining wasn't really his thing. He enjoyed his friends, but pulling everything together for a party seemed like a lot of work outside of his bailiwick.

He heard the shower shut off and began assembling some of their breakfast on plates. He flipped the bacon in the pan, then pushed the pan to the back of the stove. It would finish cooking in the hot grease while he prepared everything else.

Pulling some plates from the cupboard, he set them on the side of the counter where the bar stools would allow them to sit and eat. He almost never...actually, he'd never eaten at his dining room table. Turning his head he looked at the beautiful piece of furniture and shook his head.

Theresa entered the kitchen, and the aroma of a freshly showered woman came with her. He nodded to the counter where the place settings were waiting for them.

She grinned. "Does it matter which one I sit at?"

"Nope. Help yourself."

She sat at the one closest to her bedroom, which was what he expected. She was still uncomfortable.

He plated up the remainder of the breakfast foods and carried their plates to the counter.

"Wow, this looks fantastic," she exclaimed.

He chuckled. "Thank you. I hope you enjoy it. I have cream cheese crepes, fresh fruit, bacon, and coffee. Do you like coffee?"

"I do. Yes."

He poured them each a cup of coffee, then sat next to her at the counter. "Dig in please."

She nodded and cut into her crepe and took a bite. The appreciative hum he heard after, made his heart happy. It was his favorite breakfast food, and he was glad she liked it.

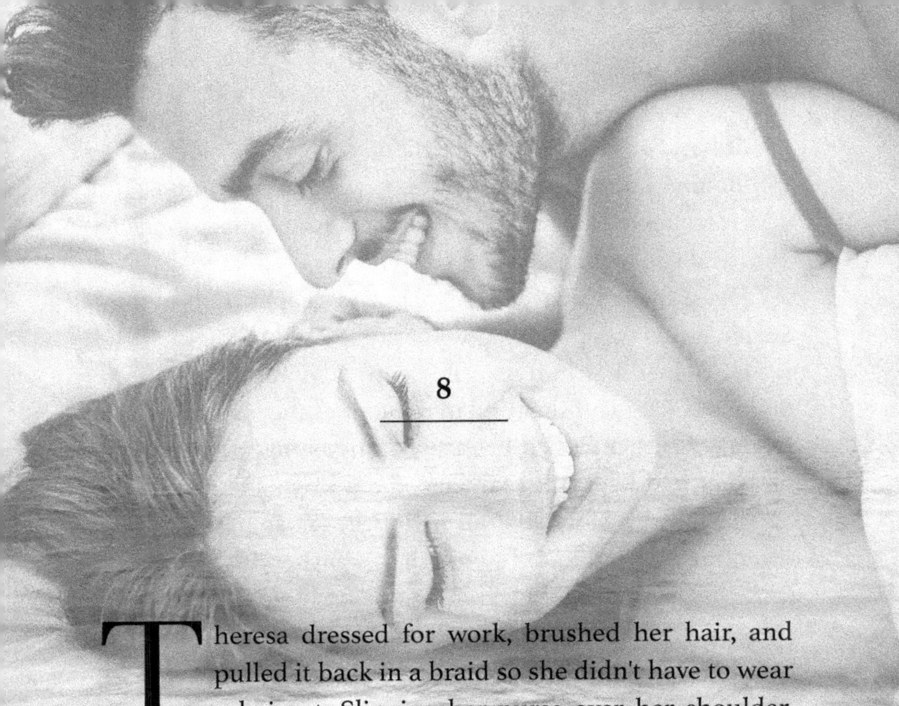

8

Theresa dressed for work, brushed her hair, and pulled it back in a braid so she didn't have to wear a hairnet. Slinging her purse over her shoulder, she sauntered out to the living room where Marco stood waiting for her.

He nodded and grinned. "Ready?"

She smiled because it was impossible not to. "Yeah."

"You mind riding together?"

She didn't hesitate. "No." She swallowed. "I don't mind."

He opened the door and waited for her to pass before stepping out and locking his door. As they made their way down the hallway to the stairs, Marco's hand was at the small of her back. She could smell his aftershave. It was the most compelling aroma. Clean and fresh with a hint of fresh-cut wood. She took a deep breath to breathe more of him in.

"Are you nervous?"

"No." Her cheeks burned. Had he figured...

"You took a deep breath. Was it to calm yourself?"

He had. Dammit. "Ah, yes. Today has been a lot."

"It has. You've handled it brilliantly."

"Really? I don't feel like I have."

He chuckled as he leaned forward to open the outside door and she managed a nice deep breath of...Marco.

"Trust me. You have." His voice was deeper than before. Sexier, if that was possible.

He helped her into his vehicle, walked around the front of the truck and all she tried to remember the last time she'd felt taken care of. It had been so damned long. Her last relationship had been six years ago. Even then, she didn't feel taken care of. More like an armpiece or something. She shook her head and intentionally pushed the negative thoughts from her mind. Her friends had told her he was a piece of crap. She thought he was smart and handsome. It took her three months to see he was a turd.

As Marco drove them down Main Street, she noticed he looked closely at the businesses in town. He turned to see her watching him and he grinned. That's when she saw it - he had a dimple in his right cheek. Gads, he had everything she liked in a man.

"I like watching the local businesses decorate their places for Christmas. Every day there's a change. Wait until we get home tonight. From the living room window, we can look down Main Street with all the lights on and see how magical it is."

She cocked her head. He looked for the magic in things like Christmas and even decorations?

"I can't wait to see it."

Turning them left toward the Sandbar, he continued to look at the surrounding buildings and she continued to try and not stare at him.

He pulled them into the parking area nearest the employee entrance. She hopped out of the vehicle, not waiting for him. They weren't on a date, she was his co-worker. But she saw his frown. Then she felt the tug in her tummy. She felt bad for making him feel bad. She closed her eyes and took in a deep breath. This situation was weird and intense and she didn't have the experience to deal with anything like this.

She stepped toward the employee entrance as he held the door for her. She smiled at him as she passed, and she saw that hint of a dimple again. Worth it.

She headed to the punch clock and clocked in. She tucked her purse in her locker and donned her black apron as Marco pulled his fresh white chef's jacket from the dry-cleaning closet and popped it on. He looked incredible in that jacket with his dark hair and tanned skin.

She hustled out to the dining room to begin setting up the condiments. She picked up the first tray of salt and pepper shakers from the kitchen when Marco entered. He opened the walk-in cooler and stepped inside. He hurried out of it and left the kitchen in a hurry. Her brows bunched together as she followed him from the kitchen, but she began setting up the tables instead of following him.

Soon Jace followed Marco from the office to the kitchen and her curiosity got the better of her and she followed them. She intended to pick up a new tray of salt and pepper shakers when Marco stepped from the cooler, Jace close behind. Jace's jaw was tight, and Marco's was tighter.

She met Marco's eyes but didn't say anything. Jace hustled toward the door, "I'll give them a call right now."

When he'd left, Marco motioned toward the cooler. "Someone slashed open the packages with the steaks. Ruining the entire order for tonight."

"Who would do that?"

"I don't know. Jace said he let them in to deliver this

morning at six. The usual delivery man came. Nothing seemed off. And he left."

She swallowed a dry knot in her throat. Marco stared into her eyes. "You need to be very careful Theresa."

"How do you know it's..."

"We don't know it isn't. Nothing like this has ever happened before."

She leaned on the stainless-steel table in front of her and tried taking deep breaths. "I think I should go, Marco. Now it's affecting Jace and Margo."

"No. You aren't safe out there on your own."

"I might not be safe here."

"But you have people here who can protect you."

Jace entered the kitchen, stopped, and stared at them. "What's going on?"

She looked into Marco's eyes and hers watered. She opened her mouth, but nothing came out. Marco waited, which made her more nervous. Damn him and his patience. He nodded to her, and she sucked in a big breath.

"Jace. I was an investigative reporter back home in Maine. I wrote an article on the Celtic Crime Family, who have politicians in their pockets. They have money laundering operations, as well as criminal activity, including trafficking and drugs. I exposed them and shortly after, I began getting death threats. I left and ended up here, which I hoped was too far away from Maine for them to follow me. However, I think they've found me."

Jace stepped toward the table and stared at her. "Why do you think they've found you?"

"They texted me last night. This morning they threw a rock through my window. Luckily Marco was there and they ran away."

Jace turned his head toward Marco. "You were there?"

"I was out jogging and saw Theresa throwing packed bags into her car to leave."

"You were packing to leave?"

"I didn't want to bring any danger here."

Jace stared at her a moment, then turned his eyes to Marco. Marco said nothing so Jace turned back to her. "But you didn't leave?"

"No." Her bottom lip quivered. "I'm staying at..." She paused and cleared her throat. "At Marco's."

Jace's eyebrows rose. He slowly turned his eyes back to Marco. Marco stared at Jace and said nothing, which was interesting to watch if she wasn't so scared and creeped out right now.

Jace nodded his head once. "Okay. So, let me see if I understand." He took a deep breath. "You exposed a major crime family, and they are after you. You ended up here, but they've found you and now you're staying with Marco. But I don't see how this has anything to do with my shipment of meat being damaged."

Marco *finally* spoke. "I think they did it to scare Theresa."

"The Celtic Crime Family? If they are after her, why haven't they tried to harm her?"

Jace looked her way and closed his eyes. "I'm sorry Theresa, I don't want that to happen, I just..."

"It's okay. I understand."

Marco finished his comment. "I think they hired someone local to scare her. And Theresa thinks the Celtics know she still has dirt on them, and they want it."

Jace woodenly turned his head toward her. He looked into her eyes for a long time and her heart beat so forcefully in her chest it nearly made her lose her breath. "Do you have more on them?"

She bit her bottom lip slightly then nodded. "Yes."

"What do you have?"

"They were instrumental in getting the president elected by dirty means."

"And you have proof?"

"I do."

Jace looked at Marco. "Holy fuck."

9

Jace stared at Marco. "What are you doing to keep her safe?"

"I've gotten Mitch De Mario involved."

Jace nodded. "That's good. What has he done so far?"

Marco looked at her and nodded. Though her voice sounded shaky, she replied. "He has taken my car and hidden it. He gave me another one to use in the meantime. He fixed my kitchen window, and he has cameras in and around my place to monitor activity. And timers on my lamps."

Jace nodded. "Okay. I have security here. I'll ramp it up though. I'll have a few more cameras installed outside watching our employee cars. And I'm going to put a couple of cameras in here to monitor deliveries. I just called The Meat Shop and they're bringing over a new shipment for tonight. We'll haggle over the damages and who pays for what later."

Marco nodded. "Okay."

"In the meantime..." Jace turned to Theresa. "Stay inside.

If anyone comes in that makes you uncomfortable, let me or Marco know right away."

Theresa's eyes met his and they stared at each other for a long while. She finally replied to Jace. "Okay."

Jace nodded. He started toward the door to the restaurant but halted. "And stay with Marco."

He left instantly.

Theresa still looked into his eyes. "What does that mean?"

"He means staying with me is a good idea."

"Oh."

He nodded. "You good?"

She bit her bottom lip once more. "I think so."

"Okay. Let's get ready for the lunch crowd."

She nodded, picked up a tray of salt and pepper shakers, and exited the kitchen. He turned the burners on the stove to heat the griddle and began pulling ground beef from the cooler to make patties for lunch. Soon the other waitstaff came in, Kaysen and Kelsey and they helped Theresa out front. He managed things in the kitchen. He liked it this way for lunch. Tonight is when he'd have helpers in here and the dishwasher. The kitchen got busy and loud at dinner time.

Theresa seemed to settle in as lunchtime came and went. Business as usual was key. He was happy to see her begin to relax a bit but knew it wouldn't last. He understood the pressure she was under.

Theresa entered the kitchen and snapped an order onto the order board he used. He grinned at her and received a smile in return.

"You doing okay?"

She nodded. "Yeah."

"Good." He nodded and plated an order.

He looked into her eyes. They were beautiful eyes, but

right now they drooped slightly. Her shoulders weren't as straight as they usually were. He stepped closer to her and dropped his voice. "Are you sure?"

Her eyes flicked to his. "I am. I guess I'm just tired. I feel like I've been awake for days."

He nodded. "Stress. You'll be safe tonight and hopefully, can get a good night's sleep. That will change things for you tomorrow. Today has been a long day and it's only two o'clock right now."

"Yeah. I guess. I felt this way when I left Maine. Always looking over my shoulder. Always waiting for the next shoe to drop."

The back door opened, and Theresa jumped. He whispered, "It's okay. I believe it's the steak delivery for tonight. If you don't want to be here while they deliver, go to the office and chat with Margo for a few minutes. I'm sure by now Jace has filled her in."

Before Theresa could respond, the kitchen door opened and both Jace and Margo entered. Jace moved directly to the delivery person who wheeled in a dolly with three heavy boxes on it.

Jace didn't wait for him to get fully in the door. "I want to know what happened this morning."

The driver's eyes grew round as he stared at Jace's tightened jaw and dark eyes that brooked no argument. "I don't know. I delivered. It must have been one of your..."

"It wasn't. No one was here but me until Marco..." Jace looked his way, then back to the driver. "Came in and found the damaged packages."

The driver stuttered a few words out then his eyes watered and his shoulders dropped. "Someone paid me to do it. I needed the money and he offered me two hundred dollars. I couldn't pass it up."

"Who!" Jace's voice grew louder and Marco moved toward the driver.

"I don't...don't...know."

Marco's anger rose but he recognized the man's complete fear. He took a deep breath. "How did he pay you?"

"C...c...cash."

"Let me see it."

The driver's hands shook as he reached into his pocket and pulled out two one-hundred-dollar bills. He held the shaking bills toward Marco. He gently took the money and held the bills up to the light in the kitchen. He moved them back and forth to see if the blue security ribbon changed with the movement.

He looked at Jace. "They're real."

Jace nodded and Marco handed the driver the bills.

Jace said, "If he approaches you again, I want you to tell me. I want to know what he asks you to do."

"Okay."

Marco shook his head. "What did he look like?"

"He had red hair. Taller than me."

Marco turned toward Theresa and Margo who stood watching. Theresa nodded as her chest rose. She blew out a breath and swallowed.

Margo put her arm around Theresa and squeezed her. "We'll do everything we can to keep you safe."

"I know you will. Thank you."

Marco moved to the stove and began cooking the new orders that had come in. Jace took care of the driver and told him if anyone asked questions about what happened after he slashed the packages, he was to say nothing happened and they ordered more food. Nothing else. And if he was hired again, he was to come directly to Jace or Marco and let them know.

As soon as the kitchen door closed behind the delivery driver, Marco stepped to the door and turned the lock. Anyone else delivering today would need to knock.

He stared at Theresa as he moved back to the stove and nodded. She nodded in return and mouthed, "Thank you."

His heartbeat increased. He rotated his head as he turned the burgers on the grill. He was getting too close.

Theresa finished setting up the dining room with Margo's assistance. The hired cleaning company would come in the morning to mop the floors and clean the bathrooms and other areas that were not food-related. Margo had insisted on staying out front with her, so she wasn't alone. She hated feeling like she needed a babysitter, but she was grateful for good friends and the concern. Despite the doors being locked, she still felt vulnerable. And exhausted. She felt totally exhausted. If anything happened tonight, she wouldn't be able to run anywhere. There was nothing left in her. She'd spent every bit of energy she had today.

A loud knock sounded against the front door, and she jumped and yipped. Two more knocks hit the door hard, and Margo's hand flew to her heart first, then both Jace and Marco rushed out to the dining room from opposite directions.

Marco nodded toward her, "It's Mitch. He just texted. Remember, knock space knock knock."

She swallowed the fear that clogged her throat and

nodded. She closed her eyes for a moment as Marco rushed to the door to open it. She focused on her breathing, reminding herself they were all okay. It was all okay.

Marco first peered out the door, using his foot as a stopper, then opened the door and let Mitch inside. As soon as Mitch stepped inside, Marco closed and locked the door once more.

Mitch glanced at her and nodded. "Hi, Theresa."

"Hi, Mitch."

He nodded to Jace and Margo who stood nearby. Mitch addressed her. "You received a call on your phone. I need you to listen to what it says and tell me if you recognize the caller's voice."

She swallowed nervously but stepped forward. "Okay."

He pulled her phone from his pocket and tapped the face of it. The caller's voice came on. "Theresa, you can run but you can't hide. Not forever. I know you have the transaction records proving what you think is the Celtics meddling with the presidential election, but you don't really know what you have there. And before you go making an embarrassment of yourself, you and I need to meet."

Theresa stared at the phone that Mitch held out. It was her phone, but right now, she didn't want to touch it. It felt like something poisonous, something dangerous and dark.

How brave was she? Was she brave enough to pretend like she didn't know what they were talking about? She wasn't sure if she was that brave.

Her eyes left the phone and slowly scanned up Mitch's arm and over his shoulder to where Marco stood. He stepped forward, then stood before her and softly asked, "Do you have something that will incriminate them?"

She swallowed. She wasn't sure how honest she should

be with anyone. Everyone seemed to want the information she had.

Marco said, "Theresa, you need to trust us, hon. We're trying to save you, but we need to know what we're up against."

Her heart beat so fast she thought she was gonna pass out. She swallowed quickly and took in a deep breath. Well, what did she have to lose, really?

"Yes, I have them," she slowly answered.

"Where are they? We need to put them somewhere for safekeeping."

She licked her lips. "I have them in safekeeping."

"But what if they find them?"

"They won't."

"Theresa..."

She hurriedly said, "Marco, I appreciate everything you're all doing for me. I really, really do. But this is something that I protected long ago when I first started to find out what was going on with the Celtics. I have the files protected in such a way that no one will find them. I have it blockchain-protected, and the only way it can be opened is with a private key. And that private key is hidden over several different sources."

Mitch grinned. He looked at Marco. "Well, damn. That's pretty fucking good."

Marco nodded. She saw him swallow, though. He was worried.

He said, "Yeah, she's good. She's good."

Jace stepped forward then. He let out a deep breath. "Okay, so you're the only one who knows where the blockchain-protected documents are, and you're the only one who knows how to retrieve the password?"

"Yes."

Mitch nodded. "And no one else?"

"Correct. No one else. Only me. And I have it further protected with a dead man's switch. So if something happens to me, it will automatically go out to law enforcement, media, television stations, newspapers, and all over the internet via a private account that no one knows I own."

Marco nodded slowly. She watched him. He almost seemed as though he admired her. That made her smile a little. Actually, speaking all this out loud made her feel better about everything. She had done the right thing. She protected the data. And if they didn't want it to get out, they had to leave her alone—or at least not kill her.

They didn't have to leave her alone, but they needed her to stay alive.

She felt stronger now. She should tell them that much. It would give them pause. Maybe.

She said, "I have everything protected to the best of my ability. It doesn't mean they can't kidnap me and try to beat it out of me. I would prefer they didn't do that. But they're not going to get it out of me, and no one else knows anything about this."

Mitch nodded. "Okay, well, that's good. I'll say this— don't tell anyone right now either, including Marco or Jace. Sorry, guys."

Marco shook his head. "Nope. Nope. That's all right. We need to protect her the best that we can, and by her being the only person who knows how to uncover this information, I think that protects her even more."

Mitch nodded. "Yep, I think it does too. So here's what we're gonna do right now. I'm gonna reply to this phone number, and I want you to say only you know where the information is, only you can uncover it, and you have no intention of doing so until you're guaranteed safety. And that guarantee will come by tomorrow night at midnight. Let's push the envelope a little bit and force these bastards out."

Theresa swallowed and nodded. "Yes. I've been living under the radar for far too long and looking over my shoulder all the time. It's time we settle this. Thank you."

Mitch nodded. He tapped on her phone a few times and held it up for her to speak, exactly as he had told her to do. She did so and felt immediately better. But she added, "I have the information dead-man encrypted. If I die, the whole world will get the information I have. All of it."

Mitch hesitated a moment and glanced at Marco. He stared into her eyes. "Are you sure?"

"Yes."

Mitch nodded and sent it.

She breathed out a sigh of relief. It was the first time she was actually taking steps to make this stop. She wasn't running. She was fighting back, and she had an amazing group of people with her.

Hopefully, no one would get hurt.

Mitch shook hands with Marco and left the Sandbar. After he was gone, Marco secured the restaurant once more and turned to Theresa.

"Do you have more to do out here?"

She looked around, glanced at Margo, and shook her head. "No, I think we're finished here."

"Okay, let's get ready to go then. He just got that phone call, so we want to get out of here before he has time to come here and react if he's close."

"Okay."

Marco looked at Jace and nodded. "You good with this?"

Jace nodded in return. "Yes, we'll all get out of here right away."

They quickly turned the lights off, shut down any equipment that was still running, and the four of them left quickly. The doors were locked up tight.

He helped Theresa into his vehicle. He heard her sigh. He knew she was frightened. Who wouldn't be? She was one woman against the entire world at this point.

He hoped she understood that she had him, Mitch, Jace, and Margo. And if he needed to bring in Quinn, Mason, or even Sid, they would all be there. Between all of them, they had contacts they could reach out to. They helped each other out. That's what friends do for each other. That's what he would do for any of them.

He climbed into the vehicle, noticing that she sat stone-still and stared straight ahead. His heart reached out to her. Poor thing. No one deserved this.

He reached over and gently squeezed her hand. "We've got this."

She looked at him and smiled. "Thank you."

"Okay, you're welcome. I know it's easy to say don't worry, and to be honest with you, I don't think I could stop worrying either if it were me. But we're gonna do everything we can to protect you. Please know that, at least."

Her smile was weak at best, but she tried. When she turned to him in this light, all he wanted to do was kiss her. He wanted to wrap her in his arms, hold her, and tell her everything was going to be okay.

And he knew he couldn't say that with certainty, but he knew he was going do everything he could to make it happen—if he had anything to say about it.

He started his truck, and they moved toward home.

As always, he looked at the Christmas lights. He pointed out two new ones. "Oh, look, the insurance office has new lights today. That looks nice."

She turned her head and stared. "That does look nice."

"It does." He grinned.

He turned his head to the other side of the street and saw the barbershop. "Ah, look at that one."

They had a lit-up pair of scissors, the height of the building, in front of the door. It looked like people could walk underneath the handles to get inside.

Theresa even chuckled a little. "That is really cute."

"Remind me when we get home to show you from the living room window when you look down the street. It's beautiful."

"Okay."

They arrived at the condo and made it upstairs without incident, which he was happy about. He was also grateful that Mitch lived downstairs and knew that security was tight right now.

So he hoped that they'd have no issues tonight.

Though they did just poke the bear.

After he locked the door, he took Theresa by the hand and gently led her across the living room floor to the big window. He left the lights off, so they were drenched in darkness, but the beautiful colors from Main Street lit up the place.

She sighed. "Oh, that is really pretty."

"It is. It was one of the things that I was first drawn to about this place. It just so happened that they were starting to decorate when I bought this place, and I couldn't wait to get here and see it in all of its glory."

She smiled and looked up at him. "I can see why. It's beautiful."

"It is. Okay. So, do you need a drink? Something to unwind?"

"No. I'm afraid to drink. I need to keep all my senses. What if we have to get up and run in the middle of the night?"

"We're not. We're not going to get up and run in the middle of the night. We have security here. Mitch lives downstairs—he has things covered. Quinn has security on the building—he has things covered. We are going to know if anyone is lingering about before they're within a mile of this place."

"Okay. Well, if it's all the same to you, I think I'd like to forego the drink and keep all of my wits about me for tonight."

"That sounds good. I totally understand that."

She turned to walk toward her bedroom, and his heart felt heavy. He couldn't take her worry away and he couldn't convince her, yet, that she was safe. Likely safer than she'd been all this time living here.

She stopped, though, and turned to face him. She took a few steps to bridge the gap between them. She tilted her head back to look up into his eyes, and in this light, with the Christmas lights twinkling down below, she was the most beautiful woman in the world.

Of course, he always thought she was beautiful, but there was something a little magical right now.

"Thank you, Marco." She paused. "I appreciate every-thing that you're doing for me. I want you to know I'm not being ungrateful. I'm just trying to be practical."

He grinned and nodded. "I know, I know. I will do anything to protect you. I promise you that."

"Thank you."

And then she stood on her toes, and her lips pressed to his ever so lightly.

While it was just a sweet, simple gesture, he would never be the same.

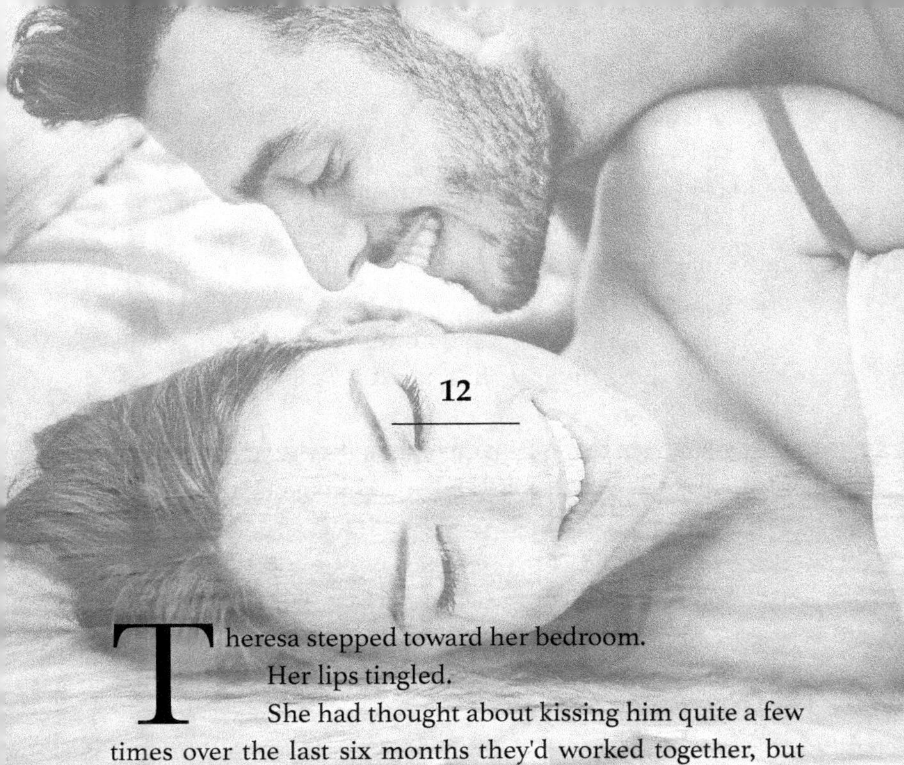

12

___

Theresa stepped toward her bedroom.

Her lips tingled.

She had thought about kissing him quite a few times over the last six months they'd worked together, but her logical mind told her not to get involved. She might have to run at any time. And as much as she hated thinking about that, she just couldn't get involved.

She knew it could break his heart. Hers too. She didn't want to break anyone's heart.

Right now, she just wanted to stay alive.

She heard Marco's phone chime, and he answered.

"Karason."

"Oh, well, I'll be damned. Do you know who?"

A pause.

"All right."

Another pause.

"Okay, I guess that'll be the first order of business. Thanks for checking into that, Mitch."

He listened for a moment, then said, "Okay, I'll do a little searching on my end too. I'll talk to Theresa about it. Maybe she's had some interaction or has seen something that would confirm that too. Talk to you tomorrow."

She halted, turned around, and took a few steps toward him in the living room. He sat on the sofa and looked up at her.

"Mitch says he's done a little investigating, and it seems as though the syndicate has ties to businesses here in Blossom Springs."

Her stomach turned. She had thought she was safe here, only to find out that they had been watching her all along.

Maybe.

Maybe they didn't realize. Maybe they had ties to every city, in every state, all over the United States.

Probably further.

Who knew?

She placed her right hand over her belly. "Oh my god," she whispered. "Does he know who?"

Marco shook his head. "No. We'll have to do some investigating here."

"How does he know?"

"Well, he doesn't divulge his security secrets, but he said he heard some chatter. He has a chatter channel. Do you know what that is?"

Her heartbeat sped up.

"Yes, I know what that is."

"Okay, well, he has a chatter channel, and he heard Blossom Springs and business partners."

She leaned down and rested her hands on her knees. She hoped it would force her mind to stop thinking of the bad things that could happen and start to formulate a plan. She'd let herself get complacent. What was wrong with her? She'd always thought her muscle memory would come back when she needed it, and she'd jump into survival mode once more. Maybe it had run out since she had been on the run for the past year. It was only the past six months here that she'd felt safe.

"Okay, so we have our work cut out for us, Theresa. We have to figure out who could be a business partner here in Blossom Springs."

She closed her eyes for a moment.

"Okay," she finally got out.

Her knees shook. She stretched her back.

His voice was soft and concerned when he said, "I'm sorry." The concern in his voice nearly made her weep. He knew how scared she was.

That wasn't good. She was not an actress—that was a fact.

Shouldn't she keep some distance?

He twisted slightly, resting his forearms on his legs as he spoke to her softly. "Hey, we're gonna do everything we can to make sure you're safe. Do you understand me?"

She nodded. "Yes, but they're here."

"Well, I guess we've known that now since last night when someone made contact with you."

"Right, but that was just by cell phone."

He nodded. "And then this morning? Someone threw a rock through your window. Do you think that was random?"

She sucked in a deep breath and blew it out hard. "No, it wasn't random. Do you think they've been watching me for a while?"

"It's possible. It's possible they've been waiting for instructions on what to do. Maybe they've been watching you to see if they could get a clue as to where you have those documents hidden. I would say it's highly probable that they are very calculated, and they are going to be very careful."

He grinned. "You have them scared, sweetheart. You have them real scared."

She huffed out her breath. "Well, now they have me scared too."

"Yeah, I understand."

Her knees still shook, and her stomach was flipping around like a fish trying to find water.

His voice was low and husky when he broke the silence. "Come on over here and sit down before you fall down."

She slowly moved to the sofa and sat on the edge of the cushion.

He scooted next to her and wrapped his arm around her. He gently leaned them back against the sofa, but he kept his arm around her shoulders. She could smell him. It was an interesting combination of food, cooking oils, and Marco. How could he still smell like himself after creating hundreds of meals tonight?

He reached over with his free hand and gently held her hand. He squeezed it gently.

She liked the comfort that she felt from his touch. She liked the softness that filled his voice when he comforted her.

Basically, she liked everything about him.

But she was in danger, and she had brought trouble to him.

His voice was deep, but solid and strong when he said, "Look, sweetheart, I know you're scared, and I know this feels like they are very close. But I can also tell you this—we're one up on them. We know they're here. They don't know we know that. So, tomorrow morning, we're going to start doing some research. You don't have to tell me where the files are, but can you just tell me this? Do you have to go somewhere to access them?"

She swallowed.

She turned her head and looked into his eyes. She held his gaze for a long time.

He didn't flinch. He didn't look away. She tried to determine if he was trying to get information out of her or if he was tried and true.

She licked her lips and inhaled. "No, I don't have to go anywhere to access them."

He nodded once. His arm squeezed her shoulders.

"Okay, that means you're safe here, and they don't know if you have the information wherever you're at or if you have to go somewhere. My guess is they're trying to figure that out."

"Okay."

He was making sense. She was starting to feel better.

"Okay." She repeated.

He grinned slightly. "Mitch is on this. He's scanning his chatter channel tonight. He's entered in some keywords, and he'll monitor it all night. And one of his employees is also on it. By the time we wake up in the morning, we should be one step closer to where they are. They won't be one step closer to where you are. Okay?"

"Okay."

He smiled. His hand was gentle as he reached up and softly brushed a hair away from her eyebrow.

His fingertips moved down her face slightly, and his fingers cupped her ear so gently.

His hand slid further down to cup her neck.

And then he slowly reached forward and gently touched his lips to hers.

And she liked it.

She returned his kiss.

She tried not to lose her breath.

Tried not to lose her head.

He was a great kisser.

She loved the way his lips felt against hers.

This was all so surreal.

Her head spun.

She was going to have to find a way to keep herself in check.

Then a thought came to her, and she reluctantly pulled away. "But I told them I had a dead man's lock on the files. They'll know they are electronic."

<h1 style="text-align:center">13</h1>

He huffed out a breath. "Yeah. I would imagine they knew that anyway. There's no way you'd run with piles of documents."

Her head bobbed slightly as she thought. It was one of the things he'd initially liked about her. She was a thinker. She was cautious though and now he knew why.

She took a deep breath. "Are you tired?"

He chuckled at the change of subject. "Not really. I normally come home wired after a busy night at the Sandbar."

"Me too."

She leaned back. "I'm going to do some research. Want to research together?"

He chuckled. "Yes. I'd love that. Do you like coffee while you research?"

"Yes."

"I'll get a pot going, you get your computer."

She stood and sauntered toward the bedroom, and he watched her. He stared at her while they were at the Sandbar every chance he got. He enjoyed watching her walk. She was strong and confident and sure of herself. It didn't hurt that she was gorgeous. A beautiful woman who was also smart and confident, though scared right now. She was confident enough to even blow the whistle on a crime syndicate in the first place. She'd get her mojo back as soon as she realized she had more power than she thought.

Marco poured them each a cup of coffee and set them at the dining room table.

He was finally going to use his dining room table, though it wasn't for a meal with his friends as he had first envisioned. It was going to be for research.

That was okay.

He was going to use it for the first time with Theresa, and there was a lot to like about that.

Theresa came in and set her laptop on the table next to his, near where he had placed her coffee cup. She opened the lid on the laptop and then settled in. He sat in the chair next to her and did the same with his laptop.

She took a deep breath and looked at him.

"What do we start researching first?"

He chuckled. "That is the fifty-million-dollar question, isn't it?"

"I think we need to look first at new businesses within the last... what, how long did you say you were on the run?"

She swallowed. "I've actually been on the run for about a year now. It'll be a year—oh, next week."

"Okay, so where were you before you came to Blossom Springs?"

"Well, I left Maine. I ran to New York City. I didn't like how busy it was, and I figured they had a lot of connections there, so I left and started heading southwest.

"I drove and drove and drove. I spent two nights in St.

Louis—just outside of the city. I didn't like that city either, then I narrowed my focus to small towns.

"So I drove into Kentucky. I found some small towns and spent some time there. Then I moved through Tennessee, staying outside of the major cities.

"Next was Georgia, and I found some small towns around the military bases. I felt safer there, I suppose— because of my military service, being near bases, it seemed like security for me. But I never really felt at home or completely safe.

"So I left Georgia and came into Florida. I spent a month in a couple of different cities in northern Florida, then decided to move farther south.

"And that's when I ended up here."

He nodded. He watched her face as she spoke.

You could see it when she mentioned certain cities—like New York and St. Louis.

The look on her face said it all.

She didn't like those cities. And likely, not feeling safe anywhere had a lot to do with it.

"Okay," he replied, "so probably not enough time in any of those cities or towns for them to follow you or trace you anywhere. Did you ever feel like you were being watched or followed?"

She put her hands on her lap and turned to look at him.

Her pretty brown eyes stared into his, and he could see right into her soul.

At least, he felt that way.

She didn't look away from him. She wasn't trying to hide anything.

"No, I don't think so. I think it was just a general fear that they would find me. And in those bigger cities, I hadn't really met anyone. So who would I call if I needed help?

" I started to feel like maybe being lost in a big city wasn't where I wanted to be, and I made the move here.

"I needed to work for a few reasons. I didn't want to chew up all my savings—that was one reason.

"And the other one is, I didn't want to just sit at home all day long and worry. So being out in the workforce kept my mind occupied. I found the job at the Sandbar in the local paper when I was up north—outside of Tallahassee—and I thought, a small-town bar on the water. Well, it's not like the syndicate is going to have people lying around the beach. So, I jumped at the chance.

"After I met Jace, I realized what his preference was for hiring military veterans and helping them. I figured I fit the bill. Not only do I have a little PTSD, but man, I was running scared. And he seemed solid and nonjudgmental, and I figured working for him would be good. So I took the job."

"Okay," he grinned.

When she talked about Jace and the Sandbar, they, Jace and Margo, really had developed a nice little community there.

"So, you started working, and you slowly became comfortable here."

"Yeah. I mean, like I said, the syndicate wasn't going to have guys hanging out at the beach or at a beach bar. And, you know, I kind of felt like no one was really going to be looking for me working in a bar of restaurant kind of place.

"And I didn't have anything happen to make me feel suspicious or worried. So yes, I grew comfortable. That was my mistake."

He nodded. "I think that's how people always get caught. They just get comfortable."

He continued, "Well, it could be—" He paused. "You were smart about the things that you did, Theresa.

"You were smart about continuing to move. You were smart about not using electronic devices. Getting a cell phone in your mom's name was smart. They could look, I suppose, for her name, and maybe they did. Maybe that's how they found you. It's not a secret who your mom is."

"She's dead."

"Honey, you're not the first person who has taken a dead relative's name when you're in trouble."

Her shoulders dropped.

"I'm not as smart as I thought I was."

"Well, you've made it a year. I mean, that's pretty good. Normally, they'd get you within the first couple of weeks. So I'd say you were very smart."

She grinned. "Thanks."

"Okay. So, in knowing all of that, let me change my mind. Let's start looking for businesses that are newer in the last year here in Blossom Springs. If you want to do some searching on that, what I'm going to search for are businesses who have had hard financial times and suddenly are doing much better."

"How are you going to find that out?" she asked.

He grinned. "Small towns are a pretty hard place to hide financial woes. Everybody knows."

She chuckled. "I suppose. It's difficult to hide a lot of things in a small town. I've noticed that. As soon as Jace and Margo started dating—oh my gosh."

"Yeah. That's a fact. It's both the bane and the joy of living in a small town. Correct?"

"Correct."

He nodded. "Okay. So, here's what I would do if I were you. Get in touch with Carley Thompson. Since she is a realtor in the area, she may have records of new businesses that have started up in the past year. She's probably helped with hundreds of transactions and might be willing to share the records. And I will work on my end with some things. I'm going to also send Mitch an email and tell him what we're doing. I'll copy you on it so you can see what the communication is. And that way, nobody is duplicating any efforts. And he'll know what we're working on, so he can focus on other things. Deal?"

She slightly chuckled. "Deal."

14

Theresa stretched her back, raised her arms in the air, and tried to release the tension in her shoulders.

She reached forward, grabbed her cup of coffee, and sipped—only to wrinkle her nose when she realized the cup was cold.

She looked over at Marco's cup. It was nearly empty.

She had dug in and started doing some real estate investigation. He drank and worked at the same time.

She stood and reached for her cup.

Marco turned and looked at her.

Man, she could look at him all day. He was such a handsome man.

"Do you want more coffee?"

He grinned. "Yes, thank you. I appreciate that. You didn't drink yours. You don't like it?"

She chuckled. "Nah, I was just noticing the difference between us. You can sip on your coffee and work at the same time. I get engrossed in my work and forget to drink my

coffee. It was merely that I got involved. That's it. I'm gonna get myself a cup now."

She reached forward, grabbed his cup, and sauntered to the coffee pot. She poured her cold brew down the drain, rinsed the sink, and then poured them each a fresh cup.

She turned and looked back at him. "I'm sorry, I didn't notice—cream and sugar?"

"Just cream for me."

She chuckled. "Me too."

She poured their cups and brought them back to the table.

She had just sat down when an email popped up from Carley.

She looked at the time on her computer.

Three forty-five in the morning.

"My god, Carley just emailed me at three forty-five. What do you suppose she's doing up?"

He chuckled. "Well, they have a puppy."

"Yeah, but isn't—" She paused. "Isn't that puppy almost a year old now?"

"About nine months, I guess."

"Oh, I suppose."

She opened the email and read Carley's reply.

Off the top of my head, I can give you the names of three new businesses in town. I didn't have a lot to do with any of them as far as the sales process goes. Two of them are just renting the buildings they're in—they didn't have a need for a realtor. The third one bought a small building but was very, very coy about what they were putting in it. They just said it was for the future growth of a business, but that's all they would say.

Theresa quickly typed out her response.

Thank you so much for that. Why are you up this early in the morning?

She sent her email.

Almost immediately, a reply popped up.

I have a nine-month-old puppy who counter-surfed last night and got a hold of some chicken. Needless to say, we've been going to the bathroom a lot. Like every hour. I'd love nothing more than to be snuggled in next to my husband, but—puppy.

Theresa read the response to Marco, and they chuckled.

"Yeah, the joys of owning a puppy," he said.

"Right."

He stopped and looked at her. "Did you have a dog growing up?"

"No. How about you?"

"We always had dogs. My brothers loved dogs. My sister wanted the dogs. We always had one or two running around."

"I'm jealous. I would have loved to have had a dog growing up, but my parents didn't want that."

"Yeah, it's nice having a dog. My parents always said it developed our sense of responsibility. We each took turns — every week it was somebody else's turn to feed and water the dogs. And if we didn't remember—oh, we got an ass-beating."

Theresa chuckled. "Yeah, I've heard about families like that."

Marco's head cocked to the side. "You're an only child?"

"Yeah, I'm an only child. It was lonely, though. I used to envy my friends and their big families, but Mom couldn't have any more children after me, so I didn't get siblings."

He chuckled. "Having siblings was nice. Sometimes it was a pain in the butt—especially a little sister. And my little sister is a little beauty. So needless to say, as my friends and I all got to be around sixteen, seventeen, eighteen years old, I didn't bring them to the house much anymore. They spent more time staring at her than they did kicking around with me."

She chuckled. "Yeah. Boys, right?"

"Yeah. Boys."

"Anyway—so did she name the three businesses?"

"Oh, yes."

She scrolled back to the first email.

"She has them listed down here at the bottom. One is a small brokerage agency. They're renting their building. One is a law office. That one's also being rented. And the last one is the one that was bought. They said it was for future business, and there's no business name for it. But the name on the file is Bradford Bennett LLC."

"Okay, so let's look into those businesses, shall we?"

"Okay. I'm thinking maybe—" He hesitated. "I'm thinking I'm going to be visiting at least two businesses. See what they look like inside."

The thought of going on a covert mission, so to speak, sent a bolt of excitement through her body. "I'll go with you."

"No, you won't. You have to stay here. We don't want them to see you, right?"

"Right. Maybe I could wear a disguise."

"No. Again, I think you need to stay here."

"Am I a prisoner here?"

"No, you're not a prisoner, but I do want to keep you safe. And you have to be smart about this. Don't put yourself out there in the open."

His phone rang.

She saw him take a deep breath before picking it up. He looked at the readout on the screen. He said, "Mitch."

He tapped the button, then the speaker icon.

"Good morning, Mitch. I'm sitting here with Theresa. We are doing some investigating."

"Right. Well—her house burned down. It's on fire right now."

Theresa's stomach twisted.

Her hand flew to her mouth.

"Oh my god. Oh my god."

Mitch continued. "I decided to test them and see how far they'd be willing to go. So I sent one of my employees into the house. They drove Theresa's car to the driveway, went into the house, and then slipped out the back door and through the back area to Hospital Drive. They circled around. I was sitting at the end of the street with my lights off, watching it all. I saw somebody come running through the woods and throw a Molotov into the window, and the place caught on fire. My employee ran and got Theresa's car out of the way. I don't know if they stayed to watch or not, but I hope she had all of her stuff out of there. And I'll say this—more than ever, she needs to stay hidden. They're beginning to get bold in their scare tactics. If that's all this was."

Marco stared into her eyes as he replied. "They wouldn't kill her until they had the files they wanted. I'm reasonably sure of that."

Mitch commented, "But of course, we can never be too sure. So, I think this was a way to flush her out and really scare her. Maybe hoping that she's going to leave town so they can catch her on the road. So that's what we're gonna let them do."

Marco's jaw clenched.

She stared between him and his phone as if she were hearing a foreign language.

She finally said, "What?"

Her heart pounded so fast she didn't even know if she could breathe. He was going to send her out there?

Mitch continued, "I think what we're gonna do is have my employee put that long wig back on and drive your car out of town. We're gonna make a few trips around town first, so they see you—wherever they're watching from—and then start to head out of town. And we're gonna be following. Maybe we can flesh out who's actually watching and how they're following you."

She placed her right hand over her stomach and took in a few deep breaths.

"Oh my god. Oh my god."

Marco's hand reached over to hold hers.

He squeezed gently to comfort her.

And she was grateful for that. But what comforted her more was his strong steady presence and the way she felt sitting next to him. She was incredibly grateful for that. He made her feel more secure than anyone she'd ever had in her life. Oddly, she felt safer now, with a cartel on her tail, than she had ever felt in her life.

15

———

Marco watched Theresa as Mitch explained his plan. Her eyes rounded and he could see her chest rise and fall in rapid succession. He held her hand for comfort, but when Mitch was finished explaining what they planned to do, Marco changed the conversation.

"Mitch, I'm watching some businesses today to see what I can find out about their activities."

"That's a good idea. What are you focusing on?"

He grinned at Theresa. "Rents that are too high. Bank deposits that are abnormally large for a small town."

"How are you going to figure out large bank deposits?"

"Usually when someone is laundering money, they take a lot of cash at the business they're laundering from, but they also make more than one bank deposit in a day to several different banks. And, if they're using a mule to transfer the money from the place of business to another location for laundering, there will be a mule coming and going. My thought is to specifically watch the new brokerage and the attorney's business. If I sit and watch the comings and goings of people in a new business, a smurf should show themselves in short order."

Theresa cocked her head. "What's a smurf?"

He grinned as he responded. "It's someone who is helping in the laundering process. He or she breaks up large transactions into sets of smaller transactions that are each below the reporting threshold. Then they pretend to invest them or take them to various banks."

"In what way?"

He turned in his chair to face her. "A smurf might pretend to be a landlord. He'll take in far too much money for rent on a building. It may be a residential rental like an apartment or Airbnb. He actually only collects the regular rent, say a place is worth a thousand dollars a month. But on the books, he writes in three thousand a month. In many cases, there are only a couple of tenants in a building so there's activity, and they are instructed to tell anyone who asks that they pay three thousand dollars a month for rent. So if authorities come around and ask, it seems legit. If anyone questions how this person can afford that kind of rent, they're instructed to say they have a trust fund or something. The other units are usually empty, so they don't have too many people on the books. But fake leases and names are used. The money comes from other sources, say drug deals or illegal smuggling, etc. But it's laundered through the apartment building."

Theresa nodded slowly. "I guess I never heard that term. I did see transactions on the ledgers I found that didn't add up and that's why. That's how I started investigating in the first place. They were also using laundromats, pizza places, and dress shops. Basically, any business. But even though I'd investigated for so long, I didn't look outside the state of

Maine. I should have. So now I'm going to go back through my information and figure out a few more things."

He grinned. "There you go."

She cocked her head, "Why an attorney's office?"

"An attorney, a bad one, is easy to bribe into working for a syndicate. They need the money, and they like the power. So, they'll launder money through their law office using fake names as clients, creating fake documents, etc. The smurf will bring money to the attorney. The attorney counts it, then doles it out into files. Those files need to have billable hours associated with them to justify the costs, so said attorney is usually very busy creating fake documents to go with the money. They make deposits to their bank for the fake clients. Many times, these clients are also the landlord, who has so many legal problems, they pay their attorney a ton of money to fix their issues."

Theresa nodded. Her pretty lips turned down into a frown. "That makes sense, doesn't it?"

"How did you channel your research?"

She shook her head. "I started looking at the money laundering, but it was clear there was something bigger at stake. I then became more focused on the millions, actually billions of dollars, being floated to the presidential and senate campaigns. I couldn't believe how much money was going to television and radio stations for ads for this candidate. I started following that trail and didn't even have the chance to look at the laundering aspect. I was more worried about the threat to democracy. If the Celtics were paying for a president and Congress, it had to be for their benefit. I wanted to know what that benefit was. That's the direction I was going. And I found some leads. A couple of them led to what I thought was human trafficking."

Mitch's voice softened. "You be careful. As you're aware, they don't want this information out."

"I'm aware, it's why I'm basically on the run. My boss began getting threats. At first, they were idle threats. She ran my story anyway. It was a beginning piece of what I had planned to be a five-part series."

Marco watched her as she spoke. Her fingers shook slightly as she began talking about her boss. He softly encouraged her to continue.

"What happened?"

Theresa's eyes stared into his for a while. Finally, her lips thinned and she bit her bottom lip. "The threats after the first story grew in urgency. They went from we'll shut your paper down to we'll burn your house down."

She swallowed and sat up straighter. "They did. Burned her house down. No one was injured and that's when she told me to get out of town. Don't contact her. Lay as low as I could and when it was safe to come back, she'd let me know."

Marco's brows furrowed. "How would she do that?"

"I check the paper once a quarter on the first day of the month. If it's safe to come back, there will be an ad in the classified section for an investigative reporter. It would say, only TM need apply."

"Have you been checking?"

"Yes." She took a deep breath. "No ad so far."

Mitch was quiet for a moment. "What's the name of the paper and your boss's name?"

"The Daily Reporter and her name is Carolyn Sutton."

"Hang on a moment, I need to check something."

They could hear the tones on his phone as he typed something in. He read on his phone for a few moments, then looked up at her and said, "I'm afraid I have some bad news."

Marco felt her hold her breath and stiffen. She sat stone still.

Mitch inhaled deeply then swallowed. "She was killed in a car accident last month."

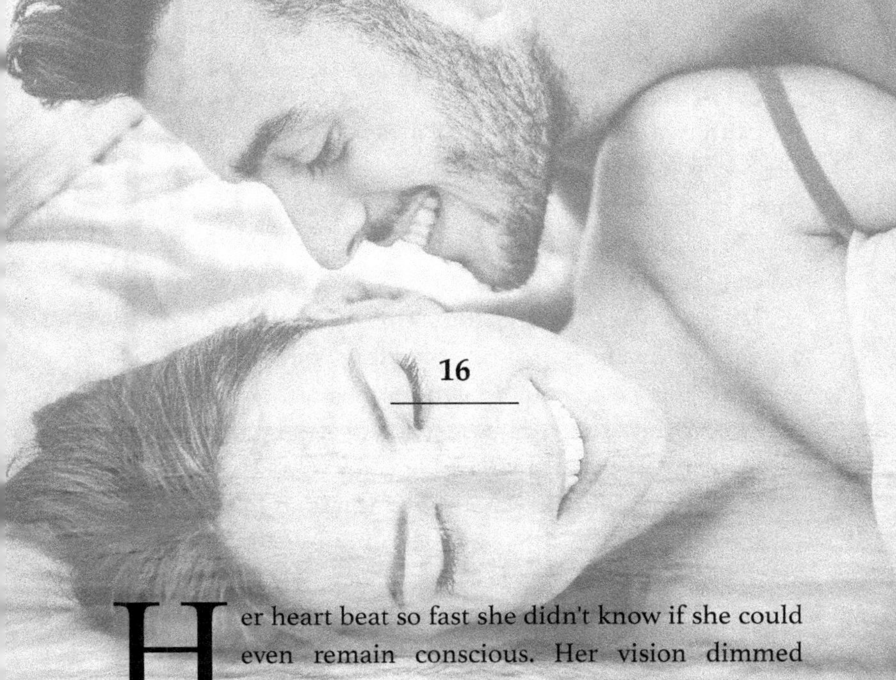

16

Her heart beat so fast she didn't know if she could even remain conscious. Her vision dimmed before her and the horrors of the past year began to bombard her brain. She could still hear Carolyn's voice as the first threats came into the office. She'd been scared but felt as though it was their job to report the news. All of it. No matter how seditious and dirty it was.

The air left her lungs as she said, "What? What kind of a car accident? I didn't hear anything about it."

Mitch was quiet a moment, then he responded. "It just says car accident, Theresa. It doesn't offer any other information. Now, I will say this—I do know someone in the area. I can give them a call, talk to them about the accident, see what the general feeling is—if it was a true accident or if foul play is suspected."

Her mind nearly went blank. She muttered, "Foul play?"

Mitch's tone was even. "Look, considering all the facts here, we have to assume that it could have been foul play, right? I mean, you're on the run for a reason. And I think we absolutely need to operate under the assumption that it was probably not an accident. That means you need to stay as close as you can to Marco. I'm gonna go so far as to say you shouldn't even go to work."

"But I need—" She stammered a little, the words refusing to come out.

Marco squeezed her hand. "Honey, I think he's right. Things are heating up. They're getting concerned that it's been a while since you've been seen—until recently. Now they know you're here. They're going to step up their efforts to get the information you have."

She swallowed a dry knot in her throat. It felt like she'd swallowed a mouthful of sand. Her mind wouldn't engage. She blew out a deep breath.

"I feel like a sitting duck here, not doing anything, just waiting for them to come and get me."

Mitch said quickly. "I can understand that and appreciate it, but you're a sitting duck if you go out there right now. Let me touch base with my contact in Maine and find out what he thinks is going on. I'll get back to you as soon as I can. Stay here. Don't leave. Let's be smart about this so no one else gets hurt."

She drew in a shaky breath and let it out slowly.

"Okay. I understand."

Her mind raced. She knew what she had to do. It was imperative now to get the word out. Marco turned to her. "I think we both need some sleep, as we've been up all night. At least an hour or two before we do anything."

"I can't..." She stopped trying to force the words from her mouth. She shook her head and swallowed. "I can't sleep right now. I have research to complete. You go ahead and get some rest."

He shook his head slightly. "I'll just take a quick shower. That's all I need."

She watched him saunter to his bedroom and she blew out a breath. If only things were different. If only she hadn't started this shit-show of a report. But curiosity was something she couldn't set aside, and once she started researching, she couldn't stop. The more insidious reports she found, the more she had to keep digging.

She turned to the dining room table where their laptops sat side by side. She sat in her chair and pulled up her blockchain account. It took four separate passwords before it opened for her, that was by design. After her account loaded, she took a deep breath. It was time to begin getting this information completed and ready to release. And to do that, she was going to have to break cover, which was already kind of blown anyway.

As soon as her fingers began typing, the story flew from her. It had been bottled up for so long. She'd thought endlessly about how to write the final two pieces of her story. She attached the links to the documents she'd set up in a file in the cloud. As soon as she released each piece of the story, the documents could be accessed and seen. Not the originals though. The hard copies of the documents they'd managed to obtain had been scanned and locked away in a safe by Carolyn. She stiffened as she realized what that meant.

Marco strode from his bedroom smelling amazing and looking even better. It wasn't fair that men could simply take a shower to look refreshed and ready to tackle the world.

He stopped near the table and stared at her. "What's wrong?"

She swallowed and blinked her eyes rapidly to keep from crying. Her nose tingled and her ears warmed. She stood and took a deep breath. "I may have gotten Carolyn killed."

His brows furrowed. "That's impossible. You're here, she was there."

"Right." She inhaled to fill her lungs. It was more to keep herself from falling apart than anything. She looked into Marco's eyes. "The documents I had on hand. The real documents that started me on this report were scanned for the story, but Carolyn kept them in a safe at her home. We were worried they'd be found and destroyed before the stories were released."

Marco's chest rose and fell. He wore a gray t-shirt that he likely didn't mean to be sexy, but it was. A simple damned t-shirt. And he wore a pair of jeans that looked amazing on him. She let her eyes roam down his long lean legs to see that he was barefoot. Good gawd, the man oozed sexy.

"Theresa." His voice was deep, soothing and she liked listening to him speak. Far too much. "She did that because she believed in the story. I assume she knew what might happen, otherwise she wouldn't have sent you off to run."

She rubbed her fingers against her temples. "I shouldn't have let her take those documents."

"They would have no way of knowing if she had them or not."

"But, they knew one of us had them. They likely asked her where I was, and she wouldn't tell them. Or they asked where the documents were."

His eyes stared into hers. "How would they know you had the documents?"

"I said as much in the first story I wrote. I emailed you a copy so you could see what we're up against."

He nodded his head and smiled. "I already read it."

Her brows shot up into her bangs. "You did?"

He chuckled. "I'm pretty good at my job. Both of them.

My former military experience taught me to be resourceful, prepared, and ready to tackle whatever I needed to take on."

She nodded. "Of course."

He stepped to her and wrapped his arms around her. She eagerly wrapped her arms around his waist. Her ear rested on his chest, the strong steady beat of his heart was comforting. The solid mass of his chest made her feel completely safe.

But she wasn't. She was in more danger now than ever.

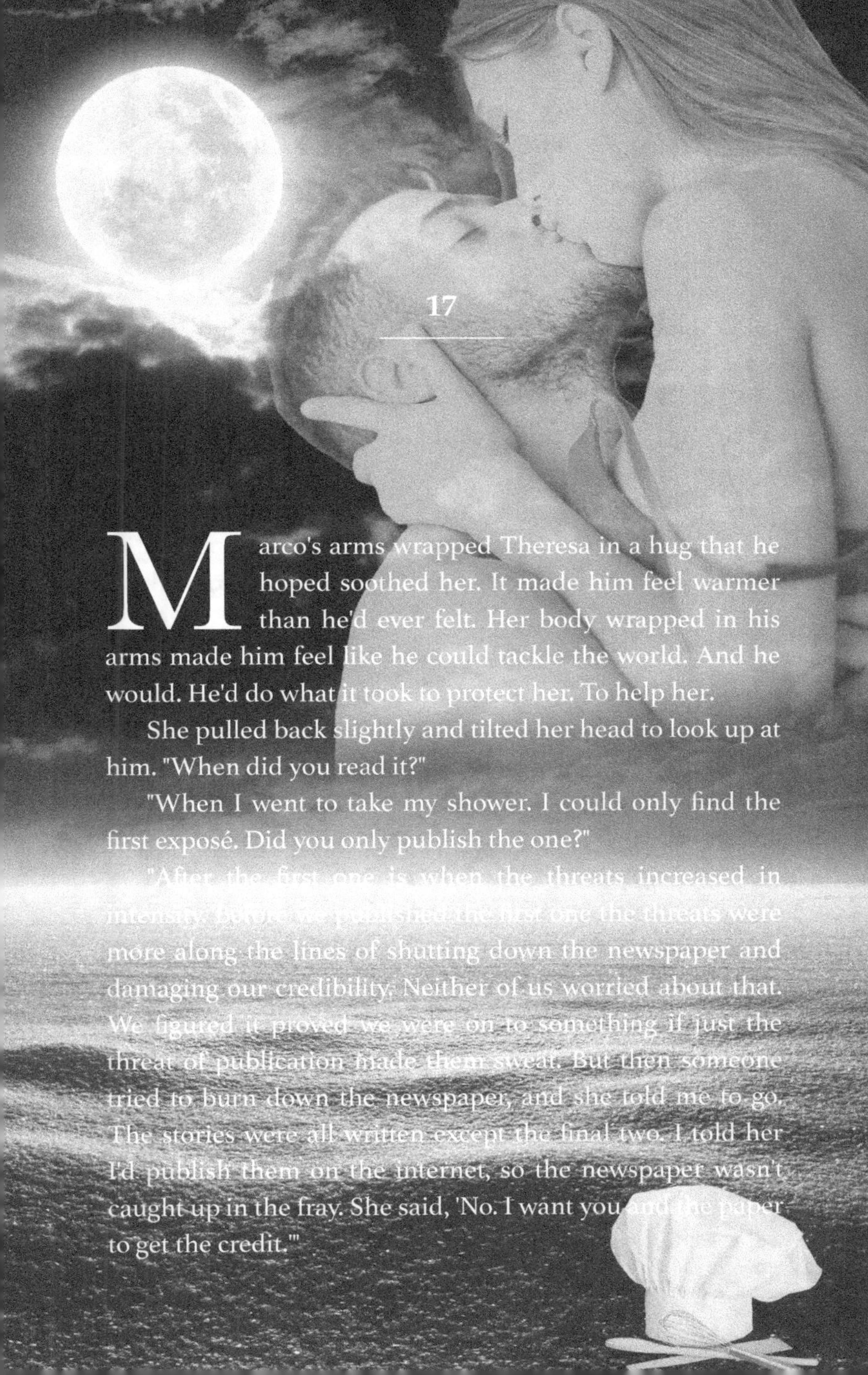

17

Marco's arms wrapped Theresa in a hug that he hoped soothed her. It made him feel warmer than he'd ever felt. Her body wrapped in his arms made him feel like he could tackle the world. And he would. He'd do what it took to protect her. To help her.

She pulled back slightly and tilted her head to look up at him. "When did you read it?"

"When I went to take my shower. I could only find the first exposé. Did you only publish the one?"

"After the first one is when the threats increased in intensity. Before we published the first one the threats were more along the lines of shutting down the newspaper and damaging our credibility. Neither of us worried about that. We figured it proved we were on to something if just the threat of publication made them sweat. But then someone tried to burn down the newspaper, and she told me to go. The stories were all written except the final two. I told her I'd publish them on the internet, so the newspaper wasn't caught up in the fray. She said, 'No. I want you and the paper to get the credit.'"

"Okay. So there are four more articles to publish?"

She stepped back. Her fingers twisted together in front of her. "Yes. I just finished writing the final article. I need to proofread it and make sure the links to the documents work, but it's written."

"Okay. So, we need a plan. The plan has to make sure you're safe, while also getting the word out about the criminality you've found. Do you mind if I read them?"

"No, I don't mind. I'd actually like your comments."

They moved in unison to the table where their laptops sat side by side. She motioned for him to sit in front of her laptop to read the stories she'd written. He nodded and sat.

Theresa sucked in a deep breath. "I have the second, third, fourth, and fifth stories in order here." She pointed to a folder on her laptop. "Just open that folder and read them in order."

Marco opened the first story and began reading, even though he'd already read it, he wanted to read them now in succession. She'd titled each story. The first one was titled *The Whisper in the Dark*. She'd recounted receiving an anonymous tip regarding the elaborate network. Millions of dollars moving through shadowy shell companies and offshore accounts, disguised as ordinary business transactions. She'd almost set it aside as some troublemaker trying to get his or her fifteen minutes of fame. Except, there wasn't a name. And some of the language made her believe there was something dark and dirty going on. She was a great writer, succinct and informative. She laid out the story as she unfolded it and laid the dirty dealings bare.

The second exposé was titled, *The Dirty Money Trail*. She laid out how she set out to dive headfirst into a maze of financial records and offshore transactions. There was a web of shell companies, each one designed to obscure the flow of cash and its origins. She painstakingly detailed the network of transfers between obscure banks in tax havens, where millions of dollars were moved. Then the link to prove the transactions were not random. There was a pattern.

He took a deep breath and clicked on the third, which was titled, *Inside the Syndicate*. This story led Theresa into the heart of the criminal network. Through a series of risky undercover interviews with former operatives and unsuspecting wives needing to feel important, she pieced together the organization's inner workings. Her source was code-named "Mercury," who risked everything to reveal how money was moved and manipulated. Mercury described a highly organized structure, with mid-level managers acting as gatekeepers and financiers directing funds from offshore accounts to domestic fronts.

His heartbeat picked up as he read the details she'd uncovered. Theresa was right to be in hiding. She should be more scared than she was. His fear for her was growing with every sentence he read.

He turned his head to see her watching him. Her breathing was stilted and uneven. He smiled at her, though it felt forced. "You've done an incredible job in your research. I'm incredibly humbled and proud of you at the same time."

She smiled. "You are?"

He nodded. "I am. You've uncovered the Madoff-esque network of this century."

She swallowed. "I'm afraid I've gotten a few people killed for it though."

His brows rose. "A few?"

Her shoulders rose as she inhaled a deep breath. She held it a moment and let it out slowly. "Carolyn for one.

But..." Her lips quivered and her eyes watered. "Mercury...she was also murdered."

"How?"

"I don't know. I only found out the week after I left Maine. I tried keeping in touch with her, we have a code, and our meetings took place in person. But sometimes it was too dangerous, so we'd meet via electronic means. Always different so no one platform could be hacked and reveal us. I contacted her via our code. It was a text that was made to look like a scam asking you to enter your social security number. But we had a code to tell us what means we'd use to touch base. I didn't hear back from her, so I scoured the internet looking for any mention of her. I discovered her house had been broken into and she'd been beaten to death."

"Geezus."

"Yes. I left where I was in case the code was somehow deciphered."

He stared into her beautiful but scared eyes. "You knew her real name?"

"Yes." A tear slipped from the corner of her eye and created a wet path down her cheek. He used the back of his forefinger to swipe it away. Her eyes stared into his for a long time. "She was married to one of the sons of the head of Celtic. Her name was Keely Benson."

A knot appeared in this throat and he worked to dislodge it before he spoke. "Did he kill..."

"I assume so. I don't know for sure and of course, there isn't going to be an investigation because everyone would be paid off. So, it'll go down as a random robbery."

His phone rang and they both jumped. He pulled it from his pocket to see Mitch's name. "Hey, Mitch, what's up?"

"Can you put me on speaker?"

"You got it." He tapped the speaker icon and nodded to Theresa.

"I found some things out. First of all, Theresa, I'm so sorry to tell you, but it does look like the accident wasn't an accident. My friend told me they're investigating and at every turn, they've had to jump over hurdles. That made him and his partner look closer at someone in the agency, and they most likely had a mole. So now there's a task force set up to investigate the mole, but that also shed light on what was going on. It appears Carolyn was strangled, put into her car, and it was pushed over a cliff into the water. By the time she was found, the evidence of murder was difficult to uncover, but a crack coroner noticed the deep contusions on her larynx and kept investigating."

Theresa swayed and reached out to hold on to the table. He reached over and took her free hand in his. "Thank you for investigating this, Mitch. How are they handling it in Maine?"

"They're keeping this investigation under wraps for right now. The mole has likely told his handlers that it's happening but they're moving forward."

Marco continued to stare at Theresa as she processed this news. He replied to Mitch but didn't look away from Theresa. "Theresa told me that Carolyn had the original documents she had uncovered. The documents were stored in a safe in Carolyn's house. Is there any way someone could go in there and see if they're still there?"

Mitch let out a slow whistle. "I can certainly ask."

Theresa took a deep breath. "Mitch, your friend isn't working for the police, is he?"

"No. He's working for a private company hired to come in and ferret out cases like this. They're off the books, so to speak. Do you suspect the police are dirty?"

"Not necessarily. But the Celtics do have some of them bought, which is likely where your mole came from. But there will be others inside. The lure of money and the sheer evilness of the Celtics is enough to turn a good cop. They'll threaten families, children, and wives. They don't care. They threaten into submission."

"I'm sorry I don't have better news, Theresa."

"Me too," she whispered.

Marco squeezed her hand again. "Mitch, Theresa finished writing her exposés. I'm reading them now. You should read them too. They're unreal and very detailed."

"I'd love to read them. They may give me and my friends in Maine something to go on."

Theresa weakly smiled. "I'll email them to you." She cleared her throat. "Once the full autopsy and investigation into Carolyn's death is finished, I'll write a story about that too."

"I'll make sure my friend gets me the documentation you need to publish it."

The line went dead, and Marco leaned forward to hug Theresa. She let out a shuddered breath and tucked her lips into the crook of his neck. He closed his eyes as feelings washed over him. He wanted to protect her. It was getting close to needing to protect her. Maybe he was getting too close but there was no going back now.

18

She inhaled Marco's scent, felt warmed by his nearness, and bolstered by his strength and courage. They could do this. She could do this with his help. Mitch's too. But she was quickly coming to rely on Marco. Not only rely on him but want him nearby.

He whispered, "Are you okay?"

She closed her eyes and let his strength seep into her a bit more. She sat upright and looked into his sexy brown eyes. "Yes. I hate what happened to her and I'll likely not sleep at night for a while thinking about what she went through. She was tough. And she said she knew the risk. But I wonder if she knew it could lead to her murder."

She watched his Adam's apple rise and fall as he swallowed. "I don't know if our brains can actually let us completely go there. We know the risk. It makes us more careful. But to actually deeply know what that might look like, I don't think we ever really know until it's too late."

"Yeah."

He turned back to her computer, clicked on the fourth article, and kept reading. She sat quietly as he read, waiting for his response. The fourth exposé focused on the fact that the money was funding political campaigns. They were putting people in power that would hide what they were doing. Would help them do it without fear of being found out. She'd titled that one, *The Political Nexus*.

She'd been inspired as she wrote the fifth one to title it, *Aftermath and Accountability - The Long Road to Justice*. At this point, they were so far from justice and accountability. She wanted this piece to spark a firestorm of public outrage that would make it too big to sweep under the rug. There needed to be a public outing of the officials who looked the other way or were actively involved in the operations of these sons of bitches who had been stealing, killing, and railroading innocent lives. She knew there would be resistance and she hoped with everything in her, especially now that she also needed to avenge Carolyn, that enough people would take up the mantle so that it wouldn't be dropped.

Marco finished reading and turned in his chair to face her. "I'm in awe of what you've done here. You have put yourself in danger beyond anyone I know to expose the wrongs of some very powerful people. And I am humbled by you."

She smiled softly, her cheeks heated hearing his words. "Thank you. But to be honest, at the time I didn't know how much danger I was in until today. I was investigating a story. Even when Carolyn told me to run, I thought she might be overreacting. In my limited thinking, I thought exposing them would make us too prominent to harm. Everyone would look at the people spurned when one of us died. Right? Instead, they have people to cover it up as if Carolyn never mattered. I'm going to expose them and make them see that she mattered. Mercury mattered. I matter."

He nodded and grinned as she spoke. "You do matter. All of you matter."

She felt the tears fall before her brain comprehended what they were. She did that sometimes. She got all worked up and passionate about a story and didn't pay attention to what was happening to her. Like not drinking her coffee as she worked.

She sniffed and swiped at the tears on her cheeks. Marco stared at her. She couldn't quite read the thoughts in his mind from his expression. It was almost as if he was proud of her.

Finally, his lips turned up in a sexy smile and he whispered again. "You're incredible and I'm so inspired by you."

"Inspired?"

"Yes. Inspired to be brave. To do what's right and important. Sometimes we tend to shrink into the background and let others carry the mantle. I'm inspired to help you carry the mantle."

She sniffed lightly. "Okay. What does that look like?"

"I'm going to do everything in my power to keep you safe and help you get these stories out there. I think we start by sending them to Mitch. Then, we dig into the businesses in Blossom Springs that are helping the Celtics launder money and expose them on a local level. Then a national level."

Her heartbeat sped up. He was really something, this man right here.

"I like that very much. I'll send them first; then, I would like to take a bit of a nap. I've exhausted myself doing all of this. Do you mind if I lay down for a bit?"

"Of course not. I'll lay down with you."

She froze. He was going to lay with her? Her brows shot up into her bangs and he nodded. "I mean, at the same time."

That sort of made her sad. She took a deep breath and sent Mitch the articles to read, then stood up and took his hand in hers. "How about we nap together?"

"I don't want you to feel pressured."

"I don't feel pressured. I feel tired and having you next to me will help me sleep better. Unless you don't like sleeping with another person."

He stood and she tilted her head up to see his face. To look into his eyes. "I don't sleep with other people. But I would like to take a nap with you."

She smiled. "I'd like that very much."

He took her hand and led her to his bedroom. Once they were inside, he locked the door. "To make you feel safe."

She smiled and kicked her shoes off. She wasn't going to tell him sleeping with him next to her would make her feel safer than a locked door. Maybe that would be for a different day. After she'd had some sleep and could think straight. Maybe then.

19

Marco woke with his arms wrapped around Theresa. Her butt tucked in tightly to his cock, which was now growing firm. She smelled good. They were warm snuggled together. Comfortable, though not any longer. He didn't know if he should move away, and risk waking her or think of something unpleasant to make his cock shrink. Unfortunately, thinking about it further and the sound of Theresa sleeping peacefully next to him made him harder.

His right arm was tucked under her neck, his left arm wrapped around her waist, his hand tucked under her arm resting peacefully on the bed. They were wrapped tightly together and no way to untangle without waking her.

He closed his eyes to think of anything else when she scooted to her back. She still used his right arm as a pillow. He opened his eyes to see her beautiful brown eyes staring up at him. They stared at each other for a long moment. Then she cupped her hand behind his head and pulled him down for a kiss. The instant their lips met, his body roared to life. Her hand roamed down his neck, onto his back as she twisted her body further, so her breasts were now pressed into his chest. No chance of his cock softening now.

Her tongue slipped into his mouth and danced along his tongue. She was tantalizing. His left hand slid down and pulled her ass in tightly, so his cock was nestled nicely against her body. She moaned slightly and his mind nearly exploded as all the times he'd thought of her this way bombarded his brain.

She moved her hips back and forth, rubbing against his erection, and his blood sizzled. He moved to lay her on her back, as he rose over her. He held himself off her slightly with his elbows resting on the bed, his hands tangled in her silky hair, his cock pulsing against her body.

She moved her hips in rhythm to the perfect dance and he felt the precum wet his jeans.

He reached down and unbuttoned and unzipped his jeans and relief swept through him when her hands immediately shoved his jeans over his hips. She then shimmied her shorts off under him. He only gave her a small space to do it because he liked feeling her wriggle under him.

He reached over to the nightstand and pulled a condom from the drawer. She smiled and took it from him. "Let me."

She ripped it open and reached between them taking his cock in one hand and deftly rolling the condom onto his cock with the other. He had to close his eyes and restrain himself as she pumped her hand up and down to secure the condom. Then she began playing with him.

He reared up, she spread her legs, and he stared into her eyes as he entered her.

She moaned. So did he. Her heat and tightness sucked him in. He pulled out and slid back in and it was like coming home. She moaned as he slid in, and he wanted to hear that over and over.

He pulled out and slid back in waiting for her sounds of pleasure, feeling his own pleasure.

"Damn, you feel amazing," he husked.

She splayed her hands across his ass and lifted her legs higher. "So do you."

He pulled out again and when he slid in, she pulled him tightly to her. That felt better. He huffed out a deep breath and she chuckled slightly. "We feel amazing together."

"That's a fact."

He moved faster and she moved with him. He pumped into her harder and she met him move for move. Their movements grew in intensity as they sought their release. His skin heated from the exertion, their aromas mingled in the air as their bodies did.

His hands fisted in her hair, and she smiled. Her hips began moving faster and he kept up with her, but he could feel his balls tighten painfully as his orgasm threatened to explode. He moaned and whispered, "Come for me, baby."

Her hips moved faster, and he kept up with her, adding pressure where their bodies met until she cried out his name and his vision dimmed as he felt the hot pulsing stream shoot from his body.

He jerked a few times as his seed spilled into the condom. Her arms tightened around his waist, her legs tightened around his ass.

Her breathing was rapid, as was his. He dropped his head next to hers, still holding himself slightly aloft. He whispered. "You'll never know how many times I dreamed of this."

She sighed. "Likely not as many times as I did."

20

Theresa stepped from the bathroom after having showered to see Marco standing at the stove making them something to eat. Her stomach growled and she glanced at the clock on the stove and saw it was now two fifteen. They should have been at the Sandbar by now and she said, "Shit. I'm late."

He turned his head and grinned at her. She'll never forget that grin, it was the sexiest grin ever. "I texted Jace before we napped and told him we couldn't come in. Mitch had already been there and informed him of what was going on. They've also met with Blossom Springs PD and gotten their take and made a plan for your safety."

Relief swept through her. "Thank goodness. But that does put a burden on them."

Marco laughed. "Jace said he missed being in the kitchen so he's happy to be back in there for a bit. It'll be like old times for them."

"I suppose."

She stepped around the counter and wrapped her arms around him from behind. He turned in her arms and moved them across the kitchen against the counter. "No need for either of us to get burned."

"Right."

His head dipped down and kissed her lips. How was it possible his kiss felt better than it had before? His body felt more comfortable against hers now. They knew each other in a different way and she liked this so much better.

He pulled away from her slightly and grinned again. "I hope you're hungry."

She smiled. "I am."

"Good. I made Chorizo steak, fried potatoes, and asparagus."

"Oh my gawd, that sounds delicious."

Her stomach growled again as if it needed to make the point clearer. She chuckled and he kissed her forehead.

"Go sit at the table. I'll get this plated up."

"You don't have to wait on me. I can help."

He nodded. "Okay. I'd love a beer."

"Perfect. I'll set that up."

She reached around and squeezed his mighty fine ass. "Tight ass Mr. Karason."

He chuckled and shook his head. Turning to the stove, he plated up their food, which smelled amazing. She pulled two beers from the refrigerator.

Theresa sat on the opposite side of the table from where their laptops still sat open. Marco set a plate in front of her and one next to her. He sat beside her, picked up his beer, and held it out to her. She tapped her beer to his, and they each took a drink from their bottles.

"This smells amazing."

He grinned. "Thank you. It'll taste better."

She cut a bite from her steak and put it in her mouth. He was right, of course.

They ate quietly for a bit and her body began to feel sated. She'd had some rest. Some exercise. Now food and clarity came to the forefront of her mind.

"What did Mitch, Jace, and the police discuss?"

"I thought I'd ask Mitch to come over after we eat and get the details."

"That sounds good."

She finished her meal, and her mind began working again.

"I think I should publish these."

Marco looked over at her. "As in now?"

"Maybe one a day to build up an audience for them. I can post them to YouTube and add links on the other social sites to that platform. I'll note the next part will be posted on the following day at a specific time. That should grow interest. The more people who know, the more support I have and the safer I am. I can also add that I'm afraid for my life and that if something happens to me, the dead man's switch will engage, and all of the stories will be released at once. That's how they'll know something happened to me."

Marco turned in his chair and stared at her. "That's not a bad idea. But we need to speak to Mitch and Jace first. They'll need to put some protections in place."

She nodded. He was right. This could blow back on the others. "Also, the newspaper in Maine. I don't know who the editor is there, but I could call them and warn them that the rest of the stories are coming."

"You shouldn't be the one calling. I'm sure they have all the phones associated with the paper altered to let them know when calls come in, and they're most likely monitoring. So, it would need to be someone else. Like me. I can call and tell them they need to set up some precautions."

"I hate to get you involved."

"Too late. I'm involved. And I'm not sorry about it."

She took a deep breath. "I hate that Jace, Margo, and Mitch are involved too. I mean this is growing."

"And you need it to. Actually, the public outrage you instill should be to your benefit. The more people who know, the better protected you are."

She nodded slightly and closed her eyes. "Okay. Let's talk to Mitch first."

They finished their meals, and she cleaned up the dishes while she got her head around all of this. After a year of hiding and feeling like she couldn't be seen, she was throwing herself into the public eye and it was frightening.

Mitch knocked on the door. Knock. Space. Knock, knock. Marco chuckled and moved effortlessly to the door and opened it up to his friend.

"Welcome. Come on in."

Mitch stepped inside and Theresa moved into the living room. "Hi, Mitch. Can I get you something to drink?"

"Yeah. I'd love a bourbon."

"Coming right up." She turned and faced the kitchen, then froze. Turning her head to Marco he grinned. "Above the fridge."

"Okay." She reached up on her toes, opened the cabinet, and pulled down a bottle of bourbon. She poured one for Mitch and glanced at Marco. He shook his head no with a huge grin on his face. "But I'll have another beer."

She brought their drinks into the living room and sat on the sofa next to Marco, Mitch opted for the chair to the right of the sofa. It was time to get the show on the road.

21

Marco took a swig from his beer and looked at his friend. "Tell us what's going on."

Mitch nodded. "I sent my employee out in Theresa's car." He paused and met her gaze. "Your car," he corrected. "The instant she drove out of town, someone tried to run her off the road. They're coming after you, and I believe it's safe to say they are going to do it right away. You've got them scared."

Theresa swallowed and he took her hand in his and squeezed. "Okay. So they are in town for sure. They don't just have a minion watching me, they're after me?"

"I believe so yes."

She nodded. "What do you think changed?"

Mitch shrugged. "I don't know."

Theresa looked up at him, then turned to Mitch. "Do you think they found something out from Carolyn? Found documents at her house?"

Mitch shrugged again. "It's a possibility. As soon as I touch base again with my friend, I'll ask if they know where she was murdered. If it was at her home, and that's where the documents were, it's possible they found something."

Marco took a deep breath. "What's the safety plan?"

Mitch nodded. "Police are aware of what's happening. They'll be circling the lot here more often and they have their chatter channels open to more signals. They also know I'm on it here and that you're taking an active role in activities. Jace for his part is open to anything we need him to do. So are Mason, Quinn, and Sid. Though we don't want to involve them if we don't have to. Jace is toying with closing the Sandbar down for a few days until he knows things are safe. But if he doesn't close, he agrees that you two need to stay out of there. For the safety of yourselves and his customers."

Theresa nodded. "Yes. I don't want any more collateral damage."

Marco turned to Mitch and said, "Theresa wants to publish the last four articles and get them out in the open. What do you see as potential threats?"

Mitch looked at Theresa, "What's your plan?"

She calmly explained her plan, and Mitch nodded. "I'm impressed. And I think it's a great idea. Get it out there and get more people to know about it to protect yourself. For once, maybe the internet is a good thing. I may be able to help you further with that. I have someone with connections to a couple of the social media platforms. I'll contact them and guarantee they don't throttle the posts or mark them spam. We'll get more eyes faster that way."

Theresa leaned forward. "Are you sure they aren't part of this?"

Mitch's brows shot up. "I hadn't thought of that."

"I've been amazed at the people who are involved. Either

willingly or unwillingly. Depending on the coercion used to get their compliance."

"Well, I guess I'll know based on their answer to this. Then, we'll avoid that platform if we need to."

Marco nodded. "That's a good idea."

Theresa took a deep breath and nodded. "I agree. And in the meantime, I'm going to pour over my documents and see if I can find anything from any business in Blossom Springs. It could be one or more of the new businesses, but that would mean they knew I'd come here or was here. That's unlikely because I didn't even know I'd come here. Not for six months. So, it's more likely that I have some information in the documentation I have here."

Marco grinned. "You're badass."

She laughed and he enjoyed watching her beautiful face transform to the happy face before him right now. She was getting her mojo back. He could almost see her strength growing.

Mitch stood. "Okay. I'm taking off to speak with Jace and tell him what's going on. If we all need to have a meeting with the police, I'll let you know. In the meantime, stay safe."

Marco stood and followed Mitch to the door. "Thanks for coming over."

Mitch grinned. "We'll keep her safe."

Marco locked the door behind Mitch, turned to her, and grinned. "Not that you can't protect yourself. But on that note, do you have any weapons?"

"Yes. I have a nine-millimeter."

"Okay. Anything else?"

"No."

Marco moved to the gun safe in his living room and opened it with the fingerprint lock. He pulled out a small canister in a pouch. Turning to Theresa, he handed it to her.

"Pepper spray. In case you need it. Never leave here without your weapon and the spray. Also, your phone."

She grinned. "Yes, sir."

He shook his head and closed the distance between them. "I want you to stay safe."

She smiled, stood on her toes, and kissed him. "Thank you for caring. I want to stay safe too."

"Good. No heroics."

"Right."

"Okay. So go through your documents. I'm going to head over and watch the attorney's office for a little bit."

"Why? If it's new it's not likely to be one of the businesses we need to be watching."

He nodded, "But I have a hunch there's something not right about that place. When Kelsey began working at the Sandbar, remember she had that old ticket she needed help with? She went to that attorney and without even listening to her he barked at her and said he couldn't help her. She came back and asked Jace for a recommendation. My point is, a good attorney would have listened to her and if he or she couldn't help, they'd refer her to someone else in town who could. That attorney doesn't need clients. There's something else going on there and I'd like to take a look for myself. Maybe stop in with an issue I need help with."

Theresa stepped into his body and hugged him. "You'll be careful though, right?"

He chuckled. "I'll be careful. I just want this to end. You to be safe. And leave it to us to see where this is going."

She lay her head against his chest for a moment and squeezed him tightly. "I want it to end too."

He kissed the top of her head and stepped back. "I'll be back in an hour. Don't open the door. Don't go anywhere. Please."

"I won't. I have enough research to do here. I'll be sitting right there in front of my computer." She pointed to the dining room table.

"Perfect."

He pulled a gun from his safe, loaded the magazine into it, and tucked it into his waistband holster. He pulled his ankle holster from the gun safe, strapped it on his right ankle, and slipped another nine-millimeter into it. He closed the safe door and turned to see Theresa staring at him.

His brows rose as he watched her. She chuckled. "Gotta love a man with a gun."

He cocked his head, and her cheeks turned pink. She was adorable. Before he decided to stay, he strode to the door. "Lock this behind me."

She nodded and sauntered to where he stood. He leaned down and kissed her before he slipped out the door and down the hall. He had a gut feeling this attorney was dirty. He hoped he could find out for sure.

22

———

With Marco gone, Theresa admitted, only to herself, that she felt uneasy. Things were heating up and with the go-ahead to begin publishing her stories, things would surely get more dangerous. Until they couldn't. If that was a thing. Maybe once all was exposed, they'd kill her for exposing them. They wouldn't care about saving her or their reputations, those would be tarnished anyway.

She shook her head to give the negative thoughts a shove out and began to focus on the task at hand. Her phone vibrated and she halted for a moment, then remembered it was the phone Mitch had given her and they didn't have that number.

"Hello."

Marco's husky voice filled her ear. "Hey, there. I'm just checking in to make sure you're okay."

She let out a sigh. "Hi. I'm good. Just thinking the worst."

"Don't do that. You need to keep your head on straight. Stay clear on the task and be aware. Though you're safe there. You have more security than the local jail."

She chuckled. "That's comforting."

He laughed and she closed her eyes to imagine what he looked like laughing. She could see his face. His beautiful smile. She'd watched him at work for six months and regretted how things were. Now they'd moved into a new phase, and she wanted to play this out.

She sat at her computer and pulled open the ledgers she'd scanned in. They used codes for where the money came from. She had a code sheet Mercury had helped her put together. She pulled up her code sheet and started color-coding the ledgers, giving each code its own color.

After an hour, she rotated her neck to relieve the stiffness in it. She stood and stretched then carried her now cold coffee cup to the kitchen. She dumped the cold coffee and rinsed her cup.

She turned to see the coffee pot had turned off. Touching the outside of the pot, she realized it had turned off a while ago.

She took a deep breath, opened the refrigerator, and found bottles of water on the door shelf. She pulled a bottle out and twisted the cap. Taking a long drink she set it on the counter and replaced the cap. Marco had mail sitting at the edge of the counter and she noted his address. What caught her attention was the zip code.

Her heart sped up and she hurried to her computer and looked at the code she and Mercury knew were attorneys working for the Celtics. She scanned the list of attorneys and found one that stopped her heart mid-beat.

She picked up her phone with shaking fingers and tapped on Marco's number.

He answered, "Hey, there, beautiful."

She chuckled. "Hey, handsome. I have a question."

"Let me have it."

"Do you happen to know if all of the extended zip codes in town are the same?"

"Hmm. Not something I ever researched fully, but I think the last four digits are specific to a building, a group of apartments, or a post office box. It helps in mapping an area for postal delivery. Why this very random question?"

"I think I have the last part of the code figured out."

"Honey, what code?"

She swallowed. "The codes in the ledgers. Mercury and I weren't sure what those codes meant. But I just saw your mail on the counter and figured it out. It's zip codes. That's how they coded where their money came from."

"Okay."

"Marco, is there a way you can find out what the extended zip code is for the attorney's office?"

He was quiet for a moment, then responded. "Yes. I'll call you when I have it."

"Be careful..." The call had ended before she managed to get the words out of her mouth.

She took a deep breath, more excited now that she'd figured it out. At least she was pretty sure. She then set up a new spreadsheet on her computer and added a column for location. She'd then drill this down further to identify exactly which buildings in their respective states and cities the money came from.

She quickly put her spreadsheet together, eager to ferret out the mysteries in her story so she could change it to add the addresses and people. If she was calling people out, she would do it fully and completely.

An explosion nearby shook the building. Theresa slipped off her chair the force was so great. She looked around and saw the bright orange flickers outside the living room window. She crawled to the window; not sure she should show herself.

She peered at the corner of the window and found the vehicle that Mitch had loaned her engulfed in flames. Sirens grew louder and people began standing in the parking lot staring at the burning vehicle.

Theresa gasped and dropped to the corner of the room. It was hard to catch her breath. They knew she was here. They'd found her. How did they know she was here? Her mind raced. Who knew she was here? Mitch knew. Marco knew. Jace and Margo knew. The police knew.

She closed her eyes and practiced deep breathing for only a moment. She didn't have a vehicle to escape with. Marco was gone with his. She was a sitting duck here.

Panic rose again and tears poured from her eyes. She was going to die tonight. Taking a final deep breath, she crawled from the window to the short hallway that led to her bedroom. She pulled her weapon and holster from her purse. She belted her holster on and loaded the full magazine into her 9mm. She may go out, but she would go out fighting. She'd riddle anyone with holes who tried coming in to get her.

She inhaled deeply and ran to her computer, staying as far from the window as possible. She checked the time. It was five-forty p.m. Her second report had been posted forty minutes ago. They acted fast.

As she saved her data on her computer, her fingers shook furiously. She logged out of her encrypted files and closed the lid on her laptop. She pulled it from the table and slid it under the stove. For however long it would be hidden, they wouldn't be able to destroy her files.

She swallowed as she heard footsteps in the hallway. Pulling her gun from its holster, she racked the slide to insert a bullet in the chamber and pulled her hands close to her body, her gun facing out. She was ready.

"Theresa?" She heard a male voice call out. She sucked in a breath.

"Theresa, it's me. Marco. I'm coming in."

She heard the key in the lock, but her brain wasn't registering everything correctly. The door pushed open and she took a deep breath.

"Theresa. I'm coming in."

Marco stepped into the living room and her heartbeat increased as if she had run a marathon.

"Put the gun down, baby." His voice was soothing. He stared at her and she finally registered it was him. She swallowed the knot in her throat and lowered her weapon.

Marco stepped inside and locked the door. She holstered her weapon, and he rushed to her and pulled her tightly into his arms.

"Thank God you're alright."

23

H e held her close and felt her shaking. "It's okay, honey. It's okay."

"They know I'm here."

"It's possible."

"Why else would they target the car that Mitch loaned me?"

"I've asked him that question. He said he'll get back to me."

"When, after I'm dead?"

His arms tightened around her. "You're not going to die."

Theresa tilted her head up to look into his eyes. "Are you sure he isn't with them?"

"I'm certain. But I don't know his employees. I trust that he's careful and wouldn't bring anyone on who was dirty, but sometimes things can take a turn."

She stepped back and when her beautiful face tipped up to look into his eyes, his heart felt heavy. The sadness etched on her face was heartbreaking.

"Marco. I'm at a loss here. We're here because you have all this security. And that's great, but they now know I'm here. How long do you think it'll take for them to bribe or threaten one of your neighbors here into letting them inside? I'm a sitting duck here. I have to go. But Mitch has my car, and the one he gave me is in flames outside. I can't run, and I don't have a safe place to run to right now."

He took a deep breath and let it out slowly. "I'll do everything in my power to keep you safe. That said, it sure doesn't look like it tonight, does it?"

Her lips turned down into a frown. "No. But I know this wasn't your doing."

"It wasn't. I swear to you."

"I believe you. You're the only person I believe right now."

"Okay. So, let's think this through a moment."

His phone rang and he pulled it from his pocket. "It's Jace. You trust Jace don't you?"

"Yes."

He tapped the answer and the speaker icons. "Hey, Jace."

"I just heard there was an explosion by your place. Are you and Theresa alright?"

"Yes. Rattled but alright."

"Thank God."

"Jace. Theresa is afraid she's a sitting duck here now. That was a clear threat."

"I read her exposé today. That's likely what escalated the threats."

"Yeah, that's what we think. Now we need to find a safe place to lay low. And, since we don't know who we can trust, minimal people should be told where that is."

"I agree with you on that. Do you have any ideas?"

He looked into Theresa's eyes and smiled. He mouthed, "Do you trust me?"

Her eyes looked deeply into his, he saw a tear form at

the corner of her eye and slowly drift down her cheek. She sniffed lightly and nodded.

He took a breath. "Jace, there's a man at the VFW, I think his name is Wes. He's mentioned a family cabin outside of town. I know his MOS was surveillance and recon. I'm guessing his cabin is set up with the very best in all of that. Anyway, can you ask him about it and not mention my name or Theresa's? Maybe see if a friend can use it as a getaway or something."

Jace chuckled. "Great plan. I'll touch base with him. His name is Wesley Charles. He's a good man. Honest and true and you're correct, his place is like no other. I've been there."

He smiled at Theresa and another tear rolled down her cheek. He swiped it with the back of his forefinger. "Thanks, Jace."

He ended the call and kissed Theresa's forehead. "We've got this. Let's pack up."

She went into the kitchen and knelt down on the floor in front of the stove. He watched her slip her hand under and after several attempts, slide her laptop out. She stood and glanced at him. Shrugging she said, "I needed to hide it and didn't think anyone would look there. Not for a while anyway."

He chuckled. "Good thinking. But your cloud account is heavily encrypted. Your laptop isn't going to matter much."

"Not for that it won't. But I have notes I didn't have time to upload to the encrypted files." She set her laptop on the counter. "Marco, I cracked the code!"

He neared as she logged into her laptop and pulled up a spreadsheet. "See, it's zip codes. I didn't put it together until I saw your mail." She pointed to his mail on the counter. "The zip code is the same as a few of these accounts. That's why I wanted the extended zip code of the law office you were watching."

He chuckled. "That's fantastic. You're as smart as you are beautiful."

He pulled his phone from his pocket and swiped to open his photos. "I took these pictures from mail in the mailbox. Luckily he didn't check it today."

She looked at the mail and found a piece with the extended zip code. "Here it is. I now know this is the code for Blossom Springs and this building. I can match up other codes with the same numbers and the first five numbers. I can then try to pinpoint where these other businesses or people are located."

He leaned in and checked over her spreadsheet. It was long and he could see the organization of her information. "That's impressive, Theresa."

"Thanks. I took it from the ledgers. I've been trying to figure out where all these operators work and where the money is from. Working briefly, it's from all over the US. They're everywhere."

He whistled low and slow. "Fucking unreal."

"Yeah. That's what I said."

His phone rang and she jumped. He turned his screen so she could see it was Jace. He tapped the icon and greeted his friend. "Hey, Jace."

"Hi. Wes is fine with you at his cabin. I didn't tell him your name but vouched for you. I'll take you out there and give you the codes and show you some of the security features. Is it safe for you two to get out of the building now?"

"I think this is the best time. Fire trucks and police are all outside. With the melee of people and frenzy of the fire, we should be able to slip out unnoticed."

"What about a statement from the police?"

"Mitch is down there handling it now. After all, it was his vehicle."

"Gotcha. Okay, load up and come past the Sandbar. It's closed tonight, but I'll be in the parking lot waiting for you. Slow down when you get here, and I'll pull out in front of you and lead you there."

"Sounds good. We're packing up now."

He ended the call and nodded to Theresa. "Grab anything you need. Don't bring anything you don't need."

"Okay." She picked up her laptop and her notebooks and chargers from the dining room table and hurried to her bedroom. He grabbed his laptop and pulled the case from his closet. Setting that in the chair in the living room he hurried to his bedroom and pulled a duffel bag from the shelf in his closet. He quickly dropped in underwear, socks, sweat pants, shorts, and t-shirts. Pulling his toiletry bag from his closet he tossed that in and carried the duffel to the living room. He dropped the duffel on the floor in front of his gun cabinet and rushed to open it and fill it with extra weapons and ammo. They wouldn't go quietly if something were to happen.

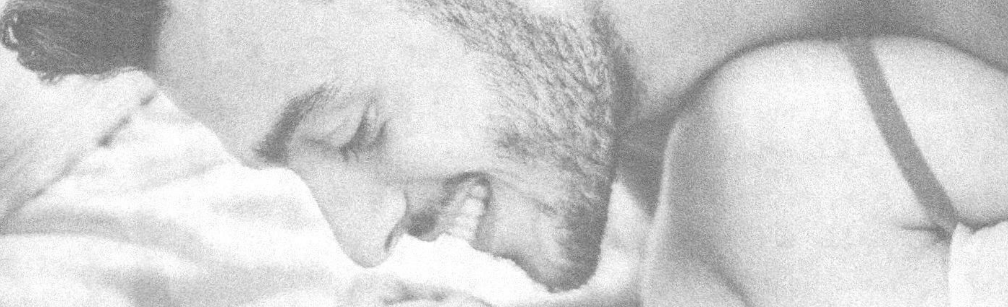

24

Theresa packed quickly and lightly. A few clothing items that would have to be hand-washed in the cabin if need be. Her top priority was to have access to her stories to finally figure out the codes and hammer that last nail in the coffin of the Celtics. She'd stew in her own juices to get that story out and she was more determined than ever. At this point, they only had twenty-two hours until the next report dropped. And life could get a bit dicier.

She lifted her backpack off the bed and slipped her arms into it. Moving into the living room she saw Marco emptying his gun safe into his duffel. She grinned.

He nodded. "Safety first."

She chuckled. "Right."

He picked up his duffel, turned off the lights in the living room and kitchen, then peered out the living room window from the corner.

She peered out next to him and saw Mitch out there talking to the police. Other people milling about were looking at the car, which now sat in a pile of steaming ashes, parts strewn around the parking lot, and police and fire-fighters trying to keep onlookers from picking up the pieces to keep as souvenirs.

She swallowed as she stared at the car. "Thank God I wasn't in it."

She turned toward the door and Marco followed closely behind her. "That's a fact."

Marco held his hand on her shoulder and whispered, "Let me go first to make sure we have the all-clear."

She let him pass her. She could clear the hall too, but she didn't want to make him mad. And, it felt so good to have someone want to take care of her. This past year, she'd been on her own looking over her shoulder constantly. Then, she let herself feel safe and get complacent. Maybe if she had kept at these codes, she would have figured it all out sooner.

Marco took her hand and led her down the hallway. They took the stairs rather than the elevator. As they reached the bottom step, he turned them to a short hall behind the stairs. "There's a back door here."

They stepped into the night air, the smell of burning fabric and paint tainted the warm breeze that blew. He hurried them around the back of the building to where he'd parked his truck when he'd gotten home. He helped her inside the truck, taking her backpack as she climbed in, and setting it in her lap. "Buckle up."

She grinned, but it was forced. She was scared right now. Her fingers shook as she fastened the seatbelt. All the what-if scenarios crept into her head. What if she had to jump from the vehicle quickly? She'd be buckled in. What if they were shot at and she had to get down? She'd be buckled in. What if they had an accident? Well, she'd be buckled in.

Marco hurried around the front of the truck and jumped

in, slinging his duffel bag over the back of the seat. That stopped her morbid thoughts.

He quickly fastened his seatbelt and started the truck. He slowly moved the truck through the parking area. He'd parked on the opposite side of the building where Mitch's car had been parked. They had easy access to Main Street. While turning onto Main Street, he watched his mirror often. She watched all around them to make sure they weren't being watched.

Her heart beat incredibly fast and her fingers still shook. That was close. Too close.

He turned his head and looked her way. "Are you okay?"

"Yes. Scared. But okay."

He nodded. "You don't have to keep releasing the exposés."

Her brows furrowed. She stared at him in disbelief. "Yes, I do."

"I just meant, you don't have to make a point. You can likely disappear as far as the Celtics are concerned. Though it may be too late for that now. But we could try to negotiate. You have the dead man's switch. We could always use that as leverage."

She shook her head. "I don't want to negotiate. These assholes are dirty. They kill people. They harm them in other ways. Threatening them or their families with harm if they don't do something. Usually making them break their own moral codes. They need to be found out. People need to know their elected officials are dirty."

He shrugged. "Don't you think most people already know that? I mean politicians have a bad reputation for a reason."

Her voice rose higher. "Right, but this is proof. Proof that they are bought and paid for!"

He reached over and took her hand. "Hey, I just wanted to point out that whatever you decide, either way, I'm with you."

She swallowed and took a deep breath. "Thank you." She closed her eyes a moment and reminded herself Marco was on her side. He was only playing devil's advocate. There was nothing wrong with another point of view.

He navigated the corner at the end of Main Street that put them on Sunset Beach Road. As they neared the Sandbar he slowed.

He nodded toward the edge of the parking lot. "There's Jace."

As if on cue, Jace pulled out in front of them. They followed him to the end of Sunset Beach Road, where there was a fork in the road. Right led to Sunset Beach Drive and left put them on Lake Street. Lake Street led them out of town where the scenery changed to lush vegetation and quiet beauty. She let her shoulders drop and rotated her head. She tried forcing the tension from her neck and shoulders, but it was stubborn.

Jace made a sharp right onto Middle Inlet and at another fork in the road, he took the right onto Nowhere Road. That's what this felt like. They were going nowhere. Or hopefully not anyplace that would get them found. A quick veer to the left put them onto Hidden Oasis.

The scenery changed again to woods of varying species of trees and tall ground cover. She shook her head and Marco asked, "What's wrong?"

She chuckled. "Nothing. I was just thinking that if anyone was willing to tuck themselves in that tall brush with all the crawly things hiding in there, they were braver than me."

He nodded. "Sometime I'll tell you about some of the dreadful places I've had to hide out."

She pressed her lips together. "That didn't help."

"I'm sorry. I wasn't thinking."

He pulled to a stop at the end of Hidden Oasis where there stood an amazing, cozy-looking cabin near the edge of a beach. It was secluded and private and so serene she nearly sighed.

Marco shut his truck off and waited for a beat. He knew Jace wouldn't set them up. He trusted his friend completely, but his training had taught him to be cautious. Watch everything. Overlook nothing. Be prepared.

Jace stepped from his vehicle and nodded toward them, then turned and strode to the front door of the cabin.

Marco turned to Theresa. "You ready?"

She took a deep breath and blew it out. "Yeah. I trust him."

"I do too."

She shook her head. "So why are we afraid?"

"Things are heating up. We're right to be cautious and afraid. It's what will save us if we need it. It's why we're here."

"Right."

She nodded and gripped her backpack with both hands. "Okay."

She opened her door, and he opened his at the same time. He strode around the front of the truck and met her there. He kept his hand at the small of her back as they marched toward the door to the cabin, where Jace waited for them.

He stepped back as they neared to let them in. Once inside they stood staring at the place in wonder. Theresa whispered, "Holy shit."

Jace chuckled.

Marco shook his head. "I didn't expect this."

Jace chuckled. "I told you it was like no other."

"You did, but holy shit, I didn't think it was like this. I expected rustic and primitive."

Jace nodded. "I get that. I was surprised the first time I came here too. Let me show you around."

He glanced Theresa's way and caught her eye. She grinned and began to follow Jace into the cabin.

Jace started their tour. "So, obviously this is the living room. The fireplace is gas. Feel free to use it. You simply turn it on here..." He showed them a switch near the left side of the fireplace and flipped it on. Flames appeared and the room instantly took on a different feel.

"The kitchen is this way." He moved toward the left of the front door. "This is all new. New appliances, gas stove, you have everything here you'll need. Pots and pans, etc. Dishes are in the cabinets. Wes said to make yourself at home."

Theresa finally spoke. "We didn't bring food. I didn't think of that."

Jace shook his head. "I took care of it. Margo shopped for you when I told her what we were doing. I have it in the truck. I'll bring it in after I show you around."

Theresa took a deep breath. "Thank you and please thank Margo for us."

Jace grinned. "I will. We're happy to help you. And we're sorry you're going through this."

Theresa swallowed and he worried she'd start crying. The stress was immeasurable at this point.

Jace continued. "Now, this way..." He walked toward the back of the cabin. "Are the bedrooms. There are three here and two bathrooms. One in the primary bedroom and one between the other two bedrooms."

The place was gorgeous. Marco couldn't believe this was tucked back into the woods along the water, yet so close to town. What a little gem.

Theresa set her backpack down inside the primary bedroom and followed Jace back out to the living room.

Jace turned to look at both of them. "Let me show you the security system. You'll love this."

He strode to a desk in the corner of the living room and opened the top drawer with a key. He held the key up, "This is the key to the desk. The other keys belong to the front door and there's one to a shed outside. But you need to unlock the top drawer to access the security system." He reached under the top of the desk, with the drawer open, and pushed a button. A computer screen rose up from the desk. Marco chuckled. "This is amazing."

Jace grinned. "Just wait, I haven't even shown you the cool stuff."

He pulled a mouse from the desk drawer and shook it to wake up the system. He also pulled a notebook from the top drawer. "This is the password. The notebook is to stay in the drawer until you need it and then put it back immediately. There are six cameras outside. Up the driveway and around the perimeter."

The computer came to life, and six squares appeared on the computer screen. "Here are your views from the camera. You can see all around the property beginning when we turned onto Hidden Oasis. There are cameras inside here..."

He pointed to the corners above the door and across the living room in the upper corner. "There are also cameras in the kitchen, pointing to the back door. There are no cameras in the bedrooms or the bathrooms. And open disclosure, Wes has access to the cameras coming up the driveway. He knows when someone is here. He doesn't look at the cameras inside here, though. Only if something were to happen. He wanted you to know that."

Jace nodded and turned to Theresa. She smiled in return.

Jace continued. "Keep this up. It'll chime if someone comes up the driveway. You can look and see who it is. There are locks on the doors and windows. The windows are bulletproof glass, the doors are reinforced steel. There's also a safe room if you need it. Once the door to the safe room is opened, Wes will get a warning and he'll send police here immediately. I'll show you that next."

Marco nodded. "Okay. This feels a bit like Fort Knox."

Jace laughed. "That's exactly what I called it the first time I came out here."

Theresa finally found her voice. "Why did he build this?"

Jace shook his head. "He enjoys it. He has the knowhow and he loves tinkering. And he felt if his family ever needed anything like this, in the event of some type of catastrophe, they'd have a place to hide."

Theresa nodded and Marco grinned at her. He could see some of the tension leaving her shoulders and her face. It was less stern than it had been previously.

Jace finished off his tour. "Here's the Wi-Fi password." He pointed to the notebook then put it back into the drawer and closed it. "And follow me to the safe room."

Marco took Theresa's hand, and they followed Jace through the kitchen to a door at the back. It was a basement door. They descended the stairs and lights flickered on. "No one sneaking up on anyone down here. The lights will come on at the movement."

Theresa chuckled. "Wow."

Jace stopped them at another doorway. He pulled his phone from his pocket and tapped a couple of times then held the phone to his ear. "Wes, we're opening the safe room. I just wanted to give you a heads-up."

Jace listened a minute then hung up the call. He tapped a number into the electronic keypad that appeared after he waved his hand in front of it. He typed in the number. "The code is in the notebook in the desk drawer. Memorize it."

Marco responded. "Will do."

The door opened and they stepped into another amazing room with bunks on the walls, a small kitchen, a bathroom, and a sitting area. "There's food down here, MREs. Water bottles under the bottom bunk. You can live down here for two months if need be."

Theresa chuckled. "Oh, my gawd. This is unreal."

26

Theresa unpacked the groceries Jace and Margo had purchased for them. It frayed her nerves a bit to see there was enough food for them to be here for a month. Her system couldn't take this type of hiding and worrying for a month. The final exposé should be released in three days' time, and after that, the cat would be out of the bag. She shouldn't have to worry about being offed, as everyone would come looking for the Celtics if anything happened to her. At least she hoped that would be her shield.

Marco stepped into the kitchen and whistled at all the food.

"It looks like there's enough food here to be locked up for a month."

She chuckled. "That's what I was thinking." She folded up a paper bag. "I won't stay sane for a month. Hiding. Being afraid of every sound."

He walked around the counter and put his hands on either of her shoulders. "The heat is on now because of the reports. They're likely hoping to stop them from being released. Once they can't, they'll need to go into repair mode, and they'll likely leave the country. At least the higher-ups will, so they can't be arrested."

"I hope you're right. If they're out of the country and their organization is fractured, they won't have time to worry about me."

He grinned. He was sexy all the time, but when he grinned, there was something that happened to her on a visceral level that made her entire body sizzle. His arms wrapped around her, and he stepped in closer to fully hug her.

Her arms wrapped around his waist, and she laid her ear to his chest. She liked hearing his heartbeat. It was comforting. It sounded so strong and solid. She closed her eyes and listened. They stood together, just taking comfort in each other. At least she took comfort in Marco. Maybe it was one-sided. What on earth did she bring to this relationship but trouble, turmoil, and upheaval in his life?

She swallowed the large knot that formed in her throat and released her arms. Marco pulled away and she felt the loss instantly.

Marco's phone rang. He wasted no time answering. "Karason."

She listened to his side of the conversation, not sure if she should. Maybe it was a personal call. Not everything revolved around her, though it seemed to lately.

Her cheeks heated as she realized she'd been rather selfish. His life had been turned upside-down the instant he offered to help her. She didn't resist enough either. She'd been caught up with the fact that Marco, this man she'd longed for from afar, wanted to help her. He likely had friends and things he did when he was off work that didn't include running from people firebombing your home or near it anyway. And, chasing off someone throwing rocks.

She started putting food into the large pantry and in the refrigerator and freezer.

Marco responded to whoever he was talking to with, "Hang on a moment. I'll put you on speaker."

He tapped his phone and strode to her. "Okay, Mitch. Say it again."

"My chatter channel has revealed some interesting information. There's a charity event in Blossom Springs this coming Saturday. On the surface, it's to raise money for funding for medical research focusing on the elimination of childhood leukemia. But it's actually a front to launder millions of dollars for the Celtics. The chairman of the fundraiser is none other than Torin Terry, owner of the PCK Meatpacking plant outside of Blossom Springs."

Marco's brows furrowed. "Are you sure he's in on this?"

"I'm ninety-nine percent sure. I did some research after I heard this on the chatter channel. I have proof he's been in recent meetings with heads of the Celtics, including the president. Chatter is that he houses several people at his place outside of town. He has a ranch, with a ranch house. It makes sense to me that he'd have available beds out there. He can direct activities from out there and his guys can be all over town in the ranch trucks without anyone thinking anything of it. They could have been watching Theresa for a time. Hiding in plain sight. Much like she was doing."

Her stomach twisted. She'd remembered some of those guys coming into the Sandbar two days ago. They'd been that close to her. They likely came in for lunch to make sure it was her.

She nodded her head and Marco's jaw tightened. "Did you see them?"

"Yes. At the Sandbar."

"How do you know it was them?"

"They all wore work shirts with the ranch logo on them. Khaki-colored button-up shirts and jeans. There were three of them."

Mitch continued. "They were likely making sure it was you."

Marco stared into her eyes. "Did one of them have red hair?"

She pinched her lips together. "Yes."

"A man with red hair threw the rock through your window. They followed you home or were watching and found you packing your car."

Her stomach twisted and she worried she'd lose the little bit she'd eaten for supper. Her hand flew to her tummy and pressed as her knees began shaking. She realized they'd been close for a while now.

Marco took her arm and guided her to a bar stool at the counter. "They've been close but until they blew up the car, they only tried scaring you. Threatening you."

"Right." She took a deep breath. "They want my information."

"They'll get it when the rest of the world gets it."

She nodded.

Marco spoke to Mitch. "I'm going to that fundraiser to see if I can find out anything more on Torin Terry, the organization, and how close he is to the Celtics. Meaning, is he a leader or is he working for them?"

Theresa nodded. "I'm going with you."

"No, it might not be safe."

"I'm going with you. You just said they don't want me dead. Not yet. If they see me there, I may be enough of a diversion for you to get the information you need. And I can't just sit here and do nothing. It might also be good for my story."

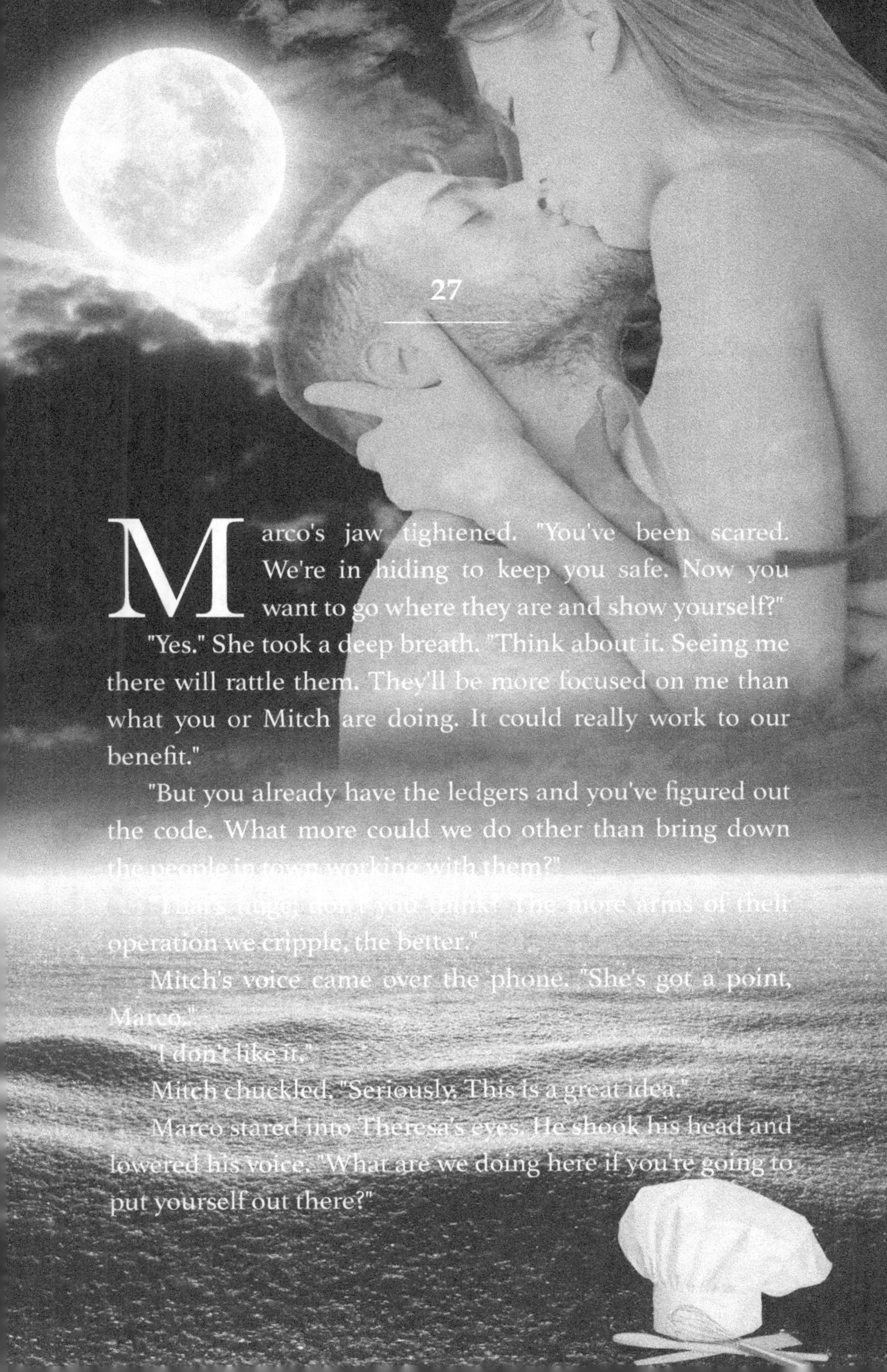

27

Marco's jaw tightened. "You've been scared. We're in hiding to keep you safe. Now you want to go where they are and show yourself?"

"Yes." She took a deep breath. "Think about it. Seeing me there will rattle them. They'll be more focused on me than what you or Mitch are doing. It could really work to our benefit."

"But you already have the ledgers and you've figured out the code. What more could we do other than bring down the people in town working with them?"

"That's huge, don't you think? The more arms of their operation we cripple, the better."

Mitch's voice came over the phone. "She's got a point, Marco."

"I don't like it."

Mitch chuckled, "Seriously. This is a great idea."

Marco stared into Theresa's eyes. He shook his head and lowered his voice. "What are we doing here if you're going to put yourself out there?"

"Here, we're safe and can eat and sleep in peace. Out there, at least at the benefit, they won't expect me and we'll be one up on them. We'll surprise them. Let's work with Mitch to have everything set so we're safe. We'll have an entry plan. We'll have our escape plan. We'll be on point at every step. What are they going to do with all those people around? Nothing. They won't expect us. They have to go through the motions of bringing in all the money to launder the Celtics money. They may also worry that there are others watching to make sure the event is on the up and up. It's perfect. I'll even dye my hair and look different, so they won't know it's me."

He stared at her beautiful dark hair. He liked her hair just as it was. He'd always admired the shine in it. "I don't want you to dye your hair."

She smiled at him and her shoulders softened. "Okay. A wig."

Mitch responded and Marco was irritated at the interruption. "We can work something out with a wig. I'll take care of getting you a dress to wear. We'll have wires sewn into it. We'll have trackers sewn into it. We'll know where you are all the time."

Marco's stomach tightened at the thought of putting her in any danger. He rotated his head and let out a breath. "Okay." He looked into Theresa's eyes. "You follow orders soldier. Every. Damned. Order."

"I will." She smiled and his heartbeat sped up.

Mitch responded. "Great. We'll get things taken care of here. Theresa, you have a couple of days to work on your exposés to get them scheduled. May I make a suggestion?"

"Sure."

"Leave something out. Something you can keep as

leverage in your dead man's switch. Once all the information is out, you need to keep something out to make sure they don't come at you out of spite."

"Yeah. I've been thinking of that. Thank you."

"Okay. Anything else?"

Marco looked at Theresa and she shook her head. "No, Mitch, we're good here."

"Okay. We'll talk later."

The call ended and he lay his phone on the counter. He spun Theresa's stool around and framed her in his arms. He lowered his head until their noses were nearly touching. "I mean it. Every order, Theresa."

"I know."

His lips touched hers lightly. Her tongue swiped across his bottom lip, and he opened his mouth for her. The instant their tongues met, he deepened the kiss. His lips covered hers. His hands held her head in place. He pulled her forward and off the stool with his left hand and her legs instantly wrapped around his ass. His cock roared to life, and his skin heated. It had been a hell of a day, but dammit if his body didn't respond to her.

He lifted her higher and turned them toward the primary bedroom. He didn't ask, he assumed, they'd be sleeping together. There was no reason not to. Not anymore. They were safe here. And he wanted to make love to her tonight.

Their lips continued to meld together. Her arms held him tightly as he carried her across the living room.

As he lay her on the bed she softly moaned, and he closed his eyes. He loved that sound.

Her fingers began pulling his shirt up his body and he helped her remove it. She tossed it over the edge of the bed and began working on his button and zipper. He rolled over as soon as she had his jeans undone and shimmied them down his legs.

He quickly rolled back and began removing her clothing. He liked this part. The anticipation. The unwrapping of his present.

As soon as her clothing was removed, he rolled onto his back and pulled her over him. Her long dark hair spilled over her shoulders and her lips turned up in a smile. It was sexy. He stared at her. Her eyes, her face, her hair. Then his eyes roamed down her beautiful body. His hands cupped her breasts and molded them with his hands. Her flesh was soft and pliable. She smelled like citrus and soap. Clean and fresh.

Her hips moved forward and grazed his thickened cock. The hairs brushed against his sensitive skin and his cock jumped. Her smile grew and she moved again. Then she reached down and wrapped her fingers around his cock and began pumping him up and down. Her hands were soft, her grip firm enough to give him pleasure, but not pain.

"Do you have a condom?"

The air rushed from his lungs. "No."

"Do we need one?"

He stared into her eyes. "I'm clean."

She nodded. "Me too."

"What about..."

"Birth control? I'm on it."

He nodded.

She rose up on her knees and positioned the head of his cock at her entrance and slightly dropped down enough to keep his cock in place, but not enough that he slid inside. He stared at her stunning face as she grinned.

"Tease."

She chuckled. "Maybe."

He placed his hands on her hips and slowly lowered her down. Incredible. Watching her face as his cock slid inside her warmth was now imprinted on his brain. The soft moan as she slid onto him added to the experience. His heart, something happened to his heart. It beat faster, but it also felt like it opened inside of him. It was reaching for her. That had never happened before. Ever.

His mind raced as he tried to figure it all out. Thoughts were flying at him faster than an asteroid shower. Then she lifted herself up and the cool air hit his shaft until she slid down once more.

He groaned as the feelings and thoughts assaulted him. Her breasts bounced in front of her as she moved. He couldn't stop watching the erotic dance they performed for him.

She rose and slid down again and again. His hands moved between her hips and her breasts, molding them in his hands, feeling their heaviness as they moved. It made him harder.

She placed her hands on his shoulders as she rode him. Her fingers dug into his skin slightly. Her lips turned up into a soft smile, her eyes became heavy as her climax came closer. Her skin was beautiful with its fine sheen. It glistened in the light of the moon that now shone into the cabin.

He didn't know where to look as she moved on him. Everything about her called to him.

"Marco," she whispered.

"Theresa," he replied.

She moaned, her fingers gripped his shoulders tightly and her body stiffened as he watched the mesmerizing display before him. His breathing came in short bursts as the excitement nearly overwhelmed him. His hands gripped her hips as his hips pushed up into her as tightly as he could. The tightness in his balls made him lose his breath for a moment, then the warm spurts flowed from his body into hers and his vision grayed as his body relaxed.

28

Theresa stepped from the shower and toweled herself off. She dressed in jeans and a yellow t-shirt, eager to start her morning. Sleeping next to Marco last night felt wonderful. She'd slept fantastically too.

She dried her hair with a blow dryer, then pulled it up onto her head and secured it in a high ponytail. She planned on tackling the codes today, finishing her reports, and starting the new story that had been brewing in her brain this past week. She'd tell her story. Of how she had to go on the run. Throwing rocks, blowing up cars, killing people. The hate and vitriol with which the Celtics operated needed to be fully disclosed and she now knew how she'd do it.

Moving from the bathroom through the bedroom, quietly, she stopped for a moment to stare at Marco sleeping. He was beautiful. He'd likely hate hearing that. But he was. All the times she'd thought about him as they worked together, she'd never imagined this. She'd always held herself back. Watching him at work, she thought he was a heartthrob. The old-fashioned term made her grin, but he was. His strong build, broad shoulders, and rippling muscles were captivating. But, watching him relaxed and sleeping peacefully now...this was incredible.

She grinned and went out to the kitchen to pour him a cup of coffee. She quietly pulled two coffee cups from the cupboard and poured them each a cup. At least she'd set the coffee up last night and used the timer. She hated waiting for coffee in the morning.

She'd unpacked some macarons yesterday. She remembered thinking Margo had fabulous taste in food. Placing two of those on a plate, she carried the coffee and sweets into the bedroom and set them on the nightstand for Marco. Taking one last look at his peaceful slumber, she tiptoed from the room and setup her laptop on the dining room table. She pulled her notes from her laptop case and began to work.

After logging into her encrypted account, she started organizing the codes by what she now believed to be zip codes. She'd group the numbers into areas and take an area at a time to fully determine how many states were involved in this corruption. Then she'd break the states down into counties, then cities and municipalities. Perhaps one day, she'd be able to dig into each municipality and find the culprits.

She froze as she thought about that for a moment. She could have people do it for her. She could place a call to action in her exposés where citizens could report corruption. Those citizens would do the work for her. She shook her head as thought after thought bombarded her brain with the way to set this up. It would have to be private. She could set up a website. And specific information would be required for anyone to submit any tips about what was happening. She could then work on the investigation of that.

Her heart raced as she thought of all the possibilities of having boots on the ground, so to speak, helping her ferret out information.

Her fingers flew across her keyboard as the thoughts presented themselves. She'd organize them later, but for now, she didn't want to lose them.

The more she typed the more energized she felt. Excitement pumped through her veins, and she couldn't wait to begin working on this.

Marco placed a warm cup of coffee near her right hand. She looked up at him puzzled and he grinned. Ahh, that grin! She could look at that all day.

"You started working again and let your coffee get cold. I thought you may want to take a break and eat something."

She smiled and he bent down and kissed her lips. "Thank you," she whispered.

"You're welcome." He stood. "How long have you been awake?"

She glanced at the time on her computer. "About an hour."

He chuckled and grinned at her. She couldn't help but smile. "I'll get breakfast ready."

"Do you need help?"

He cocked his head and grinned. She laughed. "Right. Thank you."

He nodded and strode to the kitchen while she took advantage of the incredible view. He wore jeans that fit him to perfection. His strong thighs fit perfectly into those jeans and his muscles were perfectly outlined by the fabric.

The gray t-shirt he wore stretched across his shoulders accenting how muscular he was. Damn!

She went back to her codes, despite wanting to watch Marco cook.

She finished three pages of codes, looking up each zip code to find the state associated with it. With each completed page, her excitement grew. A few more hours and she'd know more than she did now. And she'd have the codes pinpointed. Her goal was to have them finished before the next report was released.

Marco called to her from the kitchen. "Breakfast is ready."

She picked up her coffee cup, sauntered to the kitchen, and climbed on a bar stool at the counter. Marco set a beautiful omelette in front of her complete with fresh orange slices, a banana, and a sliced apple. "It looks amazing."

He grinned. "Thank you."

He picked up a plate for himself and walked around the counter to sit down next to her. They ate in silence for a bit. Both of them were hungry, and frankly, her brain was still deciphering codes.

Marco finished his breakfast and pushed his plate away. He sipped on his coffee then broke the silence. "How are you coming along?"

"Good. It's a slow process because I have to look up zip codes as I go."

"Let me help you. I need to do something, and it'll make your work easier. We'll be finished sooner."

She turned to stare into his eyes. Not a hardship. Not at all. "Okay. If you're sure."

"Yeah. I need something to do, babe."

Babe. He called her babe. Electric currents raced through her body. Her tummy somersaulted. Her nipples pebbled. She liked that. A lot.

Marco stood and stretched. He wasn't used to sitting for long periods like this. And his eyes needed a break from the computer screen.

"Do you need anything?" he asked Theresa.

Theresa typed away and absently replied. "No, thank you."

He chuckled and moved to the kitchen. His phone rang and he answered as he opened the refrigerator to make lunch plans.

"Karason."

"It's Mitch. I'd like to come out with your clothing for the benefit tomorrow night."

"Okay. We're home all day."

Mitch laughed and he did as well. It was kind of funny. "See you in fifteen minutes."

The call ended and he pulled some cheese, sausage, and grapes from the refrigerator. He began slicing the cheese and sausage, keeping an eye on Theresa from time to time. When she worked, she engrossed herself in it. Full on focus. He was grateful they were out here and safe. She'd more likely hear anyone trying to get into her place if she were working there. Not that it was a choice anymore.

He arranged their food on a plate and carried it to the table. "Take a little break, babe. Mitch is bringing our clothes for tomorrow night."

"Okay." She didn't look up from her screen and he didn't know if he should be irritated or impressed with her focus.

She finished typing, clicked her mouse a few times, and closed the lid on her laptop. She reached over and picked up a piece of sausage. "Oh, this looks wonderful."

He grinned. "Thanks."

She took a bite of her sausage and nodded. "It's delicious."

He chuckled. "You must be hungry."

She shrugged and glanced at the clock on the stove. "Oh wow. It's after three! The exposé should have posted at three."

Marco pulled his phone from his pocket and checked the internet. He had set a notification to Theresa's website and saw it on his screen. "It posted."

Theresa jumped up and rushed to her computer. She logged in, found the website, and began reading the comments. "People are thanking me for posting this. They're also sharing their stories too! Oh my gawd."

He began reading the comments on the article and grinned. People were sharing their stories. And many others were sharing and clicking the heart emoji. The article was getting attention. More than a thousand people had interacted in some way. He held his hand up. "Nice job."

She slapped her hand to his in a high-five and they both chuckled.

The security system chimed, and Marco rushed to the

computer to see Mitch's SUV pulling up the road. "It's Mitch."

He watched the vehicle make the turn and then stop in front of the cabin. Marco strode to the door to open it for him.

Mitch carried an armful of clothing in bags and a suitcase. Marco rushed outside to help him carry something inside. Mitch shook his head. "I've got it."

Marco chuckled and beat him to the door to hold it open.

Mitch stepped inside and laid the clothing over the sofa and the suitcase on the floor next to the sofa.

Theresa drew closer and picked up the dress bag. She unzipped the front to expose a gorgeous sparkly burnt orange gown. She was going to look stunning in that dress. The color next to her skin proved she would make a statement.

She grinned. "It's beautiful."

Mitch nodded. "I can't take credit for that. My employee, Gabby, picked it out for you."

Marco's brows drew close. "Why did you pick a bright color for her? She'll stand out."

"That's what I want. I want all eyes on her. If everyone can see her, there's no opportunity for them to grab her and try to drag her out. Everyone will notice."

"What will you be doing?" Marco asked.

"Watching money transferring hands. Recording people at the benefit. Recording people talking to Torin Terry."

Marco nodded slowly. "What are we to do?"

Mitch grinned. "The same thing."

Marco's brows drew close, and Mitch laughed. "Let me show you."

He picked up the suitcase and laid it on the sofa. Unzipping it he pulled a box from inside. He lifted the lid on the small box to uncover a gorgeous diamond necklace and matching earrings.

"This necklace conceals cameras and microphone." He pointed to small cameras the size of the clicker on a pen. "These will be sending footage to my office." He pointed to other small devices. "These will capture the audio. We'll be recording it all. Then we'll pour through all of it to find keywords. The video footage will help us place everyone in the room. It'll likely pick up things you aren't even aware of."

He pulled another box from the suitcase. "This is your tie clip, cufflinks, and pocket square."

Mitch handed them to Marco. Marco looked closely at the diamond-studded items and saw the small cameras and audio devices.

Mitch continued. "You two need to walk around the entire room. Chat people up. Stand near when someone is whispering. The microphones can pick up sounds from quite a distance away. Just practice turning your body in the direction of someone you're listening to. That way, we can see who is talking and hear them."

Marco glanced at Theresa. "Get your acting skills honed up."

She chuckled. "I don't know if there's enough time. But I'll absolutely do the best I can."

Marco's gut tightened. He didn't like putting her there in that place. It would be crawling with assholes who wanted her shut up. Assholes who killed and didn't flinch.

He took a deep breath. "Okay. And you'll be doing the same?"

"Yep. And if I can get into the office, I'm going to do that and find anything to tie Torin Terry to the Celtics. That will be difficult. But I'll do anything I can to stop this jackass."

Mitch continued. "Also, there are wires and cameras sewn into your lapels, and buttons."

Theresa smiled. "What about me?"

Mitch chuckled and nodded. "Yes. Along the neckline, there are minute cameras sewn in. Recorders are sewn in too."

Marco took a deep breath. He didn't like putting Theresa in danger like this, but he'd do everything in his power to guard her.

30

---

itch drove them to the charity ball. She sat in the back, practicing her breathing and telling herself she wouldn't be in any more danger here than she'd been at her rental. At least here she was aware they knew about her. At her rental, she thought she was still in hiding.

In fact, if the unthinkable did happen, she was wired, with cameras and audio, so they'd find her quickly.

Mitch and Marco spoke in the front seats about nothing in particular. Neither of them seemed nervous or edgy. She didn't know if she should be irritated about that or happy this was an ordinary day for them.

They pulled into the parking lot at Paradise Gardens. She hadn't been here before. It sure was pretty outside.

The palm trees had white Christmas-type lights wrapped around the trunks, which lit up the palm fronds. They lined a curved drive, and her brain told her nothing bad could happen in a place that looked like this, right?

Mitch parked off to the side and twisted in his seat.

"If we get separated for any reason, and you feel scared,

just say so. My employees will get in touch with me imme-diately."

He turned to Marco as well. "You too. I know you're used to this kind of stuff. At least you used to be. But I'm serious. If either of you needs me, just say so."

Mitch looked her in the eye. "Got it? Just say so."

She nodded. "I've got it."

He turned to Marco.

"And you?"

"Got it," Marco said.

Mitch picked up his phone and tapped a couple of times. Then he said, "Gabby, turn on the cameras and the mics."

Theresa heard a click, and her breathing increased. It was getting real.

Mitch turned again. "Theresa, say something in a normal voice. What color is your dress?"

"It's burnt orange. Gabby, it's beautiful."

Mitch grinned, and Marco turned and smiled at her.

Mitch nodded. "She said thank you, and she can hear you perfectly."

Then he nodded to Marco.

Marco grinned. "Test one, two. Her dress is beautiful, and she's stunning in it."

Mitch chuckled. Marco turned to her and winked.

She smiled despite being nervous. He made her feel like she was in love for the first time.

Her tummy flipped, and it wasn't nerves. It was Marco.

Mitch opened his door and stepped out of the vehicle. Marco did the same and opened her door.

She smiled as she stepped from the vehicle. Her flowing dress swished as she moved. She'd never worn a dress like this before. She'd not even gone to her high school prom. She thought they were stupid. So, this was a first for her.

During her time in the military, she wore fatigues or a uniform. During her civilian life, she wore business casual. She didn't attend fancy dinners or balls, and if she did attend a ball for the military, it was always in uniform.

She worried about how this made her feel. At the ripe ol' age of thirty-two, she was wearing a gown, an expensive one at that, and for the first time, she felt pretty. Her head swirled at this feeling, and as they began walking toward the entry door with Marco's hand at the small of her back, she felt like a princess in a fairy tale.

She wanted to hold onto this feeling for a little bit. Who knew when it would happen again?

They neared the front door, and a man stopped them.

"Names, please."

Mitch responded, "Theresa Miklovic, Marco Karason, and Mitch DeMario."

The doorman checked their names off on a sheet and opened the door for them.

Marco's hand stayed at the small of her back, and she was grateful for that. She wondered if he could feel her shaking.

After they entered, they stopped at a table and received name tags. They weren't the kind of name tags you peel and stick on your clothing. That would be frowned upon and tacky. These were cute little name tags tied to flowers; boutonnieres for the men with a white rose, and a pretty white rose corsage for the women. What a cute way to have the name tags hung. Apparently, they were sparing no expense.

After they'd had their name tags pinned on, she turned to Mitch. "Is this covering anything?"

He pulled his phone up and read a text, then he answered her, "It's covering a camera slightly, but not a problem. I don't want them to see us moving it, so we'll work with it."

Theresa nodded, inhaled a deep breath, and let it out slowly while her hand absently rested against her tummy. Those butterflies were back, only this time they weren't because of Marco.

They entered through an arched doorway into a gorgeous ballroom. There were all kinds of people standing around, small groups drinking and laughing. The women were glittering with diamonds and sparkling gowns.

There were large buffet-style tables set up all around the perimeter of the room with expensive prizes on them. It was for a silent auction. In front of each prize was a clipboard with numbers where guests added their names and how much they were willing to bid for a particular prize.

She thought that was a good thing to show Mitch's employees, so she bent down so that her cameras would pick up the names on the clipboard.

Marco was doing the same with his cufflinks.

They walked slowly along the auction tables, looking at the prizes and the names on the clipboards.

She would try and remember to do it again just before the auction prizes were called, so it would be a more complete list than this one.

Marco steered her to a bar at the back of the room.

The bartender asked, "What will you have?"

Marco grinned. "Two glasses of champagne, please."

Her brows furrowed.

He leaned down, kissed her temple, and whispered in her ear, "Sip it slowly. We need to look like we're here enjoying ourselves."

She nodded and smiled.

He handed her a glass of champagne and tapped his to hers.

"Cheers."

They each took a small sip of their champagne, and he steered them to a group of six people standing in a circle.

A man saw them approach and opened the circle for them to enter.

"Hello there. My name is Doug, and this is my wife, Connie. Also with us is David and Maxine, and over here are Glen and Sondra."

"Hello, my name is Marco, and this is my girlfriend, Theresa."

"Very nice to meet you," Doug said. "Are you from here?"

"We are now," Marco said. "We both moved from other parts of the United States and found ourselves in Blossom Springs. It's such a nice area, and we enjoy it here immensely. I'm glad we found it."

"Us too, actually. David over there owns the bank in Blossom Springs."

Marco nodded. "It's nice to know who I have my money with. Now I feel like it's in a good place."

David nodded. "Thank you, sir."

They participated in some idle chitchat, then Doug and David began talking about golf.

Marco nodded and stepped back. Theresa followed him.

"It was nice meeting you all. I see some friends over there we'd like to speak with before we sit down to eat."

Doug responded, "Yes, it was nice to meet you both." And then Doug continued to talk about golf.

They moved across the room, and Theresa saw Mitch doing the same thing they were doing, casually sauntering along, listening to conversations, talking a bit more with certain people, and then moving on.

And that's what they were here to do. She wondered if this was why she'd never participated in big fancy balls before. This wasn't her cup of tea. Not at all.

She didn't give two craps about who saw her where. She didn't need to hobnob with the elite. It seemed stuffy and phony.

She wondered how many of these people were criminals and how many of them were here just to donate to a good cause. Also, how many of them were laundering money; either for the cartel or for themselves.

It made her feel like she wanted to go back to the cabin and take a shower. Being in a room full of criminals was the most distasteful thing she'd ever done in her life.

And that was a fact.

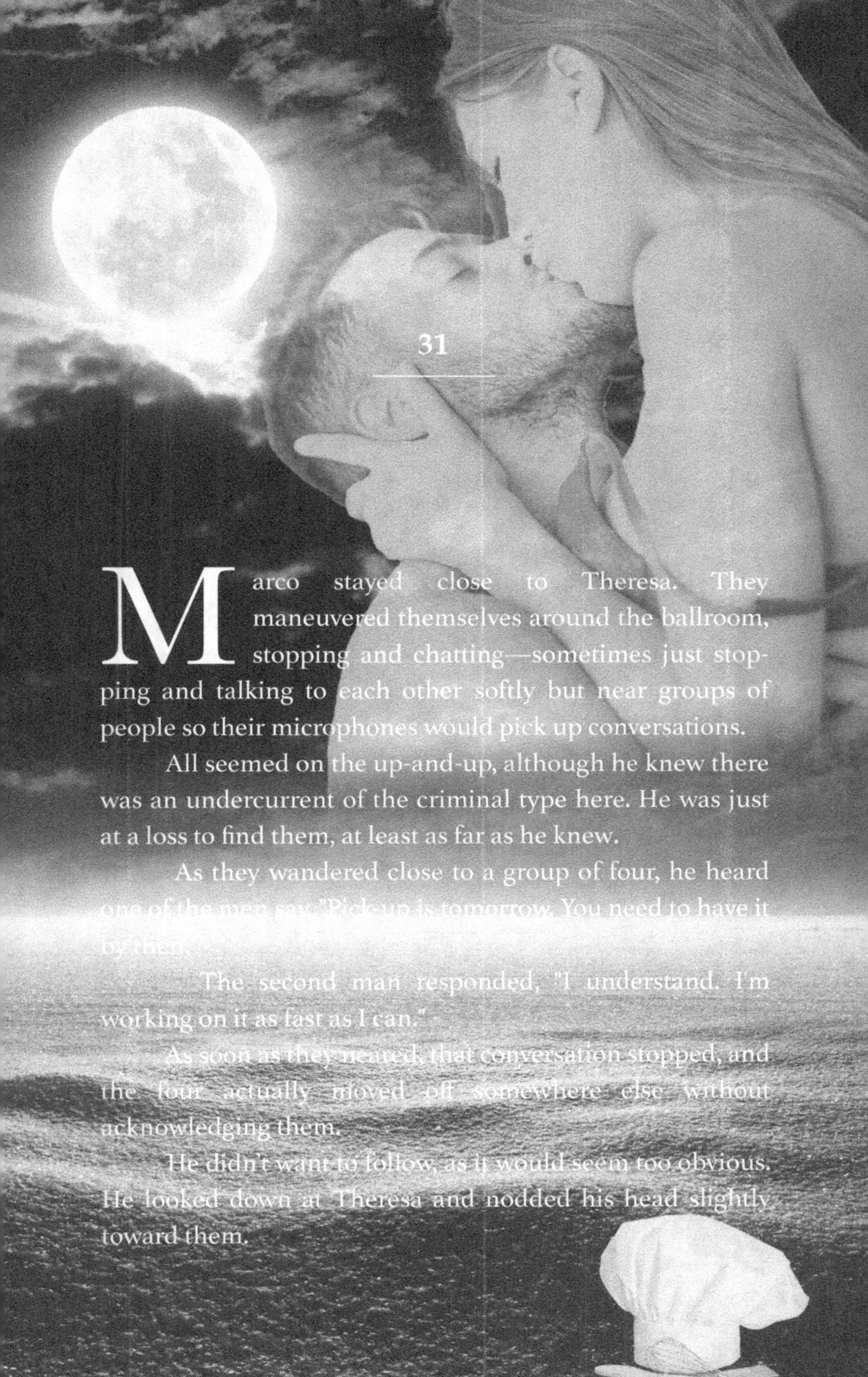

31

Marco stayed close to Theresa. They maneuvered themselves around the ballroom, stopping and chatting—sometimes just stopping and talking to each other softly but near groups of people so their microphones would pick up conversations.

All seemed on the up-and-up, although he knew there was an undercurrent of the criminal type here. He was just at a loss to find them, at least as far as he knew.

As they wandered close to a group of four, he heard one of the men say, "Pick-up is tomorrow. You need to have it by then."

The second man responded, "I understand. I'm working on it as fast as I can."

As soon as they neared, that conversation stopped, and the four actually moved off somewhere else without acknowledging them.

He didn't want to follow, as it would seem too obvious. He looked down at Theresa and nodded his head slightly toward them.

She nodded. "Let's give them a few minutes, and we can try again."

"Absolutely," he said.

Just as he started to steer them toward another group, a chime sounded, and a man dressed in a tuxedo stood on the stage. "Dinner is served. Please make your way to your seats. Your table numbers are on your name tags."

Marco steered Theresa toward the dinner tables. They were sitting at table thirty-one.

They found their table and sat, and much to his surprise, the four people who had walked away from them earlier came and sat at the same table. Hopefully, this was fortuitous.

He held Theresa's chair out for her, and she sat. He took the seat next to her and smiled at their table companions.

Four more people came to join them. The tables were ten-tops, round and large. Conversation was difficult unless you were speaking to the person on either side of you.

Across-the-table conversation in this room was nearly impossible.

The noise level was loud. That was until the chairman of the ball, Torin Terry, walked up to the podium on the stage.

"Good evening, ladies and gentlemen. Thank you for joining us here today for this great cause. The monies that are raised here tonight, and generously donated by all of you, will go to help children with leukemia. We donate the money to various hospitals that have laboratories working on the cure for leukemia, and a portion is set aside to help children whose parents can't afford their treatments. That way, we ensure that those children get the treatment they need."

Everyone at the tables clapped.

Mr. Terry nodded his head and held up his hand. "Thank you. I ask you all to open your wallets and donate generously, so we can help as many children as possible. Hopefully, the research that is done with the help of the funds you donate will end this insidious disease altogether, so no other child has to suffer through it."

More applause.

Mr. Terry continued, "Now, while we eat, we have an orchestra here to play soft music. Please enjoy yourselves. The food here is phenomenal, and when you're finished eating, I urge you to get up and place another bid for these beautifully donated auction items. Again, your money goes to a good cause. Thank you all for attending."

More applause.

Mr. Terry sat at the table in front of the stage.

Waitstaff began delivering their food, and most of the people at the table seemed to be more interested in talking only to their companions rather than engaging with anyone else. Marco was fine with that. They had microphones that could hear a lot. So, he and Theresa mostly ate in silence.

She sat to his left, and every so often, he would lay his hand on her leg and squeeze slightly, to comfort her. And himself. He wanted tonight to be successful and for him, success meant they'd gather some information and Theresa would be safe. They'd go home together and make love.

As waitstaff began removing their dinner plates and delivering desserts, they ate once more and then waited to see what was going to happen next. Their table companions promptly left the table. Marco thought that was a sign they had things they didn't want to discuss in front of others.

He looked up and saw two of the men from their table walking to the restroom together. He leaned down to

Theresa and whispered, "I'm following them to the restroom. You stay in this room. Maybe take a walk along the auction tables once more. There should be more names on them now. Don't go anywhere else, please."

She smiled. "I won't. I'm fine."

They got up from the table. They walked together until he had to turn toward the restroom. He watched her briefly as she walked toward the auction tables. As he strode toward the bathroom, he passed an empty conference room, or banquet room, whatever it was in this place, and heard men talking.

He decided to loiter outside the door and see if his microphones could pick up any of the conversation. Not wanting to seem too obvious in case someone else came along, he pulled his phone out and pretended to be texting someone. He heard: Celtics, money, late, and a few other things that he thought were important.

He sure hoped this conversation was being picked up and that it was valuable. He left the area before anybody became suspicious or came along and saw him standing too close. He went out to the ballroom.

But he couldn't find Theresa.

32

Theresa casually walked along the auction tables, leaning over to read the names on the clipboards.

The amount of money that people were willing to bid was unreal, and she wondered how much of it was ill-gotten gains.

Their bids were likely false. The amounts they were willing to bid were just for show, so the benefit could keep records, but in actuality, that money was being laundered. It made her sick they were willing to use children to hide what they were doing.

She continued walking along each table, stopping when someone called out, "Theresa, is that you?"

She looked up to see Kelsey, who she worked with at the Sandbar.

"Kelsey? Yes, hi! What are you doing here?"

Her mind whirled. What would Kelsey be doing here? She didn't come from money. Actually, she just had some issue with a ticket or something. What did Marco say? She had to have help?

Kelsey shrugged. "Oh, my dad wanted me to come in his place. He comes to this thing every year."

"Your dad? What does your dad do for a living?"

"Oh, he runs a paper company. He sells the cardboard boxes to PCK Meatpacking, and they ship their meat out in them. This is a big deal for him. He's known Torin Terry for years, and they're good friends. They golf and do all sorts of things together. So, one of us had to be here, and my dad is out of town, so he needed me to come in his place."

Theresa's mind spun. She'd never heard Kelsey talk about her family. Actually, she thought she was from out of town.

"Okay... but with me off work for a while, aren't you filling in at the Sandbar?"

Kelsey shrugged. "Margo's filling in tonight, and she can handle it. And with this thing going on, a lot of people wouldn't be at the Sandbar, so they didn't expect a big crowd, even though it's Saturday night."

Theresa swallowed. None of this seemed right. Then Kelsey spun around quickly. The drink in her hand went flying, splashing all over Theresa.

Theresa gasped. "Oh my God!"

Kelsey responded, "Oh! I'm so sorry! I'm so sorry!" Kelsey's voice was high-pitched and panicked. "Here, let me help you, oh my God, let's run to the bathroom, I can find some napkins to sop this up. I am so, so, so, so sorry!"

Theresa shook her head. "No, that's okay. I don't need to go to the bathroom."

She rushed over to the bar and asked for some napkins. The bartender handed her three cloth napkins, and she began dabbing the front of her dress, trying to soak up the mess and not pull a camera or microphone from its seated spot.

"Theresa, please," Kelsey pleaded. "Let's go to the bathroom so I can wash some of this off. It's going to stain your dress, it's very beautiful, by the way." She took a breath. "I thought you were on personal leave for some reason?"

Theresa paused. She hadn't thought about an alibi if someone asked her what she was doing here. She certainly never expected to see Kelsey or anyone she knew.

"I am on personal leave, but this was an event I had to attend. But why are you here? This is all big-money people."

"I told you, my dad asked me to come. Why are you here?"

Theresa sighed. "It was just something I had to do for a friend."

"What friend? What friend do you have that would have this kind of money?"

Theresa blew out a breath, exasperated. Usually, she was quicker at thinking on her feet. She told white lies all the time when she was in reporter mode. But this? It caught her off guard.

"Well, to be honest, I'm not sure that's any of your business Kelsey. And I'm not sure why you're asking me so many questions."

"I'm sorry! I didn't mean to seem nosy or anything. I was just surprised to see you here."

"I'm surprised to see you as well."

Kelsey sighed. "Anyway, let's go. Let's get to the bathroom so I can help you wipe this up."

Theresa's exasperation came out in a huff. "I don't need help wiping this up. It's fine. As soon as I get home, I'll send my dress off to the dry cleaners. It'll be fine."

Suddenly, Mitch appeared from nowhere. "Hello there, Theresa. Do you need some help?"

She spun around, startled. Then she realized Gabby had probably told him she was being grilled.

"Mitch, thanks. Oh, Kelsey accidentally spilled a drink on my dress. We're just trying to sop it up."

Kelsey shook her head. "I told her we needed to go to the bathroom to put some water on the stains, but she won't come."

Mitch shook his head. "That's okay. My housekeeper can help you get any stains out, if need be, and the dry cleaners will do a perfect job with it."

Kelsey huffed slightly. "I was just trying to help."

Mitch dismissed her quickly. "Yes, I can see the kind of help you were trying to offer. Theresa, how about we step into the hallway and finish mopping up this mess, so we're not in the main ballroom?"

Theresa sighed. "Yes, that would be great. Thank you."

Mitch slowly ushered her out as she continued dabbing at her dress. Her chest started to feel sticky, whatever Kelsey had in her drink was sugary. Out in the hallway, her heart pounded. Her breathing was slightly unsteady.

"Thank you for coming to my rescue," she said. "That almost felt like she did it on purpose. The way she spun around and spilled that drink, it was almost like she tossed it."

"Yeah, Gabby told me she was giving you the third degree, working way too hard to get you out of the room."

"It was so weird. And I didn't know her dad owned a paper manufacturing company."

Mitch responded. "He doesn't. At least, not this Kelsey's dad. Luckily, I'm familiar with the employees at the Sandbar, and I had Gabby do a quick check on her. She was lying."

Theresa's stomach dropped. "Oh my God. Kelsey..."

Marco rushed up to them. "There you are! What happened?"

Theresa quickly explained everything. Marco put his hands on her shoulders. He looked into her eyes as he softly said, "It's okay, honey. It's okay. Let's just finish our job and get back to the cabin, where we're safe."

Marco kissed Theresa's lips softly. "You good?"

She nodded. "I'm good. But now I'm pissed. I don't want to leave yet, not until we figure this all out. For one thing, if Kelsey is dirty, I don't want her working at the Sandbar. I don't want her getting Margo and Jace in trouble. I don't want her profiting from being dirty."

Marco huffed out a breath. "I know. I get what you mean. We can take a different approach, just tell Jace and Margo that we have suspicions."

"I don't want to do that. I want to know what those suspicions are. I want to know why she's here. We know she lied. She doesn't have a father who owns a paper packaging company."

"Okay, so what's your plan?"

"I'm going to get her attention. As soon as I see that she notices me, I'll walk out and head to the restroom. You're welcome to come and stand nearby and make sure everything is okay. If it looks like she's trying to lure me into something, you'll all be there. But I want to know what she's up to."

Marco's stomach twisted. He knew they had a job to do, and he willingly accepted their role in it. But if Kelsey was dirty, if she was working for the Celtics or someone associated with them, they could have more manpower out there than they realized.

"Mitch, what do you think?" Marco asked.

Mitch shook his head. "You know, I think it could be a setup. But as long as we're prepared and ready, we can keep Theresa safe. And Theresa, no heroics. Do you understand? Just do what we talked about. Let Marco and I handle the rest."

He watched her throat constrict as she swallowed. Her beautiful brown eyes locked onto his.

"I won't do anything heroic. I just want to flush her out."

"Okay."

Marco held her gaze a moment longer, then leaned in and kissed her lips softly.

"Okay."

Mitch clapped his hands together. "All right, give me a minute. I'm going to text some local PD friends and have them stay close by. For now, why don't you two head back to the ballroom and walk around? Get Kelsey's attention. I'll position myself in the hallway near the women's restroom and act like I'm taking an important business call. Most people here will understand that."

"Sounds good," Marco agreed.

He held out his arm, and Theresa locked hers with his as they entered the ballroom. They sauntered around the edge of the room, scanning for Kelsey. It didn't take long.

"There she is," Theresa murmured.

Marco followed her line of vision and spotted Kelsey

deep in conversation with two men he didn't recognize. Both wore tuxedos, and their discussion looked intense. Kelsey seemed almost... scared.

They moved closer, and just as they neared, Kelsey's eyes met his. Then she flicked her gaze to Theresa.

She saw them. Together. Her eyes narrowed. She said something to the men she was with, then began walking toward them.

Marco looked down at Theresa. "Here she comes."

"All right," Theresa responded. "I'm heading toward the women's bathroom. Don't be far behind."

"I won't. I promise."

Theresa turned and walked toward the exit nearest the restrooms. Marco watched her until she reached the door, then Kelsey was right in front of him.

"And what are you two doing together?" she asked, her tone sharp.

Marco grinned. "We're having a good time, thank you very much."

Kelsey shrugged. "You know what I mean."

"And you know what I mean."

Kelsey's eyes flickered with something unreadable. Then, without another word, she turned and strode toward the restroom exit.

Marco followed, careful not to seem too obvious. But he wasn't the only one watching. The two men Kelsey had been speaking to were watching him closely.

His gut tightened. He whispered, "Kelsey was talking to two men and it looked like she received a scolding. They're working together." He stepped through the same exit Theresa and Kelsey had gone through, keeping his pace measured. He murmured quietly to Mitch's people.

"Kelsey's following Theresa to the women's bathroom.

I'm following as well, and the two men Kelsey was with earlier are following me."

As he entered the hallway, he saw Theresa step into the restroom.

Kelsey was about ten steps behind. Marco moved closer to the bathroom door, not too close, but close enough. And then he thought... Why do I care if I look like a perv? This place was full of perverts. Full of disgusting criminals. Why should he care?

He took another step closer; then he heard it.

A struggle. Raised voices. A scuffle. Marco shoved forward, pushing open the door.

"Need help in the women's bathroom...now!" He yelled to Mitch's people.

When he stepped inside, rage flew through him.

34
____

The instant Kelsey entered the bathroom, she jumped on Theresa. Luckily, she was braced for the fight. And she was pissed, so that helped her tremendously.

Kelsey grabbed Theresa's hair and yanked her across the room. Rather than hitting the wall, Theresa managed to grab Kelsey's hair and pull it as hard as she could. Kelsey grunted and grabbed Theresa's throat with her free hand. She squeezed but Theresa yanked hard on Kelsey's hair and dislodged her grip.

The door burst open just as Kelsey swung and managed to punch Theresa in the side of her face. Theresa raised her knee and caught Kelsey in the gut. Kelsey expelled a whoosh of air and was then jerked back. Theresa whirled in a fury of anger to see Marco firmly gripping Kelsey with an arm around her neck and one around her waist, trapping her arms to her body.

Theresa took a deep breath and fought the urge to lunge at Kelsey. Remember your combat training. Keep your wits

about you. Don't lose control. Fighting in a gown had greatly hampered her ability to use her legs.

Her eyes locked on Marco's as Mitch entered the bathroom with two police officers behind him. The police officers put handcuffs on a fighting, wiggling Kelsey, who tried in vain to get away. Once they had her in cuffs, they eased her to the ground so she couldn't run.

Marco wrapped his arms around Theresa and her heart needed his comfort right now. Her hair was likely a mess, her dress was certainly a mess, and her dreamy feeling of being a princess had long passed.

She took two deep breaths and turned to stare down at Kelsey, who was shooting daggers at her from her position on the floor.

"Why, Kelsey?"

Kelsey pressed her lips together and looked in the opposite direction.

Marco moved them toward the door. Police officers said, "Stay close."

Marco nodded, "We will."

Mitch stopped them. "Hang on. Don't go out there until we have more backup. I saw her companions ready to enter this room until they saw the police and myself rushing in."

Theresa's heartbeat was beginning to slow. The incredible adrenaline rush had started to subside and her body shook. Marco took his jacket off without a word and hung it over her shoulders. "It's the adrenaline."

"Yeah."

Police were questioning Kelsey but were not getting any responses from her, so finally one of the cops read Kelsey her rights.

One of the cops turned to Theresa and said, "We'll need a statement from you."

Mitch responded, "I'll get them to the station for an interview."

The officer nodded. They lifted Kelsey to her feet and ushered her through the door and out to their cruiser where they'd give her a private escort to the police department and hopefully jail.

Mitch turned to them, "Okay. Her two goons..."

He stopped speaking and opened the bathroom door. "Are gone, but I don't know where. Let's get out of here. We'll head to the police station and give your statements, then to the cabin where you can get a good night's sleep."

She nodded. "That sounds good. Will you ever get the information about why Kelsey was involved here?"

"Yes. I'll get that information."

Theresa's shaking started to subside. She took a steady breath and let it out slowly. "Okay."

Mitch led the way from the bathroom, and she and Marco followed. Once in the hallway, she walked along between them, with Marco's arm securely around her, holding her tight. Her heart swelled with the protectiveness he offered. It had grown progressively over time as she worked with him, but these past few days, he'd found a place in her heart that would never leave.

As soon as they left Paradise Gardens, the cool air brushed over her face and the remaining tension left her body. The beautiful lights lit the palm trees, and the shine on the driveway glittered with the lights. It was still impressive here. Regrettably, she didn't get an opportunity to dance with Marco and that made her stomach twist slightly. She'd felt like a princess in a stunning gown with her prince in an amazing place. Kelsey ruined it all. She'd never forgive her for that. She'd also never forgive her for the duplicity and nastiness she brought to them all.

They strode quietly to Mitch's SUV, all lost in thought. Suddenly, two men jumped from between cars and attacked Marco and Mitch. She heard fists connecting with flesh and bone. Grunts and feet scrambling on the pavement. It took her mind a few moments to comprehend what was happening and then she saw another man coming toward her. He began running and she had only a few seconds to figure out what to do. Shots rang out, two in rapid succession and she saw the man running toward her fall. She was pushed down as something heavy hit her legs. Her head hit the pavement hard, the jarring pain sliced through the back of her head and ran down her back to her hip. Air whooshed from her lungs and the weight that had pushed her down, now lay on her legs.

Panic rose along with the shooting pain from the back of her head. Then, as if by divine intervention, the weight on her legs was lifted.

Marco knelt down beside her, blood trickling from his lip. "Theresa. Baby, are you okay?"

She tried to say something but nothing came out. Taking a deep breath, she then whispered, "Yes."

Her hand lifted to his lip. "You're hurt."

"I'm fine."

"You're bleeding."

"The important thing is you aren't."

"I'm not more important than you."

"I think you are." His fingers reached behind her head, still on the warm pavement. "I don't feel blood, so that's good. Are you able to move?"

"I think so."

"Move your hands for me."

She chuckled. "I just did."

"Yeah." He chuckled. "Move your legs."

She moved her legs back and forth and he smiled.

"Can you get up?"

"Yeah." She began to sit up and Marco's gentle hands lifted her back from the pavement until she was in a sitting position.

He grinned. "Okay?"

"Yeah."

"Okay. Now up you come."

He pushed the material from her gown away and displayed her feet. One of her heels had flown off, one was lying near her foot. Marco picked up the shoe next to her, then glanced around for the other. He nodded, but instead of reaching for it, he turned his attention to her. "Do you need me to help you?"

"Maybe." She took a breath. "No, I can do it." She started to move into a standing position and a slice of pain from her hip made her gasp. "Maybe some help."

He gently lifted her to her feet. "Get your balance."

She stood stock still and tested her balance. He held his arm out firmly. "Use me for balance. Let's try to walk."

She took two steps and let out a deep breath. "I'm good. My left hip is a bit sore. But I'm good."

He nodded. "Okay, hang on."

He retrieved her other high heel, then held his arm out to her. She glanced around and found the man who had been running toward her lying on the pavement face down, about three feet from her. Another man lay near her feet. Mitch had the other one, face down on the pavement with his hands zip-tied behind his back.

"You shot them." It was more of a statement than anything. She was beginning to process what had happened. Marco shot the men threatening her.

"I wasn't going to let them take you. And Mitch shot one of them."

35

Marco sat on the bumper of the ambulance as EMTs looked at his lip. It had a nice split in it, but that was it. He was going to have a shiner tomorrow, and one of those fuckers caught his ribs with a fist, but nothing was broken.

"All set, Mr. Karason."

"Thanks."

He stood and hefted himself into the ambulance with a grimace and a groan. He sat on the cot next to Theresa who already had a bruise on the side of her beautiful face. Nothing was broken though.

He took her hand and held it. She currently had a thermometer in her mouth. Her hair was askew, and her dress was a mess. But she was still the most beautiful woman he'd ever laid eyes on. He leaned over and kissed her temple. His lip ached slightly, but it was worth it.

The EMT pulled the thermometer from her mouth and read it. "Ninety-eight. You're normal."

Theresa laughed. "Hardly. How many normal people do

you know that are attacked at a charity ball and almost kidnapped?"

The SMT smiled. "Well, I'll give you that. You're all set.

Marco stood gingerly. His ribs hurt like a bitch, but it was a muscular injury and he'd be good in a couple of days.

He held his hand out to Theresa, and she took it and stood. Her shoes were somewhere else. Her adorable toes poked out from under her tattered dress.

She looked up at him. "Where's Mitch?"

"He's out there waiting for us. He spoke with the police after I did."

"Okay. Do I have to speak to them now?"

"I think Mitch arranged for you to come in tomorrow."

She nodded. "Tomorrow the final exposé releases. The heat should be largely off. At least that's my hope."

"I hope you're right."

He sat down on the bumper, dangled his feet, and eased himself to the ground. He didn't think he could lift Theresa down, and that pissed him off. Instead, he held her hand as she took the steps down. Each time her bare feet found a step, he grinned.

They sauntered across the parking lot to find Mitch chatting with a cop. He looked up and saw them coming toward him and nodded. He said goodbye to the cop and met them in the middle.

"I have your shoes in the SUV. Do you need me to get them?"

"No."

"Okay. I moved my vehicle here." He pointed to his SUV.

Marco helped her into the SUV, climbed in the front passenger seat, and heard her sigh.

Mitch's phone rang just as they pulled out of the parking

lot of Paradise Gardens. He tapped the button so the speakers would pick it up. "DeMario."

"It's Jace. Someone threw a Molotov through the front window of the Sandbar."

Marco swore. "Fuck."

He heard Theresa gasp in the back.

Mitch responded first. "Is everything okay?"

"Luckily Margo and I were there. I put it out right away. One table was damaged. And, of course, the window. And thank God no one was here but us."

Mitch nodded. "I'm glad no one was hurt. Speaking of hurt, I have Marco and Theresa in the car with me. Theresa was attacked. Marco was too. He also shot one man, and I shot the other. It's been a mess here tonight. Also, Kelsey who works for you is dirty. That's who attacked Theresa."

"Son of a bitch. Theresa and Marco, are you alright?"

Marco tried to twist in his seat, but a searing pain locked him in place. He waited a beat and when Theresa didn't respond he did. "We're okay. A bit bruised. A lot pissed."

"You have a right to be pissed."

Marco reached his hand back and Theresa took it and squeezed. He heard her take a deep breath.

"Theresa? Are you alright?"

"Yeah." Her voice was weak, but the way she squeezed his hand spoke of her strength.

Jace cleared his throat. "Are you two up for a visit tomorrow?"

She squeezed Marco's hand once and he nodded. "Yes. We'll be moving slowly but it would be nice to see you and Margo, if she wants to come out. We'll fill you in on the details."

"Sounds good. We'll see you then. I'll text in the morning for a good time to come out."

"Okay." Marco rested his head against the backrest. Suddenly he felt exhausted. He'd expelled all his adrenaline and now he needed to sleep.

Mitch took over the conversation with Jace. "I'll come out when you do, and we'll catch you up on everything."

"Sounds good. Everyone rest easy tonight."

The call ended and Mitch eased them out of town. The road to the cabin was slightly bumpy, but it didn't hurt as much as he feared it would. Mitch walked them to the cabin and waited to hear the door lock before he left.

Marco turned to Theresa who stood looking like a sad princess. The bruise was deepening in color and her lips turned down in a frown.

"It's okay. We're safe now."

"I know, but you're going to have a black eye. It's already turning purple."

He chuckled. "We'll match then."

"What?"

"Babe, you have a bruise on the side of your gorgeous face. And that pisses me off. But you're still the most beautiful woman in the world."

A tear slid down her cheek, and he swiped it with the back of his forefinger. He leaned down slowly and kissed her lips lightly.

When he straightened, he groaned softly.

He took her hand and led her to the bedroom, where there'd be no sex tonight. But he'd hold her all night. When they both felt better and could move without discomfort, they'd make up for tonight. He looked forward to that day.

Theresa softly asked. "Do you want to shower first, or should I?"

"Go ahead, babe. I'll go use the other shower."

She didn't even argue. She turned toward the bathroom, stopped, and looked back. "Can you unzip me?"

He chuckled. "Yeah. I can unzip you."

He pulled the zipper down and helped her step out of her dress. He carried it out to the sofa and lay it across. Mitch was going to have a lot to explain to the dry cleaner.

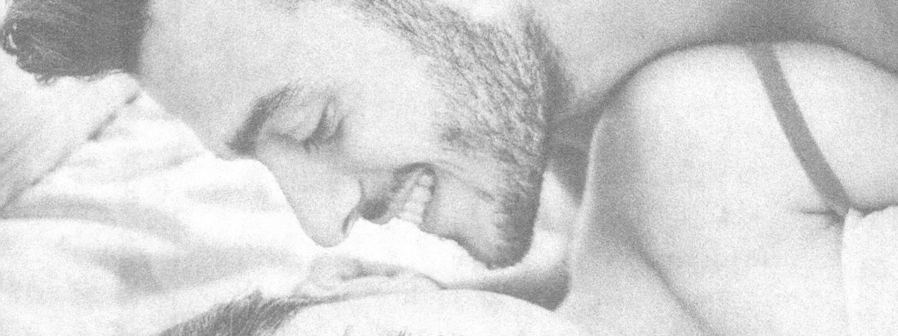

Theresa climbed into bed naked as the day she was born and sighed. Marco chuckled and slowly scooted toward her. He wrapped his arms around her from behind. She lay her head on his arm, his other pulled her closer. His warm skin touched hers and she felt wrapped in the safest, sexiest cocoon.

She closed her eyes and whispered. "I've never spooned before."

His voice, deep and sexy in her ear chuckled. "Really? I'm your first spoon?"

"Yeah. Lame right?"

"I don't think so. I'm happy to be your first."

She laughed.

He kissed the back of her head. "I love you, Theresa."

She stared across the room for a moment, though it was dark and she couldn't really see anything. "Did you mean to say that or are you sleep-deprived?"

He chuckled. "I meant to say it. Because it's true."

She could feel his heartbeat strong and solid on her

back. His arms tightened slightly. She smiled. "I love you too."

His arms tightened again and he sighed. That sounded so sweet. So lovely. A tear slipped from her eye and dripped onto his arm. She sniffed lightly, embarrassed that she cried twice tonight. His soft steady breathing near her ear told her he didn't know about this time, so she didn't have to tell him. She closed her eyes and sleep took her sooner than ever before.

SHE WOKE TO MARCO SETTING A CUP OF COFFEE ON THE bedside table and a plate graced with two macarons.

"Thank you." She stretched.

He sat on the edge of the bed and slowly leaned in to kiss her forehead. "You're welcome."

She smiled. "How are you feeling this morning? I see you're moving around, though slowly."

"I'm sore. But I'll be fine in a day or two."

His hand smoothed over the left side of her face where she likely had a nice purple mark. "How are you?"

"I'm fine. How purple am I?"

"I'm more purple than you."

She smiled. "It looks good on you though. You look all manly and primitive."

He chuckled. "Okay. I've never been called that before."

"Oh, I'm your first?"

He grinned. "You're first for a lot of things, Babe. I've never said I love you to anyone before. You were the first person I've barged into a woman's bathroom for. Attending a charity ball was another first. And I've never stayed in a cabin more secure than the White House before. I've done all of those with you."

She sat up. Some of her muscles argued but it wasn't terrible. She wrapped her arms around his shoulders because she didn't want to hurt him anywhere. "Thank you. I really do love you too. I think I have for months, but I didn't think we could ever be together, so I held back."

He grinned. "I'm glad that changed. I think I've loved you from afar for a long time too. But you kept yourself aloof and I didn't know why. I'm glad that changed too."

She lightly touched the skin around his purple eye. It was warm to the touch. "Except for this big bad boy."

"I'd do it again."

She kissed him gently. Neither of them was in any physical condition to make love. Hopefully soon though.

"Drink your coffee and enjoy your macarons. I'm making breakfast."

"Okay. I'll be out soon."

She watched him leave the room. Nice view. She picked up her coffee cup and sipped the hot delicious liquid as she nibbled the macrons. Thinking about all that had transpired in this past week, her head whirled. She never would have thought all these changes would have happened in a week's time. But she wasn't sorry. About any of it. Well, except Mitch's car and the Sandbar suffering a Molotov. And of course, she was sorry anyone was killed, but they were bad men doing bad things. Every time she thought about how close she came to being in their custody, her blood ran cold.

She pulled back the covers and stepped from the bed. Her sweatpants and T-shirts were in the dresser. She quickly dressed, picked up her plate and coffee cup, and carried them to the kitchen. As she passed the sofa and her pitiful-looking dress she stopped a moment and stared at the damage. She wondered if it could be repaired.

There were rips at the bottom and one at the waist. The sugary drink that was spilled on it stained the front. The glittering stones all over the dress now looked like sad little rocks. Their glimmer had dimmed.

Marco came to stand behind her. He took the empty plate from her hand and whispered. "It's just a dress."

"I know. But I felt so pretty in it. And we didn't get to dance last night. I felt like a princess with her prince. Now it looks like the princess partied too hard and my prince is bruised and battered."

He kissed the top of her head. "You're always pretty. The most beautiful woman I've ever known."

She chuckled. "Right."

His left arm snaked around her waist and pulled her back to his body. "I would never lie to you about that. You're gorgeous. And one day, we'll dance. I promise."

She smiled and rested her head against his chest. "Thank you."

He chuckled. "Breakfast is ready, Baby."

He stepped away and the minute he did, she felt alone. She fell harder and harder for Marco every day. She was a goner for him.

She sighed and turned toward the kitchen just as Marco set a plate in front of her stool. That made her chuckle. They'd been here four days and now that was her seat.

Marco carried a plate to his stool, and they sat to eat. Today's menu was crepes. Cream cheese and strawberries. Goodness, she'd need to begin working out again if he continued to cook like this for her. She never ate this much when she lived alone. She'd grab something at work or home, something super simple, like half a sandwich or some fruit.

"This is delicious Marco."

He grinned. "Thank you. I noticed at the Sandbar, you used to devour these."

"You noticed that?"

"Babe. I noticed everything about you."

"Did not."

He chuckled and shook his head. "You love cream cheese crepes and steak sandwiches. You don't like the seafood pasta. You love spaghetti, with meat sauce. You don't care for the fried fish sandwich. You love my steak, cooked medium rare. You enjoy my smoked pork chops. You dislike the eggs from the carton that we use for gluten-free foods. You do like my deviled eggs."

Her mouth dropped open as she stared at him. "You paid that much attention?"

"And so much more." He took a bite, chewed, and swallowed. "You usually wear your hair in a ponytail on the day you haven't had time to wash it. You wear it down when you come to work then put it in a ponytail before customers come on the day you wash it before work. It's so shiny and soft looking I've always wanted to dig my fingers in it and let them run through the strands."

He leaned toward her and his hand slid into her hair at her temple, then slid back. He pulled his hand away and let the silky strands slide through his fingers. "Like this."

He did it again. She stared at his eyes as he watched her hair flow from his fingers.

Her hand reached up and mimicked the same motion in his hair. He always wore it a bit longer, grazing his collar in the back. She let the strands fall from her fingers. She slid her hand into his hair again and he closed his eyes. She asked, "Do you like that?"

"Mmm."

His fingers slid into her hair again, but this time he kneaded her scalp gently. She closed her eyes and enjoyed the feeling of his fingers on her. She mimicked the motion on his scalp and received a gratuitous moan and a smile. "That feels fantastic."

"Yeah."

37

Marco sat at the dining room table next to Theresa as she finished up her writing. Today the final report would be published. She was now writing the end to that. Explaining the dead man's switch and that she was increasingly worried about being murdered by these thugs. Hopefully, this would help them understand she meant business.

She froze mid-type and whispered, "Shit."

She stood and moved toward the bedroom. He followed her to make sure she was okay and found her in the closet, on her knees, digging through her backpack.

"Is everything okay?"

She looked up at him, her brows pinched together. "I just found a note in my encrypted files from Keely. She told me she left a thumb drive for me in the bag of documents. I never read that far in the documents to see that note."

She dug through the zippered pouch. She pulled documents from inside and set them on the floor. Once the pouch was emptied, she opened it and looked inside. There wasn't anything in there. She squeezed the zippered pouch and felt something. He watched her comb through every inch of that bag with a thoroughness that was impressive.

"Oh my God. I found it."

She pulled the lining of the bag up and away from the bag itself and there was an invisible zipper sewn at the bottom. She unzipped it and pulled out a black thumb drive. She held it up between them and he saw her throat constrict as she swallowed.

He grinned and nodded his head. "You got it, baby."

He held his hand out to help her up and she rushed to her computer and inserted the thumb drive. A folder marked 4TJM was all that populated.

Marco leaned in. "What does that mean?"

She smiled. "For Theresa Jean Miklovic. That was a code we used. Though it wasn't much of a code."

"Oh. Clever. As long as you knew what it meant, it was a good code."

Theresa nodded. "If it was something about her husband the code would be SJBC. That meant Shooter John Benson Criminal. SJBL was Shooter John Benson Legal. He had some businesses that were legal, so things looked on the up and up. He never laundered through those businesses. But she watched what he did there anyway."

"She was brave."

Theresa's shoulders fell and she nodded. "She was incredible. But he treated her like shit, and she wanted him to be found out. All of them. She hated what they were doing."

"She's lucky she found you."

Theresa chuckled. "I was lucky to find her. We uncovered so many things about these assholes."

He watched her screw up the courage to open the folder. She finally took a deep breath and clicked the folder to open it. The open folder revealed a list of documents and one said Theresa.

Theresa looked into his eyes for a moment. She swallowed and clicked the folder. A document opened which was a letter to her.

Dear Theresa,

I write this letter to you knowing that I'm likely dead at this point. I told you from the beginning my life was always at risk. If Shooter found out what I was doing, he'd kill me. And there was always a chance that he'd kill me anyway, in one of his outbursts. They've become worse and it really is only a matter of time.

I know you've asked me why I don't leave. You see, I can't. He'll find me. No matter where I go, no matter what I do, he'd find me. I'd live my life on the run with no money and the inability to ever keep myself safe. One of the documents I have attached here is also a copy of my bank accounts. Shooter has been using my bank accounts recently to implicate me so I couldn't run. He always threatens to expose me, so I remain compliant. What he should realize is if he brings me down, it will also throw shade on him. But I believe he has the officials in his pocket and they have been paid off, so he likely would never be implicated. In a sense, this is my last act of defiance, and my death will not be in vain if you manage to bring the Celtics down. At a minimum, shed a bright light on what they're doing to the point their operations will cease or slow down and their influence will no longer be valuable. Besides the money, they love the power their influence brings. That alone is worth watching. The rats will all leave the sinking ship.

The documents in this thumb drive are bank statements from both Shooter's and his dad's accounts. Some of them are offshore accounts and many of those show money exchanges with foreign governments for arms and secrets. Shooter loved dealing in secrets and access to his father. That is always a big-ticket item for him.

Bring to light all these bastards have done and are doing, Theresa. Then I hope you find peace and happiness in life and know you did a remarkable thing in bringing down one of the biggest and most corrupt crime families of this century. It's been my pleasure to know and work with you.

Your friend,

Keely.

Theresa wiped her eyes as she read Keely's words. Marco lay his hand on the nape of her neck to show support. She turned and cried on his shoulder. The distance between them was large, so he pulled her onto his lap and he held her as she cried for her brave friend and the loss she felt all over again.

When her crying subsided, he tightened his arms around her waist and whispered in her ear. "You and Keely are the bravest women I've ever known or heard of. You should write her story."

Theresa sniffed a few times and finally lifted her head from his shoulder. "What would that look like?"

"It would be a retelling of how she contacted you and the things she's told you over the time you worked together. You can interview people who knew her. Her family, siblings, parents and others. You would tell the world who Keely Benson was. That would be a phenomenal tribute to your friend."

38

Theresa added links to some of the documents Keely had shared with her, kept some of them back, and encrypted them with her dead man's switch. She finished her story by explaining what the dead man's switch was and that if she were killed, even if it looked like an accident, the final incriminating documents would be released for the world to see. She only listed some of the foreign governments involved in the duplicity. Keeping the bigger countries, Russia, China, Ukraine, and others encrypted behind her dead man's switch. She also mentioned there were countries still to be named.

She scheduled her final exposé to release in the next hour and she stood and stretched. Marco had moved to the kitchen and was baking up something that smelled phenomenal. She sauntered toward the aroma of sweets and the lure of Marco. She moved around the counter and hugged him from behind as he stirred something delicious smelling on the stove.

She sighed. "It's finished."

He turned in her arms and kissed her lips. His was still

split, so he couldn't kiss her like she preferred. Like he wanted to. Soon.

"Nice work babe. How do you feel about it?"

"I'm happy. It feels good."

"Wonderful."

He turned to stir his sauce on the stove. "Jace, Margo, and Mitch will be here in about an hour. I wanted you to have the time you needed to write. Tonight, we'll celebrate."

She stood back and watched her man cook for a moment. "What are you making?"

He chuckled. "Steak and asparagus. I'm also baking a triple chocolate lava cake for dessert. This is the chocolate sauce to drizzle over the top of the cake."

Her hand flew to her stomach. "I'm going to have to start working out again. The way you feed me is certainly going to show soon and I'll get a huge belly." She held her hands out in front of her.

His eyes stared at her hands. She saw his jaw tighten and his Adam's apple move as he swallowed. He set his spoon down, turned the flame off under the pan of simmering chocolate, and pulled her into his body. "I love the way you look. I also love feeding you. And, I love you."

She chuckled as she stared into his gorgeous brown eyes. "I don't bring much to the table here. I don't cook for you. I do love looking at you. I also love who you are as a human."

"That's a ton right there." He bent his knees and kissed her lips.

She wrapped her arms around his waist gently, splaying her fingers open on his back. She took a deep breath and let it out slowly. Nothing felt better than a Marco hug.

He stepped back once more. "Sorry, gotta take care of dinner."

She nodded. "I'll set the table."

She proceeded to set the table in the dining room. She found beautiful woodland placemats with tiny pinecones at the corners. The plates were brown with red rims. The silverware was of high quality. The cloth napkins in the buffet were laid on the plates and she found candles in tall candle sticks that she set in the middle of the table. It was the most elegant table she'd ever set in her life, and she was proud of it.

Marco entered the dining room and whistled. "This is beautiful."

"I can't take credit for buying the dishes, placemats, and candles, but I love how they look together."

The security system chimed, and Marco hurried to the computer on the desk to check the cameras.

"They're here."

She nodded and glanced once more at her pitiful dress still sadly draped across the back of the sofa, before she sauntered toward the front door to greet their guests. She waited until Marco gave the all clear and joined her at the door.

He opened it and stepped onto the front porch as Mitch exited his vehicle. Jace and Margo were pulling items from their SUV to bring inside. She couldn't imagine what they brought.

Mitch shook Marco's hand. His eyes examined the shiner Marco sported then he nodded. "It could be worse."

Marco chuckled. "It could."

When Mitch's eyes turned to her, though, his lips turned down in a frown. "I'm sorry to see you bruised up, Theresa. I feel as though I should have protected you more."

She smiled at Mitch. "It could be worse."

He chuckled as his own words were tossed back at him,

then she took a breath. "I'm sorrier for the dress. I apologize for the damage. It is so beautiful."

Mitch held his hand up for her to stop. "Don't worry about it. We'll see if the dry cleaners can clean it up."

Jace and Margo came to the porch with arms full of goodies. Marco chuckled. "What on earth do you have here?"

Jace chuckled and Margo responded. "We brought food in case you're running out of things."

Theresa moved to the side to let Margo pass through the door. "Here let me help you with these."

She took a bag from Margo's arms and carried it to the kitchen. Margo set her bag on the counter next to Theresa's then turned to her and hugged her.

Margo's hug was warm and friendly, and it felt so good. Not as good as Marco's, but close.

When Margo pulled back, she looked at Theresa's face. "Oh, honey. Are you alright?"

Theresa nodded. "I am. It actually looks worse than it is. It only hurts when I touch it."

Margo's lips turned down. "I'm so sorry."

"It's not your fault, Margo."

Jace entered behind them with bags and set them on the counter. When his eyes landed on her face, he frowned. "How are you, Theresa?"

She chuckled. "I'm good. As I mentioned to Margo, it looks worse than it is. I think Marco took the brunt of the beatings though."

Marco stepped around the counter and shook his head. "It's all in a day."

Mitch laughed. "It used to be. These days you wrestle more with meat than people."

Marco laughed. "Truth."

Theresa remembered her manners. "What can I get everyone to drink?"

Margo pulled two bottles of wine from one of the grocery bags. "I brought wine so we can celebrate."

Theresa chuckled. "I'm all for that." She looked at her watch. "The report will publish in twenty minutes."

Margo chuckled. "We could be into our second bottle by then."

Marco and Theresa served dinner to their guests. They enjoyed the meal together, laughing and telling stories. Their guests asked for a recounting of the events of last night and Marco obliged. It took a while, as a lot of things occured.

Jace asked, "What happens with the police now? Are you in trouble?"

Marco shook his head, but Mitch responded. "I believe I smoothed things over. Theresa still must go in and give her statement. I called today and asked if she could have the day off. But tomorrow she'll have to go in."

Marco glanced at Theresa, and she nodded.

His stomach twisted though. Would she be a sitting duck in the police station? They didn't think anyone on the Blossom Springs Police Department was dirty. But then again, they didn't think Kelsey was dirty either.

Theresa sighed after Marco repeated Kelsey's involvement. "Believe me, I was shocked to see her there. She said she was there in her father's place and that he owned a paper company that supplied the cardboard boxes to DCK

Meatpacking. Since I was wired, Mitch's team did some quick checking and said she was lying."

Jace's jaw tightened. "Is that how you got that bruise on your face?"

Theresa shrugged slightly. "Yes. She spun me around by my hair and my face hit the stall wall."

Margo spat, "That bitch."

Jace reached over and lay his hand over Margo's. "Of course, she's not welcome at the Sandbar any longer."

Theresa nodded. "Of course not. I hope she sits in jail for a good long time."

Marco responded. "It's doubtful. If it's her first offense, battery doesn't get you much jail time these days."

Margo's brows furrowed. "But if she's involved in the money laundering..."

Marco nodded. "We believe she is. We don't have proof. Yet. And we aren't sure how long she's been working with them. It does explain how they found Theresa's phone number though. Kelsey had it. And Theresa recognized some of the men from PCK Meatpacking at the Sandbar. They likely stumbled on the fact that she worked there and then found someone, Kelsey, to help with what they needed. Remember that ticket she needed help with? I think she used that new attorney in town, who is most likely a front for the Celtics. So, perhaps he helped her with the ticket if she did him a favor or two. This is pure conjecture on my part, but it's all I've been thinking about since last night."

Margo looked across the table at Theresa. "Honey, I'm so sorry."

Theresa smiled. "It's not your fault. None of us knew anything. Not until last night."

As the conversation continued, Marco was reminded of what's really important in life; having people you enjoy spending time with and having a person in your life that you love and who loves you. This is what a full life looked like.

He realized all of it now.

He stopped mid-story as he was talking.

Theresa took his hand. "Marco, are you all right?"

He shook his head slowly.

"Uh, yeah, yeah, I'm fine. I just realized that I didn't have a PTSD attack last night. It didn't dawn on me till just now."

Theresa smiled and squeezed his hand. "That's wonderful."

"It is, and I'm not complaining, but I'm surprised. They'd been getting bad for a while, and then when I started working at the Sandbar, they had ceased for the most part. Once in a while, a loud bang would make me jump or make me feel as though an attack was coming on, but during all the fighting last night and the shooting, I didn't have an attack."

Theresa grinned at him. "I'm so happy for you."

He squeezed her hand. "Thanks."

Jace grinned. "It's amazing when they stop, isn't it? But be cautious; they don't always stop. It could come back. Just keep doing your therapy and what you need to do to stay healthy. Keep loving and being loved."

He grinned. "I absolutely plan to do that."

He stared into Theresa's eyes. It wasn't a hardship at all. The smile she bestowed on him was so worth it.

They finished their meal, and a pinging started, sounding like it was coming from Mitch. He reached into his shirt pocket and pulled out Theresa's old phone.

He scrolled and stopped. Text messages were coming through. His face grew stone cold.

"Looks like you've hit a nerve with the crime family.

They're texting and want to know what information you still have."

Theresa quickly looked at her watch. "Oh, the last exposé released."

Jace replied, "It's good to know they're reading it."

Theresa glanced at Mitch. "But what are they saying?"

Marco squeezed her hand and listened as Mitch read the texts.

* *You think you're so smart. We demand you give up what you have or your life is in peril.*

* *Meet me tomorrow to hand over the remaining documents you have.*

* *I mean it. We demand all documents in your possession or you won't know a moment's peace.*

Marco pulled his phone up and checked the website that Theresa was posting the exposés on. He saw so many comments from a great many people, good comments, congratulating her on taking the steps to bring this all to light. Stories of people who had had experiences with certain folks here and there. And then they started coming in, sounding different.

"I just left an encrypted message for you in the private email that you posted. I have some information on some people I think are involved."

That similar type of message... posted over and over and over again.

He turned to her and grinned.

"Well, you may have the cartel rattled, and part of that reason is people are coming forward. Your inbox is filling up according to these comments."

She ran to the coffee table where she had placed their laptops, and she pulled hers open. Typing in the passwords, she started reading.

"Oh my gosh. These stories corroborate Keely's story. They corroborate some of the ledger accounts I have. Oh my God. We can actually bring them down. If these people are still willing to come forward, we can bring them down."

Marco rushed over to the sofa and sat next to her as they started reading email after email. People who had names, dates, and similar stories of things that had happened to them. Family members who were mysteriously killed. Family members whose personalities changed one hundred percent after an encounter with this person or that person, and then after their death, finding accounts being used to launder money.

"Oh my God," Theresa whispered. "This is... this is unbelievable."

Marco bent and kissed her lips.

"You're unbelievable. Look at what you're doing. Look at the change you're going to make. Look at the people who have been affected that you're helping get their story out. See, you don't have to just write Keely's story. You could have a different chapter about every one of these people, even if you change their names. You've got to write this book, Theresa."

She smiled and looked into his eyes. He didn't have to say anything more. He didn't want to push her into it, but he knew she could make some big differences if she did, and he wanted her to be happy. He wanted her to realize her potential. Waiting tables was fine, and managing the restaurant was wonderful; she was doing a great job, but she had more to offer, and people to help. She could do that.

40

Theresa felt depleted after telling her story to the police. Marco was waiting outside for her, at least she hoped so. They'd asked to speak with him again as well. She may have to wait for him.

The officer, Tray Fielding, escorted her to the waiting area. Marco wasn't there and Theresa's knees began shaking.

"I'm sorry. Is there somewhere more private I can wait for Marco? I feel...exposed out here alone."

Tray's eyes locked on hers a moment, then he nodded. "I'm sorry. I didn't think of that. You can wait in our break room."

"Thank you."

She followed Tray through the swinging half door that led them behind the counter and through an area with desks neatly lined up. "This is the bullpen."

She grinned. "Okay. That's interesting."

He shrugged. "It's an ancient term that's been attached to these rooms all over the country in every police station that's ever existed."

She chuckled. "I was in the Army. We have mess halls for our cafeterias. Same thing."

Tray nodded. "Marine here."

She nodded. "HooRah."

He grinned and she wished she had a friend she could set him up with. He was handsome.

They turned a corner and entered a small room. The wastebasket was overflowing, the chairs weren't pushed in neatly and there were dirty dishes in the sink.

Tray turned to her. "Sorry for the mess."

She grinned and shook her head. "No need to be sorry."

Tray nodded. "Please take a seat. I'll let Marco know where you are when he finishes."

"Thank you, Tray. I appreciate it."

She sat at a table, pulled up her phone, and continued reading the messages on her story. They continued to flood in. The shares on it were astounding. Someone commented, "OMG, you're going viral. Good for you."

She smiled, but it didn't last. A lot of people, good people, lost their lives for these exposés. She didn't feel like a hero or an influencer. She simply wanted justice. Justice for Carolyn. Justice for Keely. Justice for all the people whose names she didn't know but whose lives were altered or ended because of the Celtics.

"There you are."

She jumped and turned her head to see Marco walking toward her. "You ready to go home?"

"Yeah."

She stood and met him halfway. "Was it awful?"

"Tedious. How about you?"

"Same." She chuckled.

He wrapped his arm around her shoulders and steered her to the front door of the building. He checked the outside before they exited, and it made her feel better. But really, would they be so bold as to try something at the police station?

After they'd both buckled up and Marco pulled from the parking lot he said, "Kelsey confessed."

"She did?"

"Yes. It's as I surmised. In order to get close to you, the attorney, who we now also know for a fact is dirty, fixed her ticket in exchange for favors."

Theresa stared out the windshield and took a deep breath. "Were some of those favors sexual?"

Marco's head turned her way. "Why would you ask that?"

"It's something many of them do. They have total power and they abuse it."

He nodded. She watched his Adam's apple bob. "Yes."

Her stomach twisted slightly for Kelsey. That was likely awful. But Keely had told her of some of the things they did to people. Total control to utterly humiliate them and make them believe they were dirty and in the wrong.

Marco reached over and took her hand in his. He carefully drove them to the cabin. Inside, she sighed. "I love this place. I feel like I'm in a cocoon. Safe and secure."

"Yeah. I know what you mean."

She kissed his lips. "I'm going to take a shower."

He grinned. "You want company?"

Her brows shot up. "Are you feeling better?"

"I am. But I know I'll feel much better once I'm inside you."

She smiled broadly and took his hand in hers. She sauntered to the bedroom. Marco locked the bedroom door, and she continued to lead him to the bathroom. She began taking her clothes off as Marco reached in and turned the water on to warm. He flipped on the overhead heating lamp and as soon as the warmth surrounded her, she shivered. It felt incredible.

Once her clothing was removed, she watched Marco shed his clothing. The instant his shirt came off, she saw the bruising on his ribs. Her fingers lightly touched the purple and greenish skin. She bent down and kissed his bruise. His hands dove into her hair.

She continued to kiss his bruise and then up his chest. His hands explored her body everywhere. She kissed his jaw, his cheek, his split lip. He grinned.

He pulled her toward the shower, and stepped in, gently guiding her inside with him. He moved her under the spray. She tilted her head back to wet her hair.

He pulled her from the spray and turned her around. His hands delved into her hair. The shampoo in his hand added an aromatic sensory experience to their shower. Their first together. Her first with another human. A romantic shower, that is. In the Army, they all showered together, but it was nothing like this.

His firm fingers massaged her scalp. He smoothed the shampoo down the long strands of her hair, slid his hands over her ass then slipped around and cupped her breasts. His lips kissed the shell of her ear and he whispered. "You're the most beautiful woman I've ever laid eyes on."

She closed her eyes enjoying all the sensations. "You're the sexiest man I've ever laid eyes on."

He chuckled next to her ear and her nipples pebbled.

He pulled her back into his body, his hands then slid down her tummy to her clit. She gasped as he began making small circles around it. His finger slid into her channel, then came back out and circled her clit. He repeated that motion over and over until her orgasm sped to completion. She gasped and cried his name as his fingers lightened on her clit.

Once she'd relaxed, he picked up her hands in his and pressed them to the wall of the shower. He bent his knees and slowly entered her from behind. As he filled her, the feeling was so incredible she wanted to remember it forever. So many sensations were happening at once right now that her knees shook.

He pulled out and entered her again and again, all the while whispering near her ear how much he loved her. How beautiful she was. How sexy she was. And finally, he pushed himself in and released his seed into her body. She rested her head against the warm shower wall, Marco's lips near her ear, his body holding her tightly. She never wanted to be with anyone else ever.

41

Marco finished his phone call with Wes Charles, who owned the cabin. He looked around the room as he sat at the desk, half watching the computer screens in front of him. He nodded his head slowly, knowing he was sure of his next move.

Theresa exited the bedroom and moved toward him, a sexy smile on her face. She seemed more relaxed these days. Her smile was back. Her personality was back. "I'm going to miss this place."

He grinned. "I know. It's become a Shangri-la."

"Yeah." She cocked her head to the side. "What are you doing?"

He shrugged. "I was taking a close look at the security system and how Wes has it set up. The entire place is set up perfectly."

Theresa neared the desk and glanced around. She stepped close to him and stared at the security camera outputs; each monitor was divided into four camera feeds, which showed the road coming in, the backyard, the front yard, the side yards, and three empty squares. "What are those empty screens for?"

"There are three cameras inside. One up there..." He pointed to the corner of the room above the front door. "One in the kitchen. And one downstairs pointing toward the safe room door."

"Oh. So we haven't been on camera the whole time have we?"

He chuckled. "If something had happened, Wes would have been able to turn them on and see who entered the house and where they are. But as a general rule, they aren't turned on."

"Okay."

He turned in his chair and faced her. "Do you like this place?"

She cocked her head to the side. "I do. It's very nice."

"I like it too."

He pulled her on his lap and wrapped his arms around her waist. "I asked Wes if we could stay here a while longer. He agreed. Rather than going back to my place, we can stay here and figure out our next steps."

"Oh, that's wonderful."

"We don't know what the cartel is doing right now. And it'll give you time to make plans for what you want to do moving forward. Do you have any ideas?"

He watched her swallow as she stared across the room. "I've been thinking about it a lot, of course. But I don't have definitive plans. For instance..." She turned to look into his eyes. "Are we..." She took a deep breath. "Good?"

He grinned. "I think we are. Do you?"

"I do. I mean we haven't had a normal courtship as it were. We've had more longing from afar than many folks. But being here, we've gotten to know each other a bit better and I'm hoping for more of that while we're here. What do you want?"

Marco agreed. "I want that too."

He looked into her eyes. "I mean, what do you want to do from here? As far as work. As far as living arrangements. All of it."

She took a deep breath and let it out slowly. She stared at the computer screens as she spoke. "I've been thinking about that. I wondered if I should buy a condo where you are. It's safe there. At least safer than I've been previously. I could likely have more security added to my place. I have savings. I think if I knuckle down and write that book I can get it published and start earning money on it before my money runs out. And I could always get freelance writing jobs for newspapers where I can work remotely. That will generate money." She looked into his eyes. "I don't think I can work at the restaurant anymore. I'd feel terribly exposed, and I don't want to bring anything bad to Jace and Margo. They've been so good to me."

He reached up and tucked her hair behind her ear. "That all sounds good. I was thinking of something a bit different though."

She swallowed and he felt her stiffen up. "It's not bad, babe."

"Okay."

"I was thinking of renting this place from Wes for a year. You can write from here. When I go to work, you'll have security. It'll give the authorities time to investigate the Celtics. And from there they can figure out if you'll be safe moving forward. I also thought we'd contact an attorney and have him or her reach out to the Celtics and negotiate a plan. You give up some of the information you have set aside for their promise to leave you alone."

"Marco, are you sure? That's uprooting your life."

His arms tightened around her waist. "Theresa, in the best way possible you have uprooted my life. I'm not sorry. I'm happier with you than I've ever been. I want to explore that more. I want to give us time to really get to know each other and we'll only do that by living normal lives. At least as normal as we can be given the circumstances with the Celtics."

"That's what I mean. Your life won't be normal with me in it."

"My life won't be happy without you in it. And who says normal is the only way to live life? Remember I used to be a SEAL. I'm likely not all that normal anyway."

She laughed. "Oh my God."

"What do you think about staying here? Write your book or books. You'll be safe when I go to work. We'll learn to live with each other and see if we like it."

They stared into each other's eyes for a long time. Her eyes glistened and she sniffed lightly. "If you're sure, I'd love to live here with you. As a regular couple."

He kissed her lips. "I do the cooking, you clean and do laundry."

"I can live with that."

She leaned in and kissed his lips softly. Her arm snaked around his shoulders. Her lips moved from his to his jaw, then she kissed her way to his ear. She whispered near his ear, "I love you, Marco."

He closed his eyes and inhaled her scent. His arms tightened around her again. "I love you, Theresa."

42

Theresa unpacked the last box Marco had brought to the cabin. He'd decided to rent out his condo and therefore had to pack up all his personal belongings. As for her things, she'd packed most of everything she had when she was initially leaving the house she'd rented out of town. She had that stuff here already and had unpacked it. This place was beginning to feel a bit more like home. Not her home, but their home. She looked at a photo album Marco had in a box. She'd set it on the coffee table to look at later. It was now later.

There were pictures of him in BUDS. Pictures with his fellow trainees. In uniform, and he was incredibly handsome. There truly was something about a man in uniform. Some pictures were of places that she wasn't aware of. When he got home, she'd ask him where these places were. She turned the page and saw him standing in front of a tank next to a woman. They both stood with their legs shoulder-width apart, arms behind their backs. It was how military training required a person to stand. It took a long time for that to go away. Sometimes, she still stood that way when waiting for instructions from Margo or her boss prior, Carolyn, at the newspaper. Carolyn used to laugh and tell her to relax.

There were several more pictures of this woman with Marco at various places. They never looked to be more than friends and she wondered how anyone could just be friends with him and not develop more feelings. She'd felt something different about him the instant she met him. Had her life been different, she'd have pursued things with him long ago. She hated thinking about the lost time.

She flipped through the photo album, half interested and half afraid of what she'd see. Though he said he'd never told anyone else that he loved them, and she took comfort in that. How did a person get to be forty-something and never fall in love? Some of her friends from the military fell in love every week with someone new.

She set the photo album on the coffee table and made her way to the kitchen. She emptied the dishwasher, wiped the counters down, and hung the damp rag on the faucet to dry. She squirted hand lotion onto her hands and rubbed it in as she sauntered to the dining room table where her laptop was waiting for her to be productive.

She'd thought all day about how she'd start her story. It had finally come together in her brain. As soon as she pulled up her notes her fingers began flying over the keyboard at warp speed. She let them flow, those words she wanted to get out. She'd self-edit later and clean it up. She wrote about Keely and how she so naively married someone she thought was a strong man and would be good to her forever. Her dream man, she'd said a couple of times during their conversations. How dismayed she'd been the first time he hit her. Then apologized and promised to never do it again. Then he forcibly had sex with her, apologized, and promised he'd never do it again. Then things happened more frequently but without the apology. And finally, she thought she'd leave him, only to be told he'd kill her if she ever tried that again. She then wrote about the day Keely contacted her and said she had information Theresa may like to have. Thus began Theresa's foray into the world of the Celtics.

A while later, the security camera pinged and it took her a moment to realize it was the camera. She rushed to the desk and her heart raced. She saw an SUV pulling into the driveway. Her heartbeat sped up at the sight of the vehicle, her breathing took on a shaky quality. It took a bit for her to realize it was Marco. She swallowed the knot in her throat and the door opened. Marco stepped in, the smile on his face disappeared when his eyes landed on hers.

"What's wrong, Baby?"

She closed the distance between them and his arms immediately wrapped around her body and held her tightly. "Hey, you're shaking. Are you alright?"

"Yes." She shook her head. "I'm sorry. I was absorbed in my story and heard the camera and saw a car, but it took me a bit to realize it was your car and fear ran through me."

He squeezed her tightly and whispered in her ear. "That's understandable. The stuff you're writing about is dark. I should have texted you that I was on my way. I'll do that from now on."

He released her and stepped back slightly. He bent down and kissed her lips, then he grinned. "But, your story! That is so exciting, Babe."

She smiled. "I started writing. I've been at it for..." She looked at her watch. "Oh my God. Three hours." She chuckled. "I've been writing for three hours!"

He held his hand up for her to high-five, which she did. "That's fantastic, let's celebrate."

She grinned. "Are you too tired?"

"No, I'm always wired when I get home. Let's have a drink and you can tell me all about it."

She smiled and took his hand. "How about this? You sit here..." She moved him to the sofa. "I'll get you a beer and I'd love for you to tell me about some of your pictures."

He smiled as he looked at the photo album on the coffee table. He picked it up and opened the cover. Theresa ran to the kitchen and got them each a beer and sat next to him. She handed him his beer and tapped her bottle to his. "Cheers."

"Cheers."

They flipped through the photo album, and he spoke about the places he'd been, the people he'd met, and that the woman in the pictures was a friend. Once in a while, she was a friend with benefits, but that was it. She felt that little pang of jealousy for a moment, then let it go. That was his past, she was his present, and hopefully, his future.

He yawned after an hour and a half and she did too. They both laughed, then stood and began shutting off the lights. They were a normal couple, and it felt pretty freaking great.

As she snuggled into Marco's arms Theresa's heart felt full. Setting aside her writing this past year had been from necessity. Getting back to it now, only in a different way felt so good.

She closed her eyes as Marco's deep even breathing lulled her to sleep.

A loud alarm broke into her restful sleep. Sitting up in bed, dazed and trying to figure out what was going on took some time. But not for Marco. She turned to see him alert and dressed in his sweatpants.

He pulled his phone from the charger and read the screen. He huffed out a breath and ran from the room. That panicked her more than the abrupt alarm. She scooted to the edge of the bed, pulled on her sweats and a T-shirt, and went out to find Marco sitting at the desk, watching the computer. His brows were furrowed, the alarms still going off.

"What is it?" she yelled.

"I don't know. I'm trying to figure it out."

She checked her phone, there wasn't an amber alert or silver alert on her screen. The alarms came from the house. They weren't smoke alarms.

Marco's phone rang and he answered it immediately. "Karason."

Theresa's throat clogged with worry. Her breathing came in short bursts and her brain finally caught up to what was happening. The shrieking of the alarms began pounding in her head. She hadn't had a PTSD attack in a long time. But she felt her body shake as if one was about to happen.

She scrambled to the bedroom to put her shoes on. If they had to leave, she needed shoes. Without a second thought, she grabbed her laptop and shoved it in its case, then slipped her arms into her backpack. She hurried to Marco, who was now typing something into the computer.

The alarms stopped and silence fell around them. He sat still, watching the computer screen, his fingers shook, and she noticed his body locked tight. She swallowed the lump in her throat and called out to him. "Marco."

He sat still as a statue.

"Marco. Baby, it's me, Theresa. Honey, can you talk to me?"

She approached him slowly, not sure if she should get too close in case he thought she was an enemy. She blew out a breath and moved to stand next to him. Slowly she knelt down to her knees so she wouldn't look imposing in his state, and she laid her hand on his thigh. She held herself steady, as she tried to get her own breathing under control. She felt sweat trickle down her back and temple.

Taking a deep breath once more, she softly said, "Marco. Baby, please come back to me." She squeezed his thigh gently and sobbed when his hand rested on top of hers.

She opened her eyes to see his beautiful brown eyes watching her. He turned in his chair and took a deep breath. Then he reached under her arms and pulled her up onto his lap.

Her backpack was a burden, and she slipped it off her arms and wrapped them around Marco's shoulders and her head rested next to his.

Marco's hands smoothed up and down her back and he finally spoke to her. "I'm sorry, Baby. Please forgive me."

"There's nothing to forgive." She spoke into his neck. "You didn't hurt me. I was scared but not hurt."

His arms tightened around her body. "I'd never hurt you."

"I wasn't sure if you'd think I was the enemy."

Tears spilled from her eyes and fell on Marco's shoulder and neck. She heard him sniff and felt his body shudder and she tightened her grip on his shoulders. They sat still together, holding on to each other as if their lives depended on the other. And in that moment, she felt as though hers did depend on Marco. She felt a closeness she'd never had in her life for another person. Something not even making love to him made her feel. They each shared something terrible. The ravages of war had raged through them both in different ways, but the aftereffects still haunted them.

Marco woke and immediately felt for Theresa. She lay next to him, her back to him, and she was curled up in such a way it looked as though she were cold or scared.

He rolled over and wrapped his arms around her, pressing his body to her back. She yawned and relaxed, her fingers wove themselves into his. She kissed his fingers and he allowed them a moment to just be.

Finally, he lifted up on his elbow and laid his head in his hand, then pulled Theresa's shoulder so she was on her back.

"Hey, are you alright?"

"Yeah."

"You were lying almost in the fetal position."

Her eyes looked up into his and a small frown appeared on her beautiful face. "Sometimes after I've had an attack, I do that in my sleep. My therapist said it's self-soothing. My dreams after an attack are fractured and usually dark. I curl up to protect myself."

His fingers moved a lock of hair that stuck to her cheek.

Then he caressed her face with the back of his fingers. "We both had a rough night."

"Why did that alarm go off?"

"We aren't sure. Wes is looking into it. Today I'm going to do a thorough check of things with him. He'll be out here at eight this morning. Neither of us could see anything on the cameras last night. Today we'll walk around the outside and see if anything looks out of place. We'll check all the cameras and make sure everything is good."

Her eyes stared into his. "Are you okay after last night?"

He frowned slightly then took a deep breath. "Yes. Normally after an attack, I feel exhausted. It uses up all my energy. I couldn't see anything wrong last night on the cameras, Wes confirmed the same and that's when I had my attack. It's almost autopilot for me. We were safe, no present danger, then my body has an attack, then I'm better."

Her hand reached up and smoothed his cheek, then slid around and cupped the nape of his neck, pulling him down to her lips. He kissed her softly. He loved the way her lips felt against his. It was a rush, feeling her soft lips touch his.

He lifted his head. "That was nice."

She smiled. "Yes, it was."

"How often do you have your PTSD attacks?"

She took a deep breath. Not too often anymore. It's almost as if I forbade my body from having one. I was on the run and needed to always keep my wits about me or I'd be killed. So, this is the first one I've had in about a year."

"I'm not sure how I feel about that."

She rolled over to face him. She rested her head in her hand, mimicking his pose, and stared into his eyes for a long time. "I think you should feel good. I mean, in a way. It meant I felt safe enough with you to have an attack. Somehow, I knew we were okay. I felt like you were handling it.

That might be wrong of me because if you needed me, I'd one thousand percent be here for you."

He swallowed. "I get it."

She smiled. "How often do you get attacks?"

"Since I met you, that's my first. The other night, I was surprised one didn't come on. Last night, I thought because of the way we were woken up, so abruptly and during a deep sleep, it messed with my head."

"Yeah. I think so too."

He kissed her again. "So, what we need to do is go to counseling. Mason does some counseling and between he and Jace, Quinn, Sid, and the VFW, we can find a counselor that will help us. Together. As a couple. To know how to help each other when this happens. And, who knows, maybe in the future we can help other couples."

She smiled. "Aww, I love that idea."

He kissed her again. "Regrettably, we have to get going. Let's eat and get dressed before Wes gets here."

Theresa stretched and he watched her body as she did. She was fit like a feline. Her skin so smooth his fingers itched to touch her sometimes. She rolled to her side and sat up. His body had other ideas, but he knew they didn't have time. Maybe before he left for work this afternoon, he'd make love to her again. The promise of things to come would make his morning a happy one.

He dressed and sauntered out to the kitchen to be handed a fresh cup of coffee and receive a kiss. He was beginning to love mornings.

After breakfast, Theresa jumped in the shower, and he sadly sat at the desk looking at the footage from the cameras last night to make sure they didn't miss anything. He didn't see anything out there that looked suspicious. A couple of squirrels playing. A rabbit hopped by nibbling on vegetation as it did. Animals could be identified by the cameras and shouldn't set off the alarm.

A deer ran through the backyard and that's when the cameras went off. He stopped the footage and watched frame by frame to see if anything or anyone set it off. He couldn't see a thing. He froze the footage in that spot to discuss it with Wes.

The cameras chimed and he saw Wes driving up the driveway. He moved to the front door and opened it, waving to Wes as he got out of his truck.

"Good morning."

Wes chuckled. "I'm glad you have a smile on your face and you think it's a good morning. I worried you'd be upset after the shenanigans from last night."

"Not upset. But eager to see what happened so we can rectify it."

Wes climbed the two steps to the porch and shook his hand. "Glad to hear it."

Marco stepped back and let Wes enter the cabin. "I would like to show you something I found on the cameras this morning. Maybe we can start our search out back in this section."

He moved to the monitors on the desk and backed the camera up one minute. Then he played the footage for Wes to watch with him. When the alarms went off as the deer ran by, Wes moved in closer to take a look. Marco stood, "Take a seat."

Wes sat down and replayed that footage several times. "Yep. Let's start our search out back."

They stood and began walking to the back door when Theresa stepped out of the bedroom. "Good morning, Wes."

"Morning, Theresa. You're pretty as a picture for sure."

He kept moving and Marco followed. But he stopped in

front of Theresa and grinned. "You are you know." He kissed her and caught up with Wes.

Wes stepped slowly and surely through the grass in the backyard, carefully watching the ground. Marco did the same, looking for anything that seemed out of place. They were careful to stay about an arm's length apart so they didn't overlap. As soon as Marco reached the edge of the camera's view his stomach twisted.

"Wes!"

Wes rushed over to him and whistled when he neared. "I'll be damned."

He knelt down to touch the deer lying on the ground. "He's dead."

Marco helped Wes roll the deer over, looking for a gunshot or anything that caused its death. Marco felt near the deer's neck and found a lump and a fresh wound. "What's this all about?"

Wes looked closer and pulled a knife from his ankle sheath. He cut around the wound and pulled out a small device. He held it up and heard a buzzing sound coming from it.

"This is what set off the alarms."

Marco stood and followed the path the deer had taken on the camera and came to a small area where the foliage had been flattened. A few drops of blood were visible on the leaves and a small wrapper lay under some brush. He picked up the wrapper. Omnicam. That was all he could read.

He took a deep breath and looked at Wes. The older man nodded. "I think we're thinking the same thing."

They both moved toward the cabin, locking the doors after entering. Marco rinsed the device off in the sink so they could read any markings on it. Wes washed his hands in the bathroom and was already at the computer looking up Omnicam.

Marco glanced at Theresa, typing away on her computer. Her eyes met his and she stopped. She joined him at the desk with Wes and they all stared in disbelief at the article that populated the computer screen.

Omnicam is a tracking device used mainly for spying. But it had the ability to disable security systems.

Wes looked up at him. "Is there a serial number on it?"

Marco turned the device over in his hand and found some numbers. He read them off and Wes wrote them down. "I have contacts who can trace this. Do you?"

Marco nodded. "I do. I'll call them now."

Wes nodded. "I'll call you when I find something out."

The older man left, and Marco picked up his phone and called Mitch.

"Yeah."

"I need to track where an Omnicam came from. Can you do that?"

"Yeah. Where did you find it?"

"Inserted in the hide of a deer that is now lying dead in the backyard."

"No shit?"

"Yeah. No shit. It set off our alarms last night."

"Okay. Do you have a serial number, and can you take a picture of it and send it to me?"

"Yes." He read off the serial number, took the picture, and sent it.

Theresa stood near the desk listening to all that had transpired. He took a deep breath and nodded at her.

She crossed her arms in front of her and asked. "Is it the Celtics?"

"I think so. But we don't know for sure."

"They want me to know, they know where I am, and they can get to me if they want."

He stood and pulled her into his arms. "Maybe."

She stepped back. "I'm not letting those fuckers win."

She marched to her computer.

"Baby, what are you going to do?"

"I'm releasing a bit more information about them. I'm going to let them know if they continue, so will I."

His brows rose and he grinned. "You're plucky."

"I'm pissed."

He shrugged. "I say plucky, you say pissed. Same thing."

She nodded. "Okay."

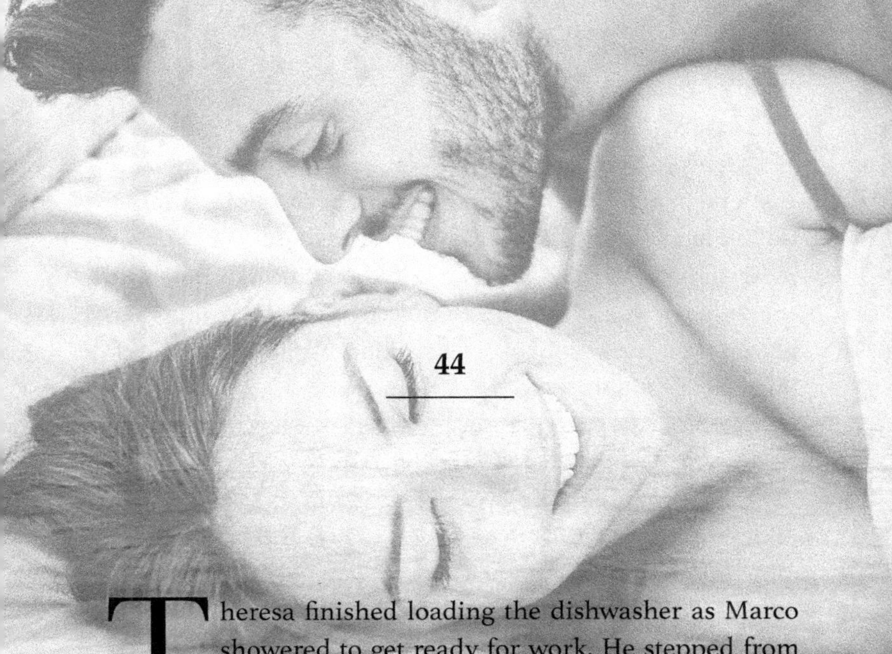

44

Theresa finished loading the dishwasher as Marco showered to get ready for work. He stepped from the bedroom smelling heavenly. She was jealous he was leaving to go to work looking and smelling like he did. He was too sexy for words.

He kissed her lips and held her shoulders as he looked into her eyes. "What's the plan?"

"If anything happens here, I'm to dial 9-1-1, and call you while I'm running downstairs to hide in the safe room."

"Yes."

The security system alerted them someone was approaching, and Marco hurried to the cameras. "It's Mitch."

Theresa opened the door to let Mitch in. "Hey there. I'm glad Marco is still here."

Mitch rushed to the desk where Marco sat, and she shrugged and locked the door.

As she made her way to the men, Mitch started talking. "I traced it to Attorney Perry Henry."

Marco's brows rose. "The new attorney in town?"

"Yes."

"How did you trace it?"

"Via an algorithm. From the moment the serial number was added to it until now, it's been tracked. But Perry Henry received it yesterday. I called Blossom Springs police to share this news with them and they are at Henry's office and home right now looking for evidence the bastard was hunting last night."

Theresa stepped closer. "What if they can't find anything?"

"We'll cross that bridge when we get to it. But also, your phone started getting texts again today. Did you release more information about the Celtics?"

"Yes. In response to this..." She pointed to the device. "If they wanted to let me know they could get to me, I wanted to let them know every time they try, more information will come out."

Mitch pulled her phone from his pocket. "I hope this doesn't backfire." He texted them in response as she watched.

> "I guess time will tell. I'm sick of being scared of them. And I have a lot of dirt left to share."

Mitch texted again and sent it off.

His phone rang. Looking at the readout, he grinned. "Blossom Springs PD."

"DeMario."

He listened then replied. "Hang on, let me put you on speaker."

He tapped his screen and spoke once more. "I have Theresa Miklovic and Marco Karason here with me. Please repeat and continue."

"Hello. This is Officer Isak Voss. I called to inform you that we have evidence that Perry Henry did indeed go hunting last night. He's in custody now. We've found a knife with blood on it and deer hair stuck to the hilt. If you can get me the proof that Mr. Henry received the tracking device, we should be able to charge him with hunting out of season. Which isn't much, but it's enough to keep him for a bit. We can also then charge him with stalking if we can prove he had the tracking device. We'll send someone out to pick up the deer so we can DNA test it for a match to that on the knife. And if you have anything linking Perry Henry to the Celtics we just might be able to make this man sing."

Theresa nodded. "I have the codes that have his zip code and some transactions related to him in connection to money laundering."

"I'd like to see that information Ms. Miklovic."

"I'll gather it together and get it to you."

"Thank you. Mr. DeMario please bring in your information as well."

"I'll be down there soon."

Mitch hung up and pocketed his phone.

Theresa moved to her computer. "I'm pulling up the information I have based on his zip code."

Marco nodded and moved to sit next to her at the table. "Also pull up anything you have that relates to PCK Meatpacking and any other business here in Blossom Springs. Let's see if we can pull up the businesses in this area and give it all to the police. If police start questioning them over and over, they'll likely lay low and perhaps ask the Celtics to leave you alone so they aren't all exposed."

"Okay." Excitement ran through her. Finally, finally it was all starting to be worth it. She searched in her codes and printed the documents pertaining to each zip code in

Blossom Springs. She then showed Marco and Mitch the money associated with each business. There were four in all. The attorney, PCK Meatpacking, a brokerage firm, and a business not named as a business but under the name of Bradford Bennett LLC. She showed them the money trail. "I don't have a way to track the money penny for penny. But a good question is, how does a business that isn't a business at all, make any money to launder?"

Marco grinned. "Damn, you're smart."

She felt her cheeks heat. "Thanks." She moved a paper. "Also, it doesn't make sense that an attorney with no business and a brokerage firm that I bet can't show you the names of five clients, have large amounts of money deposited on a regular basis into various banks."

Mitch nodded. "All good points. I think I can help in one aspect. The same algorithm I used to track this device, can possibly track money through the accounts associated with these codes."

"Oh, how can we set that up?"

Mitch pulled up his phone and tapped a couple of times. "Gabby, I want to track a few numbers. Theresa is going to send them to you. Please set them up in the algorithm and record the paths."

He hung up and looked at her. "Okay. Send Gabby the numbers, and the amounts associated as well as the names. We can get to the banks through the algorithm and it will trace everything that comes in and goes out. Typically, these accounts deposit and withdraw on the same day. Transactions that are deposited and withdrawn within 24 hours aren't traced. But the algorithm does trace them. All it knows is to follow the trail. Many times, banks can't do that for privacy reasons, and to add these algorithms to their systems is too expensive."

Theresa compiled the lists she had, complete with business names and owner's names if she had them. She eagerly sent it off to Gabby, excited that she was making progress.

45

Marco pulled his phone from his pocket and tapped Theresa's photo.

She answered, "Hello, sexy chef."

He chuckled. "Hello, sexy writer."

She laughed, which made his heart happy. "I'm on my way home."

"Sounds good. Can't wait to see you."

"Same here, Baby."

Ending the call, he drove to the cabin, soft music playing from his stereo system and his thoughts on the beautiful woman he now shared his life with. Life sure had a way of throwing curve balls at a person.

As he turned off Lake Road onto Middle Inlet, his phone rang. Tapping the button on his steering wheel, he answered, "Karason."

"It's Mitch. I received a text in response to my text, which is really Theresa's text to the Celtics this morning. They want proof she has more information to release."

"To what end? They hunt her relentlessly to get it then kill her?"

"I don't know. I'm trying to get my head around how we prove she has more information and how to keep her safe."

Marco's jaw tightened. Those fuckers were not going to harm her. They didn't care about physical threats. They all believed they'd die for this cause eventually anyway. At least most of them did. What they cared about was the power. And the money.

He cleared his throat. "In your opinion, what is their power?"

"Power as in following through on the threats they've made?"

Marco shook his head. "No, as in power over people, or businesses. What is the power they covet so much?"

Mitch was silent for a moment and Marco turned onto Nowhere Road. Finally, Mitch responded, "They like telling people what to do and them doing it. Total power over people."

Marco nodded slowly. "And the money is second?"

"It depends on the person. For some, having a ton of money is more valuable than anything else."

"I suppose." He thought about this for some time. "Don't respond yet. I'm almost home and I'll talk with Theresa and see what she has to say about it all."

"Roger that."

He turned down Hidden Oasis Rd and saw the sleepy little cabin's silhouette against the moon's rays. A slight fog hovered over the water in the lake. It looked peaceful and eerie at the same time.

Turning the key in the lock he stepped into the living room and nearly ran into Theresa.

"Whoa, where are you going?"

"I had hoped to open the door for you."

"Ah." He chuckled and kissed her lips. "Sorry to be so fast."

She laughed. "Right."

She handed him a beer with the perfect smile on her face. "Thank you."

She tapped her bottle to his and they sauntered to the sofa hand in hand. What did he like better, morning or coming home? It was getting hard to decide which was better. Maybe no decision was best. He liked them both equally.

He sat and she twisted to sit facing him, her legs tucked under her. He took a breath, "What do you think the Celtic's power is?"

"They like control. I believe it's like a chess game with him, the leader. He tells people to do his bidding, and he enjoys watching them jump through hoops to do it. After a while though, it's less about them seeking his attention or permission and more about the satisfaction of people knowing he can do what he wants and when."

"He being..."

"John Benson."

Marco's brows shot up. "As in Vice President John Benson?"

"Yes. I told you the Celtics had powerful connections."

"Okay. So they have the White House in their control and to what end?"

"Money."

"Just money?"

Theresa shrugged. "Keely said it was a slow progression just like Shooter's abuse. They slowly infiltrated everything they could infiltrate. The money was initially the end goal. They infiltrated Congress and controlled spending bills. They'd steer the spending to companies they owned and operated or businesses they controlled. The money began rolling in. Do you like war? They'll vote to help another country in a war, use their equipment or uniforms or anything associated with it, and make money. If the voters grew weary of the wars and the money being funneled to it, they'd switch to pharmaceuticals. Then switch to pouring money into education. All this brings them money via the companies they control. They get kickbacks and buy-offs from these businesses to help them make money. It's the perfect scam. All are controlled by the very people who tell you they're on your side while stealing your money via heavy taxes and lining their pockets with it. We vote for these pigs."

Marco's jaw tightened. "I know many politicians are criminals. It's why I almost stopped voting years ago. Now I don't vote until I have researched all candidates and issues. But to see that someone has proof of all of this is mind-boggling."

"Yes, and they threaten and kill people who can expose them."

Marco nodded. "Okay. So, we need to protect you. All you have right now is their minimal compliance because if it goes this high up, the stakes are high. But since it does go that high up, I think we need to completely expose all the wrongdoing."

Theresa's brows furrowed. "How do I stay safe?"

"I have a former SEAL acquaintance who can get us in to see the Speaker of the House."

She sat up straighter. "How do you know you can trust him?"

"I'll vet him first. I believe I can with a bit of tweaking. Mitch's algorithm can be modified to trace his activities over the past few years."

She shook her head. "It's really like Big Brother is watching all the time, isn't it?"

"Sadly, with cell phones, we can be tracked all the time. Watches, eyeglasses, our vehicles. Anything with a computer is an electronic trail."

"Wow." She cocked her head. "Then why did it take them so long to find me?"

He grinned. "This is simply a guess. But if they have algorithms similar to this to track people, they'd know those algorithms can be tracked too. So, an enemy could find everyone and everything they were tracking and why. It could wipe out a political campaign. It could bring down giants."

Theresa jumped up. "Let's do that. Find out if Mitch's algorithm can be modified to track Shooter John Benson. I have his phone number. I have his email address, and I have his home computer IP address. We need to track that. It will lead to John Benson and all the other scumbags associated with their dirty dealings."

She ran to her computer and brought it back to the sofa, he dialed Mitch.

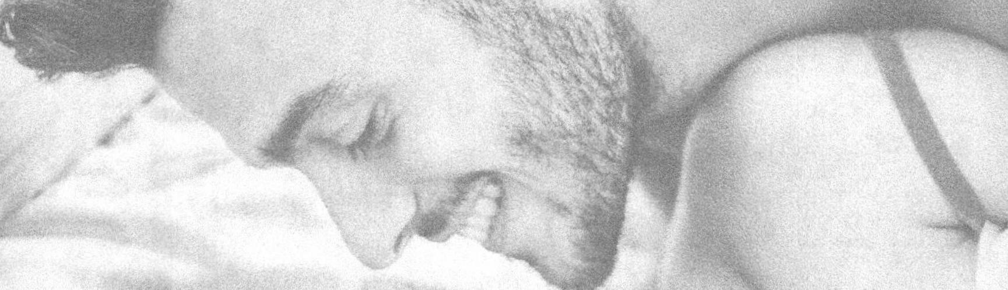

46

Theresa sat quietly as Mitch and Gabby worked on the algorithm. She and Marco had driven to Mitch's office and Gabby eagerly began coding the new algorithm to follow Shooter's trail. To say her stomach was rolling, was to compare it to a hellish roller coaster being kinda cool.

She sipped the water Mitch had given her. Marco sat with his arm around the back of her chair.

Mitch glanced at Marco. "Is your contact on board?"

"Yep. He's simply waiting for me to call with the results."

Mitch nodded and continued typing something on his computer.

Gabby clapped her hands together. "I've got it. It's working."

She turned her monitor so they all could see it. The dark screen populated with text. It rolled quickly as the information was compiled and filled the screen.

The text filled the page so quickly it was difficult to read anything. Theresa finally asked, "How long will it take to decipher what all this says?"

Gabby grinned at her. She had strawberry blonde hair and cute freckles dusted over her nose. "Once we reach current days, I'll have it decipher into readable text. I can ask it to sort it by date. By location. By travel times or when he's been in his car or away from his car or anything in-between."

"That's amazing. Can you also pull out data on phone calls?"

"Yes. Calls he made and calls he received."

Theresa pulled her laptop from her backpack and opened it on the edge of Mitch's desk. "Here are the phone numbers of Shooter's wife, Keely, and my editor, Carolyn Sutton. Can you also have it pull out times he was near these two phones, as well as calls made to and from?" She wrote the numbers on a piece of paper and handed them to Gabby.

"I sure can."

Gabby took the information Theresa gave her, and Marco leaned forward. "Are you hoping to prove Shooter was involved in Carolyn's murder?"

"Yes. And Keely's. If his phone is in close proximity and is equal to the time of death, we can also have authorities arrest him for Keely's murder. As to Carolyn, I don't know if he had lackeys do that work or if he did it himself, but I'd like to prove one way or the other his involvement or lack thereof."

Marco's fingers squeezed her shoulder and he nodded. "Super smart."

She blushed slightly. Praise from him always made her blush. Praise from a man such as Marco was high praise indeed.

She took a deep breath; her body was exhausted. Her

brain was tired too. Glancing at Marco, she could see dark circles forming under his eyes. They needed to sleep.

"Mitch. Is it possible for Marco and I to go home and rest for a few hours?"

Mitch nodded. "Of course. When you wake up, we should have this information deciphered in several different ways and be able to decide how we want to proceed from there."

"Thank you."

Marco leaned forward and shook Mitch's hand. Theresa waved at Gabby, who grinned but kept typing. She seemed to be in her element doing this, despite the late hour. Or was that early hour? She glanced at her watch; it was now two-thirty in the morning. It was becoming a bad habit to be up at this hour. She needed her beauty sleep. If not for beauty, she sure needed it, so she didn't get crabby.

Marco took her hand as they left Mitch's office. He opened her door and waited for her to get in before making his way around the front of the vehicle and getting in on his side. She buckled her seatbelt. As soon as Marco started the vehicle, she rested her head on the back of the seat and closed her eyes. She'd been working on this case for more than two years. She'd been on the run for the past year and it felt like it was starting to catch up with her.

"Hey there, sleeping beauty. We're home."

She opened her eyes to see Marco looking down at her from the open car door. "Oh, I'm so sorry. I fell asleep so fast."

He held his hand out to her, and she gratefully accepted his assistance to pull her from the vehicle. He chuckled. "You snored."

"I don't snore!"

He laughed. "You do."

He unlocked the door and they stepped inside. Relief swept over her. Marco reset the security system and took her hand once more. She dutifully followed him to the bedroom. She sat on the edge of the bed and kicked her shoes off. Without another thought, she lay back and fell asleep into a deep sleep.

She felt hot. She pushed at the covers to get some relief. A strong firm arm wrapped around her waist and a sturdy chest pressed firmly to her back helped her to relax. She managed to kick her legs from under the covers, still in her sweatpants and T-shirt from last night.

"I don't like you sleeping with clothes on." His husky voice murmured in her ear.

She grinned. "Sorry. I didn't..." Her brows furrowed. "How did I get under the covers?"

"I did that. You wouldn't wake up."

"You didn't try to wake me up."

"I did too."

"No, you didn't. I would have woken up."

"Babe, you didn't. I picked you up, pulled the covers back, laid you on the bed, and covered you. You didn't wake up."

She took a deep breath. "That's not good."

"What's not good is the hours we've been keeping. What's also not good is that two nights in a row I didn't get to make love to you."

She rolled over to face him. Her arm wrapped around his shoulder, her lips pressed to his. "Yeah, that's not good."

He chuckled. His lips pressed to hers, softly, at first. His tongue slipped between her lips and his cock grew rigid against her.

She wiggled her sweatpants down her legs and pulled her feet free while his fingers teased her clit and slipped into her entrance. Once free from her pants, she opened her legs, and he lay between them. She lifted her legs and locked her feet behind his back. He very easily slid inside of her body with a soft groan.

They moved together, each seeking the release from the other. Her orgasm came first, rushing up on her so quickly she felt cheated. His took a bit more, but every bit of it felt wonderful.

He pushed into her so easily, so perfectly as if they'd always known each other.

She whispered, "You feel so good, Marco."

He huffed out a breath near her ear. "You're like heaven."

He pushed into her a couple more times and froze as his long deep groan tickled her ear. His body shuddered once and he relaxed, careful not to crush her.

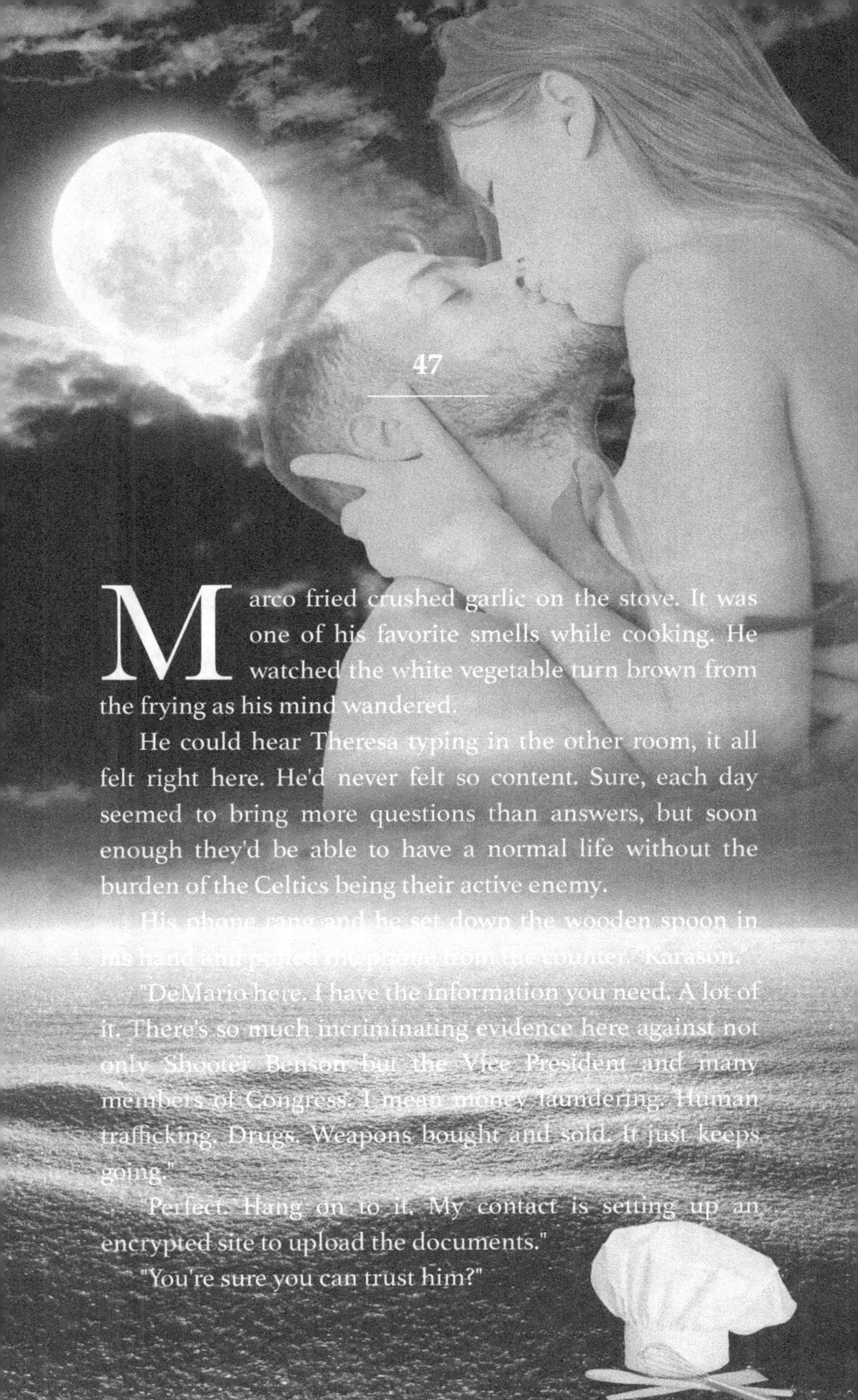

47

M arco fried crushed garlic on the stove. It was one of his favorite smells while cooking. He watched the white vegetable turn brown from the frying as his mind wandered.

He could hear Theresa typing in the other room, it all felt right here. He'd never felt so content. Sure, each day seemed to bring more questions than answers, but soon enough they'd be able to have a normal life without the burden of the Celtics being their active enemy.

His phone rang and he set down the wooden spoon in his hand and pulled the phone from the counter. "Karason."

"DeMario here. I have the information you need. A lot of it. There's so much incriminating evidence here against not only Shooter Benson but the Vice President and many members of Congress. I mean money laundering. Human trafficking. Drugs. Weapons bought and sold. It just keeps going."

"Perfect. Hang on to it. My contact is setting up an encrypted site to upload the documents."

"You're sure you can trust him?"

Marco nodded as his eyes watched Theresa. "I have two contacts, to be honest, and I have one checking on the other. I do believe I can trust him. He's always been aboveboard and honest to a fault. I know things change, but just in case, I have another friend doing a bit of research for me. I won't hand anything over until I have some assurances."

"I should have known you'd have this covered, but I needed to ask, just in case."

Marco stared at Theresa as she worked. As if she felt him watching her, she looked up at him and smiled. His heart skipped a beat. She did that to him. He hoped he did that to her.

"I'll let you know when I hear from my contact. Hang on tightly to your information."

"Will do."

Marco pulled his phone away, then stopped himself. "Hey, Mitch?"

"Yeah."

He turned to the stove to stir the garlic. But also, he didn't want Theresa to hear. "Was Shooter near Keely when she died?"

"Yeah. Carolyn too."

Marco sucked in a deep breath. He nodded slowly. "Thank you."

The call ended and Marco finished their meal. Steak, with garlic and mushrooms crusted over the top. He popped the steaks into the oven to sear the flavors together. As that baked for a moment, he pulled two plates from the cupboard and gathered his thoughts about how to tell Theresa she was right about that piece of shit Shooter.

"Did he kill Keely?"

He turned around to see Theresa standing at the counter

staring at him. He inhaled a deep breath and let it out slowly. "Yes."

"What about Carolyn?"

He swallowed a knot that formed in his throat. "Yes."

Theresa nodded. Her eyes glistened, she bit her bottom lip and sniffed. "I knew it. I could feel it. Now I know for sure, but I don't know how to feel about that. Not that I care two shits about his reputation, but part of me hoped that someone Keely once loved wouldn't be so cruel as to beat her to death."

He held his arms open and she quickly moved around the counter and filled his arms. He rested his cheek on the top of her head as his arms wrapped her in warmth. Her arms wrapped around his waist. He enjoyed the feeling of Theresa in his arms. He always enjoyed this feeling, but sometimes it just felt better than others. Maybe because he needed her here with him as much as she needed him right now.

He kissed the top of her head and rubbed his hands up and down her back. "I'm so sorry, sweetheart."

She lifted her face up to his. "It's not your fault. Being the bearer of bad news sucks too, doesn't it?"

"It does." He sighed. "Especially when you know the news is going to hurt someone you love."

Her arms squeezed him once more then she stepped back. "Now what?"

"I'm waiting for my contact to get back to me on when we can meet. He is also setting up an encrypted portal to upload the documents Gabby and Mitch have."

"Can we see it first?"

"Of course. I can ask Mitch to upload it."

She grinned slightly. "Let me set up an encrypted portal for him to upload them. I have this one covered."

He smiled and kissed her forehead. "You absolutely do."

She moved to her computer, and he pulled their dinner from the oven. He garnished the plates with asparagus he pulled from a pan on the stove.

Grabbing silverware from the drawer, he carried the sizzling plates, with the assistance of hot pads, to the dining room table and set them on placemats. She smiled as she glanced at their dinner. "Damn, once again, gonna have to work out."

He brought a bottle of wine from the wine rack and two glasses and sat next to her. "I know how to work this off."

She laughed. "Yes. I like your workouts."

She cut into her steak and took a bite. "Mmm." She swallowed. "Baby, you are a fantastic chef."

He poured them each a glass of wine, not even irritated she didn't wait for him to dig in. He smiled as he handed her a glass. "To us."

"To us."

He then dug into his steak and thoughts of what his future looked like swirled in his mind. She was his future. Dinners like this and maybe a kid or two running around the house. Mornings with her and a hot cup of coffee. Nights with her sizzling under him as he made love to her. That's what he saw when he thought of the future.

"Do you want kids?" he blurted out. Her eyes locked onto his and held.

"Do you?"

"I asked you first."

She chuckled. "Fair enough." She swallowed and took a sip of wine. "I'd love to have them. But, the way my life has been recently, I didn't think it would happen. You can't bring kids into the world if there are people trying to kill you."

"Right. Totally irresponsible."

She shook her head. "I'm being serious."

He lay his hand over hers. "I'm sorry. I understand how you've felt. How do you feel now?"

Her chest heaved as she took in a big breath. "I'd like to have one or two. But I'm thirty-two right now. My time might have passed."

He shrugged. "Maybe."

48

Theresa finished setting up the encrypted account and sent an invitation to Mitch and Gabby to upload documents. She sat staring at the screen as she saw documents begin to populate. Her stomach knotted up as the screen filled with folders, each titled with the data sorted within. Timelines. Locations. Keely. Carolyn. Money trails. And so many more.

She hovered her mouse over the Keely folder but didn't click. Did she need to see it? It wouldn't change anything. It was enough that she had the information, and Marco found a way for it to get into the hands of the authorities.

The same for Carolyn. She'd avenge their deaths and make all this public. There would come a day Shooter would be in jail, though it may not be for murder charges. He had high connections, and they would likely pardon him of any wrongdoing unless things moved too quickly to stop that from happening. At any rate, the two brave women who she sought justice for, would be brought to the forefront. Their killer would be in the public eye and her story about them would let the world know what brave strong women they were.

Maybe when it wasn't so fresh and she needed to add the details of their deaths to the stories, she'd open up the information and put the timelines together, so there was no mistake about who their murderer was.

She stood and stretched then glanced at her watch. Marco should be coming home soon. Then her day would be complete. Just as her thoughts ran to him, her phone rang.

His picture appeared on her screen and she smiled. "Hey, handsome."

His chuckle sent goosebumps skittering down her arms. "Hey, Baby. I'm on my way."

"Can't wait to see you."

"Five minutes."

The call ended and she went to the refrigerator to grab them each a beer. She pulled cheese from the dairy drawer, sliced some up, and arranged it on a plate. Pouring some crackers from the box next to the cheese, she carried it to the coffee table, then went back for the beers.

As she moved into the living room the security system chimed, and she stopped in the middle of the room looking toward the door, so he'd see her and the beer as soon as he walked in.

The lock turned in the door and his handsome face filled her vision. His smile said it all. "I love this."

She laughed. "I hoped you would."

He hurried to her and kissed her lips. She handed him his beer, and they tapped their bottles together and moved to the sofa.

"Wow, a snack too. Thank you. I'm a bit hungry tonight."

"Were you busy?"

"Yeah." He took a drink. "It isn't the same without you there."

"Aww. I feel a bit jealous when I see you going to work looking so handsome. I used to watch you all the time. Now someone else gets to do that."

He laughed. "No one is watching me. We have two new servers; both are men and the women out front are swooning over them. They both work out and have big muscles. Jace and I have been laughing about the reactions out front."

"Ohh, I'd like to go see their muscles."

His brows furrowed. He lifted his right arm and made a muscle. "This is your muscle."

She squeezed the firm muscle. "I like that muscle."

They chuckled and drank their beer.

Marco's phone rang and he looked at his watch before answering. "Hey there. How are you?"

She listened as she carried the empty cheese and cracker plate to the kitchen. When she returned, he hung up the call.

"My contact is all set with the encrypted folder. He's going to email you and would like you to begin populating it. As soon as it's all populated, he'll set up a conference call with the both of us to explain what he has and what it means."

She nodded. "I'll get it started right now; it'll take a while for everything to upload. In the morning it should be all set."

"Sounds good. I'm going to jump in the shower."

She opened her inbox and saw the email from Marco's contact. He hadn't shared the name with her and the email simply said, USDOD1. No name to decipher who it was. She was an investigative reporter, she could dig but chose not to.

He'd tell her when he needed to and she didn't want to break his trust. She loved having him in her life and didn't want to do anything to hurt what they had. Wasn't that the key to a long relationship?

She clicked on the link in the email and opened the folder using the password USDOD1 gave her in the email. Once opened, she began copying the files Mitch and Gabby sent her into this new folder. It was all in the works now. Soon Shooter Benson would be in jail. As soon as that happened, she'd celebrate Keely and Carolyn. Who knew how many others there were? Hopefully, that information would come out as investigations ensued. There just had to be justice for all the damage that pig had created.

The folders began populating and she stood and shut off the lights in the living room and sauntered to the bedroom to snuggle with her man. Life was damned good right now. Even though she was hiding in a cabin and afraid to go out. That would be something she'd work on another day.

She undressed as the water shut off in the bathroom and slipped into bed. She rested on her side, facing the bathroom door, her head in her hand, eager to see Marco come toward her.

He appeared in the doorway, naked as the day he was born, but in much better shape. She smiled as he stalked toward her. His muscles rippled as he moved. His lips curved into a beautiful smile. "My day is now complete."

"Mine too." He pulled the covers back and slipped between the sheets. His fresh scent filled the room. His arms pulled her to him, and she sighed. This really was the best way to end a day.

49

Marco pulled into the parking lot and put his vehicle in park. He turned to Theresa, "Are you ready?"

She took a deep breath. "Yeah."

"Good."

He hurried around the car and opened her door. As soon as she stepped out, he took her hand and together they walked into the counselor's office.

The receptionist greeted them. "Hello. How may I help you?"

He smiled. "Marco Karason and Theresa Miklovic here to see Devin Krill."

"Certainly. Please take a seat and he'll be with you shortly."

He still held Theresa's hand as he led her to the loveseat near the window. They sat together. He watched a dog playing outside and Theresa watched the television hanging in the corner of the waiting room.

"Oh my God," she gasped.

He looked at the television to see what was happening.

and the scroller at the bottom of the screen said, "Shooter John Benson accused of two murders and money laundering."

He pulled his phone from his pocket and checked the news stations he watched. The first article was the same as the headline. He tapped it to open the story and began reading. Theresa did the same on her phone.

His contact had set the wheels in motion after their conference call last week. The most damming evidence came first because it was difficult to refute the timelines from his telephone being next to Keely's telephone, at Keely's house, at the same time the coroner had estimated the time she died.

The article delved lightly into the charges and the picture to go with the article was of Shooter Benson in handcuffs being led from his home. The article ended with, "Vice President Benson could not be reached for comment."

Theresa turned to look at him, her mouth slightly open, her eyes rounded. "I didn't expect it to happen this fast."

"He knows the faster they move the less time they have to concoct lies and make up fake bullshit to refute the evidence. If they've arrested him, they're doing a thorough search of his home, office, and vehicle. They won't have time to destroy any of it."

She nodded her head slowly and the receptionist announced, "Devin is ready to see you."

Marco stood and took Theresa's hand once more and they followed the receptionist through a door and down a short hallway to Devin's office. Marco stood back and let Theresa in the office first. Devin was welcoming as they entered, shaking their hands enthusiastically with exhuberant greetings.

Devin motioned to a sofa that matched the one in the

waiting area and took a seat across from it as he and Theresa sat.

The meeting was productive, they spoke about their respective PTSD attacks, how they personally handled them, and what they'd need from the other for support when having an attack. The nice thing is they both understood the affliction.

On the way home, Marco stopped at the Sandbar. "I'd like to have a light lunch here if you don't mind."

She chuckled. "On your day off you want to go to work?"

"Yes, please. Are you scared?"

"No, not really."

"Okay. We don't have to linger, just order something for lunch and eat. We can leave right away if you feel exposed."

She grinned. "I'm not afraid to tell you when I need to leave."

He nodded and exited the vehicle. They entered the Sandbar together. The crowd was light, it was two in the afternoon, so lunch was over. One of the new servers, Gavin, greeted them at the door.

"Hey, Marco. Nice to see you."

"Hi, Gavin. This is Theresa."

"Nice to meet you, Theresa. Boy everyone here sure misses you."

Theresa smiled. "Thank you. It's nice to meet you."

Margo came from the office and hugged Theresa. "It's so good to see you."

Theresa hugged Margo in return. "It's good to see you too, Margo. How is everything going?"

"Not as smooth without you here, believe me. But we're managing."

Theresa smiled. "Aww, thank you."

Gavin pulled two menus from the rack on the side of the

receptionist stand and asked, "Would you like to eat outside or inside?"

He grinned. "Outside, please. Actually, upstairs."

"It's the best place to eat here."

Margo smiled as they followed Gavin upstairs. He held his hand at the small of Theresa's back as they ascended the stairs, his heart was full and he was so damned excited for this next chapter in their lives.

Gavin seated them at the middle table on the upper deck. It faced the water and the view was incredible. He laid the menus on the table and asked, "Can I get you something to drink?"

Marco looked at Theresa and grinned. "Order what you want."

"I'd like a glass of wine, please. A Moscato."

"Excellent. And for you, Marco?"

"I'll have a beer please."

Gavin nodded and walked away.

Theresa stared out at the water, her posture was relaxed and her smile was radiant. "All the time I worked here, I never got to enjoy a meal up here with this view."

"I know what you mean. It's something special up here. Jace had a vision and he's done well with it."

"Yeah."

Marco reached into his pocket and pulled a little package from inside. It was wrapped in pink tissue paper and he'd carried it for the past two days waiting for the right time.

"Theresa." She turned to look into his eyes. "I love you."

She smiled and chuckled. "I love you too."

He nodded and swallowed. "Will you marry me?"

Her eyes rounded and as she stared into his eyes, hers watered and a tear slid down her cheek. "Yes."

It was simple and perfect. His fingers shook as he opened the tissue paper to reveal a perfect one-carat round diamond on a gold band. Theresa sniffed as he held her left hand and slipped the ring on her finger. She stared at her hand adorned with the beautiful ring on it. He'd known from the beginning he'd put on her finger. It seemed to fit her, as she seldom wore jewelry. This one sparkled and didn't compete with anything else.

She stood and he did the same. They met in front of the table and wrapped their arms around each other. He kissed her lips and held her close. He could feel her body shaking. "I'm so happy, Marco."

"I am too, Baby."

He looked up to see Margo, Jace, and Gavin watching them. He grinned. "She said yes."

They clapped and Margo rushed forward to hug Theresa. After the congratulations were exchanged, they resumed their seats at the table and Theresa shook her head. "Why here?"

"It's where we met. It's where I watched you from afar wishing we were together. It's where you first agreed to let me help you and our lives together began."

She nodded and tears slipped down her cheeks. "You're amazing."

He grinned. He'd spend his life being amazing for her.

EPILOGUE

Theresa took a deep breath as Margo zipped up her wedding dress. Margo stood behind her and looked over her shoulder into the mirror. "You're beautiful, Theresa."

"Do I look fat? Marco feeds me far too well. I've been doing yoga, but he's an excellent chef."

Margo chuckled. "No, you don't look fat. You're incredibly beautiful."

Theresa smiled. "Thank you."

She took a deep breath and turned to Margo. "I never thought this would happen for me."

"He's a lucky man to have you, Theresa. Just as lucky as you are to have him."

"Thank you."

The door burst open and Effie Karason, Marco's sister and the youngest in the Karason clan popped into the room with the enthusiasm of a toddler with a new balloon.

"He's ready. Good Lord Almighty, we never thought the man would settle down. Our mamma and papa are smiling down from above on this day."

Effie stopped as her eyes landed on Theresa. "Oh my goodness, you're beautiful!"

Theresa and Margo both laughed. She'd met Effie earlier this week when Marco's family came into town, and she was a burst of energy.

Theresa held her hands out to Effie with a smile. "Thank you."

"Oh damn, Marco's gonna bust when he sees you."

Margo laughed and so did Theresa. "I'd prefer he didn't bust, but thank you very much."

Someone knocked on the door and Effie turned in a swirl of light blue as her dress flowed around her and opened the door.

"Hi, my name is Izzy Payton from Petal Pushers."

Effie stood back and held the door open as she announced. "Petal Pushers is here. I like that name. Why is it most of the businesses in town have names like The Book-keepers? The Insurance Agents? I swear there's no imagina-tion here."

Izzy entered the room with two white boxes stacked on top of each other and Margo rushed to help her. Izzy thanked Margo, then turned to Effie. "I didn't get to name my business because my father did when he started the business. But, it keeps people from having to guess as to what your business is, doesn't it?"

"I suppose." Effie seemed to shrug it off and moved to open the boxes of flowers. Izzy opened the second box and pulled out Theresa's bouquet. It was stunning. A water drop shape held white roses, blue daylilies, carnations, and blue ribbons. Effie's bouquet was a small cluster of white roses and blue daylilies with shorter blue ribbons. The men's boutonnieres were blue roses. Marco's was a white and blue rose. They'd purposely kept things simple and sleek, and she was happy. There wasn't a flurry of preparations after their engagement last month; they simply invited Marco's family because Theresa didn't have anyone left in her family. They also invited their friends here in Blossom Springs. Simple. Elegant. Private.

Izzy picked up the box of boutonnieres and stepped toward the door. "I'll go find the guys and get their boutonnieres pinned on. Where are they?"

Margo directed Izzy to the office downstairs. The women had taken over the private room upstairs to dress and get ready.

Theresa wasn't sure what to do from here. She checked her watch and saw they had ten minutes to go. She was afraid to sit down because her dress would wrinkle. She felt fortunate to have found this dress on short notice. She and Margo went shopping and as if it were meant to be, they found this stunner on the rack. It was a figure-fitting white dress with lace overlay. Sheer sleeves and lace embellishments. And she felt beautiful in it. Her hair was pinned up on her head with a few curls framing her face. Her diamond ring had to be taken to the jewelers this week to have the wedding band soldered to it and she felt naked without it all week. She'd grown fond of looking at the glittering ring on her finger.

She inhaled deeply and Margo chuckled. "Soon."

"I know. This waiting is the worst. If he's ready, we should get on with it. We can stand around for the rest of the day."

Margo laughed and pulled her phone from her purse. "Hey, handsome. Are the guys ready? The bride is."

"Okay. I'll tell her."

"The men are ready and for the record, Marco's sick of standing around too."

Theresa grinned.

Effie clapped her hands. "Okay, let's go get my brother a wife."

Theresa and Margo both laughed, and the ever-exuberant Effie hustled out the door without waiting for instructions.

Margo stared at the back of the door for a moment, then asked, "How old is she?"

Theresa chuckled. "She's a lot, isn't she? The house has been incredibly busy this week. She's twenty-seven."

"And none of the brothers are married?"

Theresa shook her head. "Nope. They seem great, but they have a family tendency to be loners. Except Effie. She says she's just picky. Her exact words are pickier than shit and I have big-ass brothers who won't let me take crap from any man."

Margo laughed and Theresa shook her head. She'd been hearing this all week. She told Marco that one day Effie would meet "the one" and that would be the end of it. She'd be head-over-heels, and those big-ass brothers would need to deal.

Izzy stepped back into the room with a pretty smile on her face. "It's time."

Margo nodded to Theresa. "Ready?"

"Yep."

Epilogue Marco

Marco listened to his older brother, Brock, tell a story about a time when he was in Fallujah clearing a house. He'd heard this story before and right now, he wanted to focus on marrying Theresa, but his younger brother, Devin, seemed completely interested in the story, so Marco politely listened. His mind wondered what Theresa looked like right now.

Jace entered the room. "The bride is ready. How about the groom?"

Marco nodded. "The groom is also ready."

Jace nodded. "Perfect, let's go get you married."

Marco chuckled and followed Jace from the office. Brock and Devin were behind him, still chatting about his mission. He loved his siblings. They didn't see each other often, maybe two or three times a year. But he sure was ready to have their house back and quiet again. And he wanted Theresa to himself. Effie badgered her constantly about everything. What did she do all day while Marco worked? Did she like dogs? Did she think they'd have kids? What would they name them if they did? It went on and on every day. Theresa was exhausted and he felt bad for her. He'd sprung his family on her and she never complained. But the wear was beginning to show. Tonight, they were heading to a hotel where they'd spend their wedding night quietly and he'd get to enjoy his new wife.

They ascended the stairs to the upper dining room and walked out to the upper deck. Theresa had asked to be married where Marco had proposed. Mason and Carley married up here and she thought it was a beautiful setting. He agreed with her. They asked Jace and Margo, who were eager to have the wedding at the Sandbar, and what a beautiful wedding it would be.

He stepped onto the deck and took in the view. Izzy Payton from Petal Pushers had wrapped the railing in white and blue flowers. The tables had been moved away for the ceremony and would be brought back for the reception. He and his brothers took their places at the front of the deck, where the minister stood. He looked out onto the small intimate crowd they'd gathered to witness their wedding today and his heart filled with appreciation for their presence. Sid and his wife Grace were here. Quinn and Hanna. Mason and Carley as well. Their counselor, Devin came with his wife. Of course, his brothers and sister were here. That was all he needed.

The music started playing. Jamie Hart agreed to play the guitar and sing a solo for their wedding and Theresa was ecstatic. He sat at the back of the deck and as he played the wedding march. Jamie smiled at Marco and he nodded.

Margo walked down the aisle first, followed by Effie, who chattered all the way down the aisle. He grinned and shook his head. That girl could talk.

The music grew louder, and Theresa stepped from inside. Her long dark hair was piled high on her head. The long white lacy gown she wore fit her perfectly. She looked like a princess walking toward him. The bouquet she carried was both simplistic and elegant.

She didn't wear any jewelry, and he couldn't wait to slip her wedding ring on her finger. He'd noticed her looking at her finger this week and frowning. She missed her engagement ring.

Her eyes locked on his and he couldn't have looked away from her if there was a hurricane approaching. His bride. His present. His future. And she was breathtaking.

Finally, the minister said, "You may exchange rings."

He slipped her eternity band soldered to her engagement ring on her finger and her eyes glittered with moisture. She looked into his eyes, "They're beautiful."

He grinned. "They don't shine as brightly as you do."

She slipped the gold band on his finger. It had five small diamonds embedded in the band and he instantly loved how his hand looked with a wedding ring on his finger. The ring that signified Theresa was his wife, and he was her husband.

The minister said, "You may kiss your bride."

He didn't hesitate. He kissed her sweetly, then he kissed her again. Her hand cupped his cheek and she kissed him. He grinned.

The minister then introduced them. "Ladies and gentlemen may I introduce you to Mr. and Mrs. Karason."

Their friends and family clapped. His brothers hugged him tightly while Margo and Effie hugged Theresa. His heart was filled with love today. He'd work hard to keep it that way for the rest of their lives.

BONUS EPILOGUE

Marco wrapped his arms around Theresa and kissed her lips. Jamie Hart started singing a slow song and Marco whispered, "It's time we danced together Mrs. Karason."

She laughed. "Yes, please."

She'd kicked her shoes off and they now danced in the sand on the beach. The weather was balmy, a light breeze kept them cool as he swayed with his bride to the tune Jamie sang.

He rested his cheek against hers while they moved to the music. "It's been a perfect day."

She giggled. "It has been."

"When you're ready to go, I'm ready to go."

She pulled back and looked into his eyes. Hers were beautiful. She'd added something to deepen the color of her lashes. They looked longer too. But mostly, her eyes looked happy.

"I'm ready when you are."

He kissed her. "Good answer."

He took her hand and started walking toward the parking area. She stopped him. "We have to be good hosts and say good-bye."

"But that'll take a long time."

She chuckled. "It might take a while, but these people came out to celebrate us. We need to thank them for that."

"Okay. I know you're right. But I feel like I've barely seen you this week and I miss you."

She stepped into his arms. "I miss you too and I know what you mean, but this is not the time to be rude."

"Okay."

She led him to the bar area out on the deck where several of their guests stood. They said goodbye to them and continued walking down the bar to Marco's siblings, having a rousing conversation about some childhood fun they'd had. "Okay, you all behave and don't wreck the house. We'll be home in the morning."

They all hugged. His heart warmed when his siblings hugged Theresa and congratulated her on joining the family.

As they reached Mitch, he finished up a phone call. "Everything okay?"

"I guess I'm needed. Did Petal Pushers do the flowers for your wedding?"

Theresa nodded. "Yes. She did an amazing job."

Mitch nodded. "Name Izzy Payton?"

"Yes. What's wrong?"

"She just called me and wants to meet tomorrow morning. Something's been happening at her shop, and she wants cameras added to her place."

Theresa responded. "Oh, I hope it isn't serious. She's an awesome person and is doing a great job with her shop."

Mitch shrugged. "I'll see tomorrow. Congratulations on your wedding today. It was beautiful."

Marco shook his hand and Theresa hugged him. The last people they needed to say good night to were Jace and Margo. Not seeing them outside he led Theresa inside. They moved toward the office and Marco knocked on the door. Jace opened the door with his shirt half undone and Margo looked sheepish as they said good night. Margo quickly hugged them both and Jace closed the door even faster. Marco looked down at Theresa. "I hope that's us years from now."

She laughed. "Me too."

They left out of the back door. As soon as they were buckled up, he backed from their parking space and headed to the hotel. She was all his now.

MITCH PULLED INTO THE PARKING LOT OF PETAL PUSHERS AT ten minutes to eight the following morning. There were flowers everywhere he looked. Outdoor pots of plants and flowers decorated the wooden front porch. The windows were graced with plants and decorative stained glass hanging items. It was pretty but an awful lot to take in. He exited his pickup and neared the front door. He twisted the handle and as soon as he pushed the door open, hanging bells chimed over his head.

"Good morning," called someone from the back of the store.

"Morning. It's Mitch DeMario."

"Hi, Mitch, I'll be right up."

Within a few moments, a beautiful woman with long blonde hair and a big, gorgeous smile came toward him carrying a vase full of flowers. He didn't know what they were called, he only knew they were yellow.

"Hi, Mitch. My name is Izzy Payton. Thank you for coming."

"Absolutely. Tell me what's been happening here."

She set the flowers on the counter near a register and moved past him. "I found this outside last night when I popped in after setting up for the wedding."

He followed her outside and she pointed to a hole in the wall near the window and a large rock laying on the ground. "Anything else?"

"No. But I've noticed tire tracks in the parking lot when I come in the morning. I don't know if it's kids just goofing around. But when they start throwing rocks and creating damage, I want to capture them on a camera to stop them from progressing."

"Okay. Let me take some measurements and get an idea of how many cameras you'll need and then I can write up the costs for you."

"That sounds good. Thank you."

Mitch followed Izzy inside. She was dynamic and energetic. "Just a couple of questions. Did anyone recently get mad at you for any reason?"

Her pretty brows pinched together. "No. I mean, I don't recall anyone getting mad."

"Okay. It helps to ask. How about anyone trying to buy you out?"

"No, not that either. I'd never sell. This was my father's place, and I inherited it when he passed away. I can't sell it. It's been in my family my entire life."

"Okay. I just wanted to check. I'll go get those measurements."

As he strode to the door, a rock burst through the

window and smacked him directly in the chest. He flew back and fell over a low shelf with plants on it. His head hit the floor and his vision turned to gray. He heard Izzy scream and that's the last he remembered.

Up next in Blossom Springs... He's grumpy and guarded. She's sunshine with a stubborn streak. When fiery florist Izzy Payton hires brooding former Marine Mitch DeMario to investigate sabotage at her family's flower shop, sparks fly, and not just from the danger closing in around them. Get ready for sizzling chemistry, escalating threats, and a battle of wills that might just end in love. **Don't miss *Smoldering Nights* — coming next!**

Looking for stories filled with heart-pounding suspense, steamy romance, and unforgettable characters? Sign up for my newsletter and get a **FREE book** to dive into right away!

It's easy: 1 Sign up below. 2 Confirm your email (we like to keep things legit and bot-free). 3 Start enjoying your free read and exclusive updates, sneak peeks, and special offers!

Love awaits—don't miss your chance to join the adventure!

https://www.pjfiala.com/subscribe/

ENJOY THIS BOOK? YOU CAN MAKE A BIG DIFFERENCE

Your Review Matters!

As an independent author, I don't have the big budgets of major publishers for splashy ads or subway posters (not yet, anyway 😊). But what I do have is something far more valuable—amazing readers like you.

Your honest review is one of the most powerful ways to help my books reach other readers. If you enjoyed this story, taking just a few minutes to share your thoughts would mean the world to me. Reviews, even short ones, make a huge difference.

Click below to leave your review and help others discover *Sizzling Nights*:

▶️ https://geni.us/SizzlingEBAll

Thank you for your support—it means everything! 

ALSO BY PJ FIALA

I'm fortunate to be able to do what I love. It's a blessing.

My list of written works has gotten so long I needed to move it to my website! How's that for blessed?

Anyway, click the link below to see the list of all of my books.

Thank you so much for reading.

https://www.pjfiala.com/bibliography-pj-fiala/

or scan the QR Code below.

MEET PJ

About the Author

Writing has always been my dream, but it wasn't until I found the courage to put pen to paper that my life changed in the most profound way. Creating stories that resonate with readers and bringing to life flawed yet lovable characters brings me endless joy—and I hope my books bring you the same.

When I'm not writing, you'll likely find me enjoying time with my family or hitting the open road with my husband, Gene. We're avid bikers who love exploring new destinations, meeting fascinating people, and soaking in the beauty of this incredible country.

Coming from a proud family of veterans—including my grandfather, father, brother, two sons, and daughter-in-law—I have a deep appreciation for service and the sacrifices that protect our freedoms. Their dedication inspires me every day, and I'm honored to share stories that celebrate resilience, love, and the American spirit.

My online home is https://www.pjfiala.com.
You can connect with me on Facebook at https://www.facebook.com/PJFiala1,

and
Instagram at https://www.Instagram.com/PJFiala.
If you prefer to email, go ahead, I'll respond - pjfiala@
pjfiala.com.

COPYRIGHT

Copyright © 2025 by PJ Fiala

All rights reserved. This book or any portion thereof may not be reproduced or used in any manner whatsoever without the express written permission of the publisher except for the use of brief quotations in a book review.

Publisher's note: This is a work of fiction. Names, characters, places, and incidents either are the product of the author's imagination or are used fictitiously. Any resemblance to actual events, locales, or persons, living or dead, is entirely coincidental.

Printed in the United States of America
First published 2025
Fiala, PJ
Sizzling Nights / PJ Fiala
p. cm.
1. Romance—Fiction. 2. Romance—Suspense. 3. Romance - Military

I. Title – Sizzling Nights
ISBN-13: 978-1-966513-07-0

www.ingramcontent.com/pod-product-compliance
Lightning Source LLC
Chambersburg PA
CBHW071401300726
48976CB00006B/1951

Where are you, Talia?

Someone took her. I can feel it in my bones. But all the usual suspects are quiet and in hiding. Everything feels so normal. As if I imagined my wife—imagined holding her luscious curves and driving into her tight heat. Sometimes I wonder if I did. Was it all a fucked-up dream? Am I in some unknown level of hell?

I swing out again, missing the Galani roach and his double. Squinting, they become one. Ugly motherfucker. Him and his blurred phantom twin.

Everything turns black for a moment and I stumble. I'm just blinking away the confusion when Adrian forcefully grabs my knife.

"Let me finish up here, Boss." He pins me with a hard glare. Why the fuck does he have four eyes?

"What'd I miss?" Aris asks, clomping down the stairs. "Yuck. A fucking mess is what."

"Kostas was just heading up to grab some coffee and a bite to eat," Adrian says. "You came just in time."

Aris rakes his gaze down my form and his lips purse together in disappointment. Same fucking way Mamá's did. My heart fucking hurts. His stare softens as he grabs my arm and hooks it over his shoulders.

"Come on, bro," Aris mutters. "Let's get you back home."

My home is empty and cold. I hate it.

"Wanna swim?" I slur, leaning heavily into him.

He chuckles. "And watch your ass drown? Maybe later."

"Let me guess," I grumble. "You gotta get home to your wife."

A snort escapes him. "Selene is not my wife."

"Yet."

"Yet," he concedes. "But she sure as fuck acts like one, always bitching if I don't get home at a decent hour."

I laugh. "At least you get laid."

"If I get home in time," he jokes.

We stumble up the stairs and he helps me into his Porsche. The drive back to my villa makes me nauseous. I'm about to puke when the car finally comes to a stop. He helps me out of the car and into my villa. I groan when I scent lemons. The maid's been by, which means she had to clean up after my latest rage. Everything has been replaced and put back together again. I fist my hands, eager to destroy it once more.

"Dude," Aris groans. "You have got to quit trashing your villa. Do you know how much money we've spent on fixing this room? I thought we were past this."

I'll never be past this.

Talia.

Just fucking gone.

"She's dead," I tell him, my words choking my throat.

He sighs. "You don't know that."

"She is."

With a grunt, he drops me onto my sofa. I fade in and out of consciousness as I hear the microwave beeping. Something savory makes my stomach grumble. Aris sets down a plate of microwaved pizza on the coffee table.

"Eat, man. You're wasting away."

I shrug. "I'm not hungry."

He crosses his arms over his chest and levels me with a serious glare. I roll my eyes as I take a bite of the pizza. My, how our roles have reversed. I think Aris secretly likes taking care of me as I wallow in my fucking misery. I'd say he gets off on it, but his concerned eyes that are exactly like Mamá's don't lie. And because of that, I eat the damn pizza.

"I really do need to bail," he mutters. "I hate leaving you like this, but Selene can be such a bitch."

"Married life," I say with a grunt.

"Not yet." He laughs. "Hell, maybe not ever."

"You bought a fucking house for her." I scratch at my jaw. "Am I an embarrassment?"

"Truly, you are," he taunts, his brown eyes lighting up with playfulness.

"Fuck off. You never have me over."

"You've been preoccupied. You think I want to rub in your face the fact I'm happy with Selene and thinking about popping the question while you're dying over here in despair? Hell no. I may think you're a dick, but I'm not going to do that shit to you."

I chew the pizza and frown before swallowing it. "Don't tell me you let her decorate."

He winces. "The kitchen is seashell themed."

"Jesus," I say with a laugh. "Mamá would be rolling over in her grave."

We both sober up momentarily.

"I miss her," Aris rumbles. "I miss her so fucking much."

I, however, have mixed feelings on the matter. She fucked over my dad. Sure, he can be a dick. Like me. But did he deserve to be cheated on for a damn decade? Did he deserve to be shot because he was angry about the affair? He sure as hell didn't deserve to lose his ability to walk because she couldn't keep from having sex with Niles Fucking Nikolaides.

Is that what happened to Talia? Did she run off with her secret lover?

No one fucking knows. Especially not me.

"Maybe when you're not getting fucked up, you can come over for dinner one day. Make some décor suggestions to Selene."

"Maybe," I grumble. We both know I'm not leaving this fucking hotel to go give interior decorating advice to my brother's whore wannabe wife.

Aris leaves the room and returns shortly with a glass of ouzo. He smiles as he sets it down next to the plate. "My peace offering."

"Who knew you could be so cordial, brother?"

He grins. "Someone has to take care of your broody ass."

I suck down the ouzo and then slam the glass back down on the table. "You out?"

"Yeah. I'm out. See you tomorrow."

"Any leads?"

A frown mars his features. "If I had any, you'd be the first to know." He lets out a heavy sigh. "We'll find her, Kostas."

Bones in a ditch.

Hair hanging from a vat of acid.

Her big diamond ring at the bottom of the sea.

That's how I imagine we'll find her one day.

I hate that I'm losing faith we'll find her alive. It's been so long. Her mother is devastated. Phoenix is damn near crazed. And me, I'm fucking destroyed.

A year.

A motherfucking year.

It's not getting better. It's getting much, much worse.

"If you want me to stay with you and talk," Aris says, "I can tell Selene we're working more leads. I don't like that look in your eyes." He clenches his jaw. "You can't do to me what Mamá did to us. Don't leave me with our damn dad all alone."

He thinks I'm going to kill myself.

It's like he doesn't know me at all.

I don't want to kill myself…

I want to kill anyone and everyone involved in the disappearance of my wife.

And if Talia left me of her own accord, well, I'll deal with her ass when I find her.

"Go," I grunt. "Go play house."

He smirks. "You're jealous."

"Jealous you're going to get your dick sucked? Fuck yes. But by Selene? Hell no. Sorry, Aris, but she's a snotty bitch."

Rather than be offended, he shrugs. "She gives good head."

We both laugh and then he lets out a sigh.

"One more peace offering and then I'm gone," he grunts. "You can get your lazy ass up off your couch if you want any more. Tomorrow, come to the office sober and we can shake up some more leads."

He disappears and once again returns with my glass refilled with ouzo. With a tip of his head, he leaves me with my alcohol and my depressing thoughts. After I suck down the drink, I stumble into the bathroom, shedding my bloody clothes along the way. I take a long, hot shower and lean my head against the cool tile. My hand rubs at my dick, but between the ouzo and my shitty attitude, it's not interested in release.

"What the fuck ever," I grunt out.

Once I'm dry, I wrap my towel around my waist and fall onto the bed. I reach into the drawer, pulling out my iPad. Turning it on, I open the pictures app and find ones I have saved of Talia.

In the photos, her blue eyes are alight with fire. She was

so alive. She loved to challenge me. I loved it right back. Loved her.

Now?

I still fucking love her, which is why this shit hurts so bad. I let her leave that day pissed at me when I should have dragged her back to bed to leave love notes with my mouth all over her body. I should have spoken those words. Maybe it could have made a difference. Maybe she would still be here with me.

Scrolling past several pictures, I find my favorite. One of her lying in bed, her hair messy and her tits exposed. They're red from my mouth and her nipples are hard. The sultry look on her face just begs me to come back to bed and fuck her again. Again and again and again. That's not the look of someone who'd willingly leave. Deep down, I feel that in my heart. But my head? My head wonders if she was acting all along.

Refusing to think badly about her when all I want is to fucking come, I undo my towel and fist my cock that's come to life upon seeing her picture. She's still my wife. Until I know she's dead or left me, I'll go on the assumption she's alive somewhere out there missing me. I stroke and stroke, fixating on her plump lips. Her full tits. Her hooded eyes. Closing my eyes, I remember back to how tight she felt when I'd push into her slick cunt. How her tits would jiggle and she'd moan so fucking sweetly. Her fingernails would scrape down my shoulders and she'd beg for release. I groan when my nuts seize up. Heat splatters on my stomach and my chest heaves. When I reopen my eyes, I realize I've accidentally slid to the next picture. It's one of her at the opening of Pomegranate that her mother took. I stole it from her mom's social media like a fucking creepy stalker.

God, she's beautiful.

She's still out there.

She has to be.

As my eyes droop, I silently make a vow.

I'm coming for you, moró mou. I'm always coming for you.

And one day I'm going to find you.

chapter
two

Talia

"I N THE UNDERWORLD, PROSERPINA HAS GROWN TO love Pluto, who treated her with compassion and loved her as his Queen. As she would have up in Olympus, she remained eternally beautiful in the Underworld. Pluto admired her kind and nurturing nature. However, Proserpina missed her dear mother greatly and wished to spend time on earth with her. When Hermes reached the underworld, he requested that Proserpina come back to earth with him to rejoin her mother and father." I turn the page of the book, and a tiny hand swats out at the page, wrinkling it slightly.

"No, no, sweet girl," I tell her gently. "We have to be nice to the book." She looks up at me with her radiant bright blue eyes and giggles, and my heart feels as though it's thumped straight out of my chest. But I guess that comes with the territory. My mom used to always tell me being a mom means removing your heart and giving it to your children.

Wiping a drop of liquid emotion from my cheek, I continue to read my favorite part of the book. "Pluto knew he could not refuse the commands of Zeus, but he also could not part from his beloved Proserpina." A golf ball sized lump fills my throat, and I have to set the book down for a minute to gather myself together. It always happens when I get to this part. Thoughts of *him* surface and I have to force them away. It's the only way.

With a deep breath, I continue to read the story. "Before she departed from the underworld, Pluto offered Proserpina a pomegranate as a farewell. This was, however, a cunning move by Pluto. All the Olympians knew that if anyone ate or drank anything in the Underworld they would be destined to remain there for—"

"That book again?" a shrill voice, equivalent to nails grinding on a chalkboard, says, ruining story time.

Without turning to face the owner of the voice, I close the book and stare out at the blue waters of Mirabello Bay. From up here, I can't smell the salt water, but I can still see the waves lapping up at the shore, and sometimes when I close my eyes, I can imagine being down there, lying in a hammock, smelling the scent of—

"You know it doesn't understand anything you're saying, right?" the annoying voice continues, snapping me out of my daydream. "It's a baby," she snarls.

"And that's why I'm the mom and you're the maid." I give my daughter a kiss on her forehead and inhale her fresh baby scent that's mixed with chlorine from our swim in the pool earlier. "*She's* not an *it*. And she's almost six months old. She's sitting up and crawling. She laughs and…" I turn around to face *the maid*, annoyed at myself for allowing her to work me up, but I can't help it. Every time she speaks of my daughter as if she's some alien, it riles up my mama bear instincts and I pounce.

When my eyes scan down her body, I notice she's dressed in a skimpy shrimp-colored dress and white heels, her face full of makeup, like she's about to go to the club instead of rotate the laundry. Her collagen-filled lips are pursed together in a mixture of hate and confusion, and I roll my eyes. I don't know why I even bother to try to explain anything to her. She doesn't have a single maternal bone in her body. I pity anything—plant, human, animal, mineral—she attempts to care for. It will be dead within days.

I shake my head, giving up on explaining to her for the millionth time, my daughter is probably smarter at six months old than she is at…however old she is. It's hard to tell. Her voice is screechy and whiny, giving off a young vibe, but all the makeup makes her appear to be older. "Never mind. What do you want?"

"Dinner's ready." Oh, dear Lord, please tell me she's ordered something. If I have to eat one more of her home-cooked meals I'm going to throw myself off this cliff. I'm going to seriously have to have a talk with Aris when he gets home. Just because she's decided she wants to try and play house, doesn't mean I have to be punished.

"I'm not hungry. I'll eat later." I open the book to read more of the story to my sweet girl.

"I wasn't asking," she informs me. "I was telling you. Aris brought dinner home and he's waiting." She rolls her eyes, obviously annoyed that the man she's in love with doesn't feel the same and would rather have my company than hers.

"Fine," I snap. "I'll be there in a few minutes."

She turns on her heel to head back up to the house, when I call her name. "Oh, and *Selene*, my daughter would like her sweet potatoes pureed with only a *hint* of butter. The last time you made them there was enough butter in them to give a grown man a heart attack."

She huffs, but doesn't argue. *Damn right, bitch, know your place.*

"You ready to eat dinner, sweet girl?" I coo at my daughter, who throws her chubby little arms in the air and giggles. It's the most beautiful, melodic sound in the world.

After taking one last look down below, I stand and carry her into the mansion of a house. With at least ten bedrooms, and even more bathrooms, it would take a map to find your way around the entire place. But lucky for me, the only room I need to be able to find is my daughter's, which is on the first floor attached to mine. I give her a quick bath to get the chlorine off her body and then feed her a bottle. When I'm done, I head to the dining room.

"Nice of you to finally join me, dear." Aris stands and makes his way over to my daughter and me.

"I had to feed her first," I explain. "But I'm here now."

"And how is my daughter?" Aris asks, taking her from me before I can stop him.

"*Zoe* is perfect," I tell him, opening the lid to her high chair, so he can set her in it. "Selene!" I call out. "I need Zoe's dinner now!"

Aris chuckles, but doesn't say a word. He never does. The only reason why he keeps her around is because he knows how obsessed the woman is with him, which means she'll do anything he asks of her.

"And how was your day?" Aris asks after pulling my chair out for me and then sitting at the head of the table. Selene saunters into the dining room, her heels *click-clacking* against the marble floor. She drops Zoe's sweet potatoes down in front of me and they spill out of the cup. They look overcooked and gross. Good thing I never planned to feed these to her.

"Actually," I tell her, stifling my smile, "she's not that hungry. She just had a bottle." I reach over and grab Zoe's container of fruit and place some on her tray. "You can take this away." I lift the bowl of sweet potatoes and wait for her to take them. Which she does. Because she's the maid.

I begin eating my chicken and realize it's from Pomegranate, the restaurant I built from the ground up. Aris is probably hoping for a reaction, but he's not going to get one.

"I asked how your day was," Aris repeats.

"Fine."

"Just fine?" he prompts.

"That's what I said."

Selene sits at the table across from me, on the other side of Aris. "My back hurts," she complains. "I swear that baby accumulates so much laundry. Can we please hire someone?"

"That's what we have you for," Aris snaps, and I snort out a laugh.

"But, Aris..." she whines.

"No buts," he tells her, shutting down the conversation.

After dinner is over, I grab one of the cupcakes from the pantry I made for today. Snagging a lighter and candle from the drawer, I take everything with me onto the veranda. When I go back inside to grab Zoe, Aris has her in his arms. It's not often he holds her...

"Can I have her, please?" I extend my arms to grab her and she shifts her body toward me. *That's my girl...*

Aris doesn't hand her to me, but instead walks outside. "A cupcake?" he asks, even though he knows the drill.

"She's six months old today." Closing my eyes so the tears that are burning my lids don't fall, I take in a deep, cleansing breath. But when I open my eyes, a couple traitor tears fall. Aris, of course, mistakes them for me being a sentimental mother.

"Don't be sad, Talia. Growing up is inevitable."

"Can I borrow your phone to take a picture?" I ask. Aris chuckles.

"How about you hold her and I'll take the picture?" He hands me back Zoe.

I light the candle and Aris snaps a picture of the two of us before I blow it out and make a wish. A wish… Every birthday when I was growing up my mom would tell me to make a wish using the candles on the cake. I used to wish for trite things like a new bike, the bracelet I wanted. For my mom to let me go to the movies with my friends. Now, though, even though they're technically Zoe's wishes, every time I blow out the candle for her, I make the same wish. For—

"Talia," Aris says, breaking me from my thought. "Selene is going into town with me tomorrow. Make sure you make a list of anything you need."

My eyes snap to Aris's, but I quickly school my features, not wanting him to have any clue what I'm thinking.

"I'll make a list. And can you please have that picture printed for me?" I point to his phone, holding the picture of Zoe and me.

"Of course. Anything for you." He pulls me into his side and kisses my temple. "Anything for you."

chapter
three

Kostas

MY HEAD THROBS LIKE A MOTHERFUCKER. There was a time, when Talia disappeared, that I was clearheaded and hell-bent on finding her. I exhausted every resource I had into looking into what happened. Nothing ever came of it, though. She just fucking vanished.

Just like Michael and Tadd.

I remember torturing those incompetent fools because someone had to pay. It was their job to protect her. They had one fucking job and they failed. Adrian and Basil brought them in, strapped them to chairs, and handed me weapon after weapon until I drained them of every ounce of life.

It didn't make her reappear. She was still gone.

Leaning back in my office chair, I ignore my phone as it buzzes. Another call from my father. It drives him insane that he's stuck at his house in forced retirement. Aris and I visit him to share meals on occasion, but whenever he tries to talk business, we shut him down. I can thank my brother for that much—having my back against our father. Father is out of touch. It's Aris and I who deal with the business day in and day out. In fact, now that I've given Aris more responsibility in the past year, we've thrived. Money just fucking floods in.

Unfortunately, I don't give a shit about money.

I'm obsessed with finding Talia.

For the millionth time, I wonder about Alex. The scuzzy American fucker she dated before she came to be my wife. I know everything about the asshole. His flavor of the week. His favorite restaurant. His shitty taste in music. I follow him on every social media outlet because I figure one day he's going to slip up. One day I'll learn he has her hidden away while they play house together, laughing at the fact I'm finally out of the picture. In those dark fantasies, I slaughter Alex and make Talia watch. Then, I fuck her back into submission. It's easier being angry with her. At least there's hope threaded in with my anger. Hope that she's alive and I'll find her one day. It's a helluva lot better than the alternative: her being dead.

My eyes drag from my phone over to the bottle of ouzo sitting on my desk. I practically shake with the need to drink. I'm not stupid. I'm well aware of the fact I'm drinking myself into oblivion. And the more I drink, the further from finding her I feel. But when it's staring me in the face, it's hard to push it away. At least when I'm drinking, my body goes numb. The bleeding in my fucking heart stops.

Ignoring the ouzo, I grab my phone and pull up Alex's Instagram. He's back in Florence with a brunette tucked under his arm. His eyes are hooded as he smiles crookedly at the camera. It boils my blood that Talia was once with this idiot. I've often thought about dragging him here to my hotel so I could cut off every part of his body that may have once touched her. Adrian's eyes grew wide at my suggestion, which is the only reason I didn't follow through. I know Adrian looks out for me and with one wild expression, I knew I was acting like a madman and not like the cunning mobster I am.

But so help me if that fucker Alex has Talia or knows where she's at…

I scrub my hand down my face and begin scrolling through my contacts. I find Talia's mother, Melody, and stare at her name. This woman used to hate me, but now we share a common goal: find Talia. Melody wears her heart on her sleeve when it comes to her daughter. If she were hiding her or knew where she was, I'd know about it. I put the phone on speaker and dial her. She answers on the first ring.

"Kostas," she greets, her voice tight with concern. "Any word?"

She always answers right away, hopeful I've found Talia.

"No," I grunt out. "Any news on your end?"

A heavy sigh escapes her. "None."

We share a long moment of silence, both of us brooding.

"Emilio hasn't heard any chatter?" I'm always hopeful with his governmental position and contacts with the police, he might hear of some organization somewhere bragging over the fact they got Kostas Demetriou's wife.

"Nothing," she says. "I spoke with him today and nothing. Niles?"

I wince at his name. "Still missing also."

Another long moment of silence. It's a theory we've discussed before. Niles taking her and hiding her away. The motive is unclear, but it's one that makes a lot of sense. She is his daughter and he hates our family. It could be a way to stick it to us. He's just not smart enough or rich enough for that shit. It doesn't add up.

"I will be visiting Phoenix soon," I tell her. "I'll see what I can find out."

"Don't hurt my son."

I smirk. She's like Talia in that sense. Bossing around a crime lord like it's not a big fucking deal. But, because it reminds me of her daughter, I give her allowances I shouldn't. "We'll see."

She must not hear any threat in my words because she lets out a relieved sigh. "What about on Crete? My father said not long before she was taken, Ezio had an attempt on his life by the Galanis. Could they be behind this?"

It irritates me she knows so much about our world, but again, she's her daughter's mother. I can't fault her for being dedicated to plucking up every stone to see if it leads to her daughter. I'll take all the help I can get at this point.

"Most of the Galanis are gone," I bite out. "The dickless one is still out and about, but he doesn't have the spine to do something grand like kidnap my wife. Plus, he'd love to gloat. If he had her, he'd torment me with that fact. Since everything is silent, it tells me it's someone new or someone who couldn't care less about taunting me, but maybe someone with their own agendas."

"She's such a beautiful woman," her mother breathes. "What if someone kidnapped her and sold her into a sex trafficking ring? Do you know people who do that sort of thing?"

No, but your ex-husband does.

"I doubt that's it." I fucking hope that's not it. "But to be safe, I'll bring it up to Phoenix at our meeting. Niles admitted to allowing passage with some new clients who were into that shit."

She lets out a ragged breath. "Kostas, we have to find her. If she's with sex traffickers…" A loud sob escapes her. "I worry we'll never get the Talia we know and love back."

I scrub my face in frustration. "Whoever has her will fucking pay," I growl. "I will skin them all alive."

My words don't frighten her. "Good. They deserve it for taking my baby girl."

Voices echo down the hallway just outside my office and I sit up straight. "I need to go."

"Okay, *cara mio*, take care and let me know if you learn anything new."

I hang up and let her words sink in. Lately, she calls me *her darling* like I really am her son. And fuck if I don't correct her because it makes me miss Mamá.

Frustration churns in my gut. I rise from my chair and stalk outside onto the veranda. This afternoon, the air is warm and the salty sea scent evokes memories of my honeymoon. Taking Talia on the beach for the first time. The look of pure adoration on her pretty face as I made her mine. It's times like these, when I'm sobering up, everything feels so crystal clear. I think back to that week when we located Estevan Galani in that apartment building. How he'd eyed up my wife like she was trash he wanted to burn. The fact he survived his injuries I gave him wasn't surprising, but the fact he remains in hiding and not fucking with me is a disturbing fact. It feels important. Like I need to pursue why he isn't fucking with me. I shot his dick off, for fuck's sake. If someone shot my dick off, I'd try to destroy them, and would die doing it too.

Think, Kostas.

My mind wanders to the day she disappeared. We fought like fucking hell, but it wasn't a relationship ending fight. Too many times I've allowed myself to blame it on that. That she was pissed and finally left me. She'd met up with Selene and asked for money. Another big mystery.

I'd assumed she took the money and used it to get away.

But what if she was being blackmailed?

Rushing back inside, I sit at my desk and unlock my computer. When she went missing, I made sure the backups of our security footage were being stored in another place. I've scoured through tons of it, but often, I get frustrated sifting through hours and hours of footage that leads to nothing. The footage that never made sense was the night she supposedly took the money from Selene. I want to view it again. I pull back the footage to that night and find where we last enter the villa. Then, I skim through the night, waiting for her to leave. It eventually skips to the next day when she storms out to leave for school. I check all the cameras surrounding the villa, and nothing shows up.

Selene claimed Talia borrowed money from her, but it didn't happen that night.

She never left.

Which means either Selene confused the events or lied to me.

Why?

I assess Selene's behavior over the past year. She's obsessed with Aris. I bet she was even jealous of Talia, even though Talia was my woman and not Aris's. Would she lie to us to make Talia seem like a bad person who left me? And why?

She's a catty cunt, but she's not smart enough to pull off

some grand kidnapping of my wife and keep it from me all this time. Most likely she just wanted to make Talia look bad. Regardless, I'm going to find out why the fuck Selene would lie because it doesn't help me get to the bottom of this shit with her meddling.

"Frown any harder and your face may stick that way," a familiar voice booms from the doorway.

As soon as I see my brother, I click out of the video footage and pop open Google on my browser before turning to him. "This is my face. It's been stuck this way since I turned thirteen."

He snorts. "I can't believe Dad actually gave us lessons on how to look fierce and intimidating."

"You failed," I grunt out.

"And you passed with flying colors. But seriously? What kind of father teaches their kids that?"

I shrug and glance at the clock, before watching every tick of my brother's face. "Want to have dinner?"

His brown eyes flash for a second before he schools his features, not taking my bait. "Of course."

"Actually," I mutter. "I need to get ready for my trip to Thessaloniki."

Aris's shoulders relax slightly. "Raincheck then. We could always go visit Dad and have dinner with him."

It's sad how much he desperately tries to gain Father's favor. Even now. Even with Father being practically an invalid and meaner than a snake. My mother's death has killed him more than he'll ever let on.

"Sure," I tell him with a shrug.

"Anything new?" He walks over to the wet bar in my office and pulls out two tumblers. After he fills them with ice and a little water, he heads back over to my desk. I'm silent as I watch him fill them with ouzo. He pushes a glass my way and then he proceeds to sip his.

Not touching the glass, I cross my arms over my chest and lean back in my chair. "Nothing."

His lips purse together. "We'll come up with something eventually."

My stare on him must unnerve him because he waves a hand at the ouzo. "Drink up, man. I have to get home to Selene soon or I'll never hear the end of it."

"Sure are pussy-whipped," I say, picking up the glass and swirling the ice around in it.

He snorts. "She knows her place."

"Where is Estevan Galani?" I ask, setting my tumbler down.

His eyebrows hike in surprise at my question and then he gives me a one-shouldered shrug. "Your guess is as good as mine. Went silent after you blew his cock off."

I scrub at the scruff on my face. "Galanis aren't known for their silence. They have the biggest goddamn mouths on Crete."

His lips press into a thin line. A worried line. It makes me scrutinize him further. "I'll look into it."

"Good," I grunt. "So will I."

"Cheers to dealing with the Galani infestation," he says, raising his glass and imploring me to drink.

I rise from my seat and walk over to the door. "I'll never toast to a fucking Galani. Go on and get out of here before your viper girlfriend tries to make a meal out of your balls."

He drains his glass and slams it down with a hard clunk. Then, he stands, shooting me an unreadable expression. With a deep breath, he inhales and then exhales whatever was threatening his composure. A wide grin spreads across his face.

"Have a good night, Kostas," he says with a smug grin. "My night will be a helluva lot better than yours, I can assure you."

He walks out without another word.

I glance over at my untouched ouzo and straighten my spine. I've been a cloud for far too long.

It's time to wake the fuck up and find my goddamn wife.

chapter
four

Talia

"I NEED MORE FORMULA," I YELL OVER THE SCREAMS of my pissed off daughter.

Selene glares my way. "I was just in town a few days ago. Aris told you to make a list." She eyes me accusingly, but I just shrug nonchalantly, not bothering to settle Zoe down. Her screaming always flusters Selene. For the sake of the human population, the woman should be sterilized so she can never reproduce.

"I did make a list." Zoe's screams get louder. "But Zoe had a growth spurt and I ran out sooner than I expected. Babies grow," I challenge.

"And you don't have any left at all?" she questions. I can see it in her features, she's about to reach her limit. Her hands are shaking, and her eyes are twitching. Come on, bitch…

"If I did I wouldn't be asking. Look, if you don't want to go, I can." I shrug with a smirk that I know will piss her off. "Zoe isn't going to stop crying until she's fed." As if on cue, Zoe's screams get louder. Every wail from her squeezes my heartstrings, but it's for the greater good.

"Jesus!" Selene shouts over the loud crying. "Fine. I'm going." She knows damn well she'll be in trouble if my daughter is unhappy in any way. A pissed off Zoe leads to a pissed off Aris. And a pissed off Aris never ends well. We've both learned that the hard way. The only difference is Aris actually cares about me since I'm the mother of his daughter, whereas with Selene, he views her as nothing more than a human pincushion. Poking every hole when he feels like it. The thought has me gagging. Better her than me, though.

Frustrated, she quickly unlocks the key box right in front of me, just as I hoped she would. Seven-two-two-four. She grabs a set of keys, slams it closed, then heads over to the garage door. I watch as she types in the code. Four-nine-nine-five. The light flashes green and she opens then closes the door behind her. I wait until I hear the garage door open and close and then I run into the kitchen. I type in the code to the key box and it clicks open. Grabbing the pair of keys, I pull one off the ring and put the other one back. As I'm closing the box, I spot Selene's cell phone on the counter. Holy shit! She forgot her phone.

Grabbing it, I tap the screen. It comes to life, but there's a password. No problem since I know it. Four-six-three-six. I type it in, but it's wrong. What the hell! I type it in again, but it's still wrong. I saw her type it in myself. This has to be right. The phone prompts I only have one try left before it locks.

I hear the garage opening back up. Damn it! She must've realized she forgot her phone. What do I do? Then it hits me. I bring up the passcode screen and hit the emergency button. The car door slams closed as the call connects.

"What is your emergency?"

I run with the phone in one hand and Zoe in the other

to hide in another room. "My name is Talia Demetriou and I need you to—"

Before I can finish my sentence, my head is yanked back and the phone is snatched from my hand. "You bitch!" Selene yells. She raises her hand to slap me, but I duck. Zoe is now screaming bloody murder, and I'm running to get away from Selene so she doesn't inadvertently hurt my daughter. I make it into Zoe's room and slam the door just before Selene can touch either of us.

The door doesn't lock, so with my weight against the door, I grab the rocking chair and wedge it under the doorknob so Selene can't get in. Once I know we're safe, I make Zoe a bottle and feed it to her. She calms down right away, and once she's full, falls asleep in my arms.

Since there's no way I'm going back out there until Aris gets home, I use the time to go over my list. Stealing Selene's cell phone wasn't my original plan anyway. I just saw it on the counter and figured it was worth a try. Pulling the small diaper bag out from under my bed, I double-check everything I've accumulated over the last several months. Formula, bottles, diapers, wipes, clothes for Zoe and me, three knives, over two hundred euros. Reaching into my pocket, I add the spare keys I stole to Aris's SUV. Selene and Aris will be so focused on me trying to steal her phone, they won't even think about the fact my entire purpose was to steal his keys.

Not wanting to risk the bag being seen, I shove it back under the bed. While Zoe naps, I read a book, and once she wakes up, I spend the rest of the day playing with her in her room. It isn't until I hear Aris's voice on the other side of the door, I move the chair and open the door.

"I heard you've been busy today," he says, eyeing me with annoyance.

"I was scared for my life," I cry out. "Selene is psycho, Aris. The only reason I tried to call the police was because I was scared." Tears prick my eyes, but Aris just rolls his.

"Stop your shit, Talia. Your little stunt today was stupid on your part." Aris smirks. "Want to know why?" I don't bother to answer. I know he'll tell me. "Since I now have to worry about you trying shit, I had to give Selene a gun." Jesus fucking Christ. Is he serious?

"If you try anything, she's been told not to hesitate." Aris steps forward and grabs ahold of my ponytail, jerking my head up to look him in the eyes. "I don't give a shit if you live or die, Talia," he hisses. "The only reason I keep you around is so you can take care of Zoe. You're her mother and I didn't want to take you from her. But if you're going to become a problem…" He lets his sentence linger, releasing my hair. "Now, dinner is ready. Let's try to have a good night. I've had a long day at work. My brother has become a raging alcoholic and I'm now having to do both of our jobs." Aris rolls his eyes then walks out of the room.

Kostas has become an alcoholic… My heart squeezes in my chest at the thought of what he's been going through this last year. It's hard to believe anything that comes out of Aris's mouth. I knew the night he raped me, he was a wolf in sheep's clothing, but I had no idea just how deadly of a bite he had until the day I was taken.

I'm sitting in the auditorium, waiting for rehearsal to begin. I've only been here for a few minutes, but I want to go home. When I left this morning, Kostas and I were fighting. I know part of it is my fault. I'm overemotional and haven't told him why yet. Mostly because I'm scared of how he's going to react. But it's also his fault because he's so damn jealous. I have to kiss Macbeth in the play and I know Kostas is going to kill him if I do, which means I'm going to have to either tell my professor I can't play the role as Lady Macbeth or figure out a way to fake-kiss my partner, so my husband doesn't rip his heart from his chest. I want to be mad at him for being such a possessive asshole, but then he sends me a sweet text and I turn into a pile of mush.

Kostas: I miss you even when you piss me the fuck off.

Okay, well, sweet for Kostas... It's crazy to think how quickly he's become my entire world, and not because I was forced to marry him, but because I love him. The problem is, while I'm not sure if Kostas loves me back, I do know he wants to own and possess every part of me. At this rate, there is going to be no me without Kostas, and I'm scared of what will happen when I can't put him first. When I can't give him all of me. Will he still want me? Will what I can give him be enough? Or will he do what my father did and stray? The thought has me wanting to throw up.

"You are going to make the craziest Lady Macbeth," Penelope says, sitting next to me. When I glance up at her, she frowns. "What's wrong?"

"Nothing." I shake my head. "I'm okay."

"No, you're not," she insists. "You're crying." She reaches over and swipes a tear off my cheek I didn't realize was there. "Talk to me."

As if the dam that was holding back my flood of emotions caves, I let out every thought and feeling without holding back. Penelope wraps her arms around me and listens as I pour my heart out to her. She doesn't say anything the entire time as I tell her about everything I'm feeling and how much I miss my home and my family, especially my mom. When I'm done, she hugs me tightly.

"What is it that will make you okay right now?" she asks.

After a moment of thinking about her question, I say, "I-I think..." I hiccup through my sobs. "I think I really just want my mom." We both break out into a fit of giggles at how much of a child I sound like in this moment.

"Moms do make everything better," Penelope agrees.

I stand and wipe the tears from my face. "I'm going to go use the restroom and wash my face. Thank you for listening. Honestly, I think I just needed a good cry." I choke out another laugh and Penelope joins in.

Grabbing my purse, I throw my phone into it and walk through the side stage doors that lead to the bathroom. Setting my purse down on the sink, I wet a paper towel and wipe under my eyes until I no longer look like a raccoon.

Leaving my purse on the sink, I head into the first stall to go pee. I hear the bathroom door open and then a masculine voice yells, "Talia! You in here?" Aris? What the hell is he doing in here?

I swing open the door and find him standing in front of the door.

"We need to go now."

"What? Why?" I'm so confused.

He grabs my arm and yanks me from the stall and out of the bathroom. "I'll explain once we're in the car. Kostas sent me to get you. There's been a threat and he needs to know you're safe."

"What about Michael and Tadd?" My head is spinning.

"They are the threat," Aris says as he opens the side door to the building. Something isn't right here.

"Aris, wait!" I shout, but he doesn't listen. I reach for my phone and realize it's still in my purse...in the bathroom. Shit! "Aris, I want to speak to Kostas," I demand, but he ignores me. When I dig my feet into the grass, refusing to walk, he turns around and whips a gun out.

"*Get in the fucking car, Talia,*" *he says.*

Instantly, my hands go to my stomach, fearful not only for myself, but for my baby. "Okay," I tell him. "Okay, just please don't shoot me."

The entire drive, my only thoughts are that there's a good chance I'll never see or speak to Kostas again. My last words to him were said in anger. He texted me to tell me he misses me, but I never texted him back. He'll never know how much I love him, and that I'm pregnant.

chapter
five

Kostas

THE ENTIRE THREE-HOUR FLIGHT FROM HERAKLION to Thessaloniki was difficult. Being trapped in my private plane with nothing but a stocked bar and a building rage, I was about to explode. I wanted to drown out my thoughts, but something keeps niggling at me—something I need to keep a clear head for. Like the answer is right in front of me, but I can't seem to put my finger on it.

Aris.

I want to say Aris has something to do with it, but he's afraid of me. Deep down, I know he is. Where he might willingly sleep with my wife just to show he could, he'd never kill her. And hide her away for a year, that's just bullshit Aris couldn't keep from me. I see him every day, all day. If he was hiding something huge about Talia, I'd know.

Wouldn't I?

When she was taken, I was blinded by determination to find her. Then, anger that I hadn't. Now, drowning in grief also known as fucking alcohol. Alcohol that Aris has no qualms about offering me anytime he's around.

Which is exactly why I need to keep a clear head. For the first time since she's been gone, I feel alert and aware. I didn't get to where I am today for being a blind fool.

I'm brooding on my thoughts while we hit the tarmac. The staff on the plane is accommodating, but I'm distracted by Talia. Always Talia. Once I step out of the plane, I'm irritated to see Phoenix leaned against a door-less Jeep. He's dressed casually in a pair of jeans and a black T-shirt showcasing all his tattoos and looking like a fucking escaped convict. I hate how much he looks like Talia. It's a painful reminder of my loss of her.

"Where's my car?" I grumble.

Phoenix shrugs and hops inside. I follow suit and climb into his metal death wish. I'm sure I look out of place in my Armani suit.

"Where are your men?" he asks, nodding at the plane.

"Where are yours?" I challenge back.

"I don't need them," he sneers, side-eyeing me like I'm a minnow he can easily scare away.

"Same," I bite back like the shark I am.

He smirks as he throws the Jeep into drive. We haul ass down the road into the city. It's been a while since I've come to meet him about the taxes. In the beginning I did, right after he took over for Niles, but then, when I was losing my ever-loving mind over Talia, Aris took care of business.

"Where are we going?" I demand upon realizing we're not headed toward the city where his office is.

"We can do business anywhere with our phones," he grunts out. "I'm hungry and I figured you are too."

It's noon and I didn't touch the refreshments on the flight. He's right, but I won't tell him that. He takes us to a small restaurant outside of the city. It has horrible curbside appeal, but the moment we exit the Jeep and I get a whiff of the savory garlic scents in the air, I know looks will be deceiving.

He greets the man up front and then ushers us to a dark corner booth. When he orders ouzo for the both of us, I change my order to water, which gets a lifted brow of surprise from him.

"Got a problem?"

His nostrils flare. "Nope."

As soon as the waiter runs off to fetch our drinks, Phoenix crosses his arms over his bulky chest and glowers at me.

"What?" I demand.

"Nothing," he sneers. "Just finally looking at the man who let my sister get taken. The same man who can't find her." He's pissed and his jaw muscle keeps flexing. If I had any thought that he'd taken her, it's squashed in this moment.

"You're looking at the man who will cut your throat for fucking disrespecting him," I growl, cracking my neck. "Watch your tongue, Nikolaides. Seems you forgot who you were talking to."

He grinds his teeth but relaxes his posture. "I just don't see how after all this time you haven't found her." His eyes narrow. "Unless you don't want her to be found."

"Me?" I snap. "If I wanted to get rid of her, I would have, and I'd gladly fucking tell you. I don't play little girl games."

"Then where the fuck is she?" he bellows, leaning forward, fire gleaming in his eyes. "Where the fuck is my sister?"

"Maybe she's with your father," I bite out. "Since you

can't find him and all. Maybe they're in the same magical hidden realm of the earth."

"What are you, a fuckin' fairy?" He shakes his head in frustration. "Dad is quiet, but if he had her, I'd know about it. For one, she'd drive him insane. He'd make me deal with her. Dad and Talia haven't gotten along in some time. I'm the peacemaker between the two."

The waiter brings our drinks and we order from the menu.

"What about those men who were supposed to be guarding her?" he asks bitterly. "Could they be in on it?"

I crack my knuckles before picking up my water and chugging it down. With a slam of the glass on the table, I level him with a hard glare. "We can't exactly ask them because I skinned them alive."

His brows furrow, but his eyes flash in appreciation. "Mom keeps yapping at me about the Galanis. You two chat an awful lot."

Fucking Melody.

"I want answers," I grit out.

"And Mom has them?" he challenges.

"Fuck no, she doesn't have them."

"Then why do you call her?"

Because she reminds me that Talia was a good woman who wouldn't just leave me.

"I check every lead." I lift my chin and meet his glare. "Can I say the same for you? What about the traffickers your dad was letting come through?"

"That shit ended when I took over. And I look for her every damn day, Kostas. I think that's the only fucking thing we have in common. Well, that and the inability to find her." He lets out a heavy sigh. "We'll find her."

I hate that we have a common goal. Nikolaides and Demetrious working together. It's a shitshow, clearly.

"*I'll* find her," I amend, my fierce stare begging him to argue.

"Glad you put the bottle down, man. I was tired of dealing with your arrogant brother. At least with you, I know what the fuck you intend to do. With him…" He frowns. "With him, I don't know what to think."

I'm not about to buddy up to Phoenix Nikolaides of all people and share a drink gossiping like two teenage girls over how much my brother is a sneaky bastard. No, I can think about that all by myself.

"Where's my money?" I demand, putting an end to all things Talia related.

He rolls his eyes like the fucking teenager I pegged him for and pulls out his phone. "I'll wire it over right now."

"I know, Selene," Aris grits out, his voice booming from his office. "I said I know, dammit."

Her annoying, screeching voice can be heard all the way into the hallway. I lean toward the door, hoping to catch her end of the conversation, but I hear nothing.

"Is that all?" he asks in a bored tone. "I have shit to do."

She must end the call because he slams the phone down on his desk and curses. I choose that moment to saunter in. He shoots me a weary look and then sighs heavily when I sit in front of his desk.

"Trouble in paradise?" I ask as I rest my ankle on my knee and lean back.

Ignoring me, he stands and checks the clock. "Your meeting with Phoenix went quickly. Back before five? Was he even there?"

"We had lunch and took care of business. He's not a cheating bastard like his weasel father."

Aris is rigid as he pours two drinks. When he sets down the tumbler with amber liquid in it, I pick up my glass and inhale the familiar scent.

"What's the special occasion?" I ask, swirling the alcohol around in the glass, eyeing him.

"Can't a man enjoy a nice bourbon with his brother and not need an excuse?" He knocks back the drink and dips his head, indicating for me to do the same.

I set it down and push it across the desk to him. "You look like you need it more than me."

His jaw clenches and he picks up the glass, slamming it back as well. "What do you want, Kostas?"

"My wife."

He tenses. "What the fuck do you want me to do about it?"

I shrug. "You asked me what I wanted. I told you. No need to get defensive."

"I'm not defensive," he growls.

I grew up with you, motherfucker. Don't play games with me. I taught them to you.

"Hmm," is all I say. "How come you never invite me over for these wonderful dinners your blow-up doll wannabe wife is always making?"

"I've invited you more times than I can count over the past year," he bites out. "Not my fault you chose to drink your dinner instead."

"Yes."

"Yes, what?"

"I accept your dinner invitation."

His gaze hardens. "You called my future fiancée a blow-up doll. Consider the invitation officially rescinded."

I lean forward in my seat. "Are you hiding something from me, brother?"

"Fuck off," he scoffs. "If you want to come to dinner, come to fucking dinner. Don't say I didn't warn you that Selene is a terrible goddamn cook and you'll probably die of food poisoning. Just make sure you give me a proper warning so she can get to the store and buy what she needs."

I stare at him for a long moment, watching him intently. Each facial tick. Every twitch of his lips. The slow reddening of his skin. Finally, once I've infuriated him to the point his carotid bounces along his neck, I stand.

"I'll let you know." I give him a wide grin that I know unnerves him. "Tell Selene I said hello."

Walking out of his office, I wonder how exactly he and Selene have made it this long. What does she offer him that makes him stay? He doesn't like her. At best, he barely tolerates her. Sure, she has tits and dick sucking lips, but you can find nicer women with those same physical attributes who don't sound like a donkey in heat.

I'm going to find out.

I settle back in my own office. Back to scouring video surveillance footage from the time Talia was with me around the time she was taken.

Taken.

I know it deep in my gut.

She wouldn't leave me.

Talia Demetriou may have been pissed as fuck, but she

loved me. She may have never spoken the words, but I felt them. Now that my head is clearing, I remember that part of our relationship without a doubt. With each look, each caress, each kiss, I knew.

And whoever took her will pay so fucking dearly for every second I've lost with her.

"I'm out of here," Aris says, peeking his head into my office. "Sorry about earlier. Selene is a bitch and she pisses me off."

"She must give amazing head," I say with a wicked smile.

He sneers. "I wish."

With a wave, he bolts before I can taunt him anymore.

So, the blow-up doll doesn't even suck cock well. Again, I wonder what the fuck sort of value she provides my brother with. He can get any fucking woman into his bed with his stupid smiles and charm. He certainly doesn't hang onto any woman for very long, much less a bitch like Selene. It's more than sex with my brother. It always is. I've seen him fuck the wife of a local gangster just to piss him off. I've seen him fuck around with the Minister of Police's daughter just to anger our father. I've seen him flirt with my wife and grab her ass because he wants to irritate me.

But Selene?

What's the end game?

Marriage, babies, white picket fence.

Yeah, fucking right.

I don't buy it for a second.

Swiveling around in my chair, I decide to dig into Selene a little. I'll find out what the blow-up doll has been up to. If the past year has taught me anything, it's that I can be quite the resourceful stalker when I want to be. I will tear apart Selene's past and present. I'll learn every damn detail about her. Who her family is. Who she's connected to. How she remains tethered to my brother.

And then I'll invite myself to fucking dinner.

chapter
six

Talia

TODAY IS THE DAY. I'VE SPENT THE LAST YEAR learning everything I can about where I am and what it will take to get out. I can either keep waiting, or I can make my move. At this point, I don't think there's any more preparing I can do. If it weren't for my precious cargo, I would've already tried to run, but with her in tow, I have to be twice as careful. I can't risk anything happening to her.

I'm sitting on the lounge chair out by the pool like I always am. Zoe is sleeping on the chair next to me on her belly, under the umbrella, sucking on her pacifier. My little girl loves the pool and sun. I bet she'll love the beach as well.

"I'm leaving for work," Aris says. "Do you need anything while I'm out?"

"I can have Selene pick up anything I need." I wave him off, knowing full well he won't let that happen anymore.

"She's not running any more errands for you," he says, just like I knew he would. "I'd hate for you and Selene to get into it again, and I come home to a bloodbath, so whatever you need, I'll pick it up."

Exactly what I was hoping he would say.

"Zoe hasn't been feeling well. Can you stop by the pharmacy to pick her up Tylenol?"

Aris's gaze lands on Zoe.

"She's teething," I add.

Her body shifts, and her pacifier falls from her lips, landing on the ground. I lean over to grab it, but I can't reach. "Can you hand me that, please?"

Aris picks it up off the floor and offers it back to me.

"It's dirty now." I shake my head. "Just throw it in the sink on your way out. I need to clean it before I give it back to her."

He shoves it into his front pocket. "What the hell does teething mean?"

I roll my eyes at his lack of parental knowledge. "It means she has teeth coming in and it hurts. Tylenol will help the pain."

"Fine, whatever. I'll pick it up on my way home."

"What time will that be?" When he glares, I add, "There are a lot of different kinds. I need you to take a picture of the different ones and send them to Selene so I can let you know which one."

Aris groans. "All right, I'll send her the pictures when I'm there. It probably won't be until five or six o'clock. I have a late meeting."

Perfect!

"Thank you," I say, dismissing him.

I wait for him to acknowledge his daughter before he walks away, but as always he doesn't. He never hugs or kisses or gives her any attention. Not that I'm complaining. I'd rather him stay the hell away from both of us. It's just that I find it odd. I think back to when I told him I was pregnant. In life, we have choices to make, and a lot of times when making a choice, it isn't about which choice is the right one, but which one will keep you alive…

"What the hell is wrong with you?" Selene screeches.

I lift my head from the inside of the toilet and glare at her. "Get out," I demand.

When she doesn't leave, I reach over and slam the door in her face, so I can finish throwing up in peace.

A few minutes later, I hear yelling in the other room. Aris must be home and he and Selene must be arguing. They're always arguing. Tiptoeing out to eavesdrop, I listen to what they're saying.

"You never said you planned to keep her here forever!" Selene whisper-yells. She's meaning to whisper, but her screeching voice carries.

"It's not forever," Aris explains. "It's only until my brother completely loses his shit and I take over the business. It's only been a month and my brother is already on a downward spiral."

"Then what are you going to do with her?"

"I haven't decided yet."

"Why don't you just kill her?" Selene whines. When Aris doesn't say anything, she says, "Aris…you don't like, like her, do you?"

"No, I don't like her, but I'm not going to kill her. Then I would be as much of a monster as my brother and father. Plus, she's pregnant, and it's either my baby or my brother's."

Oh my God! He knows! He knows I'm pregnant.

"She's what?" Selene screeches.

"Are you that fucking stupid?" Aris accuses. "Haven't you seen her throwing up since we brought her here?"

"And it could be yours?" Selene sounds like she's crying.

"Yes, now stop asking fucking questions. I need to go check

on her. When I come back, you need to be waiting for me in bed, with your legs spread and your mouth closed."

Footsteps across the wood floor have me scrambling back to my room. I've just dropped onto my bed, when Aris enters the room.

"Did you hear all of that?" he asks. My eyes widen in shock. "Good, then I don't have to repeat myself. You're pregnant. You know it and I know it. The question is, who is the father?"

I have a choice to make…right here, right now. If I tell him the baby is his, he can take it from me after he or she's born. If I say it's Kostas's, his hatred toward his brother can lead to him hurting it. Either way, I'm possibly screwed…

"It's yours," I admit.

"I call bullshit."

"Call it whatever you want." I shrug.

"If I find out you're lying, you will pay," he threatens.

"More than what I am now?" I challenge. "How long do you plan to keep this up, Aris? You know I heard you…you're not going to kill me, so what are you going to do? Keep me prisoner forever?" I scoff. "It's not like Kostas loves me. It was an arranged marriage." But even as I say the words, I refuse to believe them myself.

Aris chuckles darkly. "If you believe that, you're either dumb or blind. Until you, I didn't think my dear brother was even capable of loving anyone besides our mother, but I was wrong, which is why I took you."

"You took me because you think he loves me?" I don't get it. There has to be more to it.

"I took you because my brother destroys everything he touches and he's not going to get a chance to destroy you the way he destroyed our mother."

"Aris…" I begin, but I don't even know what to say. I hate

him. He raped me. He hurt me. He stole me. But my heart still breaks for the man who lost his mother. He's grieving and he's broken. He's not thinking clearly. My only hope is that he'll eventually come to his senses and let me go. And hopefully before this baby is born.

That was a year ago. He was a monster the day he took me, but now, it's as if he lives for destroying Kostas. He feeds off it. He's never going to let me go, which means I have no option but to run.

Zoe's tiny body stretches, telling me she's waking up. Her fisted hands rise above her head, and her chunky little body rolls to the side. Her beautiful blue eyes open and she grants me the most beautiful smile.

"Mommy's going to get us out of here, *cara mia*."

After I feed her and give her a bath, I get dressed in a comfortable outfit. I don't have any tennis shoes, so I make do with the pair of flip flops I have. I tie my hair back in a ponytail and then pull my bag out from under my bed.

When I tiptoe out of the room, I spot Selene on the couch watching TV. I need to be smart about this. Aris's dumb ass gave her a fucking gun. If I play this right, that gun can become an asset to me, but if it goes the other way, it can be the very thing that kills me.

I spot the gun on the end table next to her. Laying my bag down behind the counter, near the garage door, I set Zoe in her high chair. "Be a good girl," I whisper, placing a few cereal puffs on her tray.

"Hey, Selene," I call out.

"What?"

"Aris is supposed to text you a picture of the different Tylenols for Zoe when he's on his way home. Has he texted you yet?"

"No." Good, that means he's still at work. I have time.

Grabbing a frying pan from under the sink—yes, I'm about to be cliché as hell—I tiptoe up to Selene. I'm not sure if the pan will actually knock her out, but my intention is just to knock her off her game long enough to grab the gun. Once I have it, I can make a run for it and she won't be able to stop me.

I spot her phone in her lap. I want to grab it as well, but the gun is more important. Raising the heavy item to the side, I swing it as hard as I can at the side of her head.

"Ahhh!" she screams, falling from the couch and onto the floor. Without looking back at her, I snatch the gun off the table, dart back to the dining room, grab my daughter and bag, and haul ass. I quickly type in the code to the garage and it works! Using the key in my hand, I hit the fob to unlock the doors. The SUV lights up and I throw Zoe into the seat next to me. I hate that I don't have a car seat for her, but there's nothing I can do. With a click of the garage door, it rises, and we're free.

chapter
seven

Kostas

"BASIL?"
Adrian nods at my question as he pulls into the driveway of my father's estate. Once we're in park, he levels me with a hard glare. "Basil is loyal until the end."

There was a time when I almost questioned Basil's loyalties. When he did my brother's bidding. But when I'd looked in his eyes, I'd seen he was simply doing his job. For me. At the time, it felt like betrayal, but he was only doing what I'd asked long before.

Keep the enemies close.

And since I've always seen Aris as an enemy who happens to share my blood, my two best men, Basil and Adrian, have always kept an extra close eye on him.

"Any news from Basil then?" I ask, climbing out of Adrian's SUV.

He follows me and lets out a grunt. "Just normal comings and goings to and from the hotel. His house is pretty quiet during the day. On occasion, his slut leaves to grocery shop and shit."

"Galani? Niles? Does anyone besides the skank go in and out?"

"Nope, just her."

I don't like it. Feels too easy.

"Call him and have him see if he can find anything out from the hotel staff. I want this quiet and discreet. He'll need to do it in person."

"I'll text him and send him that way," Adrian assures me. "You sure dropping in on your dad like this is okay? What if we're interrupting his nap?"

I bite back a snort of laughter. Adrian, even though he's one of my best men, has always been more like a brother to me than Aris ever was. He's the only motherfucker I'll allow to get away with making fun of my father.

"Good to keep the old man on his toes," I say with a chuckle.

We walk through the massive estate looking for him. Things are strained with my father. He thinks I should run things differently than I do, but I do them the way I want and there's nothing he can do about it. He is my father, though, so I don't disrespect him by just ignoring him. I make sure he's taken care of and check in on him from time to time like a good son does.

When I hear moans coming from down the hallway, I pause to shoot Adrian a confused look. I stalk down the hall to the source of the sound. At my father's door, I hesitate for a fraction of a second before pushing into the room. The sight before me has bile crawling up my throat.

Some young blond bitch is riding my father in my parents' bed. He may not be able to walk, but his big hands dig into her pale ass as he urges her to fuck him. She moans and rocks her hips. All I can do is see fucking red. My mother has barely been dead a year and he's fucking sluts in their bed.

"Father," I boom. "What the fuck?"

The woman cries out in surprise and slides off him. Her big tits bounce as she scrambles to find her dress that's been discarded on the floor. I stand there glaring at my father, who looks like a pathetic old man with his dick at half-mast.

"The money's in the usual place, Lyssa," he grumbles out, his eyes cutting to mine as he pulls the covers over himself. "Why the hell are you here unannounced?"

Money?

My father is fucking a goddamn prostitute?

I block the doorway when the blonde comes my way. She casts a glance over at Father, as if to ask him what she's supposed to do.

"A whore, Father? Really?" I guess it's better than him actually dating so soon after my mother. The fact it's just sex seems to soften the blow a little. Still pisses me off. Feels like just yesterday my mother was buried.

"Lyssa is more than a whore," Father bites out. "She's a friend. We go way back."

Pull the fucking brakes. "What?"

"What'd I miss?" Aris demands from behind me, finally gracing us with his presence. "Fucking gross. Do I smell pussy in Dad's room?"

Father's face burns red with fury when Aris scoots past me and into the room. My brother shakes his head.

"Why are you two here?" Father barks out.

"Kostas said we should meet with you," Aris says, his gaze raking down Lyssa. "Who are you?"

"Father's whore," I hiss.

"Another one?" Aris asks.

I snap my head his way. "What do you mean another one?"

Aris sneers at me. "Why are you acting like this is the first one you knew about?"

Darting my eyes back to my father, I fist my hands. "So Mamá dies and you fuck as many whores as you can? I didn't think your dick even worked anymore."

Aris snorts. "Since Mamá died? Where the hell have you been all our lives, man?"

All our lives?

He's fucking with me.

Our mother may have cheated on Father, but my father was loyal to her. He's the whole goddamn reason why I'm so obsessed with loyalty. It's been drilled into my head for as long as I can remember.

"Lyssa's been on the payroll for years, Kostas. Don't be obtuse." My father scowls my way.

Obtuse?

Don't be fucking obtuse?

The woman in question shrugs as if it's no big deal to fuck a man three times her age who can't even go to the bathroom by himself.

"What about Mamá?" I hiss.

Father's face softens. "I know you're having a rough time since your wife left you—"

"She didn't fucking leave me," I roar, making the woman jump.

Aris seems pleased as hell to see me lose my shit over our father's indiscretions. The smile is wiped off his face when his phone rings. As he scrambles to pull his phone from his pocket, something hits the floor and bounces. A pacifier. For a baby. I stare at it in confusion as he picks it up and shoves it back in his pocket. He answers the phone in a hateful tone that makes me wonder, again, if he even likes that woman he's shacked up with. His dumbass bitch can be heard screeching on the other line. He pales and then pure fury morphs the charming Demetriou prince into a dragon. For a split second, his hateful eyes find mine, and if they had the power, he'd slay me where I stand.

"Emergency with Selene," he growls out as he pushes past me, knocking his shoulder into mine on the way out.

Lyssa takes his exit as her cue to leave as well. As she steps past me, I grab her bicep. She shoots me a panicked look.

"You fucked him while he was married to my mother?" I demand in a cold tone.

Her eyes flicker over to my father, but he doesn't save or defend her. I can see it in her eyes. The answer is clear as day. Yes.

"Lyssa is a tigress in bed, son. You can't tell me you haven't fucked anyone since Talia left."

"She. Didn't. Leave. Talia was taken."

"And with all those pretty maids walking around, you're telling me you didn't get your dick sucked not once this entire time?"

"I'm fucking married, Father!"

He snorts. "Marriage is something for everyone else to see. It's an illusion of happiness. Everyone fucks around. Even me."

But what about loyalty to your motherfucking wife? He's drilled loyalty into my head since I was old enough to learn what the word meant. It was all a fucking lie.

"Adrian," I bark out.

His heavy footsteps thud down the hall. "Sir?"

"Take Lyssa home. The *long* way."

He doesn't argue or balk at my orders. Adrian's a good man. Without explanation, he'll do what needs doing and that's burying this dirty little secret today.

I release her once he has her in his grip. He stalks away with her. My gaze falls to the stack of bills on the dresser—money she'll never touch again.

"You lied to me," I tell him, bitterness creeping into my tone. "My entire life I thought you were devoted to my mother."

"Don't be an idiot," he bites out. "You know your mother slept with Niles fucking Nikolaides of all people."

I couldn't understand it before. How she'd even step out of her marriage in the first place. But now I wonder. Did she know about my father's whores? Was she trying to hurt him like he hurt her?

"When did you take your first whore after marriage?" I ask, my voice deadly and cold.

He glowers at me and his jaw clenches. My eyes skirt over to the pillow beside him. My mother's pillow. A smear of Lyssa's lipstick taints the pillowcase. A framed picture of my mother on the nightstand faces the bed as though she's punished even in death to take my father's abuse.

"This is none of your business," he says, cutting through my thoughts.

Slamming my gaze back on his, I crack my neck. "Everything's my business now."

His nostrils flare at my words. The double meaning behind them. "I'm still in charge here," he seethes. "You're my son, but you mustn't forget who built this empire from the ground up."

His skin is grayish and his muscle tone is gone. Father is

nothing but a decaying bag of bones. It's a wonder his dick still works because his legs sure as fuck don't. He's a pathetic excuse for a man lying in his bed, unable to do a goddamn thing but listen to what I have to say.

"You're not in charge," I state coolly. "I've been running this shit ever since the accident last year."

"Accident? Your mother's attempted murder was an accident?"

"You provoked her," I bark.

"You're insane, boy."

I crack my neck again before sliding my jacket off and draping it over the back of his wheelchair. His eyes track my movements. When I unbutton my shirt at the cuff, he narrows his gaze.

"You're going to beat an old man up? What kind of son are you?" Despite his rage, fear glimmers in his eyes.

I slowly roll my sleeve up to my elbow. The muscles in my forearm flex and the veins throb with the need to inflict pain.

"You're my father," I hiss. "I'd never strike you."

He relaxes some, but his weary gaze remains fixed on my actions. I take my time rolling up my other sleeve as well.

"This is my empire, Kostas. *I* am the Demetriou name. You can't forget that," he tells me with false bravado.

"What happens when you're gone?" I ask, already knowing the answer. "That's right, everything goes to me."

"To both my sons," he lies.

Now that I don't have the alcohol buzzing through me and wreaking havoc on my brain, I took the time this morning to analyze every facet of my life. According to our family attorney, I'm still listed as sole heir to the hotels, the Demetriou fortune, everyfuckingthing.

"I used to think loyalty was the backbone of our family name." I make a tsk of disapproval. "I was wrong. It's lies. Lies are woven into every aspect of our lives like fucking snakes in a garden." I smile at him. "It's time to cut the head off the biggest viper in the nest."

"You won't cut me open like I'm one of our victims in the cellar," he growls. "I know you better than that, Kostas. In case you've forgotten, I'm your father. We're exactly the same."

"You're right," I admit. "I won't make you bleed." My gaze drifts to my mother's picture. "But where you're wrong is that we're not the same. You may have destroyed Mamá, but you will not destroy me." I flash the picture a sinister smile. "This is for what you couldn't finish, Mamá. I heard your dying wishes loud and clear. I won't let you down."

"What the f—"

Father's words are silenced when I reach across him to grab Mamá's pillow that's stained with another woman's lipstick. I shove the fluffy pillow down on his face. His attempts to drag the pillow away and then trying to hit at me are futile. I'm a monster. A motherfucking fire-breathing beast. He's a lowly snake in the grass waiting to be stomped on. With my eyes on my mother's picture, I smother my father with her pillow. He should have died when she shot him. It's my duty to end the disloyal bastard's existence. My father struggles for longer than I expect given his weakened state. I'll give him that. At one time, I thought he was the most powerful man in the world. I fucking looked up to him. And the way he looked after Mamá and loved her was admirable.

Lies.

All lies.

Mamá may have broken my heart when she killed

herself, but she opened my eyes. She tugged on the veil of deception my father had slipped over my head. She made me see there was more to life than money and mayhem.

Love.

She wanted me to see that love was more important than so called loyalty.

It was hard to believe considering she'd deceived my father, but now learning he was the root of everything, I feel as though I finally understand her message.

Love is everything.

Love is loyalty and forgiveness and hope.

The rest is just bullshit.

I'm not sure how long I hold the pillow over Father's face, but when he's stopped moving for some time, I pull the pillow away and gently put it back where it goes beside him. His eyes are glazed over but still open. I slide my fingers down over his lids, closing them. When I check his pulse, I learn he's, in fact, dead.

I feel nothing.

Not victory or sadness.

Fucking nothing.

Once I undo my sleeves, I pull my jacket back on. I grab the picture of my mother and then head downstairs. As I wait for Adrian to return to pick me up, I make some coffee and sit in the kitchen on a barstool. My mind drifts to times when Mamá would busy herself in here, despite the fact we had a cook, and try to give us some semblance of a normal life. She'd sing and teasingly brush flour on my nose as we baked together whenever Father was away on business. I loved those simple moments with her. When I forgot I was destined to be a mob boss and could just be her little boy. Back when I would dream of racing cars in Monte

Carlo and surfing with sharks. I was innocent and my father ripped that innocence away from me no matter how hard my mother clutched me to her, trying to preserve it.

I'm not innocent anymore.

But it doesn't mean I can't be the man my mother would have wanted me to be.

I'll never be good, that's for damn sure. I'll be good enough for love, though, just as she would have wanted. I'm good enough for Talia. And one day soon I'll find her.

"Good afternoon," Tammy, a nurse of Father's, greets as she enters. "How's Ezio?"

I clench my jaw and think about my mother. About how devastated I was when she pulled that trigger on herself. Real emotion shines in my eyes as I regard the nurse.

"He went to be with Mamá during his nap," I choke out.

"Oh, honey," Tammy cries out. "He died?"

I nod and the woman hugs me. I let her. To be honest, it feels good to be drawn in a motherly hug. Resting my chin on top of her gray head, I let out a heavy sigh.

"You know Father. He's so proud. It was his wish to keep his death quiet when the time came. Cremation. No service."

She pulls away and furrows her brows as she cups my cheeks. "I'm discreet, honey. We'll get it sorted together. Just tell me what I need to do."

"Let me be the one to tell my brother," I mutter. "To tell everyone."

"Do what you have to do, dear. I'll go upstairs and make sure he's decent."

"Thanks, Tammy. Don't worry about not getting paid. I'll have Aris wire you a bonus as a thank you for all you've done."

She smiles at me. "The Demetriou men are good men. I'm proud to have worked for this family."

We're bad men, but I don't want to spoil the moment with the truth.

I give her a nod, dismissing her. I sip on my coffee as I watch out the window for Adrian. It takes a quick call to Franco to have him come deal with Father's body, and another call to the family attorney, Thomas, to inform him of the official change of power. The next person to know needs to be Aris. And it'll need to be told in person. No one wants to hear their father is dead over the phone.

I'll go back to the office, deal with some other affairs, and then drop by this evening to deliver the news over dinner. Kill two birds with one stone. It's time to see what lies Aris has been telling, and if I know my brother, the lies are plentiful. I've just never really cared too much until now.

But now?

Now I care a whole lot.

I'm going to uncover every hidden truth.

And once everything is all laid out on the table, I'm going to make those who've been playing games against me pay.

Blood. Sweat. Tears. Limbs.

They. Will. Pay.

Every last one of them.

chapter
eight

Talia

As I drive down the driveway, the winding road takes us to the front gate. I hold my breath, praying it opens from the inside. Over the last year, I've planned the best I could, but because I couldn't see this far, I could only plan to leave. As the gate slowly moves to the side, I spot a black SUV driving up behind me. What the hell? There's no way Selene caught up that fast. When I glance in my rearview mirror, I spot a man in the driver's seat.

Without waiting for the gate to completely open, I press my foot on the gas, refusing to let this guy, whoever he is, catch up to us. Damn it! How did I not see him? Aris must have someone guarding the house, but he's never been where I can see him. I've checked so many times.

Zoe sits in the passenger seat, babbling to me, as I drive down the curvy roads. I have no clue where I am or where I'm going, but my goal is to get to the city so I can ask someone for help.

I look in the mirror again, and the SUV is catching up

to me. There's no way I'm going to make it out of these hills unless I pick up my speed. I glance over at my little girl and she smiles up at me. I need to protect her. I need to get us to safety.

With one hand on the wheel, I reach over and grab the seatbelt, drawing it across her lap. It's not ideal, but it's the best I can do in a shitty situation. I press my foot harder on the gas and increase my speed, but when I glance back, the SUV is less than a car away from me now. I'm never going to make it.

All this work, all this planning, and I missed something. I slam my fist against the steering wheel. I was so fucking close. Aris is never going to give me this much leeway again. I had one chance and I messed it up.

The front of the SUV hits my back bumper and the vehicle swerves.

No!

My eyes briefly fly to Zoe to make sure she's okay before they're back on the road.

I can do this. I can get away.

He lays down on the horn. He wants me to pull over. I make it around the bend before his bumper hits mine again. Zoe lurches forward and I use my hand to hold her against the seat. I can't keep going. Whoever this guy is isn't going to stop until I pull over, and I can't risk him driving me off the road. I can't put my daughter's life in jeopardy.

Prickly tears of defeat burn in my eyes as my heart rate races.

I don't want to give up. I'm not ready to give up.

When my gaze flits back over to my little girl, my eyes land on the gun in the center console, and my thoughts go to Kostas. He wouldn't even hesitate. If he were in my shoes right now, he would kill this asshole. It's me and Zoe or him. And I'm choosing me and Zoe.

I can do this.

I am Talia Demetriou, wife of a fucking mob boss.

I pull over on the side of the road and get out, not wanting him to make it over to where my daughter is. I flip the safety off and wait for him to exit the vehicle. And when he does, I'm momentarily stunned. Estevan Galani. The man my husband shot in the dick. Of course Aris would hire a damn enemy to guard his house. Those two roaches deserve each other. At least one of them is about to be exterminated. Kostas can deal with Aris.

Pointing the gun right at him, I pull the trigger.

Pop!

The gunshot echoes loudly, making my ears ring and Zoe scream. He stumbles back, but doesn't fall. Fucking damn roach. Crimson swells where I clipped his shoulder.

"You bitch!" he growls, pulling his own gun out.

Before he has a chance to hurt either one of us, I pull the trigger again and again and again. Until he hits the ground. I stare in shock at the bullet holes littering his chest.

I shot him.

I fucking shot him.

My hands are shaking, and my body is numb. I just killed a man. One who would've done the same to me, I remind myself. As I turn around to run back to my vehicle, I run right into a hard wall. No, not a wall…

"That wasn't very smart," Aris says.

I lift the gun to shoot him, but before I can, he snatches it out of my hand.

"Get your daughter from the vehicle, now," he barks, "and get your ass in my car."

My eyes dart around me, wondering if there's any way I can still escape. There are woods on both sides, but there's no way I'll make it to grab Zoe and run without Aris stopping me.

As if reading my thoughts, he snarls, "Don't even think about it. Get your fucking ass in the car."

We walk a few feet, when I hear a moaning sound. That asshole is seriously not dead?

Aris hits me with a hard glare, then stalks over to him. With the same gun I used, he points it at Estevan's forehead and shoots. His brains explode, and I lose everything in my stomach.

Everything's a blur as I pull Zoe from the seat and clutch her to my chest. I can feel the tears falling, but I'm numb to them. I sit in the front seat of Aris's Porsche and inhale my sweet baby's hair.

Please don't hurt us.

Please don't hurt us.

Zoe is no longer crying now that I'm soothing her, and she babbles to Aris when he falls into the front seat. He says something to her before peeling out and taking us back in the direction we came. When we get back to the house, Selene is sitting on the couch with an icepack pressed to the side of her head.

"You fucking bitch!" she hisses.

"Enough!" Aris booms. "I have to go clean up the fucking mess you made," he says to me. "And since you can't play nice with Selene, and I can't risk you trying to escape, you can now consider yourself a prisoner."

"Oh, *now* I can?" I scoff. "I've been your damn prisoner for the last year."

Aris smirks wickedly. "No, Talia, you were my guest. Now, you're about to see what it means to be my prisoner." He forces me into my room and I set Zoe in her crib, so I can deal with him, but when I turn around, the door is slammed shut and it's locked from the outside. Motherfucker! I race through the bathroom to see if that door is unlocked, but as I twist the knob, the lock clicks in place. He locked me inside! With a hopeless sigh, I slide down the door and press my head against the wood. This was it. This was my one chance. And it's gone. And now we're worse off than before.

Zoe's babbling has me standing and going to her. Lifting her out of her crib, I bring her over to my bed and lay her next to me. Holding her tight, I stroke her soft black hair until her eyes flutter closed and she falls asleep, and then I let myself fall asleep as well.

Knock. Knock. Knock.

My eyes shoot back open.

Knock. Knock. Knock.

Is someone knocking on the door? Nobody ever knocks on the door. Carefully edging off the bed, so I don't wake Zoe, I go to the window to see who's there. I can't see the front door, but I can see part of the driveway.

Maserati GranTurismo.

Charcoal-gray.

Black on black tires.

It can't be… There's only one man I know who has that exact car…

Kostas.

He's here. He's going to save us.

And just like that my hope is restored. Like a sliver of light illuminating my dark world, I can finally see again. I'm chasing it. Running toward the brightness.

I don't bother trying to open the window because I already know it's nailed shut, but I watch the vehicle, refusing to look anywhere else. The house is quiet. Selene must be outside talking to him. Does he know I'm here? I listen with bated breath until I hear the front door close.

Is he in here? I can't decide whether to abandon the window to go bang on the door, or stay by the window to catch a glimpse of him. Before I make a decision, though, I see him. In his signature suit, he stalks back to his car. Strong, powerful, handsome. I miss him so much it hurts. My palms hit the glass, hoping he will somehow hear me.

"Kostas!" I cry out, knowing it's futile.

His hand freezes on the handle, and he turns. Did he hear me?

"Kostas!" I yell again, my palms smacking so hard against the window, they're stinging. "Kostas! I'm here!"

His eyes assess the area before he opens the door and folds himself into his car. And then he's gone. And as quickly as the light came, it's now gone. Leaving me stumbling through the darkness alone.

A flood of tears gush down my cheeks as I watch my fucking husband's headlights get farther and farther away until they're completely gone.

One year and he's never been here. And when he finally does show up, I'm locked in my fucking room. He must know something. That's why he came here. He's looking for me. I know he is.

Oh, Kostas, you're so close. Don't give up, please. I'm here, waiting for you.

Crawling back to my bed, I snuggle back up with Zoe. She's awake now from me yelling, but as soon as I comfort her, she falls back asleep. Such a good girl. She deserves more than this. More than being held prisoner.

"It's okay, *cara mia*, we're going to be saved."

"Wake up," Aris barks. His voice startles Zoe and she lets out a loud cry. I glare daggers his way, but he doesn't care. "It's time to eat."

"I'm not hungry. I'll eat later."

"You'll eat now, or you won't eat at all," he threatens.

After changing Zoe's diaper, I grab a bottle to bring out to the table. When I get out there, Selene and Aris are both at the table, already eating their dinner. Steak, broccoli, and potatoes au gratin. He must've brought it home because Selene can barely make grilled cheese without burning the shit out of it.

When I walk past the table, Aris's hand lands on my thigh. "I'm going to grab a jar of food for Zoe."

"I'll get it," he says. "Sit down."

"Fine." I set Zoe in her high chair and place a bib around her neck. She giggles her delight, slapping her tray in excitement.

Aris brings over a jar of sweet potatoes and a spoon and sets them in front of Zoe before sitting back down. Zoe grabs the spoon and bangs it against her tray. "Da-da-da," she babbles. Aris's eyes meet mine. "Da-da," she continues. She's too young to know what she's saying. She's just making random noises, but the thought that she's calling him da-da has me feeling sick to my stomach.

I open the jar and begin feeding it to Zoe, when Aris finally speaks. "Until further notice, you will be locked in your room while I'm not home."

"Are you seriously going to keep me and your *daughter* locked in a room for hours at a time?" I shoot him a glare.

"Or I can have Selene take care of her and just keep *you* locked up…" Aris smirks with a shrug.

Selene huffs, and when I look at her, the entire side of her face is black and blue. I can't help the grin that splays across my face. That pan got her good.

"Fuck you," she spits. "Hope it was worth it."

"Oh, it was," I volley. "Looks like you're going to be needing another visit to the plastic surgeon. Probably for the best since they fucked up your face the first time around anyway."

"Aris, haven't you had enough of this bitch? Your brother was here today! He's snooping around and he's going to find her."

My gaze swings over to Aris, whose eyes widen.

"Kostas was here?" he growls, venom in his tone. "Why the fuck didn't you tell me?"

"I just did!" Selene screeches. "And he was asking questions. How long until he figures out you have his precious Talia? Just kill her already. We can take your baby and run."

At her words, I snatch the steak knife off the table and dart around behind her, putting her into a headlock before she can even think about what to do. With the knife against her throat, I meet Aris's gaze. "You let this woman touch my fucking baby and I will slice her throat."

"Enough," Aris stands. "Put the damn knife down." He steps toward me and I press the blade against Selene's throat.

"Aris!" she cries.

"Talia, calm down." Aris's eyes dart over to Zoe. When he steps toward her, I have no choice but to let go of Selene.

"Don't you touch her." With the knife still in my hand, I lift my daughter out of her high chair.

"She's my daughter too," Aris sneers. "And if I want to fucking touch her, I will."

He steps toward me and I take a step back. When he doesn't make another move, I continue backing up until I'm back in my room.

"We'll deal with this tomorrow," Aris says. "Clearly shit needs to change around here."

Without saying another word to him, I slam the door in his face, and then I pray to God that Kostas comes back for me and Zoe. Because if he doesn't, I'm not sure how much longer Aris is going to keep me alive.

chapter
nine

Kostas

I'M SEEING SHIT.

Losing my goddamn mind.

It. Was. Her.

I pinch the bridge of my nose and debate on what to do next. Either I can drive my ass back over to Aris's house and find out for sure, or I can sit here like a pussy wondering.

I'm just downing the rest of my dinner in a restaurant between the hotel and Aris's, when my phone rings. I could answer it and tell him right now that Father is dead. Most days, I'm a dick, but even I won't do that to him. No, I'll do like I intended when I drove over there earlier and tell him to his face. I send his call to voicemail. Seconds later, I get a text.

Aris: *Did you come by?*

The next text comes immediately after.

Aris: *What did you need?*

Aris: *Want to meet up?*

I groan and before I can reply, he continues blowing up my phone.

Aris: Selene said you had something important to talk about.

Aris: I don't hit her if that's what you're wondering. She fell.

Fell?

I'm not stupid. That bitch did more than fall. Someone bashed her fucking head in.

My mind drifts to earlier.

"What do you want?"

I lift my brow and sneer. "Excuse me?"

"How did you even get on the property?"

"I used the fucking code," I growl. "Were you trying to keep me out?"

Selene has the sense to stand down once she remembers who she's talking to and shakes her head in vehemence. I'm not some pushover like Aris. I will drag her skinny ass back to the cellar by her fake-red hair to remind her if I need to. Luckily, she replaces her snotty expression with one of healthy fear.

"What'd you do to your face?" I ask, nodding to indicate the giant ass bruise that looks fresh and is forming beneath her swollen-red flesh.

She purses her fat lips before letting out a huff of exasperation. "I fell."

Says every woman hiding the fact she's being hit by a man.

"The floor must fucking hate you."

"And I hate the fucking floor too," she snarls out. "Aris went to...run an errand. Is there something I can help you

with?" Her venom bleeds away as her green eyes skim down the front of my body in appreciation.

"Nah," I grunt out. "I'll come by another time."

When I turn to leave, she grips my bicep. "Call him first."

I glower over my shoulder at her. "Are you his keeper?"

"W-What? No. He's just always busy and rarely home. You should call him first so you don't miss him."

"Hmmm," is all I say before breaking from her hold and walking away.

The door slams shut behind me. I'm almost to my car when I feel eyes on me. Stopping, I turn and look back toward Aris's massive house.

Blond hair.

A woman.

Talia?

But when I squint, the vision vanishes. That's all she is to me now. A fucking ghost.

God, I miss her. I'd give up my entire fortune to have her in my arms just so I could inhale her hair. I don't know that I even remember what she smells like anymore. The fact I'd give up everything to see her once more is disappointing. I'd always thought of myself as someone powerful. Someone who doesn't need anyone else.

Like my father.

Turns out, I was never like him.

I was always like my mother.

After I pay my bill, I leave the restaurant and inhale the early fall air. The sun has gone down. It's only just hitting me that my father really is gone. I extinguished him from this earth. Remorse or guilt should flood through me, but all I feel is relief. I was never allowed to figure out who the real Kostas was. He bred me into his monster. For his favor over my brother, I gladly heeded every instruction. And now I'm nothing but a shell. I don't want to do anything but fill up my entire being with her.

My wife.

Fuck, I'm losing it.

I need to tell Aris Father is dead and then move the fuck on. At some point, I will have to accept that Talia probably is too. A year is a long time—too long in my world—to be missing without a word. If she'd run away, I would've known about it. Someone would have tattled.

She's dead.

It's a hard pill to swallow.

One I have trouble choking down because too much uncertainty rattles around inside my head.

I pull up to the gate and punch in the same four digits Aris uses for everything. It'd been a no-brainer when I'd come earlier, but after the way Selene acted, it made me wonder if they were trying to keep me away.

So I wouldn't see that he beats on her?

Like I give a shit. She probably runs her fucking mouth too much and earned that knock to the head. We're villains, not goddamn heroes. Who am I to judge?

No, if they wanted to keep me away, it's for other reasons.

Reasons that niggle and tug at me, desperate to be thrown out in the open.

I pull up to the house and park in the driveway. Lights shine from a window in front of the house and then some upstairs. Climbing out, I pause to listen. Nothing but the breeze picking up as a fall storm rolls in. The wind whistles and I scent the promise of rain.

As I walk toward the front door, my eyes drift of their own accord to the window where I'd thought I'd seen someone. When a figure stands in front of the glass, the light shining around them, my heart does a squeeze in my chest.

I blink several times to clear my vision.

Still there.

Blond hair. A woman.

I'm storming over to the window before I can stop myself. Wide, teary blue eyes meet mine. Familiar blue eyes. Her blue eyes.

No. Fucking. Way.

"*Zoí mou.*" *My life.*

Her bottom lip trembles—lips I've ached to kiss for so long it's maddening. This can't be real. She can't be staring back at me from behind the glass of Aris's fucking house. It makes no sense. I'm truly losing my goddamn mind.

"Kostas."

The voice of an angel carries through the glass, shattering what little bit was left of my heart. She's alive. She's alive and well and standing right in fucking front of me.

"Open the window," I rumble, my words barely a whisper.

She looks over her shoulder and shakes her head. "I can't."

Fury swells up inside me to incredible heights. "Open the fucking window."

Tears race down her cheeks as she moves her plump lips rapidly, speaking in hushed tones that are somehow supposed to send me away.

I'm not going anywhere.

Bending, I try to open the window, but it's locked shut.

I point at the lever and thump the glass hard. "Talia, unlock the window."

"I can't."

I slam my fist on the window, making her cry out in surprise.

"I said open the window or so help me I'm coming right through it," I growl. "Open it. Talia, open it!"

When she steps away, turning to look toward the door again, I lose it. With a swift swing of my elbow, I bust out a pane of glass. I reach my hand inside and flip the lock. It still won't open.

Talia rushes back over to me and reaches her hand through the glass pane. Her touch is soft as she runs her fingertips along my cheek. "I can't, Kostas. It's nailed shut."

Nailed shut.

What in the actual fuck?

I grip her wrist in a tight grip and then lean in to kiss her palm. I'm afraid to let her go because she might just fucking vanish again, but I need to get to her. I need to hold her.

"Stand back," I order.

She jerks her hand back and steps away from the window. I could go beat on the front door, make my brother answer, and demand he hand her over, but right now I'm on a one-track mission. Get to my fucking wife. Hiking my leg up, I kick hard along the metal strip along the middle of the window.

Crunch. Crunch. Crunch.

I kick over and over until the metal frame of the window is mutilated and folded in, glass broken all over at my feet. Once I've weakened it enough, I slam my shoulder into what's left of the window and send it and myself careening to the floor. I'm on my feet in the next second, prowling after Talia.

Anger. Betrayal. Sadness. Confusion.

My emotions spin around and around like a fucking tornado. I'm ready to cause massive destruction. I want to destroy everyone.

Gripping Talia's throat, I walk her back until her ass hits the door. I bury my nose in her hair, inhaling the scent of her shampoo mixed with her natural sweat. The growl rumbling through me is a possessive one bordering on rage. My thumb traces along the vein in her throat that's pulsing rapidly.

"Why?" It's the only word I have. It's a loaded question.

"I don't know."

I pull away and glower at her. "You want to be here?"

She shakes her head, fat tears rolling down her red cheeks.

"You're trapped here?"

A sob escapes her. "We have to get out of here."

I'm distracted by her bottom wobbly lip, and now that I know she's a captive for some fucked-up reason, I need her like I need my next breath.

"*Zoí mou,*" I whisper over her lips. "I've fucking missed you."

Slamming my lips to hers, I take the kiss I've been craving since the moment I let her walk away from me after our fight. I slide my hand up to her jaw, gripping her tight so she can't escape me as I ravish her perfect mouth. She moans as I devour her lips and tongue. Her fingers thread through my hair, cradling me to her. My other hand finds her hip and I slide it to her ass that's fleshier than I remember. I want to strip her down right here and inspect every part of her body to see if she's changed. A choked sound escapes her when I rotate my hips, rubbing my aching cock against her body.

"Da-da-da-da."

I freeze mid-kiss. When I hear an excited shriek, I yank away from Talia, my head darting around to find the source. My eyes land on a baby. A fucking baby. With bright blue eyes like Talia.

Talia steps toward me. "Kostas, listen—"

"A baby?" I growl, snapping my head back to look at her.

Her chin is tilted up and her watery eyes are fierce. "My baby."

I stumble back, feeling as though she's kicked me in the gut. A baby. Her baby. And Aris's? The baby makes another sound and I can't help but look over at her.

"Kostas," she says, walking over to the baby and picking it up. "Her name is Zoe."

All the air is sucked from my lungs as I snap my eyes back to the little girl.

Zoe.

Zoe.

Zoe.

"Zoe, *zoí mou*?"

Tears well in her eyes and she nods rapidly.

Holy shit.

Our baby.

We had a fucking baby.

All happy thoughts come to a screeching halt. I'm going to murder them. Slaughter both Aris and Selene. Right the fuck now.

"Kostas," Talia says, her voice shaking as she rushes over to me. "We have to go. Now."

The baby—Zoe—grabs the lapel of my suit and tries to pull it her way. I'm stunned for so many fucking reasons. All I can do is lean forward and inhale her dark hair.

Mine.

She's fucking mine.

They both are.

I'm eerily calm as I say, "I'm going to kill them."

"And I want you to," she whispers. "But we need to get Zoe someplace safe. Selene has a gun and she's not afraid to use it."

My mind wars with what I should do. The mobster inside me craves violence and blood and vengeance. The husband—*and father*—in me has an overwhelming urge to protect what's mine.

I can't have both.

Not in this moment.

So I choose them.

Pressing a soft kiss to Talia's lips, I murmur, "Let's go."

She hands me Zoe and I freeze. I've never held a damn baby. But Talia doesn't give me a chance to argue. The moment the tiny flailing thing is in my arms, Talia starts throwing stuff into a diaper bag. I can't help but hold Zoe close to me, kissing the top of her head.

Those motherfuckers kept this from me.

My wife. My baby. My goddamn family.

Rage surges violently inside of me, but I don't unleash it. Talia's right. I need to get them out of here and make a plan. I'll get the full story of what's happened and then shed blood when my family is safe. Within minutes, Talia is packed and we head out the broken window. She rushes over to my car and tosses the bag into the backseat. Then, she takes Zoe from me and sits in the front seat. As soon as

I'm seated and the engine fires up, the reality begins to sink in.

They're here.

I have them.

My first instinct is to call Melody. She doesn't know she has a granddaughter. The fact I want to call her should be alarming, but it's not. Not after spending the last year leaning on this woman for emotional support under the thin veil of questioning her on the whereabouts of my wife.

"Hurry," Talia says. "I didn't make it very far last time."

Despite her words, I don't gun it like I normally would. The baby doesn't have a seat. I finally understand the term precious cargo.

"You escaped?"

"Today," she breathes. "Finally. But he caught me." A pained sound rattles from her. "I shot someone, Kostas. I was protecting me and Zoe. H-He's dead. I'm sorry, but I'd do it again and again to protect her."

Reaching over, I give her thigh a squeeze. "I don't know what the hell has been happening right under my goddamn nose, but I want you to tell me everything." I shoot her a hard look. "And don't ever apologize for protecting our little girl."

Our little girl.

I'm in fucking awe right now.

A dad. I'm a dad.

And I have my wife back.

chapter
ten

Talia

FOR THE FIRST TIME IN OVER A YEAR, I CAN FINALLY take a deep breath of relief. Oxygen can enter my lungs without a lump the size of a boulder blocking my airway.

Because Kostas is here.

He didn't give up on me, and he found me and Zoe, and we're finally safe.

Thunder booms and lightning strikes, lighting up the entire sky. The clouds open above us, and rain begins to pelt the windshield. It almost feels metaphorical, as if the rain is washing away every bad moment from this past year, hydrating the life back into us. For the last year, I've felt dead inside, but now, with Kostas here, I feel like my body is finally thriving once again. I was struggling to make it through each day, pieces of me slowly dying, but now I'm alive and can breathe easy.

Zoe's head lands on my shoulder, her body snuggling into my chest. When she babbles softly, Kostas glances over at the two of us, and for a brief moment our eyes meet. His hazel eyes tell me everything I need to know. Everything is going to be okay. He's going to make sure of it.

"When we get home, you're going to tell me everything that's happened," he says.

But my thoughts are stuck on one word. *Home.*

We're going home. Where we belong. Where we should've been this entire time.

And then it hits me. Home is the Pérasma Hotel. The hotel Aris part owns.

"We can't go back there." I sit up straight, and Zoe whines. It's late and she's exhausted. "Please, Kostas. We have to go somewhere else. Somewhere far away." My blood pressure is rising, and my heart is thumping against my ribcage.

"*Moró mou*, calm down." Kostas squeezes my thigh.

"Don't tell me to calm down, please." I'm working myself up. My head is feeling fuzzy, and it's hard to breathe again. "I can't risk Aris getting to Zoe and me again."

Kostas pulls into the parking garage, swings the car into his spot, and slams on the brakes. "Nobody is fucking taking you again. They're not going to live to have a chance."

Kostas pulls his phone out of his pocket and dials a number. Because we're still in the car, it rings over Bluetooth.

"Boss," Adrian says, answering on the first ring.

"I found Talia," Kostas says. "At Aris's house."

"Fuck."

"He and his bitch were holding her and my daughter captive."

Adrian curses under his breath again, but doesn't question anything Kostas is saying.

"I need you to go there and get *both* of them. Bring them to the cellar. Call me when it's done."

"Yes, sir."

Kostas hangs up, and after grabbing the bag I packed for Zoe, walks around and opens my door for me.

When we enter the villa, it's as if time has stopped. Everything is the same as it was the last time I was here. My flip-flops are still by the door where I left them. My favorite blanket to cuddle with is still thrown over the back of the couch. My school papers I left on the table in the foyer are still in the same spot. My purse I left in the bathroom when Aris took me is under the table. Kostas must've found it.

When I walk into our bedroom, one side of the bed is made. *Kostas's side.* The other side is how I left it. Messy sheets thrown about because I was in a rush to get to rehearsal that morning. My robe is still draped over the sitting chair. My pajamas are still on the floor next to the hamper because I missed when I tried to throw them in and told myself I would pick them up when I got home.

Only I never came home.

Because I was taken.

Because Aris fucking took me.

Took a year of my life.

"Kostas," I begin, in shock. "Did you live here while I was gone?"

His eyes meet mine, and with one look, I can feel everything he doesn't need to say. Pain. Loss. Confusion. Relief. I assess his features. There are dark circles under his gorgeous, glassy eyes. He's still as beautiful and captivating as he was a year ago, but he looks exhausted. Like he hasn't slept since I was taken.

"I couldn't do it," he admits, stepping toward me. Zoe's head is back on my shoulder. When she's nervous, she snuggles into me. And this is the first time she's ever been away from the only place she knows as home, so she's nervous.

Gently, Kostas rubs the top of Zoe's head and gives it a kiss before he leans over her and kisses my forehead as well. The sweet action has me momentarily closing my eyes, relishing in his touch. My body thrums, needing more of him.

"I looked for you every fucking day, *zoí mou*," he says softly. "At first, I was too pissed to sleep in here. I thought you ran. So I slept in the guest room. Then every day I searched, the signs pointed to you more than likely having been taken. I looked everywhere. I didn't think I left a single stone unturned." He curses under his breath. "I didn't even think to look in my brother's house." His jaw clenches in fury. "Fuck, he's been helping me look for you." He rubs his knuckles down the side of my cheek, his hand trembling with rage. "I couldn't bring myself to sleep in here. To move anything of yours. It would mean accepting you might not ever be back. I told myself once I got you back I would sleep in here again with you."

Be still, my heart.

This man. So powerful and controlling and cold. Shows zero mercy for anybody he comes across. And he couldn't sleep in our bed without me.

"Every day Aris would come home from work and tell me things about you. That you were a drunk and you stopped caring. That you had moved on. I didn't believe him, Kostas." Tears leak from my eyes. I'm finally here. Back in my home. With my husband. "I knew you would find me."

"It took me a fucking year, *zoí mou*. I failed you and our daughter."

"No, don't say that. You found us." He can't blame himself for this. The guilt will eat him up inside. I need my strong Kostas.

"After you put Zoe to bed, you're going to tell me every fucking thing my *brother* did to you and our daughter, every lie *he* told you, and I can promise you, I will make him regret every single goddamn thing he did and said."

If words weren't so matter-of-fact, the steely look in his eyes would tell me he means exactly what he says. When he finds Aris, he's not going to quickly kill him. He's going to slowly torture him for every day he held me prisoner, every lie he told me, and the thought has me almost smiling.

"I want to be there," I tell him. "I want to see Aris and Selene get what's coming to them."

Kostas grins. "Fuck, I've missed you." He gives me a chaste kiss on my lips.

Zoe stirs in my arms and it reminds me… "I don't have anywhere to lay her down." I glance at the bed. I suppose I could lay her in the center and line pillows along each side…

Kostas, of course, is already calling someone. "Thomas, this is Kostas Demetriou. I need a portable crib brought to my villa right away." He hangs up, and one side of his lips tip into a playful smirk. "The perks of owning and living in a hotel."

While I'm feeding Zoe, Kostas makes several phone calls in the other room. He's barking orders left and right, cursing and making threats like the mob boss he is, and my heart tugs in my chest. You don't realize how much you love your life until it's taken from you. And this life, the one with Kostas yelling at people, while our daughter snuggles in my arms, is all I want.

"What the fuck do you mean?" My body stills at his words and tone. Something is wrong.

Zoe knocks the bottle out of the way and climbs up

into my lap. Kostas enters the room and points to the sitting room attached to our bedroom for the gentleman to set up the crib. He quickly rolls it in, pops it open, and scurries out.

"Let me tell you something, my fucking wife was locked in that fucking house for the past goddamn year. Are you telling me you had no idea?"

"Kostas, who is that?" He shoots a glare my way and I give him one right back. At one time, his glare would've scared me, but now, it only turns me on. "Kostas." He ignore me, which pisses me off. I understand he's mad, but I am too. I was the one taken. "Kostas!"

"It's Basil," he barks out. "They got to the house and they're gone." The blood running through my veins goes cold. My eyes dart around us, and I find myself hugging Zoe tighter. They got away. Kostas wanted to take them out right then and there and I begged him to get us to safety first. And now they're missing. They can be anywhere. On their way here…

Kostas puts him on speakerphone. "Go ahead, Basil. Tell my wife how you were assigned to watch over that house and you never managed to find out she was in there."

"Boss, I swear," Basil sputters. "I never saw anything out of the ordinary. They came and went like everything was normal."

"Kostas, there's no way he would know," I tell him. "I was never allowed to leave the house. I even gave birth there." At my words, Kostas's eyes go to our daughter, and they soften slightly. "Unless Basil was able to get inside, he couldn't have seen me. Aris even had Selene drive across town to buy Zoe's stuff. I didn't even know that guy…Estevan, the one you shot his dick off, was guarding the place."

At my words, Kostas roars, "What in the actual fuck. Did you hear her?" he barks at his men. "Estevan was there?" he asks me, needing me to confirm.

"I heard her," Adrian says. "We'll find him."

"He's the guy I shot," I admit. "Several times. And then Aris finished him off. He's dead."

"Jesus fucking Christ," Kostas growls. He scrubs one of his hands over his face in frustration.

"Several of their drawers are empty," Adrian speaks. "And stuff is missing from the closet."

"They took both vehicles," Basil adds. "They're gone."

"Dammit." Kostas punches a hole in the drywall. Zoe jumps and starts crying. "Shit, I'm sorry." He gives her a pleading look, trying to convey how sorry he is.

She snuggles her face into the crook of my neck. "It's okay. She just doesn't know you yet." My words aren't meant to hurt him, but I can see it in his eyes how much they do.

"Adrian, you still there?" he growls.

"Yeah, Boss."

"Call the Minister of Public Order. Tell him I've found my wife and it was Aris and his cunt girlfriend who took her. I want every goddamn man searching for them. Every fucking available badge. They couldn't have gotten far," he barks out before he hangs up.

While I change Zoe's diaper and get her ready for bed, I can feel Kostas's eyes on us. I double-check the locks on the windows in the bedroom. With Aris and Selene missing, I'm scared they're going to show up here.

"Nobody is getting in here," Kostas vows.

"I know. I just need to make sure."

Once Zoe is comfortable in her temporary bed, with her pacifier in her mouth, her eyes roll back in her head. I laugh softly at how fast my baby girl falls asleep, and Kostas smiles.

"We made her," I tell him.

"She's perfect."

"That's because she's the best part of us."

"Let's talk." Taking my hand in his, Kostas leads me out to the living room. I glance back at the bedroom, but Kostas squeezes my hand, telling me it's okay.

When he sits on the sofa, I stay standing, needing to double-check the rest of the locks myself. Kostas watches as I go from the front door to each window, unlocking and re-locking every lock. "I'm scared, Kostas," I tell him once I'm done, sitting on the sofa next to him. "They could be anywhere, planning their next move, and Aris thinks Zoe is his daughter."

"Why the fuck would he think that?" Kostas barks. Huh? Oh, shit! There's only one reason a man would think a baby is his. "You two had sex? When?" His eyes burn into mine. "While you were living under my roof? Fucking me? You were also fucking my brother?" Kostas tries to stand, but I grab his arms to tug him back down and climb into his lap, needing to be close to him. I can't let him push me away. I only just got him back. "What the fuck, Talia."

"Stop yelling, please," I beg, glancing back at the bedroom. "You're going to wake up Zoe." My hands frame his face. He hasn't shaved in some time, so his cheeks are all stubbly just the way I like it.

"I don't give a fuck," he says, but I know he does because his voice is now several notches lower than it was a minute ago. "Tell me why the fuck my brother, even for a second, would believe our daughter is his. Did you fuck him, Talia?" His eyes plead for me to tell him no, but I can't lie to him. It's time for the truth to come out. Maybe if I had told him the truth from the beginning, Aris never would've had a chance to take me.

"Kostas…" My heart is pounding like a drum in my chest.

"It's a yes or no. Tell me. Did. You. Fuck. My. Goddamn. Brother?"

I need to explain, but he's not giving me a chance to. "Kostas, please just let me explain," I beg. "It's not that simple."

"Yes or no!" he roars.

"Yes!" I blurt out, "Yes, I had sex with your brother."

chapter *eleven*

Kostas

Her words chill me to the bone. But they're wrong. The words don't match the pain in her eyes. Despite the rage thrashing at me, I can't unleash it.

Talia is here. Straddling my thighs. Imploring me to understand.

I reach up and grip her delicate neck. Her bottom lip trembles as a tear races down her cheek. Tightening my hold, I draw her close to me until our lips nearly touch. I almost kiss her but pull away, hardening my glare.

"Take off your shirt and show me what he touched that's mine," I growl.

She stares at me for a long moment before grabbing the hem of her shirt and pulling it away. Her tits are full and nearly spilling from her plain black bra. I give her a nod to continue. She unhooks the bra, freeing her perfect breasts. The nipples are peaked and a lovely rosy color. I want to suck them until they're an angry shade of red.

"Did he touch you here?" I ask, cupping her breasts and running my thumbs along her nipples.

Another tear races down, dripping from her jaw. "I don't remember."

"One time?"

She gives me a clipped nod.

That. Motherfucker.

"It was your first time." I can barely contain the hate surging through my veins, burning just under my flesh begging to blaze.

"Kostas," she chokes out. "My first time was with you." More tears leak out. "You told me that. I need to believe that."

I close my eyes.

He raped her. He fucking raped her.

Before our honeymoon at some point. This whole time I thought it was some asshole she dated. Not my own goddamn brother.

"H-He, uh, he was d-devastated after your mom k-killed herself. Y-You were gone and I w-wanted to help. I went to check on him." A sob escapes her. "He was c-crying and I was crying. And…and…"

I open my eyes and slide my hands to her hips. "And…"

"I had t-to get the b-blood off him," she sobs, trembling. Her hands frantically cup my face. "I had t-to help him."

Sweet, innocent fucking Talia.

"Kostas, don't hate me." Her face crumples. My heart crushes.

I hastily swipe away something wet on my cheek. The ache that settles in my muscles dulls the fury. He hurt her. He hurt my fucking wife.

"Kostas," she whimpers.

I grip her throat again and pull her close. Our lips brush against the other. "Tell me all of it."

Her fingers slide into my hair as she steals a kiss. Soft. Sweet. Apologetic.

I hate it. I hate the apology in her kiss. It's dirty and wrong.

"Tell me," I whisper. "Talia, fucking tell me."

She needs to say it and I need to hear it.

"I was worried about him," she whines. "And then…I don't remember how it happened. He was j-just on me. K-Kissing me. The towel was g-gone and…"

Her body wracks with sobs. My fingers trace over her ribs and then my palms slide to her back, pulling her closer. She rests her forehead against mine. Salty tears fall on my face, mixing with my own.

He broke her.

He broke my fucking Talia.

And in doing so, he broke me.

"Tell me," I plead. I need her to say the words. To hand me the proverbial sword. I need to destroy and wage war. I need blood. I need fucking vengeance.

"He was so strong," she breathes. "I was scared."

Her lips press to mine, attempting to distract me. I nip at her bottom lip in warning.

No distractions. No more lies.

I need the truth.

"And then…and then he forced his way in." She sucks in a sharp breath before breaking down. "It hurt s-so bad, K-Kostas. I hated it. I was scared you would hate me."

I grip her jaw and kiss her hard before pulling away. Our eyes lock. Intense. Vicious. Feral.

"I could never hate you. I love you, goddammit," I growl, enunciating every word. "I love you so much it's killing me to hear this."

"I wanted to tell you," she whimpers. "But he said you'd kill me."

My chest feels like she cracked it open, shoved her hands inside, and scooped out my fucking soul.

"Talia…" My voice is low and deadly. I need her to understand me. "I would never fucking hurt you. Ever. Even if you slept with the motherfucker of your own free will. Fucking. Never. Don't you see? I'm under your goddamn spell. You got inside me. It was so fucking dark and, Jesus, Talia, you were all light. I wanted that light so bad I could taste it." I kiss her supple lips. "I'd never hurt you. Do you hear me? Never."

Her kiss is frantic—thankful and desperate—as she claws at my tie. I rip her pants roughly down her ass as she sits up to aid in my effort. We're both clumsy and overly eager as we yank off our offending clothes that stand between us. I manage to get my jacket and tie off by the time she pulls away her pants and underwear. She works on my slacks as I pull hard on my shirt, and the buttons go flying. As soon as my cock is free in her hot, soft hand, I grab her hips, pulling her to me. My hand wraps around hers to hold my cock as she slides down over my length. With a hard thrust, I drive into her from beneath her. We both groan in unison.

"Kostas," she cries out. "I missed you."

Our lips crash together as her fingers claw at my bare skin on my chest. She pushes the fabric down over my shoulders so she can dig her nails there too. My fingertips bite into her hip as I guide her to fuck me rough and fast. Being inside her is the best fucking feeling in the world.

Sliding my free hand between us, I find her clit to offer her some quick pleasure. I won't last long. Not after a year of celibacy. I'm going to come like a teenage boy. Soon.

Her pussy clenches around me when I rub her clit in firm, rough circles. I hiss in pleasure, spiking my hips up harder. She bites on my lip and rakes her nails down over my pectorals.

"Fucking come, Talia," I bark out. "I need you to come before I embarrass myself in front of my wife."

She smiles against my lips and rocks her hips in unison with the way I rub her. When sweet whines begin climbing out of her throat, I know she's finding ecstasy with me. I pinch her clit in the way she used to love and am rewarded with a full-bodied shudder. My name screeches past her lips as she comes wildly. The frantic, feral way in which she does it is enough to send me over the edge. I lean forward and suck on her neck hard enough to mark her as my nuts seize up. Grinding up into her, I groan as I flood her with a year's worth of pent-up release.

Her arms circle around my neck as she hugs me to her. I bury my nose against her flesh, inhaling her sweaty, unique scent. I lick her salty skin and brand her with my teeth. I'm already hardening again like I'm fifteen years younger.

Fuck.

She does this to me.

I stand with her in my arms and kick out of my slacks and shoes. She holds on, worshipping me with her kisses as I carry us to our bed so I can return the favor. We fall into the bed—where we fucking belong—and I kiss her deeply. She helps me rip my shirt off the rest of the way and then I'm driving into her slowly, my eyes glued to hers.

I want to see her.

I want to look at her for-fucking-ever.

We spend hours tasting and teasing and fucking. I

can't keep my dick out of her. We're sweaty and messy and fucking exhausted. And yet, we can't part ways. It isn't until we've showered and I'm about to bend her over the bed again that we're dragged from our sex-fest haze.

"Da-da-da-da-da."

The baby babbling in the other room warms me to my soul.

"I'll get her," I grunt as I yank on some boxers. Talia grabs one of my T-shirts from the drawer to wear as I leave to get our baby.

When I turn on the light, Zoe watches me with wide blue eyes. Fuck, she's so damn perfect. I stalk over to her and pluck her from the crib. Hugging her to me, I inhale her hair.

"I love you, *agapiménos*," I whisper. "I will kill that motherfucker for stealing you and your mother from me."

I consider telling her all the horrible ways I will torture that monster, but then I figure that's not a fatherly thing to do. It's something *my* father would do. And I'm not him.

Carrying her back to the room, I can't help but smile when I see Talia cozied up in our bed. She's so fucking beautiful with her hair wet and messy. Her lips raw from kissing. Purple bruises from my mouth littering her skin.

I settle on the bed and adjust the little one so she's nestled between us. On my side with my arm propped under my head, I admire the cute as fuck kid we made. Talia mimics my position and smiles proudly at our daughter.

Aris—my goddamn brother—took from me.

Took and took and took.

Never again.

As soon as I find him, *and I will find him*, I'm going to take from him.

Skin. Hair. Teeth. Organs.

I'm going to take from him until there's nothing left to take.

A slap to my face erases all murderous thoughts. The little angel with the blue eyes and brown hair swats at me again as though she's trying to touch me. Leaning in, I let her abuse me. She's vicious as she grabs a handful of scruff and tries to pull me to her mouth.

"She's hungry?" I ask because I know fuck all about babies.

"She's been teething, so it could be that. Or she's curious. Usually she cries when she's hungry."

"What do I do?" I grunt. "Fuck, she has a good grip."

Talia laughs and untangles the tiny fingers clawing at me. "For one, don't offer your face as a chew toy."

Zoe's face pinches and she lets out a pouty cry.

"But she likes it," I argue.

"She also likes hair and blankets and shirts."

I grin down at my baby. "Don't listen to Mommy. You can eat my face if it makes you happy."

Zoe coos and wriggles more, attempting to grab at me. I offer her my thumb and she sets to trying to pull it to her mouth.

"I'll make her a bottle," Talia says with a laugh.

While she's gone, I stare at my perfect daughter. How is it this afternoon I was wallowing in despair and murdering my fucking father with my mother's pillow and hours later I have my wife back and a daughter I never knew about? I feel like I'll blink awake and this will be some cruel as fuck dream.

The baby swats at me with her other hand.

"You're distracting like your mother," I grumble but smile at her.

Talia walks in, messy hair, perfect nipples poking through the thin shirt, and bare legs on display, carrying a fucking bottle.

"Distracting," I whisper to Zoe. "You're both bad news for the bad guy."

Talia grins as she hands me the bottle and climbs onto the bed, flashing me her naked pussy beneath her shirt. "Out there you're the bad guy. In here, you're Daddy." She leans in and kisses me. "And spoiler alert, he's the good guy."

chapter
twelve

Talia

THE SOUND OF MY DAUGHTER BABBLING HAPPILY from beside me wakes me from my deep slumber. I open my eyes and find Zoe lying on her back, her feet in the air, and her fists in her mouth. Kostas's side of the bed is empty, but in his place are a dozen pillows entrapping Zoe. I laugh, imagining him building a barricade to keep her safe in the bed. He doesn't know she's fully crawling and could climb right over that wall if she wanted to.

"You're awake." Kostas walks through the door, freshly showered and shaved, dressed in his power suit. God, he's so sexy. Zoe spots him, and wanting off the bed, turns over on her belly and crawls toward him. Kostas's eyes widen, and I laugh.

"Yeah, she can crawl." I nod toward the makeshift wall. "That wouldn't stop her, but that was a good try." I stretch my arms over my head. For the first time in over a year, I feel well rested. It's been too long since I've felt safe enough to get a good night's sleep. "I slept so well," I tell Kostas. His lips curl into a boyish grin.

"I did too."

"I missed this bed," I joke, and he laughs good-naturedly.

"Is that all you missed?"

"No," I admit, "I missed lying next to you… Too bad when I woke up you were gone." I pout playfully.

"I've had a busy morning," he says, picking Zoe up. She reaches for his scruff, but it's gone, so instead she pats the sides of his face.

"Any news?" I sit up, suddenly remembering that this feeling of safety and comfort is only an illusion.

"Not yet," Kostas says. "But I've removed Aris's name from all the accounts, so other than his personal account, which he can't use without leaving a trail, he has zero access to any of the Demetriou funds." He glances down at Zoe, who is chewing on her fist again.

"She's hungry." I climb out of bed to grab a bottle for her. When I'm done making it, I take Zoe from Kostas and sit in the chair near the window to feed her. "What does your dad have to say about all of this?" I know he's not a fan of me. He used me to get back at my dad for having an affair with his wife, but it backfired when Kostas and my marriage became real.

"My dad is dead and he left me in charge of the organization. He no longer has a say."

My eyes fly to meet Kostas's, but he's not looking at me. He's standing in the same place, glancing down at his phone nonchalantly, like he didn't just tell me his father is dead.

"What?" I ask in shock. "Your dad is dead?" When he doesn't look up, I say, "Kostas, look at me." His eyes lift from his phone. "Stop what you're doing for two damn seconds. Since when is your father dead? Aris never mentioned that. He would've mentioned it. Did he know?"

Kostas tucks his phone into his pocket, finally giving me his undivided attention. I can hear his phone vibrating from over here, but he ignores it. "You almost sound like you care about how Aris might feel…"

"Don't go there." I shoot him a glare. "It's just the last year, every time Aris would go on one of his rants, if it wasn't about you, it was about your father. He was obsessed with bringing him down. When he finds out he's dead, he's going to lose it." Instinctually, my eyes graze the room. If he can't focus on destroying his father anymore, his entire attention will be on destroying his brother.

"He's not going to touch you," Kostas growls. "I'm going to kill him, just like I killed my father. Only, unlike Father's death, which was quick and painless, Aris's is going to be drawn out. He's going to feel every ounce of fucking pain we felt this past year from him taking you and our daughter."

Oh, shit! *He* killed his father? What the hell happened while I was gone? "You killed him?" It should worry me that I'm more shocked than upset that my husband killed his own father, but it doesn't. I know Kostas, and if he killed his dad, there was a reason why. My husband might be cold and cruel when he needs to be, but he's also smart and calculating. Everything he does is for a reason.

"Turns out he and my brother have far more in common than anybody thought. He was cheating on my mom for years before she had her affair with your dad. And Aris knew the entire time." He scrubs his hand along the side of his face in frustration. "He instilled loyalty into us from the time we were born, but he was anything but loyal to his own wife. I walked in on him yesterday getting fucked by some whore in the bed my mother slept in, so I made sure the last breath he ever took was in that same bed."

Yesterday… "That was why you were at Aris's. To let him know your father is dead."

"He invited me to his house a million times over the last year, but I always declined. Didn't care to hang out with him and his skank. But I felt I owed it to him to tell him in person. Showed up unannounced and that's how I found you. I saw you looking out the window. Thought I lost my fucking mind." Wow, the death of his father was what led Kostas to finding me. Had he not killed him, he may not have ever found us. No, I refuse to believe that. It was only a matter of time.

"I'm glad you killed him," I blurt out, and Kostas grins. "Because it meant finding us," I explain.

"I would've found you," Kostas says, his tone filled with conviction. "But yes, I suppose his death was meant to be."

Zoe finishes her bottle and bats it away, sitting up and then crawling off the chair and onto the floor. When she gets to Kostas's shiny expensive shoes, she scratches her tiny nails along them, curiously. Kostas picks her up and gives her a kiss on her cheek, and my heart warms. This is all I ever wanted, and now we're so close to having it. All that's in our way is Aris and Selene still on the run.

"It's Aris's entire purpose to make you and your father pay," I tell him, remembering all the times Aris told me how much he despises them.

"He can try." Kostas shrugs, as if my words barely deserve acknowledgment. "But now he has limited resources to do so. It won't matter anyway because I have every man out there searching for him. We'll find him soon."

"Like you found Niles?" I accuse. I shouldn't poke the hornet's nest, but I can't help it. He's so sure he's going to find Aris, yet my father has been underground for even longer and he still hasn't been found.

Kostas glares. "I don't give a fuck about finding Niles. He's a waste of air. Your brother has taken over and is turning a nice profit. But finding Aris will happen, and when I do he will regret ever fucking with what's mine." He gives Zoe another kiss on the top of her head.

"And until you do? What if it takes months or even years? Are Zoe and I going to be held captive here as well?" If my dad was able to hide out, I can't even imagine what Aris is capable of.

Kostas glances over at me. "You will never be held captive again. I have men surrounding the villa, and if you want to go somewhere, we go. I'll make sure you're safe."

"I'd like to take Zoe to the beach." I stand and walk over to them. Her gaze flits over to me and she leans toward me, so I can take her. "Every day I was stuck in his house, I would watch the waves and wish I were back down here. We spent a lot of time at the pool, but it wasn't the same. There were walls holding us in. I want Zoe to feel the sand between her toes. To feel the waves hit her body. I want her to know what it's like to be free, even if she's too young to understand it."

"Then to the beach we'll go. But first, you need to call your mother and brother. They've been almost as worried about you as I was." Kostas pulls his phone out of his pocket and hands it to me.

Wow, things have changed. Kostas is telling me to call my family... "Have you spoken to them?" I ask, taking the phone from him.

"Your mother and I speak almost every day," he says. "I guess you can say we formed a sort of truce. We both wanted to find you. And your brother is nothing like your father. He actually handles business the way it should be handled."

"Thank you." I bring myself up on my tiptoes and give Kostas a kiss.

"For what?"

"For finding and saving us." I give him another kiss. "For loving us."

After calling my mom, who cries when she finds out I'm safe, then cries even harder when she finds out she's a grandma, then tells me she's coming to visit, and Phoenix, who—without the tears—also promises to visit soon, Kostas, Zoe, and I head down to the beach. Since Zoe doesn't have a suit, we grab one from the hotel store.

I notice a few men following us, and Kostas notes they're our guards. I still can't help but glance around. Maybe this wasn't a good idea after all. But I still keep walking toward the beach. After a year of being held prisoner, I think I just need a moment to feel free.

Kostas has one of the cabana boys set up lounge chairs and umbrellas for us. I throw a blanket down, and Kostas sets Zoe down on it. We watch as she crawls to the end and reaches for the sand. She fists a handful and is bringing it up to her mouth when Kostas swoops in and saves her.

"No, no, *agapiménos*," he says softly. "That will taste bad."

Zoe's face scrunches up in confusion, and Kostas laughs. It sounds so carefree, so unlike Kostas. Being a father really does bring out the best in him. All she has to do is look at him and he transforms from hard to soft. "So curious, just like your mother." He taps her nose with his finger and she giggles.

Grabbing his phone from the blanket where he tossed it along with his shirt, I open the camera and take a photo of the two of them. When Kostas leans in and kisses her cheek, I snap another one.

I don't realize I'm crying until Kostas looks over at me and frowns. "What's the matter?"

"Nothing." I wipe the falling tears. "Everything is perfect." I step toward the two people who are my entire world. "Every day when I was stuck in that house, I would imagine what it would be like when you found us. But my imagination didn't do it justice. Getting to see you hold our daughter in person is better than anything I ever dreamed of."

When I click on the photos I just took, I notice a tattoo I didn't see before. Glancing from the phone to Kostas, I spot it on the side of his ribcage. "That's new," I point out. Dropping the phone onto the blanket, I step toward him and bend so I can get a better look at it.

"I got it a few months after you disappeared," he says. The tattoo is of a grenade, cracked open at the seams, and inside of it are bright red beads…no, not beads. Seeds. From a pomegranate. "I thought you left me," he admits, and I stand back up.

"What?"

"We were fighting that morning and then you disappeared. I thought you left me."

I glance back down at the tattoo. I'm almost positive the seeds symbolize Proserpina—me—being forced to stay in the Underground, but… "What does the grenade mean?"

"My world being blown apart." Kostas swallows thickly. "The day you went missing my entire world exploded." And just like that, I fall even deeper in love with my husband.

The day is spent playing in the sand and swimming in the ocean. We order lunch to be brought down, and only when Zoe is so exhausted, she can't keep her eyes open, do we go back up to our villa.

After laying her down in the new crib—yes, while we

were at the beach, my crazy husband somehow had an entire nursery of furniture brought in—I find Kostas on the phone in his office. It reminds me of the time he fucked me on his desk, and that thought has me wanting him to take me there again. We've lost so much time together. All I want is to spend all my time with him. Create new memories to push away every memory that was created this past year.

When he spots me in the doorway, he abruptly ends his phone call.

"That was rude," I joke. "Won't whoever you were talking to wonder why you hung up on him?" I saunter over to him and he spreads his muscular thighs to let me in. He's still in his swim trunk sans shirt, and I take a moment to memorize every hard ridge, every tattoo on his body, including the tattoo he got while I was gone.

"I'm the boss," he says, running his hands up the sides of my hips. "I answer to no one."

"Do you answer to me?" I ask, my voice flirty.

His fingers find my pebbled nipples through my thin bathing suit top and he pinches them roughly. Waves of pleasure shoot through my entire body.

Kostas lifts me up and sets me on his desk. Papers crinkle under my weight, but he doesn't seem to care. "You and me aren't business," he says, pushing the material aside. He leans in and wraps his lips around my nipple, and the coolness of his breath sends a shiver straight down my spine. "But yes, *zoí mou*, I answer to you." He bites down on my nipple, then darts his tongue out to lick it, as he continues to pinch and pull at the other one. When I let out a low moan, tugging on his messy hair, he glances up at me with a wicked smirk. "I may not know a lot about this whole marriage thing, but I do know one thing…"

He pulls my bottoms down my legs, dropping them onto the floor, and I spread my legs so I'm completely exposed to him. "What's that?" I prompt, needing him to get to his point before I lose all my focus.

"Any smart man knows his wife is in charge." With his hands pushed against my thighs to keep me open, he dips his face down and swipes his tongue up my center.

"You're wrong," I tell him through a moan. He sucks my clit into his mouth and bites down playfully. "You do know a lot…" Kostas pushes two fingers into me, and I arch my back, craving more. Always more. "You're a really good husband…" I breathe. He adds another finger, stroking my insides in a way that has me squirming in pleasure. With every touch, every lick, every stroke, he works my entire body into a frenzy, until I'm coming all over his face and fingers, screaming his name.

"You only think I'm a good husband because I make you come." He smirks playfully as he stands and pushes his swim trunks down. I can't help but laugh. I love when my husband is playful.

"That's not the only reason." I reach forward and grip his hard cock. It doesn't need any preamble, but I stroke it a few times just because I want to.

Kostas watches for a few seconds before he loses his patience. With my hand still gripping his shaft, he steps closer, allowing me to guide him inside of me. As he slowly enters me, his thick, long length stretches me until he's buried to the hilt. "Fuck, *moró mou*." He groans. "I've missed your sweet cunt so fucking much." His hands land on either side of me, and with his strong arms caging me in, he fucks me hard and deep.

His mouth finds my neck and he suckles on my flesh. I

can smell myself on his breath, and it sends me over the edge once again. Kostas's head lifts, and his eyes meet mine. "I'm never letting you out of my sight again," he vows. And with one last thrust, he finds his own release.

His movements still momentarily, and then he pulls out. Glancing down, I spot his cum dripping out of me and onto the desk. "Kostas," I breathe. We were too wrapped up in each other last night, and then again just now… "I'm not on birth control."

Kostas smirks, his gaze focused on the mess that's now dripping onto the floor. I try to close my legs, but he grips my knees, forcing them to remain open. He swipes at the liquid, gathering it onto his fingers, then smears his cum along the hood of my clit, as if he's claiming me all over again. The thought has my insides clenching in need. "Kostas," I repeat breathily. "I could get pregnant…"

"That's good, *moró mou*," he says, looking me dead in the eyes. "Because I intend to knock you up again as soon as fucking possible."

chapter *thirteen*

I FLICK THROUGH THE SCREENS OF THE VARIOUS cameras on my app. My newest obsession. Nothing. Nothing is better than something. It's been nearly a week since I got Talia and Zoe home, but we're on edge. Not Zoe, of course. She's cute as fuck and learning the lay of the villa. I didn't know babies could be so goddamn fast. I've been tempted to build her a little cage to keep her safe from furniture and decorations and tiny things she seems to find on the floor to put into her mouth. Talia says no to cages.

My phone rings, and I answer Adrian's call on the first ring.

"Anything?" I grunt out. I swivel around in my chair to glower at the rain. My beach babies are restless stuck inside. Thank God Melody and Stefano showed up yesterday. Otherwise, I'd never get any work done. Now, they can visit and catch up with Talia while I hunt down the motherfuckers who hurt her.

"There's some chatter…"

I stand abruptly, nearly crushing my phone to my ear. "Spill, Adrian."

"With Estevan's body turning up, his people are pissed. They're not loyal to Aris like Estevan was. Estevan kept them in check because Aris's dime insured that. Now that he's gone, the roaches have scattered. Basil and Bronn have been following one of his men named Gutter."

"Gutter?"

He snorts. "Rats. Roaches. They're all pieces of shit. Anyway, Gutter seems to be planning something. Rallying his troops."

"To do what?"

"Not sure. I've been fed information that maybe they're waiting for you to fly out to Thessaloniki again. Might try to take out the private jet or put a hit on you while you're there."

"Why not here and now?"

"You're vulnerable there because you travel with minimal security. Here, at the hotel, it's a fuckin' fortress."

"Is Gutter calling the shots or is Aris still pulling strings? Aris is a sneaky sonofabitch."

"Aris is a ghost. But…"

"But what?"

"I got a tip about an older man who fits Niles's description staying about thirty minutes from here."

My entire body tenses. "What the fuck, Adrian? You could have led with that."

"It's just a tip. Nothing's confirmed. I was going to check it out. Didn't want to leave the king of the fortress unprotected."

I smirk. "The king can handle himself. Plus, security on the hotel is extra beefed. I'm about to head back to my family. Call me if you get Niles. Bring him to the cellar. Tell Basil and Bronn to keep me informed."

"Later, Boss."

We hang up and I stride through the hotel. It's pouring down rain and I hate to get out in it, but I miss my wife and our precious little angel. I grab one of the hotel umbrellas and pop it open as I step outside into the nasty weather. Wind hits hard from the west, soaking my slacks with rain. I grumble as I stalk along the pathways toward my villa. When I arrive, Melody and Stefano are just leaving.

"The weatherman said it's only supposed to get worse," Melody says in greeting. "Stefano and I are going to call it an early night. Maybe order room service. Breakfast tomorrow, though?"

"Pomegranate has an excellent brunch menu. We can meet there in the morning," I agree. "Stay dry."

Stefano holds the umbrella over her as she leans in and hugs me. I'm stiff as I accept her embrace.

"You two made a beautiful baby," she says. "Thank you for being such a wonderful husband to her. I knew you had it in you."

Stefano nods at me as she pulls away. Then, they disappear into the rain. Once on the front stoop of the villa, I close the umbrella and prop it against the wall. I mash in the code and then push through the door. It smells like coffee and Talia. Two warm, comforting scents.

I kick off my rain-soaked shoes and then walk through the villa on a hunt for them. I find Talia in Zoe's bathroom, running her a bath. Zoe splashes from her little seat inside the tub. With Talia's blond hair curtaining her face as she looks down at the little angel below her, I can't help but think she looks like an angel herself. *And Daddy is from the depths of the Underworld.* Somehow, our opposites attract. When she sees me, she grins, and her brilliant blue eyes glitter with love. It's a punch to the chest every time she knocks me over with her intensity. There's no questioning our feelings anymore.

"Someone is soaked," Talia says, smiling. "Why don't you go grab a hot shower and we'll eat after? I'll preheat the oven to cook a frozen lasagna once I'm done with her bath. It won't be homemade, but it's better than getting out in that weather."

I walk over to her and kiss the top of her head. I ruffle Zoe's dark hair. "I'll make it quick."

"Any news?"

"A lead on Niles. Maybe some other shit, but I won't know until Basil and Adrian check it out."

She purses her lips together. "Are we safe?"

"Of course."

Her brows pull together as though she doesn't believe me. It makes me bristle, but I don't let it get to me. After the hell she's gone through, she's allowed to have anxiety. One day, hopefully, it'll fade completely. I quickly shed my soaked clothes and breeze through a shower. Since we're not going anywhere, I pull on a pair of gray sweatpants, some socks, and a white T-shirt. Talia likes it when I'm dressed down. With my hair still wet and messy, I pad through the house to find her in the kitchen, Zoe propped on her hip.

"Here, hold her," she instructs.

I take my baby, who now smells sweet and clean, bouncing her in my arms as Talia peels the plastic film away from the lasagna and sits it on a tray. She then busies herself with making a salad while the oven preheats. Zoe and I walk over to the window where the storm seems to worsen.

Boom!

Thunder crashes loud and hard enough the windows rattle.

"That was intense," Talia exclaims from behind me. "This storm—"

Boom! Boom! Boom!

My blood runs cold. Thunder doesn't sound like that. It doesn't hit that quickly either. What the fuck?

"Get in the closet," I bark out, grabbing Talia's arm and rushing her through the villa as the booms continue.

"Kostas," she cries out. "What's happening?"

"We're being attacked."

"W-What?"

"Turn the lights off. Hide in the closet," I bellow as I grab my phone from the bedroom. I dial Adrian and he doesn't answer. When I call Basil, he picks up. "We're being fucking hit."

"We're five minutes out and I have Caymon on the other line. He says Aris's Porsche is at the front. Explosives are going off near the front entrance. Bold ass motherfucker," Basil huffs. "Want me to take him out, Boss?"

"No kill shot. He's mine. I want him in the cellar," I bark out.

Basil says something to Bronn and then grunts, "Bronn says Caymon's men have the Porsche surrounded."

"I'm on my way." I hang up and shove my phone into my pocket.

I stalk into the closet to find Talia and Zoe watching me with wide eyes. I shove my feet into a pair of tennis shoes and shove my suit jackets aside to get to my gun safe. After punching in the code, I pull out a Glock, check the magazine, and then hand the weapon to Talia.

"Shoot first, ask questions later," I hiss before turning to pull out my AR-15. "They have Aris's Porsche surrounded."

"Be careful," Talia cries out. "Please."

I rush over to her, planting a kiss on her lips and then one on Zoe's soft head. "Shoot anyone who walks through that closet, Talia. I have my phone. Call me if you need me. I'll be back as soon as we have that motherfucker detained."

As I leave, I turn off all the lights, to keep them safe under the cover of darkness. The doors are all locked and I slip out the front into the pouring rain. Wind violently whips at me, slashing me with rain and soaking me to the bone. I sprint through the downpour, racing toward the front of the hotel under the cover of shadows and between buildings. I'm not letting my guard down for an instant.

"Boss," Caymon hisses from between a building. He stumbles out, holding his side. "It's a fucking—"

His head explodes in front of me as he collapses to the dirt. I lift my AR and turn toward the direction the bullet came from. Spraying bullets into the trees, I try to mow down the attacker. This isn't Aris's style, which means he has his men doing his dirty work. Someone grunts from the trees and I charge after them.

I tackle the man and lay a hard punch to his kidney. He groans, attempting to roll away from me, splattering us with mud, but I'm stronger. I flip the man and shove the barrel of my AR against his Adam's apple, making him gag and cough.

Niles motherfucking Nikolaides.

The urge to shoot his head right off his spine is strong, but I need answers. I kick him hard in the stomach, making him howl.

"Get the fuck up and walk," I bellow.

He groans and unsteadily makes his way to his feet.

"Turn." As soon as his back is to me, I poke the gun in between his shoulder blades. "To your left." My phone buzzes and I quickly answer it. "What?"

"It's Adrian," he barks out. "Where are you?"

"Walking Niles to the goddamn cellar. Where are you?"

"Standing behind the Porsche. We can see them inside. A man and a woman. Call it and I'll put a bullet in their heads."

"No," I growl. "I want my brother alive. I'm going to tie down this fucker and then I'm on my way."

"Hold on," he bites at me as he talks to someone. "No fuckin' way. Basil has Phoenix."

That traitorous motherfucker.

"Tell Basil to bring Phoenix to the cellar to keep his daddy company and to watch them both. You keep Aris there."

We hang up just as I storm into the groundskeeper's house with Niles leading the way. The groundskeeper sits on the sofa, soaked to the bone, holding pressure to his stomach as blood blooms over his hands. He gurgles out something to me, but it's too late. Hot pain slices through the back of my arm, just as I'm turning. Whoever nearly stabbed me in the goddamn back, missed a deadlier hit when I moved at the last minute, but it still hurts like a motherfucker. With my gun still trained on Niles, I swing out with my leg, taking down my assailant. They hit the ground with a loud grunt.

I sling the AR to the guy's face and pop him right in the mouth with three bullets. Niles tries to run, but I crack him hard in the back of the head with the butt of the AR. He falls hard on his knees but doesn't go completely down.

"Get your ass down those stairs or I'll kick you down them," I roar, shoving the barrel into his back. "Move."

He groans and curses all the way down to the cellar. I

force him into the chair and tie him tight enough around his wrists, his hands turn purple. I'm about to head back upstairs when Basil and Bronn manhandle Phoenix down the steps. His face is beat all to hell, but he's raging like a beast. Not taking any chances, I stay until they get him subdued with an elbow to the face and tied down.

"I'll be back soon with my brother and his bitch. Don't let them go anywhere."

Basil and Bronn both nod as I take the steps up two at a time. My arm hurts like a motherfucker, but I'm high on adrenaline. I've thirsted for vengeance for what feels like forever. I'm finally getting it. Fucking finally.

I run through the rain toward the front gate with my AR raised and ready to fire. My staff are trained in the event we're ever attacked, so the guests should be fairly safe, although it's going to be a helluva PR nightmare. I'll have Josef pissed as fuck having to cover our shit, but there's nothing money won't buy—even the Minister of Public Order's compliance.

When the Porsche comes into view, flashes of light can be seen in conjunction with pops of gunfire. My men are shooting into the vehicle against my orders. What the fuck!

Racing toward them, I nearly mow down Adrian in the process.

"They shot him against direct orders—"

"Something isn't right, Boss!" Adrian barks out.

I shove past him toward the Porsche. Pushing a guy out of my way, I fling open the door. A man and a woman are slumped over, the entire interior splattered with their blood. The guy is an older man with his hands tied behind his back. The woman has gray hair and her arms are bound too.

Fuck.

Fuck.

Talia.

Bullets spray at me and I dive down into the mud, wincing at the pain searing through my hip where I've been clipped. The guy I'd pushed away splats beside me, his head blown off.

"Boss," Adrian calls out from nearby. "Stay the fuck down. I'm gonna get the bastard!"

Rolling onto my back, I wince when my arm screams in protest and my hip burns like a motherfucker. I strain my neck, searching for the shooter. The rain is relentless and it's dark as fuck. I work myself into a squat and rush around to the back of the car. Popping can be heard just north. I see Adrian's big form not far away. We make eye contact and I nod at him, pointing in the direction of the shooter.

We're coming for you, asshole.

And you're going to wish you'd never been fucking born.

chapter
fourteen

Talia

With Zoe clinging to my chest, I listen to the front door slam closed. Zoe, the six-month-old that she is, squirms, wanting to play in the closet. She doesn't understand what's going on, or that she was born into a world where the villains and monsters I read to her about, the ones who always get taken down by the white knights, are real, and they don't get taken down as easily in real life as they do in her books. Sometimes, in fact, they don't get taken down at all.

Once upon a time I thought Kostas was a monster. But now that I've seen Aris in action, I know the difference. Whereas Kostas is powerful and smart, and makes calculated decisions, Aris is cruel and vindictive, and makes decisions based on his emotions. His need for revenge. Kostas may not be like the knights in Zoe's books, but he's still *my* knight. And I know without a doubt my dark knight will do everything in his power to make sure his princesses are safe.

Where is he?

What's taking so long?

The booms we heard sounded like explosions. I pray Mom and Stefano are safe someplace. I should try to call and check on them, but not until Zoe and I are in the clear. Kostas would lose his mind if I left the closet to look for them. I have to trust my stepdad will take care of Mom.

Fear clings to me and I can't shake it off. An ominous feeling washes over me. I'm not safe here in this closet. Deep down, I know it's Aris. He can't let his brother win. It's all he's bitched about for a year. Destroying him. Toying with him. We're Kostas's weakness and Aris is smart enough to know that. He'll hunt us down. Nothing will satisfy him until he has us.

Over my dead body.

I'll shoot him in the face before I let him take us again.

I can't live as a captive ever again. I won't do that to Zoe.

"Ba-ba-ba," Zoe babbles around the pacifier I keep trying to push back into her mouth to keep her quiet. She's getting annoyed that I won't let her loose to play. In a few minutes, she's going to get frustrated and will soon be screaming her tiny little head off. My daughter doesn't do well with being confined. Hopefully, whatever is happening, will be over by then.

Hope is worthless at a time like this. My brain trumps the hope flittering in my heart. These people are mobsters, not normal men. That means hope is useless, unlike the gun beside me.

Feeling around in the dark, I find a shoe and try to hand it to Zoe to distract her. She takes it for a second before she drops it to the ground and wriggles, trying to get free.

"Ba-da-da," she babbles some more, frustration evident in her tone.

Come on, Kostas.

We don't like being alone without you.

"Shh, baby, let's go night-night." It's close to her bedtime, so maybe she will go with it. Lifting her into my arms, I start to rock her back and forth, when I hear something shatter. Zoe hears it too because her head, which was lying against my arm, pops up, smacking me in the face.

Crunch. Crunch. Crunch.

Footsteps on glass.

Oh, God.

Someone's in the house.

Grabbing the gun from beside me, I'm preparing to do as Kostas said—shoot first, ask questions later.

I strain my ears, hoping it's just the storm. But I can hear voices inside. Whispers. Something crashing to the floor. A door slams and more voices. The bedroom light turns on and shines in under the crack of the doors.

People are here.

They're going to find us.

My body trembles with fear and adrenaline courses through me. If we can be quiet, maybe they won't think to look in the closet.

"Ba!" Zoe screeches, and I wince. If someone is in here, Zoe's voice just gave us away.

"Shh," I whisper. "Shh, baby."

But she's not quiet and starts to screech as she squirms.

Come home, Kostas!

When the closet door swings open, momentarily blinding me with the new light shining in, I let out a choked sound of horror. I have no clue who is standing there, but if it were Kostas, he would've made his presence known. So, with Zoe wrapped tightly in one of my arms, I raise the gun with my other and shoot.

Bang. Bang. Bang.

Three shots go off, making my hand go numb and my ears ring.

My eyes adjust just in time to see Selene stumble back. I hit her somewhere based on her howling, but she's still alive.

"You fucking bitch," she screams, stalking toward me like one of those crazy zombies who can't be brought down. "You shot me!" Blood seeps from her lower abdomen and it's hard to tell if I got her good or just clipped her.

I aim again, hoping to hit her in the heart, and—

"It's over." Aris comes out of nowhere and tackles me. Still trying to hold Zoe in my arms, I hit and kick at him. But he's stronger and quickly disarms me, before pinning me to the floor. Zoe is flung out of my grip, and before I can grab her, Selene plucks her off the ground.

Blood curdling screams.

Zoe! My baby!

She's screaming for me and I need to get to her.

"No!" I wail. My drive to get to my daughter takes over, and grabbing the first thing I can get my hands on, I plow it into Aris's face. He's caught off guard long enough that I'm able to roll over and get out of his grip. I'm about to stand, so I can run after Zoe, when Aris tackles me from behind. With his weight on top of me, my arms give out, and my chin hits the hardwood floor. Something metallic swarms my mouth.

Zoe's screams go louder, spurring me to focus on her instead of the pain.

My baby. I need to get to her.

But before I can move forward, Aris's strong hands grip my biceps, and he flips me over onto my back, smashing the back of my head in the process. He crawls up my body, wrapping his legs around my torso. With him hovering above me, I can make out his features.

His eyes scream hate. Fury. Revenge. But the way he's smirking, it sends shivers down my spine. He's enjoying what's happening. Just as I thought he planned all of this, and he's confident enough to believe he's going to win.

Not if I can help it.

"Did you really think I would let you and that baby leave that easily?" He chuckles darkly.

"Fuck you!" I spit the blood that's been building up in my mouth in his face.

"Been there, done that." He cocks his hand back to hit me, but I see it coming. And lifting my butt into the air, I knee him in the back, forcing him to fall forward enough to lose his balance.

Taking advantage of his current state, I slide my body backward then knee him in the dick as hard as I can. He groans and rolls to his side, as I roll to mine, determined to get to my daughter. We're both on our feet, running out the bedroom door, when something heavy smacks me in the side of my face.

I fall forward, my face catching the side of the end table. Gray. Blink. Gray. Blink.

Everything fades so quickly as the sounds grow muted.

"Payback's a bitch," Selene screams as my vision goes blurry and then fades to black. I try to fight it, but I can't.

Wake up!

Open your eyes!

But I can't. Oh God.

The last thing I hear before everything goes silent is the sound of my daughter, *zoí mou,* crying for me. Needing me.

Needing to be saved. And I pray that Kostas is somewhere close. And that, just like in Zoe's storybooks, the monsters lose, and the dark knight saves the princesses.

But sadly, we all know too well that reality rarely imitates fiction.

chapter
fifteen

Kostas

M Y MIND IS ON ONE TRACK. FIND AND KILL THE man shooting at us. The quicker I can eliminate this threat, the quicker I can find my fucking brother.

"Radio to everyone," I hiss out to Adrian, though I can't see him. "I want this place surrounded. No one leaves."

The static of his device can be heard as he makes the command. My phone buzzes in my sweats' pocket, but I can't answer just yet. Not when I'm crouched and running between vehicles hunting down a man.

Pop! Pop! Pop!

Bullets whiz past me, but I duck down just in time. It's dark and pouring down rain, so most likely he's just shooting in our general direction rather than having eyes on us. Something crunches ahead and then a man makes a grunting sound as though he fell. I charge his way. A form is rising to his feet and I don't waste any time.

Pop!

My bullet hits him in his lower stomach and he groans

from the impact. He drops his weapon to apply pressure to the wound. Adrian flies up out of nowhere and tackles the fucker.

"Get him to the cellar," I growl. I'm blinded by the rain that's running from my hair into my eyes and everything fucking hurts. I'll need to get my shit dealt with because I won't be able to run on adrenaline forever.

I stumble a little, my hip screaming in pain, but manage to keep myself upright. My phone buzzes again. "I need to check on Talia," I bark out at Adrian. "Let's get this asshole there for questioning. Aris is still missing." My blood runs cold with fear that he might have gotten to her.

Men are staked out around the villa.

Aris would have to go through an entire army of men to get to her.

She has a gun and knows how to use it.

It provides some semblance of relief, but not much. Just as we push into the groundskeeper's house, I dig my phone out of my soaked pants pocket. Adrian hauls the fucker to the cellar while I wait in the living room. My hands are shaking and it takes a few tries before I'm able to enter my code to open it.

The door flies open behind me. I'm on autopilot as I sling my AR around, ready to spray bullets into my assailant. As soon as I see who it is, I nearly fall to my knees in relief.

"Kostas!"

It takes me all of two seconds to take in her appearance. She's soaked to the bone from the rain, but so many things click into place all at once.

Blood smeared all over her teeth and running down her chin.

Blond hair matted to her face and clothes clinging to her form.

Giant bruise on the side of her face.

Sobbing. Sobbing. Sobbing.

Gun shaking hard in her grip.

No baby. No baby.

No. Fucking. Baby.

"Where's Zoe?" I demand, terror burning through me like accelerant to an already out of control inferno.

She falls against me, nearly knocking me over. I toss the AR to the couch to hug her to me.

"Talia, where the fuck is our daughter?" My chest hurts and violence thrums through me.

"T-They took her," she sobs. "You said we were s-safe. We were n-not safe."

Guilt and fury wage war inside me.

I left them alone. I thought I could eliminate the threat.

"Who?" I ask, my voice low and deceptively calm.

She looks up at me, her bottom lip wobbling. "Aris and Selene."

I should have known Aris wouldn't storm the gates so brazenly. That he'd have a plan of attack that would throw me off.

"Adrian," I bellow. "Get a car and let's go."

Three seconds later, Adrian storms into the living room. I don't have to say the words because he takes in our appearances and mutters out, "Motherfucker!" He rushes out into the night as I walk Talia out the door to wait for him to bring up a vehicle. Soon, he arrives with an SUV and I pile into the front while Talia jumps in the middle row seating behind us.

"Where to?" Adrian demands.

I scrub my palm over my face to swipe away some of

the water. The asshole hid from me for an entire year right under my nose. He's a sneaky bastard like that. But now it won't be so easy. He'll have an infant in tow and a mouthy bitch. Someone will see him. I need every goddamn person looking for him.

"Airport," I utter, though I'm not sure he'll try that. The jet is always fueled and ready. At the very least, I want to make sure he's not leaving Crete Island.

Adrian hauls ass through the dark. My fingers tremble as I dial Basil.

"Yeah, Boss?"

"Make them talk, but don't kill them. I need answers." I close my eyes and breathe heavily. "They took Zoe."

"Aris?" he growls.

"I need you to have the men eliminate the threat at the hotel. Get the bodies out of there and make sure the hotel guests are okay."

"Minister of Public Order?" he asks.

"I'll call Josef. Just clean up the fucking mess and keep the roaches on a leash in the cellar. I want to know anything, no matter how insignificant."

"Talia?"

"She's safe with us but have someone check on her mom, please."

Talia squeezes my shoulder from behind in thanks.

"On it, Boss."

After we hang up, I dial Josef. My body feels cold and I fight a tremble. Awkwardly, I fumble for the heater. Adrian shoots me a worried look before swatting my hand away to do it for me.

"This better be good," Josef growls. "I have everyone blowing up my goddamn phone."

"Terrorists after a politician," I lie. That's the lie he'll spin for me too and he'll be paid handsomely for it. "Set up a press release for the morning. They took my daughter."

He barks out some orders to someone before saying, "No shit?"

"I need…" I suck in a deep breath, blinking away a wave of dizziness. "I need you to have your men out there looking for my brother."

"Aris did this shit? Your father would be disappointed."

No, Father would have already found him and put a bullet through his skull. I'm softer than Father and it shows. I can't hold onto anything precious to me. Not my mother, not Talia for so long, not my daughter.

"Have the police looking for her. Brown hair. Blue eyes. Six months old. I'll text you a picture to send to your men."

"I'll keep it discreet. We'll find her."

I wince as I adjust my position in the seat. Blackness eats at my vision.

"And if we don't by the time of the press release tomorrow…" Josef trails off.

Adrian shakes his head at me in warning.

"Then what?" Josef asks.

"We go wide with it," I bite out. Tell all my enemies I have something I want back, even it if means presenting to them my weakness.

Josef is silent. I pull the phone away to make sure we're still connected before pressing it back to my ear.

"You heard me?" I rasp out.

"That puts a big target on your most vulnerable possession."

My heart pumps fast and furious. "Right now, I need that target to find her. Make it happen."

"Of course," he says with a sigh.

We hang up and I fade in and out the entire trip to the airport. Adrian keeps getting calls and barks out orders. My phone buzzes a few times with texts from Basil. Eventually, he sends me a text with a picture of two very freaked out looking people, but they're alive. I lift my phone to show Talia and she sobs in relief.

Melody and Stefano are okay.

My phone slips from my grip and tumbles to the floor. Talia picks it back up. Her hand is warm as it brushes along mine.

"Kostas," she cries out in alarm. "Your hand is like ice." She runs her palm along my cheek. "What's wrong with you? Are you hurt?"

"He's been hit," Adrian alerts her. "Took a bullet outside and not sure what got his arm."

"Knife," I hiss out.

Talia practically climbs onto the console to look me over. Adrian pulls up to the airport and exits the vehicle.

"You're bleeding everywhere," she whispers. "And you're so pale."

"I'll be fine," I grunt out.

"We need to get you to a hospital."

"Fuck that," I snarl. "They'll hold me when I need to be out here searching for Zoe."

Her lips press together in a worried line. "I want her just as bad as you do, but we can't look for her while you're dying on me. I need you." Tears leak from her eyes and her chin wobbles.

"But Zoe," I choke out.

"Aris never hurt her or was cruel to her," she assures me, though I hear the doubt in her voice. "He still thinks

Zoe is his. We have to have faith she's going to be okay with him."

I close my eyes, suddenly very tired. "I'm sorry I failed you."

Hysterical sobs escape her and she slaps my face, forcing my droopy eyes back open. "Don't you dare fucking take the blame for what your brother did. You have done nothing but try to protect us."

Lifting my weak arm, I swipe away her tear. "He fucking hit you."

"I hit back," she tells me icily.

"Good girl."

"I shot Selene," she whispers. "But she got away anyway."

Energy surges through me. "You put a bullet in that bitch?"

"Yes."

Gripping her neck, I pull her to me and kiss her mouth that still tastes of blood.

"You're so cold," she whimpers. "You've lost too much blood."

"I'll be okay," I assure her as I text Josef.

Me: Selene—Aris's bitch—got hit. She might need medical attention so keep eyes on the hospitals.

A wave of dizziness has my head thunking against the window. Talia slaps my face again, rousing me.

"Wake up," she says firmly. "Tell me what you need me to do."

"I need Basil to…check the footage…" I blink hard.

She grabs my phone and dials Basil. "Check the footage. See what they drove off in. Send the information to Josef."

Fuck, she listens well.

Basil says something to her and she huffs.

"If they find him, I want to see his face," she hisses. "And then I want to stab him to fucking death."

Adrian climbs back in and shakes his head. "Nothing. They didn't come here. What now?"

"We neeeed toooo," I slur, my head pounding as I try to make sense of what I'm trying to say.

"Get back to the hotel. He needs medical attention. Call his doctor because he already nixed the hospital idea. Basil's pulling up the video footage to get the make of the vehicle to send to Josef. We're going to go torture fucking answers out of the men you guys caught. And then we're going to find my baby."

"Damn," Adrian says as he peels out of the parking lot. "You've been busy."

"Oh," she sneers, "and when we find Aris, I'm going to kill him."

Adrian snorts. "You got it, Boss."

Her warm lips press to my cheek as blackness pulls me under. Hot words are whispered against my flesh that have me relaxing. "Rest, baby. I need you to get better so we can fix this. Until then, we'll take care of what we can."

I didn't marry a weak Nikolaides.

I married a goddamn mafia queen.

A Demetriou in heart and now one in soul.

chapter
sixteen

Talia

THE DRIVE FROM THE AIRPORT BACK TO THE HOTEL is spent with me begging Kostas to stay awake. Scared if he falls asleep he might not ever wake up. His forehead is glistening with sweat, and his skin is cold and sticky to the touch. He needs a doctor sooner rather than later. I can't make out exactly where he's been shot, or how extreme it is, but based on his pale complexion, I have a feeling it's bad.

A myriad of emotions are running through me. Fear that I'm going to lose my husband and daughter. Anger that Aris would stoop this low to involve Zoe in his revenge plan. The man barely even paid attention to her the entire time we lived with him. What I told Kostas was the truth. Aris was never cruel to Zoe, but he also barely acknowledged she existed. The only reason he was keeping us there was to get back at his brother. He never even once tried to have sex with me or spend any time with Zoe, even thinking she was his daughter. Zoe and I are nothing more than tools to him. Tools to hurt his brother.

What I don't get, though, is why he didn't take me this time around… Taking me would mean hurting Kostas. And then a thought strikes me. Selene wanted me out of the picture, so the two of them could play house. Did he only take Zoe so he could keep her for him and Selene to raise? But he can barely even stand Selene. He treated her more like she was a warm body to sink his dick into when he was horny than like a potential wife.

Maybe he's hoping to use Zoe as a bargaining tool, and it was easier to take her than the both of us. Kostas did cut him out of all the business assets. Maybe he's planning to get somewhere safe and then he'll contact Kostas to make a deal. But even as I consider that, I know deep down Aris cares more about revenge than making a deal. Unless the deal involves Kostas losing everything and Aris ending up with everything.

Would Kostas give up everything he's worked his entire life creating to make sure our daughter is safe? Of course he would. But hopefully it won't come to that. I would rather find Aris and Selene and put a bullet through their cold, black hearts than hand anything of value over to them. They don't deserve anything. Not a single dollar. And definitely not the business. Hopefully whoever Kostas and his men caught will have some answers.

Kostas groans softly, his head lulling to the side, and I'm brought back to the present. Before we can do anything, we need to make sure Kostas is okay.

Adrian pulls in front of the groundskeeper's house and jumps out of the car. Basil comes running out, and between the two of them, they carry a stumbling Kostas into the house and lay him across the couch. While we wait for the doctor to arrive, I grab a knife from Basil and cut open

Kostas's shirt, needing to see how bad the damage is. As I'm assessing his body, the doctor and his assistant walk in. I've met them both when we first got home. Kostas wanted to make sure Zoe was healthy since Aris wouldn't let anyone see her. The doctor was helpful and gave her the necessary vaccines she needs.

"He has what looks like a bullet wound to his right side and a large knife gash on the back of his arm," I tell him.

He nods once and sets to work. Opening his duffle bag, he seems to have everything he needs. He begins working on Kostas's side, just above his hip, while his assistant helps him, grabbing various tools and such.

Needing to feel like I'm doing something, I grab a washcloth from a cabinet and wet it with cool water. Without getting in the way, I sit next to Kostas's head and pat his forehead with the cool washcloth.

His eyes flutter open just long enough for our eyes to meet before they close again, and my heart squeezes in my chest. I've never seen Kostas look so vulnerable and weak. He must be in so much pain.

"Did you give him pain medication?" I ask, worried he's suffering.

"Yes," the doctor responds. "But only the minimum. He doesn't like to be sedated."

His words make me realize this isn't the first time he's had to fix my husband. And that thought has me wondering how many times he's come close to dying. How many more times will his life be at risk? How long do I have with him until one day his life—or mine—is taken? I married a powerful man, who many people would love to see brought down. Every day I spend with him is on borrowed time.

The thought has me choking back a sob. If I were with

a man like Alex, this never would've happened. We'd be safe at home, running lines for an upcoming play. No, that's not true. If I were still with Alex, we would've already graduated.

But then I would've never met Kostas. I would've never known what it's like to fall in love with a man who has the ability to consume every part of my mind, body, and soul.

I would've never found myself. My sense of purpose. What I had with Alex, might've been safe, but it was boring. Alex didn't make my heart pound against my chest the way Kostas does. Going to school was fun, but it didn't pull the passion out of me like creating Pomegranate did. Alex was sweet, but he didn't challenge me the way Kostas does.

I would've never had Zoe. With her dark hair identical to her father's, and my blue eyes, she's the perfect mixture of the two of us. She's only a baby, but I can already see both of us weaved through her. My sass and determination, and Kostas's strength and bravery.

I didn't understand it at the time, but it wasn't until I married Kostas that I finally found my place in this world. It's not spitting lines in a playhouse, or traveling with friends. It's right here on this island, at this hotel with my husband and daughter. I love being Kostas's wife, being Zoe's mom.

And all I want is to be given the chance to continue to be both. Which means I need my husband to live, and I need to get my daughter back.

Right now, the only possible lead we have to go on are the men being held in the cellar. If Kostas doesn't wake up soon, I'm going to have to interrogate them myself. There's no way Kostas would want everyone sitting around waiting for him to get better while that asshole and his evil sidekick are getting farther and farther away with our daughter.

Moving the washcloth off Kostas's forehead, I lean down

to give him a kiss. "I love you," I whisper. "I need you to be okay."

Kostas groans. "You're not getting rid of me that easily." He gives me a lazy smirk that shoots straight to my belly. Butterflies. Even hurt, he can still manage to turn my insides out. He just has that effect on me.

I watch in silence while the doctor works on Kostas's side and then turns him slightly over to work on the back of his arm. After what feels like hours, the doctor sits straight and pulls off his latex gloves, handing them to his assistant.

"All done," the doctor says. "The bullet that entered his side has been removed, and he's been stitched up. An inch more to the left and it would've hit a kidney." He hands me a bottle of pills. "Here's an antibiotic for him, so it doesn't get infected."

"And the arm?" Kostas asks, shocking me when he opens his eyes and attempts to sit up.

"Whoa," I chide. "You can't move." I place my hand on his arm, and thankfully, he doesn't try to sit up anymore.

"It was deep, cut through some muscle," the doctor says. "Needed twenty stitches. But it could've been worse. Could've hit a lung." He turns his attention to Kostas. "You are very lucky. It's going to take some time for it to heal." Kostas nods in understanding. "Try to make sure not to use that arm too much while it's healing."

His assistant hands me a tiny bottle. "There's some healing cream. Apply it to both areas. The stiches will dissolve on their own in a couple of weeks."

I take my first deep breath of relief. Kostas is okay. "Thank you," I tell them both.

"Thanks, Doc," Kostas adds.

"I'll walk you out," Adrian tells them.

When Adrian returns a minute later, he reaches for Kostas, who extends his arm.

"What are you doing?" I hiss. "Lie back down!"

"Like fucking hell," Kostas says. "I've been through worse."

Stupid, stubborn fucking man!

Adrian helps my husband to his feet.

"Anything?" Kostas asks him, already back to sounding like himself. If it weren't for seeing him wince in pain, I wouldn't even know he was recently shot and stabbed.

"Nothing. None of them will speak," Adrian says. "Phoenix is still claiming he wasn't a part of it."

Phoenix? Oh my God! Phoenix was coming to visit. "You can't possibly think my brother had a part in helping Aris kidnap our daughter. She's his niece!"

"And what about Niles?" Kostas grunts. "He was brought in as well, after trying to take me out."

What the hell! "Niles is here?" I glance around, even though I know exactly where he is. "He's here, in that fucking cellar?" I shout, my blood boiling.

Kostas nods, his dark eyes flashing with violence.

"I want to see him now." I don't wait for Kostas as I stomp down to the cellar. I swing the door open and find Basil and a few of Kostas's other men standing guard. In the center of the room are three men, all tied with thick rope to their chairs. The first one I recognize as my brother. His flesh is bloody, and his head is quirked to the side, like he's slightly out of it. His eyes are closed, but I can see his chest heaving up and down. He's still alive.

The second is Niles. His face is also covered in blood, both eyes puffy and black and blue. His eyes are also closed, but he's not breathing heavy like Phoenix, so it takes me a second to determine he's still alive. For now.

The third guy I don't recognize, but he's in just as bad of shape as my brother and Niles. His eyes are open and he's glancing around him, as if trying to figure a way out. Not happening, fucker.

"Niles, wake up!" I kick his legs and his head pops up. The moment his eyes meet mine, my body trembles with anger. "You fucking asshole." I stalk closer to him and slap him across the face. "How dare you!" I cry. My hands are shaking, and my heart is beating erratically against my ribcage. How could he do this to me? To his own flesh and blood? It wasn't bad enough he used me to pay off his debt, but now he works with Aris to help steal my daughter?

"Sunshine," Niles cries out, and the nickname he used to call me has me seeing red.

"Don't you ever call me that!" I backhand him this time, and his face whips to the side. "Do you have any idea what you just did?" I grab his chin between my fingers and force him to look at me. "Do you?"

"I had to," he chokes out. "Aris has been holding me captive. It was either help him bring down Kostas or die." He thinks he chose his life over Kostas's…

"You didn't help take down Kostas," I spit. "You helped kidnap my daughter!" With no outlet for my built up aggression and frustration, I smack him across the face again. "He took my baby! And you helped him!"

Niles's eyes go wide. "Kostas's men said you had a baby, but I didn't know. I swear, Talia, I never knew anything about a baby. Aris never said a word."

I stare into his eyes for a long moment to gauge his reaction. He's telling the truth. I can see it in his eyes. The pain of knowing he helped take my daughter. It doesn't excuse what he's done, but it means he's no help. Useless.

"He doesn't know anything," I whisper, mostly to myself. Niles not knowing anything means there are only two other people in here who might know something about where Aris and Selene have taken Zoe.

I turn my attention to my brother. "Phoenix." When I say his name, he lifts his head. I don't even need to ask him. I know my brother. He loves me and would never do anything to help Aris in taking my daughter. I heard his voice over the phone. He was excited to be an uncle.

"You know damn well I wasn't a part of this," Phoenix growls, his voice strong and deadly.

"And why the fuck should we believe you?" I turn around to find Kostas standing behind me. "It won't be the first time you've followed in your daddy's footsteps," Kostas sneers. I'm not sure how long he's been here—I was too focused on Niles—but his color is almost fully back, and he's wearing a new shirt.

"I would never do that shit to my sister," Phoenix hisses.

"Kostas, I don't think he would do this," I tell my husband, needing him to believe me. Otherwise he's going to kill my brother. Phoenix might have spent his entire life working for Niles and the business, but he would never purposely put my life or my daughter's at risk. I believe that with my entire being.

"I didn't do it," Phoenix says again.

"Then prove it," Kostas says, his eyes locked on Phoenix as he slowly walks over to him. Once he's standing in front of him, he glances at Basil. "Hand me your knife."

Adrian steps forward. "Boss…" I know what he's silently not saying. *Let me handle this.* Kostas is too weak to torture anyone. But if Adrian says it out loud it will make

Kostas appear weak. And Kostas would rather die than ever appear weak in front of his men, or especially, his enemies.

"I got it," Kostas hisses. He snatches the knife out of Basil's hand and slices the rope holding Phoenix down. Then he slices the rope holding his hands together. "You say you didn't have a part in helping my brother kidnap my daughter… Okay. But your fucking father did. Caught him red-handed with a fucking gun, shooting at me. You have a choice to make."

Phoenix clenches his jaw, and his furious gaze flits from Kostas, to me, and then to Niles, who is now wide awake and staring at his son.

Phoenix stands and stalks over to Kostas, until their chests are practically touching. "I don't have to prove shit to you," Phoenix says.

I hold my breath in fear of what's to come. If Phoenix doesn't do something, Kostas will kill him without hesitating.

Phoenix's hateful glare leaves Kostas, and he turns toward Niles. "You did this shit to yourself," he says in a lowly, distant voice.

"Son, please," Niles begs. "I didn't have a choice. You have to believe me."

"Shut your fucking mouth!" Phoenix roars. "You chose yourself over your fucking daughter for the last time." My brother stalks toward the guard standing closest to Niles, grabs the gun from his holster, and aims it at Niles's chest.

"This is for everything you've done to Talia."

Pop!

Crimson bleeds through Niles's shirt as he cries out in shock. He hit him in the stomach, not the heart—keeping him alive. Before he can beg Phoenix not to kill him, Phoenix aims the gun at his forehead.

Instinctively, I slam my eyes closed, already knowing what's coming.

"And this is for Zoe."

Pop!

I open my eyes back up. Nile's head has been blown to bits. Several of the guards have blood splattered on them. My stomach roils at the sight, but I force the bile down, refusing to look weak in front of all these men. He got what he deserved.

My gaze goes to the third man. He's staring at Niles, his eyes wide-open in shock and fear.

"What do you know about Aris taking my daughter?" I ask him.

"I don't know anything!" he exclaims. "I was just told to come here and kill as many men as possible."

"He doesn't know shit," Kostas growls. "Nobody fucking does because Aris was too smart to let anybody know."

Kostas pulls the gun out from behind him and shoots the guy dead in the heart. His life ends so quickly, his eyes remain open as if he's frozen in place.

My eyes flit back and forth between the two dead men as reality hits. "Kostas," I cry. He turns his attention to me. "If nobody knows anything, how are we going to get our little girl back?"

Kostas walks over to me, and as tightly as his broken body can, he wraps me in his arms as I sob into his chest. We have no more leads. There are no breadcrumbs to follow. Nobody knows anything. It's as if Aris and Selene have vanished with Zoe. "Shh," Kostas coos, his body shaking from the pain he must be in. "We're going to find her. I promise."

chapter
seventeen

Kostas

I STARE AT MY REFLECTION AS I BRUSH MY TEETH. COLD. Furious. A monster. Certainly not one who looks like the father of a small, perfect baby. Or the lover and husband of a beautiful woman. I'm ruthless. My father's son. Every bit the Demetriou I need to be to face the media.

Because *they* will see.

My enemies.

And I need them to see who the fuck they're dealing with.

Talia enters the bathroom as I angrily scrub the film off my teeth. I barely slept two hours, but the press will be here at eight sharp this morning, and if I have any hope for making it through today, I need coffee and a motherfucking bagel.

"I've never heard anyone growl while brushing their teeth before," she says, her eyes squinting and her voice gravelly from sleep.

I spit, then rinse, before drying my mouth off. I've already showered for the day, which was agony on my wounds, and am in just a towel. My wife looks stunning somehow in one of my oversized T-shirts. Her blond hair is in disarray. But what has me seeing red is the awful bruising and split lip. The entire side of her face is dark purple and blue.

He touched what's mine.

He *has* what's mine.

Aris always thought he could battle with me, and because he was fucking blood, I played his games. Enjoyed taunting him whenever I could. In a way, it was our screwed-up way of bonding. But then he crossed the line. Raped my goddamn woman. Stole her and kept her from me. And now he took my child.

Loyalty means nothing to that Demetriou.

Loyalty means everything to me.

This means fucking war.

When Talia was gone, I drifted. Lost in a fog of confusion and anger. Aris played me. Dangled me by his strings and reveled in my torment. Talia made me soft. I *wanted* to be soft for her. Only for her. But clearly, I softened in a way that exposed my weakness. I may as well have given Aris a fucking gun and said, "Point and shoot here."

For the last year, he's had a "blind me" on his side. He had money and resources. He had my lack of knowledge.

But now he's no longer battling a brother, he's in a war with a monster. He thought he could sneak into my compound and get away with this shit. Sadly, he was mistaken. I will gut Greece. Burn it to the motherfucking ground. I will fill every hole with gasoline and light it on fire. Every roach will come out of hiding and I will smash them until I find the rat.

Aris will be mine.

And I'll get my daughter back.

"Kostas," Talia says, her brows furrowing. "Are you okay?"

I gently grip her jaw and tilt her head to the side so I can inspect every dark shade of the abuse she endured yesterday. With the barest of a kiss, I whisper it over her sore flesh. My words of hate are breathed against her skin.

"He will pay for this."

She shivers and grips my wrist. I turn slightly to find her lips. Despite the cut on her lip, I kiss her hard enough to split it back open. The sweet, metallic taste of her mixes with the minty toothpaste, making me hunger for her more than any bagel this morning. If I had more time, I'd turn my aggressions into passion so I could whisper all my evil promises against her skin—promises to take out our enemy and bring home our treasure.

My phone buzzes and I nip at her sore lip once before I pull away.

> *Adrian: Press is already lined up at the gate. Josef is waiting, too. Where are we doing this?*
>
> *Me: Hotel lobby. Send Josef to my office. I want to meet with him before we go public.*
>
> *Adrian: On it.*

"I have to meet with the Minister of Public Order. Then, I'll be doing a press release." I stroke my fingers through her hair that hangs in messy, natural-dry waves after the shower she took alone last night while I crashed into bed. "I need you to look the part of an angel."

Not that she'll have any trouble doing so.

Her brows furrow. "Why? What's going on?"

My perfect Talia and her never-ending quest for answers.

I drop my towel and nod at her to follow me while I dress. Throwing on some boxers and socks, I then make my way into our closet. The mess had been cleaned up by hotel staff before we went to bed, but the feeling of failure washes over me.

Zoe was taken from this very closet.

Talia lingers in the doorway, no doubt feeling sadness over last night and what went down in here. As I dress in a suit, she runs her fingers over one of her white dresses. She pulls it off the hanger and holds it up.

"This one?"

I rake my gaze down the serene, silky white material. "Perfect. And don't you dare cover up what he did to you. They need to see."

Her blue eyes dart back and forth. "Who? Who will need to see?"

Snagging a blue tie that matches her eyes, I slide it around my neck and begin knotting it. Once I've tightened it at my throat, I let out a heavy sigh of resignation.

"You are married to the monster Greece knows. Well, at least the one all the scum knows. *I* will reach them. I'm a Demetriou, it's what we do. But you," I say with a smile as I grab my jacket off a hanger. "*You* will reach the regular people. Every man, woman, and child in all of Europe. We're going to hit them from all sides. Just be you and you'll do exactly what I need you to." I step into my shoes and then walk over to her. "And you're going to have to let me be me."

"What exactly does that mean?"

"It means, I'm soft with you. In here, with our family, soft is good." My features morph into something wicked and furious. "But out there, I need to be a blade forged in stone. I need to be unbreakable. I need to be powerful." I start to put my jacket on, but my arm winces in pain.

She purses her lips before dropping the dress in favor

of helping me. She takes the jacket and holds it open so I can gingerly slide my bad arm into the sleeve. Once I have it pulled on and buttoned, I turn to regard her.

"You're hurting," she breathes. "Physically and in here." Her palm presses to my chest between my pectorals. "It's okay to be vulnerable. Our daughter is gone. They hurt us."

Sweet, innocent, pure angel.

I slide my fingers beneath her chin and tilt her head up. Blue eyes sparkle at me. She's so fucking strong. Only a woman like Talia could ever have the backbone and fire to be able to stand beside a Demetriou. She's fearless and determined. A fucking storm.

"Out there, I can't be. It's the only way to get Zoe back. The public needs an angel and the Underworld needs a fiery, unstoppable king." I kiss her nose. "Are we in this together?"

She smiles. "Since the day I saw you in that courtyard."

"You tried to run," I say, in a slightly playful tone.

"I wanted you to catch me."

Reluctantly, I pull away, needing to get a move on the day. "Make sure you grab something to eat. Basil will escort you. There'll be coffee and bagels in the lobby if you want that."

"I was thinking fruit. A pomegranate sounds good."

She pulls off her T-shirt, revealing her round tits and rosy nipples. Fuck, she does my head in when all I need is to focus.

"A pomegranate?" I ask, my voice husky as my dick strains in my slacks.

She bends to pick up the dress from the floor and holds it to her chest. Her blond hair cascades over one shoulder as she tilts her head to the side. "An angel can live in hell."

"Not without getting burned."

Sauntering over to me, she stands on her toes and kisses the corner of my mouth. "The devil wouldn't allow that."

"He already has," I growl, my palm finding her hip and squeezing possessively.

"But he won't let it happen again."

So confident and sure.

She's right.

"Go be the badass we need right now," she says, pushing on my chest to break us apart. "I'll be at my restaurant sucking on seeds until you let me suck on you later."

"Are you trying to kill me?"

"You'll need to relieve some tension and then you'll need a nap." She shrugs. "Because then we're going to go get our girl."

"Damn right."

I let my stare linger on the swell of her breasts and then up her slender throat before I latch my eyes to her parted lips. Fuck, how I want to yank her to me, drag her to the floor, and drive into her wildly. The desire to claim and own is fierce, but we have more pressing matters to attend to. And once we have our daughter back, I'll demand my fucked up happily ever after, one orgasm at a time.

Adrian flanks my right and Josef is on my left as we walk into the hotel lobby as a united front—the mob and the police coming together for the same agenda: take down Aris and find a baby. Talia will enter soon with Basil. I need to say what I need to say without her weakening my resolve. As soon as the press sees us, flashes start going off like rapid gunfire. The lights blind me, but I ignore them as I make my way to the podium that's been set up. Josef steps to the microphone first.

"Dear citizens of Crete Island," he starts, holding up his hand to end the buzzing chattering of questions being barked our way. "We're not here to answer questions, but to instead deliver a series of statements."

More flashes snap.

"Last year, good men and women of Cretan General Hospital were gunned down in a tragic terrorist event. The Demetriou family, while dealing with their own familial tragedies, were instrumental in eliminating the threat at that time." Josef gives me a grim smile to which I nod so he'll continue. "His father, the late Ezio Demetriou, was a friend to me and a pillar in this community. The philanthropic donations of this family have been what's kept the island profitable and successful. With…" He flashes me another look and I nod. "With Ezio's recent, natural passing—something the family had wished to keep quiet so they could grieve in private but are no longer able to—we are faced with terrorism once again. There are those who see the Demetrious' efforts as something to destroy, making these attempts when they are down. Last night, they tried to do exactly that. But they are wrong. Our people and the Demetrious aren't broken so easily. We will fight for peace and profit."

He steps away from the podium and gestures for me to take his place. I keep my features cool and impassive. Whenever I lock stares with a reporter, they cower under my gaze and look away.

"My family is the proud owner of the Pérasma Hotel. Last night, men stormed our gates and tried to destroy what we built." *Men ordered by my brother.* "Because we take security extremely seriously, none of our guests were hurt or even saw the terrible situation unfold. We lost a few good men protecting the people at our hotel."

More flashes go off as reporters demand to know the names.

I raise my hand, effectively silencing them all. "They were hired on to do a job for the Demetriou family. And they did it well. But now we need for you all to do your job."

A flash of white in the back of the room indicates Talia has arrived. She's clutching a soft pink blanket and a newly framed picture of Zoe. Basil escorts my wife past the curious onlookers and to the podium with me. I pull her close, sharing the microphone with her.

"I'm a private man," I say, my voice hard as steel. "I keep my personal life out of the spotlight. Because of my influence in Greece, people think they can use my personal life as a weakness against me." I lean over to inhale Talia's sweet scent before kissing the top of her head, earning more pops of flashes. I turn back to the crowd, my glare once again affixed. "Last year, I wed the woman I loved in a secret ceremony for just the two of us. But then she was taken from me." People demand to know by whom, but I ignore them. Everyone underground knows it was Aris and that's all that matters. "When I found her again, she brought home a Demetriou princess. My strong, resilient wife survived the atrocities of capture, delivered our daughter while in captivity, and found the strength to make her way back to me."

Talia starts to cry and clings to me, which sends the media into a frenzy.

"Last night, while we worked to keep our people safe, the terrorists came in and took our daughter."

The press starts shouting, horrified and demanding answers.

"She's…" I trail off and swallow hard. "My wife, Talia, would like to speak about her."

She sniffles as she pulls away slightly. "Our little girl Zoe was kidnapped." Her body trembles as she holds the blanket to her and shows the crowd the picture. "She's sweet and curious and laughs and…" A sob chokes her. "Oh God, I just want her back in my arms."

I stroke my fingers through her hair in a possessive way while staring down every camera in the room, commanding them with one look. *Find my fucking daughter and bring her to me alive.*

"I beg of you," Talia pleads. "If anyone knows anything, please help us. We need her. She doesn't deserve this."

"Our fine Minister of Public Order has set up a call center to take any and all calls. Calls leading to the finding of our daughter will be handsomely rewarded," I say into the microphone. This is for the normal, everyday citizens. They'll look for her because that's what good people do, money or not. They want to reunite a child with their family.

But I need the bad people looking too.

"Fifty million dollars."

The room explodes with excitement.

"She was last seen with Aris Demetriou and Selene Vincent." The crowd gasps again. I ramble through their physical descriptions while deliberately leaving off the fact Aris is my brother. They all know this. I don't need to fucking say it. Everyone underground will see this as one concrete fact: Aris Demetriou is dead to me.

"Twenty-four hours. If she's found within that time frame, I'll reward the finder additionally in ways I see fit."

Meaning, they will get a favor with the Demetrious, which is priceless. "Thank you all for your help."

The group goes wild with questions, and seven of my men have to flank us to get us away from the crowd. Once we're safely inside my office, I give Adrian a nod to clear the lobby of the press and tell him to apprise me of any new developments. The moment I have the door closed and locked, I collect my emotional wife in my arms.

"You did great," I murmur against her hair. "We need everyone's help in finding her."

"I miss her," she whimpers.

"Me too, *moró mou.*"

She tilts her head up to look at me, her eyes red and swollen from her crying. "The people who hate you know everything now. That your father's dead. That you're married. That you have Zoe. That your brother betrayed you. You showed your hand, Kostas."

I sweep my palm delicately over her bruised cheek and then run my fingers through her hair. "It was the only way to get her back. We *will* get her back."

"What if someone hurts her to get back at you?" she whispers, a fat tear rolling down her cheek.

I kiss the wetness on her skin and close my eyes. "We have to trust that money talks. The only one who cares about revenge over money is Aris. The citizens of Crete Island and every piece of scum who knows the Demetriou name will be hunting for our little girl. There's no way we can know where Aris went and turning over every stone would take precious time we don't have. All we can do is let the people do what we can't. We have to trust this will work."

"What if it doesn't work?"

"It's our only option, Talia."

"I'm scared."

"I know," I breathe against her soft lips. "I'm doing the best I can."

"I know you are and I love you for that."

Her lips press forcefully to mine as a fierce growl leaves her throat. The kiss takes me by surprise, especially when her hands begin frantically sliding my jacket off my shoulders and sending it to the floor before yanking at my belt. My cock—ever ready to play with his favorite pussy—stiffens in my slacks. Pre-cum leaks from me as the desperate need to fill her overtakes me. She pulls my dick from its confines and kneels before me.

"Talia," I rumble, my fist grabbing into her hair, ready to pull her back up to my level. I pause to admire how fucking gorgeous she is.

Her blue eyes are intent and dark with lust as her tongue slides between her plump lips and flicks against my wet tip. A hiss rushes past my teeth as I stare at the angel queen who bows before her evil king. Pure wickedness gleams in her eyes as she circles my slit with her hot tongue, her expression equal parts hungry and taunting. I could pull her up to her feet and fuck her senseless, but I'm mesmerized by her devious stare and pretty mouth that's stained the color of pomegranate from breakfast. She slides her mouth over the crown and a growl rumbles from me. I close my eyes, dizzied by the bliss. Her mouth bobs up and down over my length as she desperately feeds my cock into her hungry mouth. When her teeth scrape my tender flesh as she tries to take me deep in her throat, the need to have her completely overwhelms me.

"Stand up," I command. "I need to be inside you."

Her mouth pops off my dick as she shakily rises to her

feet. I waste no time grabbing her full ass and lifting her. She fuses her swollen lips to mine and kisses me just as she was my dick a moment ago. I shove her against the wall as I reach between us to grip my cock. She moans when I slide my tip along her wet slit over her panties, seeking the tight warmth only her body can gift to me. I push the head of my dick under the side hem of her panties to tease her bare flesh with my own and seek entrance. With a painful flex of my hips, I drive all the way into her, her wet panties rubbing along the side of my dick as lubricant. As I fuck my wife against the wall, I can feel the burn as my stitches tear free. I could opt for a better position, but only one goal is in my mind.

Take Talia.

I grip her ass with one hand and squeeze her tit with the other as I drive into her hard. Her mouth owns mine as she fucks my mouth with her tongue. Her thighs tighten around my waist, only further irritating my wound. I'm about to come, but a wave of dizziness has me struggling to keep Talia upright. With her still on my dick, I carry her over to my desk. I sit her ass down on the surface and then push her back, breaking our kiss. She whimpers at the loss.

"Pull your dress up your hips and let me see what I'm fucking," I rasp out, ignoring the pain lancing through my body.

She yanks up the material, fisting it just under her breasts that jiggle each time I drive into her. Her heels rest on the edge of the desk and her thighs are parted open in a dirty, inviting way that makes me want to recreate this moment later when our life is back to normal and I can call her filthy names like my "needy little slut." Names I know will turn her on while getting nasty in my office, but names that don't quite fit the moment.

"Touch me," she commands, her blue eyes intense as she drags me away from the fact that our daughter is still missing and nothing will be normal until she's found. "Right now, it's just us, Kostas."

Failure and loss fade for the moment as I run my fingers along her throbbing clit over her panties. She cries out in surprise when I rip the fabric apart and toss it away. Her hips lift and she clenches around my cock. I easily circle my fingers in a way that strums my wife into having the most beautiful sounds leave her lips.

Someone knocks on the door and we both grind out words at the same time.

"Go the fuck away!"

"We'll be out in a minute!"

Our eyes lock and I thrust hard against her, pinching her clit in tandem with each glide inside her. When I notice blood on her leg, I run my free fingers through it, marveling at the smears along her tanned flesh. Her body seizes with pleasure and her breasts jut forward as her back arches. I'm captivated with how wild and so damn beautiful she is as her pussy squeezes the fuck out of me. I groan, nearly collapsing as my balls tighten and then my release spurts furiously inside her. Cum leaks out as I slide in and out of her, filling her with everything I have. When I'm wrung dry, I slip from her hot body and stagger back, trembling and my still-hard dick dripping.

"Fucking gorgeous," I hiss, my eyes raking down her perfect body and settling at her pussy.

Bright red and raw from being fucked hard.

Thick, white cum runs down her used slit toward her ass crack.

Shaking thighs as she recovers from her orgasm.

I step closer despite the spinning around me and collect my cum on my finger. Our eyes meet when I push it back into her needy body. She whimpers and squirms as I fuck my jizz back into her cunt with just my finger. Once I'm sure it's deep inside where it belongs, I curl my finger up and seek out the part of her that'll make her scream. She shakes her head as though she can't take any more, which only urges me to show her she can. I add another finger and press the hot, throbbing spot inside her until she grips the edge of the desk with both hands and bellows my name. Her hips ride up, doing their own little dance to meet the movement of my fingers until she comes down from her high. I slip my hand away from her and admire the dark, pink depths that remain open and inviting to me. With one clench, she hides that part of herself from me, sending more cum pushing out of her pussy.

"I need…" she whispers, closing her thighs. "I need to shower and change and eat and…oh my God, you're bleeding!"

I shrug as I glance down at my white dress shirt that's seeping with blood. "It was worth it."

She sits up and then stands in front of me. Her dress falls into place and I want to pout over the fact that I can't watch my cum slide down her inner thighs. "Let's go home and get cleaned up so we can find our girl."

"Talia," I growl as I grip her throat and draw her to me. I press my lips to hers. "I love you."

Her lips break into a smile—one that's been missing the past twelve hours. "I love you too."

"We're going to find her."

"I know we are."

chapter
eighteen

Talia

IT'S BEEN FIVE DAYS SINCE KOSTAS AND I STOOD IN front of all of Greece and pleaded with the people to help locate our little girl. Five days since he offered them millions of dollars to locate Aris and Selene. And it's been five long as hell days of sifting through the thousands of leads that end in nothing but dead ends. Everybody wants a chance at the money, which means everybody thinks they've seen our little girl. I've sat in Kostas's office with him and his men for hours upon hours, clicking on lead after lead, blowing up image after image, hoping to spot one of them. I've seen several dozen redheaded women, hundreds of men in suits, and I've looked at enough babies that they all have blurred into one of the same. But none of them are the people we're looking for.

It wasn't until my eyes were itchy and I felt like I was going cross-eyed that Kostas ganged up on me with my mom and made me go home to take a break. I begged and pleaded, but they insisted.

"*Cara mia,*" Mom coos. "Please, you have to eat

something." She pushes the homemade chicken soup closer to me. The aroma fills my nostrils and my stomach growls in hunger. I can't even remember the last time I ate something besides an energy bar. "You need to be strong for your little girl, and in order to be strong, you must take care of yourself."

She leans in and rubs her thumbs along my cheeks and then under my eyes. "You have dark circles under your eyes. You need to sleep."

"I have slept," I argue, pulling my face out of her grasp.

"More than a couple hours," Phoenix adds. He's been staying at the hotel, helping to check out any leads that come through that Kostas feels are worth investigating further, which is almost all of them. My husband is determined to find our daughter, and if there's a slight possibility someone's lead could be the one that takes us to her, he wants it investigated. He has hundreds of men scouring the country on top of the thousands of leads that are being emailed and called in.

And with each passing hour, each lead that hits a wall, I get more anxious that Aris has disappeared where nobody can find them.

"Talia, please," Mom begs. "Just a few bites."

Not wanting to argue with them, I bring the spoon to my lips. But before I can take a bite, I imagine my daughter locked up somewhere with Aris and Selene, hungry and tired and cold, and a sob racks through my entire body. I drop the spoon back into the bowl, and hot liquid splashes out, burning my hand. "How am I supposed to eat when I don't even know if my little girl is being fed?" I push the bowl away. There's no way I can eat until I know she's safe in my arms and her tummy is full.

I stand at the same time Mom does. She envelops me in her arms and I breathe in her floral scent. "What if she's hungry?" I cry out. "Or lonely?" My entire body shakes against my mom's as she holds me tight. I can feel an anxiety attack coming on, but I already know I won't be able to stop it. I've been having them every day since Zoe was taken. "What if they've hurt her…or worse…" I can't even finish my sentence. My words are cut off with my cries. My head pounds so hard it feels like my entire body is vibrating. My heart is racing, and my legs feel like noodles.

"Talia, you have to calm down," she says as I begin to hyperventilate. She walks us over to the couch and helps me to sit. I try to take in gulps of air, but it's hard to breathe. My sweet little baby is somewhere out there with two crazy psychos who don't love her. They don't even care about her. Anything can happen to her, and every second she's gone is less of a chance of ever finding her alive.

Stefano appears in front of me with a glass of water. "Here, sweetheart, take these." He extends his hand with two pills, but I shake my head.

"No, I need to be awake and lucid in case a solid lead comes in." The last thing I want is to be out cold when my daughter needs me.

"Talia, you can't keep going like this," Mom demands. "Please, it will help you to calm down and rest. If a lead comes through, we'll wake you up. Kostas is handling it."

I want to argue with them, but they're right. I haven't slept in what feels like days. My body is over exhausted and shaking like a leaf in a storm.

With trembling hands, I take the glass and pills from Stefano. After swallowing them, my mom pulls me back into her side and rocks me until my body gives up and my eyes close.

My eyes flutter open, and when I look around, I see I'm in my bed. I listen for Zoe. The villa is quiet. Is she sleeping? What time is it? Does Kostas have her? And then I remember she's not here. She's missing. And my heart cracks all over again.

My phone vibrates on the end table and I grab it to see who is calling. Kostas. I check the time. It's ten o'clock at night. I've been sleeping for almost eight hours thanks to the pills Stefano gave me.

I quickly answer the call, hoping he has good news. "Have you found her?"

"No, there's been no leads that have panned out."

My heart falls into my stomach. No leads. In a couple hours, it's going to hit midnight and it will be another day without my baby girl.

"I was calling to check on you," he adds. His voice sounds worried. My mom must've told him I had another anxiety attack.

"Are you in your office?" I ask, sitting up and throwing the blankets off me.

"I am, but you need to get some sleep," Kostas says softly.

"I've been sleeping all afternoon. I'll be there in a few minutes."

I shower quickly, get dressed, and brush my teeth to get rid of the bad taste in my mouth. Then, I head to Kostas's office, Basil hot on my trail. I'm thankful for my ever-present shadow. Mom and Stefano must've gone back to their villa for the night.

On the way, I see Phoenix walking down the pathway. He gives me a sad smile. "I was checking out another lead," he says. "Another dead end."

"Thank you for helping." I wrap my arms around his waist and give him a hug.

"There's nowhere else I would be," Phoenix assures me. "We're going to find her, Talia."

I want to believe him, but with each passing day, my hopes are shattered more and more. None of it makes any sense. If Aris wanted money, he would've contacted us by now. If he wanted to use her as a bargaining chip to steal the business from Kostas, he would've reached out. And since Kostas made sure to announce publicly that Ezio is dead, Aris has to know by now that his father is no longer alive.

But he's been completely silent. And that's what worries me. If he took her with the intent to keep her, he could be anywhere by now, and we may never see her again. At least if he took her with the purpose of using her to negotiate, we could give him what he wants and get our daughter back. The problem is Aris believes Zoe is his. A lie I told at the time to save us, but now regret.

As I walk through the doors of the office, I see Kostas and a thought hits me. "Kostas." He glances my way and walks toward me. "You told the world that Zoe is your daughter."

"Yeah…" Kostas gives me a confused look.

"Aris thought she was his. If he heard your speech, he knows she's not his." My hands cover my mouth as I remember what Aris said to me when I told him Zoe was his.

"Talia, talk to me," Kostas demands.

"Aris warned me that if he ever found out the baby wasn't really his, I would pay." I lied to him for over a year, swore up and down the baby was his… "What if he took her to use her as a bargaining chip, but once he found out she wasn't really his, he changed his mind?" My heart begins to race, and my head feels cloudy. Another anxiety attack is surfacing. "He could be keeping her just to make me pay." This could be all my fault. I never should've lied to Aris.

"Talia, calm down," Kostas says, taking me in his arms. "It doesn't matter what Aris knows or doesn't know. It changes nothing. You told him what he needed to hear to keep you and our little girl safe. We're going to find her."

"Boss," Adrian calls Kostas over. "Check out this image." He blows up a picture on the computer screen. It's of a man who meets Aris's description carrying a baby, but we can't see any faces.

"Where was this taken?" Kostas asks.

"The airport about thirty minutes ago," Adrian says.

"He wouldn't just walk through the airport," I say out loud. Aris is too smart for that, even if the man holding the baby looks almost identical to him.

"Probably not," Kostas agrees. "But we're following every possible lead."

He looks over his shoulder. "Phoenix," he barks. "Airport." Without asking any questions, Phoenix comes over and gets the information from Adrian then takes off.

We spend the next couple hours going through emails and calls of leads. When it's nearly four in the morning and I can tell Kostas is dragging, I tell him we need to go home. He looks like he wants to argue, but doesn't.

When we get home, he takes a quick shower and meets me in bed. With his arms around me, I snuggle into the crook of his neck. "Six days," I whisper. Tomorrow it will be a week.

"We're going to find her," Kostas says for a millionth

time, his voice filled with as much conviction as the first time he said it.

As my eyes are closing, his phone rings loudly throughout the room. He leans over and answers it. "Yeah." He sits up straight, knocking my head off his body. "You sure?" I can't hear who he's speaking to, but whoever it is, is talking fast. "I'll check right now."

Kostas places the phone on speaker and pulls up his email app. Peering over, I look to see what was emailed, and right there in color is a picture of Selene holding our daughter.

"That's her!" I gasp.

chapter
nineteen

Kostas

"ON MY WAY," I GROWL, SLINGING MY BODY OUT of the bed on a frantic hunt for clothes. "Pick me up in front of my villa in two minutes."

Talia flies out of the bed and starts dressing. "I can't believe they found her. Is it close? How long until we get there—"

"Not we," I bark out as I button my jeans and yank on a white T-shirt. "Me."

"Hell no," she screeches as she throws on her own clothes. "I'm going."

I don't have time to fight with her on this. All I do have time for is to grab my Glock from the bedside drawer and stalk out of the bedroom. Talia comes trotting after me. When I open the door, Basil is standing beside Adrian's SUV, talking to him.

"Hold down the fort," I bark out to Basil.

He nods before stepping away. I open the rear door and assist Talia in getting in before climbing into the front passenger seat.

Talia starts to sob in the back seat. When I glance back, I see that Adrian already loaded up the car seat. He feels it too. We're bringing her home. Thank fuck we have the cover of the dark, early morning. The last thing I need is for someone to tip Aris off.

Adrian hauls ass out of the hotel property and gets onto the main road. When he'd emailed me the pictures, he also emailed the location. Two hours from here on the other side of Crete Island near a small airport. Aris may have thought about trying to leave via plane but decided against it at the last minute because he has to know I have eyes everywhere, especially ports and airports. The motel we're headed to is a piece of shit one that hookers and johns use. I cringe thinking what sort of cesspool my baby's living in right now.

"Who'd the tip come from?" I ask as we drive.

"A maid."

"Just a maid?"

"Just a maid."

"Good," I grunt. "We won't owe any roaches shit. You'll have to get the maid to safety. The moment we wire her the money, she'll have a target on her back."

"Zoe first, maids later," Talia offers from the back seat.

I look over my shoulder and smile. "Zoe is always first."

The two-hour drive is tense and quiet. I answer calls and check in on different people. My main concern is Aris and Selene getting tipped off before we arrive. Soon, we're creeping through a small town twenty minutes from the coast. The sun has risen and a few restaurants blink their signs offering hot breakfast, making my stomach growl.

Zoe first, coffee and bagels later.

"It's up here," Adrian says.

"I'll go around front and you check the back," I order to him.

"I'm going with you," Talia says, trying her shit with me again.

I whip around and reach for her hand, pulling her close to me. With my eyes burning into hers, I kiss the back of her hand. "Not today."

"But—"

"I need you safe inside the SUV ready to drive off. Understood, *moró mou*? If Adrian and I should get injured, I need to be able to pass Zoe off to you and you get the fuck out of here. Please, for once in your stubborn fucking life listen to me." My words are spoken harshly to her, but I can't keep my wits about me if she's behind me. No fucking way. I need to be able to act without question.

Fat tears well in Talia's blue eyes, but she nods, sending them loose from her lids and skating down her cheeks.

"I love you," I whisper to her. "I *need* you to do this."

"I *can* do this," she says fiercely, swiping at her tears with her free hand. "I love you too."

I kiss her hand once more before releasing her to pull my Glock out of the center console and readying myself to act. Adrian parks a little ways up the road where we can see the small, aging, and decrepit motel, pointed toward the main road for a fast getaway. Several cars litter the parking lot.

"Which unit?" I demand.

"The maid said room six there on the end of the east side."

"We'll walk over to the west side and split around the building from there. Shoot first, ask questions later. At this point, put a bullet in Aris's skull. We can't risk him getting away. Zoe's safety is our primary concern." As much as I want to torture the fuck out of him, I can't let it cloud my judgment.

Adrian and I climb out of the SUV. When I glance back, I can see Talia scrambling to the front seat. Good girl. With my Glock ready, I nod at Adrian and then quietly walk along the front of the motel. He disappears around back. I pass by rooms one through three without incident, but when I get to the fourth room, I hear muffled crying not far off.

Zoe.

Panic swells up inside me and I quicken my pace, no longer worried about hiding. My sole focus is my daughter, whose crying gets louder the closer to room six I get. When I make it to the door, I press my ear to it.

"Shut up, stupid baby! Just shut the fuck up!"

When I hear what sounds like a slap, I step back and kick the door in. It slams against the wall and I charge inside, my gun drawn. Selene has Zoe in her arms and picks up a gun beside her. Zoe is red-faced and squirming, clearly pissed at being struck by this psycho cunt.

"Give me my fucking baby," I bellow, my gun aimed at Selene's face.

She presses the gun against Zoe's side. "Get the hell out of here!"

I don't move. Quickly I take stock of the situation. It smells like dirty diapers and hard liquor. Beside Selene on the end table are several empty bottles of alcohol. Between those are a few of Zoe's used bottles. My daughter wears a diaper and it's full of piss, hanging off her little body. A red handprint on her little thigh makes me want to bash Selene's head into the corner of the nightstand.

"Put Zoe down and I'll let you live."

"Liar," she snarls. "That's why I'm keeping this baby."

When she digs the barrel of the gun into Zoe's side, she screams bloody murder.

Fuck.

I could put a bullet in her head, but she's holding Zoe too close to her. With the way Zoe flails and squirms, I could accidentally hit her. I can't take that chance.

"Money? You want money?" I ask, my gun still trained on her. "I'll give you money and ship your ass to another country. You don't fucking deserve it, but that'll be my trade. It's the best goddamn offer you have."

Her eyes dart to the window, her brows furrowing. "I need this baby. I need him."

She looks like shit. Her red hair is dull and stringy and she's not wearing makeup. A big blackish purple bruise mars her throat. Someone grabbed her neck hard enough to leave a mark. If I had my guess, it's that my brother's been hitting the bottle and lost his temper on her. I just hope they didn't hurt Zoe. The red mark on her leg is infuriating enough. I can't imagine more.

Zoe's screams get louder and louder. She's pissed. I'd like to think it's because she hears my voice and wants me, but she's only six months old, so that's probably not right. I don't know much about babies. What I do know is she'll be one happy kid the moment she's in her mother's arms rather than this cunt's.

"He doesn't want you," I grind out. Delusional bitch. "You were always a cover for him." That much I realize now. Had I thought he was remotely interested in Talia, I would've shaken him down a lot sooner. But the fact he pretended to love Selene and I thought he wanted to marry her, he was able to fool me.

"He does want me!" she cries out. "He loves me and one

day I'll give him a baby of our own. We won't need that stupid bitch's baby anymore!"

This is taking too long.

Adrian is probably outside wondering what's going on but won't enter, especially if he overhears me trying to talk her down. But Talia? She's probably panicking. I know her. The last thing I need is her flying in here like a loose cannon upsetting the situation even further.

"Put the gun down," I command, my voice loud and sharp.

Crash!

The motel shakes as something explodes nearby. It's enough to distract Selene to jerk her head toward the sound, dropping her guard.

Pop!

I put a bullet on the part of her body farthest from my daughter. Her foot. She screams, dropping Zoe, who rolls to the floor with a loud thud. My daughter screams—which is music to my fucking ears considering the drop to the floor—and I stalk forward. She's okay. Selene raises the gun and I put a bullet into her shoulder. Another one pierces her throat. I want to make her hurt. She gurgles, grabbing her throat as blood sprays. With my eyes on her, I scoop up Zoe, tucking her under my arm like a football. Selene gapes at me as she tries and fails to stop the blood flow.

Pop!

I hit her in the stomach. I want her to bleed to death, thinking about what she did. How she struck my goddamn daughter. How she hurt my wife. How she aided my brother in an unimaginable crime.

Tucking my gun into the back of my jeans, I pull Zoe to my chest and kiss her sweaty head. "Shh, I've got you."

Selene has slumped against the headboard of the bed, but she's still alive, trying desperately to hold onto her life. I stalk over to her and grab a handful of her greasy red hair. Slamming her head down, I connect it with the corner of the end table, ending her misery early. Her skull cracks and she'll be dead in seconds. If I had more time or if I didn't have my daughter in my arms, I would've tortured her.

Turns out, I'm a family man now.

Torture can't happen at every enemy encounter. Sometimes I need to be quick and efficient to get back to what's important.

"Let's go see Mommy now," I coo to Zoe. "Daddy's here. No need to be upset."

Zoe grabs my shirt and screams, still super pissed at being slapped, screamed at, and then dropped. Fuck, I'd be pissed too. Holding her to me, I step outside the door I kicked in and frown when I see Adrian's SUV rammed into the unit beside this one. Talia is sitting behind the wheel looking every bit like a mafia queen. Wild eyes. Furious stare. Protective motherly aura rippling toward me in hot waves.

"What did you do to my fuckin' car, woman?" Adrian gripes as he comes up behind me.

"I stayed in the car!" she yells out. "I obeyed! Now bring me my baby!"

Zoe screams harder and tries to flip out of my grip.

Someone wants their mother.

chapter
twenty

Talia

MY FIRST THOUGHT WHEN I SAW KOSTAS STALKING toward the SUV with our baby in his arms was that she's alive and safe and I can finally breathe again. My second thought was how fucking sexy my husband looked holding our daughter to his chest like she's his entire world. Those hands that are capable of killing and torturing are also capable of being gentle and loving. When his eyes met mine, I could see the hardness in his light eyes—quite the contradiction—but the moment he looked down at Zoe, who was crying, his eyes went soft. The same way they go soft when he looks at me.

Once I stop staring at his eyes, and how precious our little girl looks in his arms, I notice the blood. Blood everywhere. All over their clothes, and splattered across their flesh.

"Is that blood?" I jump out of the driver's seat and run around the back, needing to get to Zoe and Kostas. "Is she bleeding?" I snatch her out of Kostas's hands and start checking her for injury. Her face is red and swollen from crying and there's a handprint mark on her thigh, but there're no cuts.

"It's not hers," Kostas says. "We're both okay."

"Who the fuck slapped her?" I bring her thigh up to show him. I'm seeing red. I don't see Selene or Aris anywhere. Did those fuckers touch my baby and then leave her here? That blood better be theirs.

"Selene did," Kostas says through a growl, his jaw tightening.

"Please tell me that bitch is alive," I hiss. "I'm going to fucking kill her."

Kostas shakes his head. "She's dead."

"Did she at least suffer?" I rub my daughter's thigh while holding her close to my chest. Her crying is already calming down.

"This is her blood," Kostas tells me. "I made sure that bitch was in pain before I ended her life."

"And what about Aris?" I glance around, suddenly realizing we've only been discussing Selene.

"He wasn't here," Adrian says.

"What?" I screech. Zoe jumps in my arms, and I remind myself I need to stay calm. "He can be anywhere." My gaze flits around us, hating that we're standing outside. He could be about to pounce.

"We're going to find him," Kostas promises. "Right now, we need to get our daughter home."

Kostas is right. Zoe's diaper is filled to the brim and leaking. She probably has a diaper rash. Who the hell knows when she was fed last. If that bitch wasn't already dead, I would torture and kill her my fucking self. Aris better run far because when I get my hands on him, I'm going to make sure he suffers for the both of them.

"We need to find a hotel," I tell the men as we climb into the SUV. Luckily, when I drove into the front of the building, hoping to create a diversion, the siding was rotted wood and no major damage was done. "We need to get her diapers and clothes and formula. She can't go two hours like this. I need to give her a bath."

The heaviness of everything that's happened is hitting me like a two-ton weight on my chest, and it's hard to breathe. "We need to get her to a doctor," I say through a sob. "What if…what if they hurt her?" I'm supposed to put Zoe in her car seat, but I can't let her out of my arms. She's clinging to me like a little koala bear.

Kostas tells Adrian to stop at the store, and while he runs in to grab stuff for Zoe, Kostas calls a local hotel and makes a reservation. The entire time, Zoe's tiny, chubby arms are wrapped around me with her face snuggled into my chest.

Oh, God, I finally have her back in my arms.

My heart is racing.

I need to get her as far away as possible. To somewhere safe.

What if Aris is following us? Waiting to make his move. What if this is all a trap?

I'm so tired, and all I want to do is snuggle up with my baby, but I need to make sure she's safe.

As I watch her, I notice she's fighting sleep. She's probably too scared. Whatever those pieces of shit did to her has my baby too scared to let herself go to sleep.

When we arrive at the hotel, Adrian checks us in and then both men flank me as we ride the elevator to the top floor. Only my husband would book the Presidential suite when we're only going to be here for a couple hours.

Adrian remains outside, while Kostas and I head

inside. While I give Zoe a bath, checking to make sure there's nothing visibly wrong with her, Kostas rinses off as well. Adrian must've gotten him clothes because when he gets out, he's in a plain white T-shirt and a pair of gray sweatpants.

Once they're both cleaned up, I sit on the couch with Zoe while Kostas makes her a bottle. I hold her close and take in her sweet baby scent, thankful to have her back in my arms.

Her eyes are almost closed at this point, most likely exhausted from everything she's been through, but she's still fighting to stay awake.

My strong fighter. Just like her daddy.

The second the bottle touches her lips, she sucks it down. Her eyes begin to droop, and her stiff body loosens in my arms.

"She was so hungry," I mumble, trying hard to stay strong for my daughter, but inside I'm a mess.

Something worse could've happened to her.

We could've lost her.

"She's a baby," Kostas says. "She'll soon forget what they did to her." He runs his fingers through her head of soft dark curls.

"I'll never forget," I tell him.

And I won't.

Not until the day I die.

Every thought in my being is fueled by the urge to hunt Aris down and punish him for this.

For putting my baby in harm's way.

One day we're going to find him, and when we do. I will make him pay.

"As soon as we get home, we're going to get shit

organized and find Aris," Kostas promises. His words hit me. *Home.* The hotel. The villa where Zoe was taken. The thought of bringing her back there has my heart racing.

"I can't go back there," I blurt out, and Kostas's eyes widen. "I know it's your home, but…"

"*Our* home," Kostas growls out without letting me finish.

"Kostas…"

"If the next words out of your mouth are to tell me you're leaving me, so help me fucking God." Kostas stands, towering over me. Zoe's bottle is empty and she's sleeping soundly in my arms. "You're my fucking wife, and that's our daughter, and if you think I'm going to let you leave me, you better think twice," Kostas chokes out. "I know I fucked up, Talia. Her getting taken is on me." He pounds his fist against his chest, and his eyes bore into mine. "But you aren't fucking leaving me. Ever."

"Kostas, that's not what I was going to say." I consider laying Zoe down, but I can't do it. So instead I stand, still holding her, and walk over to him. "I'm not going anywhere without you."

Kostas's shoulders drop slightly in relief. "Tell me what you need, *zoí mou.*"

"A place where we'll feel safe. A home where Aris hasn't touched and soiled. Maybe one with a pool, so I can take Zoe swimming. But it needs to be secure so nobody gets to us." I just need a damn break. A moment to be at peace with my family without living in fear. It can be months or years before we find Aris, and the hotel no longer feels like my safe place since it's where he stole our daughter. There's no way I'm going to be able to sleep at night, knowing that's where she was taken from.

"I'll handle it," Kostas assures me, already pulling his phone out. "Why don't you and Zoe go lie down and rest and once she wakes up, we'll head out."

Before I head to the room, I step closer to Kostas, and with Zoe sleeping between us, give him a soft kiss. "I don't blame you for any of this. Never think that. I blame Aris and Selene."

Kostas nods once, but I can tell by the way his eyes flinch slightly, he'll always in some way blame himself for not keeping Zoe safe. And I get it, because I'll always blame myself as well.

When we pull up to the house—no, house isn't the right word, more like castle—Kostas gets out and unbuckles Zoe. She's awake now and goes willingly with him. Unlike where Aris kept us, this place is backed up to the beach. I can smell the salt and hear the waves. My heart already feels steadier. My body already feeling lighter.

Surrounding the home is a tall block wall with a wrought iron fence running along the top. From what I can tell, it runs around the entire perimeter of the property. The house is at least three stories tall.

"Nobody is getting in or out of here without my knowledge," Kostas says. "The home is owned by a well-known politician. It's equipped with cameras and has a surveillance room. Once Adrian sets it all up, we'll be able to see every inch of this place right from our phones. And those fences"—he points to the walls—"they're wired with five thousand volts of electricity. One touch and it will knock a person the fuck out."

"Thank you," I tell him, feeling like the weights have been removed from my chest and I can finally breathe again.

"Let's go inside."

The inside is completely furnished. Beautiful shades of cream and bright blue. White wash wood everywhere, giving the entire place an upscale beachy vibe. To the left is a huge living room and dining room—a massive floor-to-ceiling fireplace separating the two. To the right, from what I can tell, is the kitchen. In the middle is a stunning white wash spiral staircase that leads to the upstairs.

"Can we stay here forever?" I joke.

Kostas doesn't laugh, though. "If you want to."

My head whips around to face him. "Are you serious?"

"If this is where you'll feel safe, then it's yours." He shrugs like it's no big deal, when it is in fact a huge deal. This house must cost millions, and he'll buy it just because I love it.

It doesn't matter what I ask for, he always makes sure I get what I want. He said it in his vows that he would make sure I'm always happy, and while I didn't believe them at the time, I know now he meant them. Even back then, when we barely knew each other, he was promising to put my happiness first.

Before I can say anything back, the front door opens and in walks Mom, Stefano, and Phoenix.

"Oh, *miei cari*," Mom cries out. *My darlings.* She runs straight toward Zoe and me and wraps her arms around us. "I was so worried," she cries, which makes me cry.

"We're okay, Mom. Zoe is okay."

Zoe wiggles in my arms and her bright blue eyes pop open. She grants my mom the most beautiful gummy smile, and Mom's and my tears fall even harder.

"Da-da-da," she coos, and Kostas laughs. Of course the only sound she's still making sounds like *Dad*.

"She already knows who she needs to call to get whatever she needs," Kostas says, taking her from me and holding her to his chest.

I sigh, watching him whisper something to our daughter. I don't think I will ever tire of watching him hold her.

"This house is gorgeous," Mom says. "How long are you staying here?"

"Until we find Aris," I tell her at the same time Kostas says, "As long as Talia wants."

We spend the day by the pool—yes, the house has a stunning infinity pool and Jacuzzi—enjoying Zoe. Kostas frequently takes calls, no doubt determined to find Aris. For the first time in months I feel safe and don't even bother to ask him for updates. I'm simply content living in this temporary bubble.

For dinner, Kostas has one of his men pick up groceries and Stefano grills burgers while my mom and I make the side dishes. Everything feels so normal. I know being with Kostas means nothing will ever really be normal, and there will always be threats. My husband is a powerful man who runs a dangerous organization. But seeing another side to him today—him sitting on the lounge chair in his swim trunks, eating a burger and baked beans, and swimming in the pool with Zoe—gives me hope that after we find and kill Aris, we will be able to finally start our life as a family.

After dinner, everyone leaves, and it's only Kostas, Zoe, and me. While we were out back, he of course had her furniture brought over. Her room is upstairs, directly next to ours, but he also had a portable crib put in our room for now.

"Thank you for putting a crib in here." I lay Zoe in her

bed. "It's going to take some time until I'm comfortable with her sleeping in her own room." She's been fed, has a fresh diaper, and is sucking on her pacifier, already half asleep.

"She'll stay with us until you're ready," Kostas says. "But I promise you, she's safe in this house." He locks our bedroom door. "Come shower with me."

When I give him a look, silently asking why he locked our door, he says, "I want to make sure none of my men accidently walk in and see my sexy wife naked. Then I'll have to kill them."

I laugh even though I believe he really would do just that.

With my hand in his, he guides us into the bathroom. From here, we can still see Zoe's crib.

I watch as he pushes his trunks down his muscular thighs, and his thick cock springs free. His eyes meet mine, and the love that shines in them takes my breath away. I've always thought Kostas was sexy, but seeing him as a father, interacting with our daughter, makes him beautiful. And when he looks at me the way he is right now, knowing that underneath all that darkness is a lightness only reserved for Zoe and me to see, makes my heart swell.

I strip out of my bikini, keeping my eyes on Kostas as his heated gaze runs over every inch of my body. If looks could burn, I would be on fire.

"Come here, wife," he demands. He turns the water on and steps into the shower first. There are several showerheads raining down on us, so no matter where we stand warm water hits us.

"How are you feeling?" he asks, framing my cheeks with his strong hands. Our bodies are flush against one another, and he has me backed up against the wall.

"I'm good," I tell him honestly. My eyes flit out of the open shower and into our bedroom, thankful I can see Zoe. "I'm not sure I'll ever be able to let her out of my sight."

"Does that mean when she's a teenager, we can keep her locked up?" Kostas asks, his lips twitching in amusement. I love every side of him. The serious, the sweet, the silly.

"Don't rush my baby growing up." I pout, and Kostas grins.

With his thumb and finger on my chin, he tilts my head up and his lips descend on mine. My arms cling to his neck as our mouths tangle and our tongues duel with one another. Tasting. Coaxing. Getting lost in each other. I didn't realize how much I needed his touch, to feel him until now. We kiss until the water turns cold, and then after quickly washing our bodies, Kostas carries me out of the shower.

With both of us dripping wet, he sets me on the sink and spreads my thighs. His mouth goes right back to mine, his tongue massaging mine. His hands grip my hips, and he pulls me toward him. My hot center rubs against his pelvis. My fingers wrap around his hard shaft, and I stroke it, getting it hard, before I guide it into me.

Kostas's mouth leaves mine to watch as he enters me slowly, filling me with every inch of him. We both watch as we become one. When I'm filled to the hilt with him, he pulls out slowly.

"Do you see this?" he asks, already knowing I do. "Your cunt was made just for me." My insides tighten at his dirty words, and he smirks. He pushes himself back into me, hitting my G-spot.

"Faster," I beg, desperate to find my release. My breasts are heavy and my nipples are painfully erect. I need more, but he's refusing to give it to me.

"There's no rush, *moró mou*," he purrs, continuing to push in and out slowly. Every time he enters me, the head of his cock hits me deep. Little by little, like a hurricane on the horizon, my orgasm builds higher and higher. With every thrust, I can feel it getting closer, gaining momentum.

Kostas finds my clit, and he massages it in circles, still watching as he enters me deeply and then draws out slowly. In and out. Bringing me to the precipice and then taking me away from the edge before I can fall.

"Kostas, please," I beg. Can one die from being denied an orgasm? I'd rather not find out.

When his eyes meet mine, his gaze is filled with lust and love. Heat and desire. My back arches slightly, and my breasts are thrust in his face. He takes a nipple between his lips, and when he bites down on it, my body convulses in pleasure.

His thumb leaves my clit, and he cages me in, somehow filling me even deeper than before. That's all it takes for my body to detonate. His mouth covers mine, muffling my screams of pleasure as he drives into me. My hips rise to meet his thrust for thrust as we both come completely undone.

My legs are shaking, and my body has gone limp. It takes a few minutes to calm my heavy breathing. Kostas pulls out of me and smirks at what I'm sure is his cum dripping between my legs. There's no doubt he's going to have me knocked up soon…and I can't fucking wait.

chapter
twenty-one

Kostas

"YOU KNOW WHAT? FUCK HIM." I scrub my palm down my face before leveling Adrian with a hard glare. "I'm done going after him. It's what he wants."

"No," Adrian argues. "What he wants is to toy with you."

It's been days since we rescued our daughter. Days since we've used up all our energy looking for my brother. I'm over it, dammit.

"With what resources?" I demand. "I get that he could do that shit when he had access to the Demetriou fortune. When he had a bitch who worshiped the ground he walked on. When he had a fucking car. But now? He has fucking nothing. I'm done wasting precious time with my family to hunt down this motherfucker."

"I'll have Basil continue to probe his contacts. Just because you don't want to actively search for him doesn't mean we can't still keep an eye out for him," Adrian says.

A year ago, I would've fucked over a man with just my knife if he'd undermined my authority. Now, I think a little differently. Besides, Adrian means well and has my best interest at heart.

"You got anyone besides Basil?" I ask, irritation clipping my tone.

Adrian's brows knit together. I know they're like brothers, but brothers can fucking turn on you. I of all people know this. "Wesley is there. He's one of my best and most trusted."

"Give Wesley the same job. Then, we can compare notes on what information they give back to us."

Adrian is clearly annoyed, but he nods before texting. While he busies himself with the affairs of the dark side of my business, I have to deal with the legit side. I call and make arrangements with the hotel manager, Carla. She'll get started on hiring a construction crew to repair the damage Aris and Selene inflicted upon the hotel while also updating some areas of the hotel that need it. We'll be down for the season, but our other hotels in Crete and Santorini will bring in plenty of profit.

"Where's Phoenix?" I ask once he's done firing off messages.

"Last I saw, he was out by the pool with the girls."

I exit my office and make my way to the back door. As I exit, one of the men, Fowler, bows his head in respect. Phoenix stands by the pool like a sentry, looking more formidable than the five guards I have placed all over the backyard. He's dressed in a suit that fits his style unlike that shitty stuff he and his father always wore. It's like he belongs here. And I know he'd do anything to protect Talia.

Which makes him perfect for what I need him for.

Pushing through the door, I nod to him before walking over to the edge of the pool. Melody waves to me from a pool lounger. I crouch to give my wife a kiss and to grin at my daughter. She lets out a squeal of laughter, melting away all my anger and irritation. If I didn't have so much shit to do, I'd go swimming with them. But, even bad guys have to fucking work.

"My beautiful girls," I say before leaving them to play. I click my tongue and nod into the house, motioning for Phoenix to follow me. "Watch them," I bark out to Fowler.

"Always, sir," Fowler says back.

As soon as we're in my office with Adrian, I close the door and pull out the ouzo. I'm not the lush I once was, but now that I have my family back, I can relax with a drink from time to time. I make the three of us a drink and then settle in my office chair. Phoenix is guarded but stoic. I study him for a long while and decide that both he and Talia have Melody's strength. I tapped into her strength when Talia was missing, so I know this firsthand. With Niles gone, it's easier to note the similarities between the siblings. He's lucky. The fucker is growing on me. Talia sure as hell did.

"Your duties in Thessaloniki are over." I sip my ouzo and watch for his reaction.

His jaw ticks, but he doesn't show anger. "Is that so?"

"It is." I reach into my drawer and pull out a set of keys. "The Land Rover in the garage is yours. Trade it in for what you want."

He lifts a brow. "Okay. You going to elaborate?"

"Your father is dead. Your sister is here. What more do you want?"

"Not bullshit answers," he grumbles, frowning just like my fucking wife.

I let out a heavy sigh. "My brother betrayed me. You'd

die for your sister. I need someone like that on my team. Someone who would give up anything to protect my wife. Is that someone you?"

"You want a Nikolaides to come work for a Demetriou?" He scoffs, shaking his head. "Never thought I'd see the day."

Adrian snorts out a laugh. We never saw this coming either. But here we are.

"Technically, you already did work for us in case you've forgotten," I grit out. "Again, are you willing to trade your glorious life back in Thessaloniki for one on Crete Island? You'll be paid handsomely."

"Like I've ever given a fuck about the money," he bites out. "All I care about is my family."

"Then that will be your reward, Phoenix. You'll have unlimited access to both my wife and my daughter. I'll bring you into the fold—erase your fucking Nikolaides past, and give you a Demetriou future. But once you're in, there's no getting out."

He leans back in his chair and gulps down his ouzo before setting the glass down hard. "What do you want me to do? Guard my sister?"

As much as I would love that added layer of protection, I need Phoenix for more.

"You've handled the taxes quite nicely. You have a flair for numbers, correct?"

He nods. "Dad sure as hell didn't. I learned at an early age how to run numbers to help his ass out."

"Good. I've just lost my numbers man." My chair creaks when I lean forward, placing my elbows on my desk and steepling my fingers. "The moment you're given the key to the castle, there is no turning back. If I even sniff one ounce of you turning coat, I will fucking destroy you, Phoenix. I will make Talia cut into you and remove each organ for me. Are we clear?"

Adrian laughs again, earning a scowl from Phoenix.

"You're such a fucking psychopath," he grumbles. "And, no, I'd never do that shit to my sister. You have my word."

"Wonderful. Now run along and go trade that expensive ass car in for another stupid Jeep. We have to go over a mountain of shit. The sooner you get back, the sooner we can get to it." I wave him off with a flick of my hand.

Phoenix rises and gives Adrian an incredulous look. "Does he talk to you like that?"

"He grows on you," Adrian says with a snort.

"Right," Phoenix grumbles. He stops mid stride and turns to glower at me, making me tense. "And Jeeps aren't stupid. They're practical."

Adrian laughs. "Go on, boy, before you get bitch slapped."

"You assholes can fucking try," Phoenix says with a smirk that reminds me of Talia. Ornery fucker.

As soon as he's gone, I pull up my laptop and dive back into business, both legit and nefarious. A villain's work is never done.

I wake up in the dead of the night to my phone ringing off the hook.

"What?" I snarl into the line.

"Your father's place," Adrian barks out. "I'm on my way. Meet me there."

He hangs up on me. What the fuck? I slide out of bed and start throwing on clothes.

"Where are you going?" Talia asks, her voice raspy from sleep.

I lean over the bed and kiss her mouth. "Business. Phoenix and the men will be here. Your gun is in your bed-side table. Use it if you need to."

As I start to pull away, she grabs my wrist. "I love you."

"Love you too."

Within five minutes, I'm dressed and locking the bed-room door behind me. I stalk down the hallway to the guest room where Phoenix is staying before pushing inside. When I flick on the lights, he snags his Glock and has it aimed in my direction. Good reflexes.

"Need you to keep an eye on Talia and Zoe. Something's happened at my father's place," I tell him before turning on my heel.

He pads behind me. "Another diversion?"

I stalk into the spare room where we have a gun safe and turn the dial on the lock. "I don't know, but we can never be too sure. Just in case"—I toss him an AR-15—"use brute force to protect them."

In nothing but boxers and socks, Phoenix still manages to look formidable with a Glock in one hand and the AR in the other.

"You think he's coming out of hiding?" he asks.

"Nah," I grunt as I push past him. "He's just fucking with me. It's what he does."

"He'll slip up one day, Kostas," Phoenix calls out after me. "And we'll make him fucking pay."

"Damn right we will."

The drive to my father's is quick as our new home isn't

too far from there. I'm less than a mile away when I see what the fuck happened. That asshole set our childhood home on fire. I push back memories of my mother and me in the kitchen. Many nights when I was small and she'd read stories about heroes to me. The scent of her perfume that still lingered even a year after her death.

Fuck Aris.

It was his mother too.

This just proves to me he's nothing but a sociopath. All he cares about is number one. Himself. And his favorite way of pleasuring himself is to fuck with me. Sick bastard.

By the time I reach the home, it's completely engulfed in flames. The firefighters are already doing their best to control the fire so it doesn't spread elsewhere. I pull up next to Adrian's SUV and hop out.

"What the hell?" I snap, trotting over to him.

He scowls at me. "Aris."

"No fucking shit."

"And, Boss…" He pinches the bridge of his nose. "I can't get ahold of Basil."

My blood runs cold. "It's the middle of the night. Understandable."

"Wesley says he never came back to the hotel last night."

"Aris took him?"

Adrian's features pinch. "He packed his shit, man."

A rat. I had a hunch before and I was right. Unfuckingbelievable.

"Put Wesley in charge at the hotel. I want you on point hunting Basil down."

"I thought we were done hunting," Adrian huffs, irritation making his voice gruff.

"Aris. Basil is a different story. We find Basil, we'll find

Aris. Find out where the fuck he went, when he went there, and why he thought fucking me over was a smart plan. We find Basil, and I'll bleed out every detail he knows about Aris."

Adrian scowls but nods. "Yep."

I clutch his shoulder and give it a squeeze. "Brothers can turn. But you and I? We don't fucking turn. You feel me, Adrian? We're better than brothers."

"I'm gonna find his ass and haul him in myself. This shit will end soon," he vows. The exhaustion from this entire Aris debacle over the past year has worn down on my longtime friend.

As soon as he gets in his SUV and leaves, I pull up my security cameras. Talia is asleep in the bed and she's moved Zoe with her. Phoenix paces the hallway right outside their door dressed all in black, the AR slung over his shoulder. Thank fuck. The rest of the men are stationed around the perimeter of my house. At least they're safe.

But they won't be until I deal with my fuckface brother.

I'm going to find his crazy ass and end him because I'm getting too old for this shit. Can't a man just settle the fuck down and have one goddamn week to be a normal fucking husband and father?

Until I drag Aris's ass into that cellar, I won't.

I need to start thinking like him. If I were Aris, what the hell would I do next to fuck with me? Cars are a dime a dozen. He doesn't know the location of our new home. That leaves the hotel. I text Adrian to secure the property from every angle. Next, I text Josef.

Me: I want every cop hunting down Aris Demetriou. Every fucking one of them.

Josef: And compensation?

Me: Money. Lots of it.
Josef: And?
Me: Reelection.
Josef: Done.

If Josef leads me to Aris, I'll get him into any political position he so fucking desires. My next text is to a low-level punk gangster with a big mouth—someone I pay to get messages out.

Me: Aris Demetriou to me alive. 50 mil. Spread the word.
Jaws: Poppy needs a new pair of shoes. On it, Boss.

I don't care if my brother drains me dry. I'd gladly lose every dime if it means having him strapped to a chair in the cellar. Every goddamn dime. Because once he's dead, I'll just make more fucking money. I'm a Demetriou. It's what we do.

chapter
twenty-two

"**G**UESS WHAT TODAY IS?" I ASK ZOE AS I PICK her up out of her crib. She flails her chubby arms and babbles like crazy, excited to see me.

Last night was the first night in her own room and I swear I got up thirty times throughout the night to check on her. I know she needs to sleep in her own room, but it's hard to be away from her.

With Aris having burned down their family home recently, Kostas has our home on lockdown. Nobody is allowed to come or go except for him and his men. Stefano had to leave for Italy to get back to work, but my mom has extended her stay. Thankfully, we have a beautiful pool house, complete with its own kitchen and laundry room, so while she's here, she's staying there.

"What's today?" Kostas asks, stepping behind me. I lay Zoe across her changing table so I can change her diaper and get her dressed.

"Today, Miss Zoe is seven months old." I lean over and

blow raspberries on her belly. Her giggles ring out through the room. "Every month when I lived with…" I stop myself, not wanting to bring up Kostas's brother. With Aris still missing and wreaking havoc all over town, Kostas's frustration has been at an all-time high. The last thing I want to do is add to that.

"What?" he prompts.

"Never mind. She's seven months old today, that's all."

"Talia." He picks Zoe up from the changing table then turns to face me. "Whatever happened while we were apart, I want to know. It fucking kills me that I missed out on everything. Your pregnancy, Zoe's birth, the first six months of her life…"

He's right. I can't help what happened while I was being held captive by Aris. And stopping my tradition just because it began while I was at Aris's house only gives him power he doesn't deserve.

"I started a tradition when Zoe turned a month old. I would bake cupcakes and after dinner, I would light a candle in one and make a wish. Then afterward, I would take our picture. I would make Aris get it printed and I put each one into a scrap book."

Kostas smiles softly. "What did you wish for?"

"For you to find us." I take a breath, not wanting to cry. I started my period this morning, so I know I'm being overly emotional. We're home and safe, and there's no reason to cry.

Kostas steps toward me and pushes a wayward strand of hair out of my face. "Looks like this month you'll have to make a new wish." He bends slightly and kisses me. It's sweet and quick, but it still lights my belly on fire.

"Do you still have the scrapbook?" he asks.

"I do. I snatched it when I grabbed our stuff."

"You'll have to show it to me," he insists.

When he steps back, I notice he's dressed in his suit. "Are you leaving?"

"I need to handle a few things at the office. Handle my parents' house."

"Will it be able to be saved?"

"No, but it was fully insured. I need to meet with the agent today to go over everything." He gives Zoe a kiss, then hands her to me. "I should be home for dinner. Save me a cupcake." He winks playfully, and I laugh at how damn sexy he is when he's playful.

After seeing him out, I head into the kitchen to make the cupcakes. My mom comes in as I'm setting them in the oven with a cup of coffee in her hand.

"Did you sleep okay?" I ask, grabbing my own cup of coffee and sitting at the table across from her. Zoe is sitting in her high chair, playing with her new sippy cup and eating her cheerios.

"I slept very well." She smiles. "That bed is so comfortable. I'm going to have to tell Stefano to buy us one." She glances into the kitchen. "Baking this early?"

"They're Zoe's seven-month cupcakes. I make them every month to celebrate her birthday."

Mom grins from ear to ear. "Kind of like your birthday pancakes?"

"Yeah." I laugh, remembering when I was growing up I would insist Mom make pancakes like every day. Not wanting to make them all the time, she would say they were only for special occasions. So, every time I would ask, I would make up an excuse, like it was my twelve-year, two-month birthday. She could've totally told me I was full of shit, but she never did. Instead, she would make them every time.

"How's Kostas doing?" she asks. I hate that I was gone for over a year, but I love that something good came from the shitty situation. A friendship of sorts was formed between Kostas and my mom. And not just between them, but also between Kostas and Phoenix. Well, maybe not a friendship between Kostas and Phoenix per se…but definitely a mutual understanding. Kostas even gave him a job and a place to live at the hotel.

"He's okay. Just stressed. Aris is still missing, and instead of keeping quiet, he's apparently trying to create destruction at every turn to bring Kostas down."

"Has he done anything else since he burned down their parents' home?"

"Last night they think he tried to burn the hotel down. Some wires got tripped, but Kostas was ready for him and they caught it quickly, so no damage was done. But, of course, they didn't see who did it. So, now Kostas thinks there's a rat."

Mom huffs in disgust. "I hope they catch him soon."

"Same, but until they do, I think it's safe to say Kostas will be on edge. I just wish there was something I could do."

Mom takes a sip of her coffee and when she sets it down, she grins. "What if I take Zoe to the pool house with me tonight, so you can make him a romantic dinner? You can spend some time just the two of you."

My first thought is there's no way I'm letting Zoe out of my sight, but then, after I take a deep breath, I remember the pool house is only a few yards away and my mom did raise me. She's great with Zoe.

"I'll even ask Phoenix to come over," she adds, obviously sensing my reluctance. "I can spend some time with my son and granddaughter, and you can have a nice, peaceful dinner with your husband."

The buzzer goes off, indicating the cupcakes are done, so I head over to the oven and take them out.

"What do you think?" she prompts.

"I think that would be great." I open the fridge to see what we have. Upon inspection, I find I have everything I need to make Kostas's favorite: chicken parmesan.

"But not overnight," I tell her. "Once we're done, I'm coming to get my baby back."

She laughs and shakes her head. "It's so hard to believe that *my* baby is all grown up." She stands and walks over to me, enveloping me in one of her comforting hugs. "You've grown into such a beautiful woman, Talia," she says. "A loving mother and a devoted wife. I'm so proud of you."

"Thank you, Mom." That means a lot coming from her because she's not only my mom, but my best friend, and growing up, I always wanted to be just like her.

After cleaning up the kitchen, we get changed into our swimsuits and head out to the pool. It's a perfectly sunny day with not a cloud in sight.

While Mom holds Zoe, I swim some laps, and once I'm done, I take Zoe around in her little inflatable boat that has an umbrella top on it to provide shade. She giggles and splashes in the water. Only getting out of the pool to eat her snacks and drink her juice.

When lunchtime rolls around, I give Zoe back to Mom, so I can grab us something to eat.

"Need help with anything?" a masculine voice asks. Bending to grab my towel, I glance over my shoulder to find Fowler standing right behind me with his gaze pointed directly at my butt.

Since Basil has gone MIA, Kostas and Adrian are out more, so that leaves Fowler and the team watching over us.

At first, when I would catch him checking me out, I thought I was seeing things, but the more he does it, the more I realize he's a fucking perv. And a dumbass because once I tell Kostas, he's going to kill him. I almost feel bad.

I stand back up and turn around. "Nope, I got it."

"You sure?" Fowler steps closer and the small hairs on the back of my nape rise.

"Well, if you really want to help, you can start by watching *my family* instead of watching *me.*"

I know he gets what I'm insinuating because he smirks. It's smarmy and sends chills up my spine. I glance around, hoping to see another one of Kostas's men, but it's just us. I know they're all over the grounds, but only one usually stays with us inside the house or out back.

"Sorry, I'm a flirt by nature. Nothing meant by it." He shrugs, not even bothering to look guilty, despite his words, for staring at my body. "It's hard to focus when you're dressed like that." He grins boyishly and nods toward me. I'm wearing a two-piece bikini, and sure, it might be on the small side, but I'm in my own home, and even if I weren't, I should be able to wear whatever the hell I want without being ogled by Kostas's men.

Just as I'm about to give this asshole a piece of my mind, I hear my husband call out my name.

Perfect timing.

"*Moró mou,*" Kostas says, pulling me into his side. He kisses my temple then addresses Fowler. "How's everything?"

Fowler's gaze flits from me back to Kostas and I swear I see a hint of a smirk playing on the corner of his lips. *Does this guy seriously want to die?* "Absolutely perfect," he says.

"Kostas, can I talk to you for a minute?" I ask.

"Of course." He turns his attention back to me.

When Fowler doesn't take the hint, I add, "Alone."

Kostas's brows knit together. "What's the matter, Talia? If there's an issue, Fowler needs to know as well. Did something happen?"

"No, nothing happened." I glance over at Fowler, who's still standing there, with his arms crossed over his chest, and his eyes roaming my body. Is this guy for real? "Well, actually something did happen." I look pointedly at Fowler. "This guy keeps checking me out, and it's making me uncomfortable."

Kostas's brows dip further. "Is this true?" he asks Fowler. "Are you checking out my wife?"

"Sir, it wasn't like that," Fowler sputters. His back goes straight, and finally, his eyes are no longer on me.

"Either you did or you didn't check my wife out. It's simple."

"She's wearing a skimpy bikini, sir, and I might've noticed. I didn't mean any offense."

I scoff at the way he's downplaying this. He was totally perving on me.

"Where's Greg?" Kostas asks him.

"In the security room," Fowler says.

"And Kip?"

"Guarding the front."

Kostas steps toward Fowler, and since Kostas is a good half a foot taller, he looks down at him. "I don't give a fuck if my wife is naked, you don't ever look at her in any way other than to make sure she's safe. Understand?" His voice is calm, but I can see it in the way his jaw is ticking, he's about to lose his shit.

Good! Serves that asshole right.

"Yes, sir," Fowler says like the good soldier he is. Gag.

"Go take over for Kip and tell him to get back here."

What? That's it? He's just assigning him to a different location?

After Fowler leaves, Kostas's eyes swing back over to me. "Talia, is that the only bathing suit you have?"

Oh, no, he didn't.

"No, but—"

"Go change into something more appropriate, please."

I glance over at my mom, who is lying on a chaise lounge with Zoe in her arms. I can tell by the look on her face she can hear everything that's happening.

"I'm not changing," I tell Kostas, crossing my arms over my chest in defiance. "This is my home, and I'll wear whatever the hell I want."

Kostas's brows rise in shock. "Talia, it wasn't a suggestion. Go fucking change. I'm not going to have you prancing around here so my men can ogle what's mine."

What's his? Like I'm a goddamn piece of property!

"You're a chauvinist pig, and if you don't walk away right now, I'm going to push your ass into that pool." I walk around Kostas and over to Mom. I take Zoe out of her hands, so I can lay her down for a nap.

"Talia," Kostas growls, but I ignore him, because if I don't, we're going to fight. And I'm choosing to chalk his dumb ass remarks up to stress because of Aris.

"I'll see you tonight!" I call out behind me.

"So, that's it?" he shouts back. When I keep walking, he says, "Real fucking nice, Talia. I'm so glad I came home to see my family for lunch."

Too pissed, and afraid I'll say something I might regret later, I don't bother answering him. And the smart man he is, doesn't follow me.

While I'm laying Zoe down, I think about everything

he said. While he's in the wrong, he also made a valid point about being appropriate in front of his men. Not wanting to fight with him over something so trivial, when I get back downstairs, I look for him to apologize, but he's already gone. Great, now I'm going to need to make sure this dinner is extra perfect because if I know my husband, he's going to come home cranky as hell later.

Chicken Parmesan-check.

Pasta and sauce-check.

Salads-check.

Wine-check.

Oh! The bread.

Remembering I placed it in the warmer, I run back into the kitchen to grab it. Since my mom has Zoe, and I'm making this dinner for Kostas, I frosted Zoe's cupcakes and put them away. I figure we can make our wish tomorrow. One day won't make a difference. Plus, with Kostas being all growly, I figured the best way to calm him down will be to ply him with his favorite food, since I'm on my period and can't have sex with him. If he's extra cranky, I'll give him head. That always softens him up.

I hear the door open then slam shut, and then Kostas's voice booms throughout the house.

Great, just as I thought…he's cranky.

"I don't give a fuck what he said," he barks into the phone. "I've had enough of this back and forth bullshit. I want answers!"

With the bread basket in my hands, I'm stepping into

the dining room, when I see Kostas already in there. He yells some more at whoever he's on the phone with, and then, like it's happening in slow motion, his fist comes out and swipes at the items on the table. The wine glasses shatter, the chicken parmesan splatters, and the salads fly through the air.

I gape at the destroyed table, my eyes fixated on the red sauce that will stain the wall it's slowly trekking a path down. The entire meal I just spent hours making is completely ruined.

Kostas's eyes meet mine, and he looks around, as if now realizing what he did.

"Talia," he breathes.

"My mom's watching Zoe for us… I made you dinner," I choke out. "And it's ruined." I don't have to feel my cheeks to know I'm crying. I know it's just food, but I worked hard on it to make him feel better and with one swipe, he destroyed it all.

"Shit." He scrubs his hands over his face in frustration. He's always frustrated. Always mad. When he found us, it was supposed to be the beginning of our life together, but instead, because of Aris, it's as if our life is on hold. Kostas tries so hard not to let this side of him show in front of Zoe and me, but I've been watching it build and build, and he's finally reached his boiling point.

"I didn't mean to," he says, stepping toward me, his brow furling and his eyes shining with remorse. "It's just…it's been a bad fucking day."

chapter
twenty-three

Kostas

TALIA RUSHES OFF AND I FEEL LIKE A FUCKING animal. I scrub my palm over my face and laugh bitterly. Aris has infected every part of my relationship with Talia straight from the beginning. He's like a bite from a zombie and as time passes, I'm becoming infected too.

I want to hack him away from me.

Sever him like a diseased limb I'll be better off without.

We're at war, my brother and me, and it's fucking bloody.

But I will win.

Winning means keeping my wife happy. Because when we're happy, Aris has lost. The loser in a game where he didn't get the girl. Even when he stole her, she was never his. She will never be his.

I can be pissed as fuck at my brother, but allowing him to creep into our evening time alone and ruin our dinner is too much. He doesn't deserve that win. And my wife deserves more than that.

With a heavy sigh, I clean up the mess. Sure, we have

people to do this, but I need to be the one to do it. To smell the heavenly sauce I won't get to eat. To curse over the expensive bottle of wine that's ruined and never tasted. To face the consequences of my destruction. And to clean it all up.

Talia is next.

I'll kiss her and make it all better.

Once the dining room is cleaned up, I grab a bottle of vodka from the cabinet and set it on the counter. Then, I pull out some salami, several cheeses, crackers, and grapes. After arranging them on a giant plate, I locate the can of leftover frosting in the fridge. Shoving a spoon into the top, I then place it in the center of my plate of apologies. I tuck the vodka under my arm and grab up the plate. I don't find her right away because she's not in our bedroom. Eventually, I locate her in the theater room. Sitting in the dark. Crying. Fuck.

I turn on the lights and she buries her face in her hands. Setting down the plate and alcohol on the table beside a vase filled with fresh Gerber daisies, I pick up the remote to turn on the giant eighty-five-inch screen. It takes some scrolling through Netflix, but I find a version of *Romeo + Juliet* I can handle. Leonardo DiCaprio and Claire Danes. I kick off my shoes and sit down beside her.

"I know you don't want to hear me tell you I'm sorry again," I say softly, gripping her thigh and squeezing. "So I'm not saying it. You don't respond to that shit anyway."

She hisses at me. "Fuck you!" she bellows, kicking out and sending the goddamn vase on the table flying across the room. Her fucking periods will be the death of me.

"What I mean," I growl, staring at yet another broken vase, "is you do better with actions. I made you a charcuterie board."

"You can't win me over with your fancy cheese plate,"

she bites out. "Not after you threw my dinner to the floor, Kostas Demetriou."

I snort, which earns me another hiss from her. "You didn't even look at it."

She peeks out between her fingers that still cover her face. "Is that chocolate icing?"

I'm a smart fucking man.

"I bet the grapes taste good dipped in the chocolate icing," I offer, reaching over to pluck a grape from the vine, and then run it along the fudgy sweetness. "Should I taste it first?"

She pops her lips open like a petulant toddler finally giving in to receiving her medicine. I pretend to put the grape to her mouth, but then replace it with my lips at the last second. Her gasp is one of surprise, and before she can push me away, I nip at her bottom lip.

"I love you," I murmur before finally treating her to the chocolate grape.

"Mmm," she moans, her eyes fluttering closed. "I still hate you, but just a little less."

"Then I better keep feeding you."

"You better."

"I put your favorite movie on," I tell her.

She laughs, but it's a mean laugh that gets my dick hard. "I hate this version."

"But you know all the words," I argue. "Your eyes light up when you watch it."

"It's cheesy," she grumbles.

"I'll show you cheesy."

"Oh my God." She fights a smile as I pile salami and cheese onto a cracker. "You're totally cheesy. This is ridiculous. Twenty minutes ago you were furious and slinging shit around our kitchen. Now you're telling me dumb dad jokes and watching corny chick flicks? This is why I hate you."

"You love me," I explain as I shove the whole cracker in her mouth to keep her quiet so I can speak. "You love me because I am nothing without you."

Her brows crash together as she chomps on the cracker in such an unladylike way it makes me want to lick every single crumb that falls onto her thighs.

"You make me want to be better than I ever thought I could be. I never cared to be *better* until you. Now, this villain thinks he can be your hero." I lean my forehead against hers. "I'm going to be really honest here. I'll suck at it at first. You'll hate me at least once a week. But I'm fucking trying, Talia. For you. For Zoe. For our family."

She swallows and pouts. "You make it sound like I don't appreciate you. I do, even when you're an asshole."

"I see your pretty face and every horrible thing I've ever done is forgotten. All that matters is you and our daughter. I fucking bask in your presence, whether you're beaming at me or burning me with your anger. As long as you're the one doing it, I fucking want it. All the warm, happy moments and the raging, hot terrible ones. You, Talia. I want you."

"I want you too. I hate that we're being deprived of our happiness because of him."

I grip her jaw and kiss her softly. "I'm going to try harder. To leave the stress at the door. By bringing it in our home, I'm letting him win. I'll be damned if I let that weasel win."

"We win," she tells me firmly. "You and me, Kos. We're a team. A filthy king and his adorable queen." She laughs and it sounds like music.

"Accept my apology," I demand, nipping at her bottom lip. "Now, woman."

"You're such a prick," she says with a sigh. "My prick."

I grip her hand and run it over my cock. "Your prick's right here."

"Your prick is being punished," she tells me primly. "Go on. Feed me some more. I'm enjoying the groveling." She leans forward to grab the vodka and makes a seductive show of unscrewing the lid before wrapping her dick sucking lips around the bottle.

With my eyes on her so I don't miss the way her throat bobs as she swallows down the burn, I fix her another cheese and meat cracker. The movie plays in the background—the soundtrack working in my benefit to seduce my wife. As the food disappears and the bottle empties, I warm my woman up. All anger has dissipated as giggles take over.

"What's so funny?" I murmur, my lips tracing kisses along the side of her neck. "Romeo and Juliet is a tragedy."

"This version is," she snorts.

"A man tries to be romantic and this is how he's rewarded." I bite her warm flesh. "Maybe I should stop wooing you and just ravish you instead." When I slide my palm up her bare thigh to just under her dress, she lets out a sharp breath and grips my wrist.

"I'm on my period, remember?"

"So?"

"Kostas!"

"You think I'm afraid of blood?"

"Don't be gross."

"Nothing about fucking you on your period is gross."

She gapes at me when I push her dress up her hips.

"Lie back," I order.

"Kostas…"

I reach under her dress and grip her panties. Her breath hitches when I tug them down her thighs. Once they're tossed away, I kiss up her naked thigh.

"Kostas," she whines. "I have a tampon in. This is weird."

Ignoring her half-ass pleas to get me to stop, I run my tongue up her inner thigh. She moans when I suck on the apex of her thigh. Gripping her knees, I spread her open. The string of her tampon remains within reach, but I leave it alone to seek out her clit.

"I like the way you smell." I lick her clit, loving the way she shudders. "I like the way you taste. You think I was a vampire in another life?"

"Do not go there," she breathes. "Please."

Maybe not today.

There's always next month.

"Can I go here?" I ask, circling her clit with my tongue.

"Y-Yes. Go there. Mmm."

Smiling against her pussy, I tease her bundle of nerves until she's squirming on the sofa. I listen to the sounds of her breathing and pay attention to the way her hips lift each time she gets close to orgasm. When I know she's about to fall over the edge, I suck hard on her clit. She screams in pleasure as her whole body detonates. I press kisses to her perfect pussy as I tug on the string of her tampon.

"What are you doing?" she hisses, her chest heaving.

"This." I gently pull until her body releases the bloody plug. With my eyes searing hers, I drop the thing onto the empty cheese plate and then yank at my belt. Her pussy is open and inviting.

A little blood doesn't fucking scare me.

I'm a goddamn villain.

Blood turns us the hell on.

I unfasten my pants and pull out my aching cock. After I shove my pants down my thighs and rip at the buttons on my shirt, I prowl over to her, deciding that's enough stripping. I want inside her before she changes her mind.

"See this pussy?" I ask, teasing her opening with the tip of my dick.

She nods, frowning.

"It's mine," I growl with a hard thrust of my hips.

My dick slides into her warmth and I groan. Her lips are parted, her eyes soft. I want to fucking devour her. She cries out when my lips crash to hers. I kiss her hard and urgently, making her feel my apologies for what I've done and my hope for how I want to be. She kisses me back, equally as passionate.

Talia meets my fire with gasoline.

She taunts and draws out the beast inside me.

And rather than being fearful of the man I can be, she lets me own her with my mouth and punish her cunt with my cock. Begs and moans for it. Fucking loves it.

The sounds coming from her body are juicier than normal and it makes me hard as stone. It takes everything in me not to come without at least attempting to make her come again. Luckily, my girl is needy and tipsy, and the moment my fingers touch her clit, she clenches around my dick as she yells my name. I thrust into her several more times until my balls draw up, desperate for release. With a groan, I spill my seed in her bloody cunt. What a fucking mess we are. A beautiful mess.

With a peck to her lips, I pull out slowly, loving the way her blood is smeared over my thickness. If I didn't just come, I'd have the urge to wrap my hand around my dick and use her blood as lubricant, bringing myself to climax. Talia fucking undoes my mind.

"I can't believe I let you do that," she complains, but her voice is breathless and happy.

"Believe it. Because in about five minutes, I'm going to regroup and do it again in the shower."

"It blew up last night."

You've got to be fucking kidding me.

"Planes don't just blow up," I growl to Adrian. "Fucking Aris. What did airport security say?"

"They're investigating and looking through video footage to see what happened."

"We know what happened. Aris wanted to fuck around with me."

He lets out a heavy sigh. "I'll look into it. But good news is, I have a lead."

"Oh?"

"Wesley said the vehicle Basil took had less than a quarter tank of gas."

I lean back in my office chair. "And?"

"And all the service stations have been checked. He never arrived to refuel."

"So it means Basil is close. Aris is close."

"Any hideouts within fifty miles or so?" he asks. "I could start checking in on some."

We pretty much own everything worth owning within that radius. My mind flits to a few motels that we don't. One particular shithole is known for shady motherfuckers staying at. It would be stupid for Aris to go there, especially with a fifty-mil price tag for his head, but that doesn't mean he wouldn't try it.

"Let's check it out," I order.

After a quick kiss to Talia and Zoe who are napping, I grab my keys. I find Phoenix in a heated discussion with Fowler, but I don't stick around to break it up. Phoenix has taken command over these men, so if Fowler with the wandering fucking eyes needs an attitude adjustment, who am I to step in and interfere.

Adrian and I climb into my Maserati before zipping through town toward the shitty motel. Fifteen minutes later, we creep up to the building. On the side, a vehicle is parked with a blue tarp covering it.

"Basil's car," Adrian growls, jumping from my car before I get it in park.

We didn't have a plan coming here, just following yet another lead. Most leads are pointless. It's surprising as fuck this one might lead us right to Aris.

"I want at him before you kill him," Adrian hisses over his shoulder. "Give me that. I want to ask him straight to his face why he'd turn on his best friend."

I follow him along the sidewalk. We creep, listening in at each door. Nothing seems of interest until I hear him. Moaning. Lifting my leg, I kick in the door hard. Adrian rushes past me, his gun drawn. When he stops suddenly, I slam into his back.

"What the fu—" My jaw drops, ending my words.

"No," Adrian whispers. "No."

Basil, in nothing but his boxers, whimpers at the sound of our voices. Aris, that sick motherfucker, did this to our friend. A friend who we wrongfully thought was a rat was nothing more than a victim. He's lying on the bed, his tor-so cut from throat to groin. His body has been pulled apart to expose his organs. I step closer and notice that he's been freshly packed with ice. Lots of it.

"He's here," I hiss.

"N-No," Basil croaks. "Gone."

Adrian jolts from his stupor and sits beside Basil on the bed. I mimic his actions, coming up on the other side. As Adrian grabs Basil's hand and lets out a choked sound, I drag my stare over his open torso. His intestines have been pulled out some and hang over the sides of his ribs, dripping in sticky blood. He has to be in agonizing pain.

"We need to call an ambulance," I mutter, fixated on the horrific sight.

Adrian jerks his head my way. "That shit isn't fixable, Boss." His cheeks are wet with tears. "I thought he was a rat."

I sit down next to Basil and frown at him. "We didn't think you were a rat," I explain. "We just figured you were with one. And we were right. Where's he headed next? Give me anything and I'll put you out of your misery."

Basil's face scrunches. "H-He wants b-back at the h-hotel…"

"Why?" I growl. "We've not even been there."

"Info…info…" He groans.

"Information?"

"Yesss," Basil whispers.

Aris is nothing without his numbers and he wants them back. Makes fucking sense. Over my dead body.

"You served me well," I tell Basil. "Say goodbye to Adrian."

Adrian makes a growling sound of a pained animal. He leans forward and presses his forehead to Basil's. "I love you, brother," Adrian tells Basil. He sighs hard and then he's gone, leaving me alone with Basil.

"Thank you," I mutter, pulling out my Glock. "A promise is a promise."

Holding the barrel against his temple, I stare into Basil's dark eyes so he doesn't have to die alone, and I pull the trigger.

Aris will pay for this.

His time is running out.

chapter
twenty-four

"How are you doing?" I ask Kostas. He's standing in front of the mirror, tying his tie, and looks like he's a million miles away. When he got home last night, he filled me in on everything. His private plane has been blown to bits, and Basil was found in a shitty motel, alone and dying.

I didn't know him well, but from what I've seen, Kostas, Adrian, and Basil were all close. As close to friends as three men in this world can be. The way he looked at me, with sad, distant eyes when he told me about his death, had me wanting to hold him close.

Kostas won't ever say it, but I think he blames himself for Basil's death. If he had looked harder, maybe he would've found him in time. My poor husband has suffered so much loss in his life, I don't know how he even gets out of bed in the morning. If I were knocked down as many times as him, I don't think I would be able to get up.

But in typical Kostas fashion, he quickly schooled his features and pretended like everything was okay. He made love to me slowly and told me no less than a dozen times he's going to catch his brother.

"I'm okay," he says for the millionth time, glancing at my reflection in the mirror. "How about I pick up dinner on my way home to make up for the one I fucked up the other night?"

He walks over and sits on the edge of the bed where Zoe and I are still lying. Zoe likes to wake up at the crack of dawn, have a bottle, and then come back to bed with Kostas and me for early morning snuggles. I warned Kostas the first time she did it, she would keep doing it. He just shrugged and said he hoped so.

"You already made up for that dinner." I smile, recalling the way he made up for it several times. First with his tongue, and then a couple more times with his cock.

Kostas smirks, knowing what's running through my head. "Still, I'll pick up dinner." He leans over and kisses my lips. Groaning into his mouth, I grab his lapels and try to pull him back into bed.

He chuckles and stands. "Not happening, *moró mou*. I have another appointment with the insurance adjuster."

"For the plane?"

"Yeah." He pecks my lips one more time. "I should be home early. Behave."

A little while later, Zoe wakes up drooling and cranky. I think another tooth is coming in. After she's changed and fed, I give her to my mom to hold so I can find one of the men to go to the store to pick up medicine.

As I'm opening the front door, I run straight into Fowler. Our bodies collide and his hands land on my hips. Not wanting him to touch me, I move out of his reach, but his fingers are digging into my skin, preventing me from moving.

"Let go of me," I hiss, swatting at his hands.

"Would you rather I let you fall?" He smirks evilly.

Anger burns through me and I'm seconds from clawing his face apart.

"Get your fucking hands off my sister," Phoenix growls, walking up behind Fowler. "Now."

Fowler stares me down in an arrogant way that leads me to believe he thinks he's powerful and untouchable. But based on the fury rippling from my brother and when Kostas gets wind of this, this asshole will learn his place in my home—in my world.

"My bad." He releases his hold on me and raises his palms into the air.

"Why the fuck were you touching her?" Phoenix accuses. "Didn't we already talk about this?" He steps into Fowler's face.

Fowler grins wide, as if they're two old friends in on a joke. "Bro, I didn't touch her—" Fowler begins, but Phoenix cuts him off.

"I'm *not* your bro."

Fowler just laughs. "Look, *man*, she ran into me and I caught her so she didn't bust her ass. Next time I'll just let her fall." He shrugs and walks around Phoenix.

"Two strikes," Phoenix calls over his shoulder.

He says it loud enough that Fowler can hear him, but he keeps walking, pretending he doesn't.

"That guy seriously rubs me the wrong way," I tell Phoenix.

"Yeah, he's a punk."

"What's with the two strikes?" I ask, curious.

"Three strikes and he's out." He looks over his shoulder then back at me. "Why were you coming out here?"

"Zoe is teething. I need someone to run to the store to buy her pain medicine."

"Is she okay?" Phoenix's brows furrow in concern. I never imagined I would ever have my brother in my life, let alone my daughter's. And I definitely never thought Phoenix would be such a hands-on uncle. Growing up, I only got to see him for a short time over the summer, or for the holidays when he would visit. I always assumed he was just like Niles—selfish and irresponsible. But he's actually nothing like him. His only fault was that he was loyal to his dad—until he wasn't.

"She's fine. I just want to make sure she's not in pain. She's whining and being cranky."

"Sounds a lot like her mom." Phoenix smirks.

"Hush it." I push his shoulder playfully.

"I'll send Fowler to go get it." He laughs. "He's not doing shit anyway, so he can play errand boy. Make himself useful."

"I think it's time for me to go home," Mom says. We're sitting on the floor in Zoe's nursery, watching as she crawls all over the place, knocking blocks over and smashing the keys to her soft play piano.

"Already?" I pout. I love having my mom here with me. Once she goes back to Italy, who knows when I will see her again.

"Already?" She laughs. "I've been here for a month."

My pout deepens, my bottom lip jutting out dramatically. "But I'm going to miss you, and so is Zoe."

"I know, *cara mia*, but Stefano isn't good at fending for

himself. He's complained every day that the cook isn't making what he likes." She rolls her eyes in mock annoyance. "Imagine if you were away from Kostas for a few days? Or a week?"

I laugh at the thought. Kostas would never let that happen. He'd be all growly and then demand he either goes with me or I don't go. "I get it. So how much longer do I get you?"

"Stefano found a flight for next week. So we have a little more time together." She gives me a soft smile.

"Okay, I'll take it."

Zoe stops banging on the piano and turns to me. Her eyes well up with tears and she shoves her tiny fist into her mouth. Fowler should be back by now with her medicine.

"I'm going to go see if Fowler is back with Zoe's medicine yet. Can you hold her?"

"Of course," Mom says, taking Zoe into her arms. "You know, when you and Phoenix were babies, we just rubbed whiskey on your gums."

I bark out a laugh. "I think we'll stick to good old Tylenol."

I run downstairs and spot one of the men on the phone in the kitchen. Not wanting to interrupt him, I head out the front door. The vehicle Fowler uses is parked in the driveway, so I go in search of him. I find him standing on the side of the house. I'm about to call out his name when I see he has his phone pressed up to his ear. Instead, I walk forward a few steps so I can listen.

"The plane is totaled," he says then stays quiet, listening to whoever is on the other line. I'm curious as to who he's speaking to since all of Kostas's men already know the plane is totaled.

"The bitch and the baby? That's going to cost you big

time. Last time I checked you don't have that kind of money. If you want me to grab them, I'm going to need to see the money first."

Oh my God! The bitch and the baby? There's only one bitch around here with a baby, and that's me. I consider sticking around to hear whatever else he's going to say, but decide I've heard enough to know this guy is bad fucking news. It's why he doesn't give a shit about anything Phoenix or Kostas threaten. He's not working for them… He's working for Aris. He's a damn rat!

Needing to get to my daughter and mom to make sure they're safe, I turn and run back into the house and up the stairs. The first thing I need is my gun. There's no way I'm chancing that asshole kidnapping Zoe and me and bringing us back to Aris.

Since my bedroom is before Zoe's, I pop in there to grab my gun from the nightstand. But as I'm grabbing it, I hear footsteps behind me, and a chill runs up my spine. Somehow Fowler knows I heard him.

Not chancing him either killing or kidnapping me, I quickly flip the safety off and turn around with the gun aimed directly at him. He has his aimed at me as well.

"Easy, girl," he starts, an evil glint in his eye as he steps forward.

Pop!

I choke on a gasp as the blood swells, blooming like a flower. Holy shit. His eyes widen as he grabs his side. He wasn't expecting me to be packing and he sure as hell didn't expect me to shoot. He should've, though. I'm married to the most powerful mob boss in the country. Of course he's going to make sure I can defend myself.

Pop!

I waste no time squeezing on the trigger again. This bullet goes through his arm and he drops the gun.

We both go after it at the same time, but as I'm diving down to grab it, Fowler drops to the ground. When I look up, I find Phoenix standing in the doorway with a gun in his hand.

"Thank you," I breathe. I glance over at Fowler and he's knocked out, the side of his head bleeding. Phoenix must've hit him with the butt of his gun.

"I'll always have your back, sis," he says, reaching his hand out to help me up.

"How did you know?" I ask, standing and handing him the gun.

"Overheard him talking on the phone. Saw you listening as well, but I didn't want to draw attention to you. As soon as you ran, he turned around, and I knew he saw you." He kicks Fowler in the stomach so he rolls over onto his back. He's bleeding heavily onto my carpet. Great, I'll probably never get that stain out.

"I'm so glad you're here." I run into Phoenix's arms.

"Eh, looks like you were handling yourself just fine." He kisses the top of my head.

"I need to go make sure Mom and Zoe are safe," I tell him. "I don't know who we can even trust. I'm going to have her lock herself in the room. Can you tie this fucker up and call Kostas?"

Phoenix's lips curl into a wide grin.

"What?" I ask, confused.

"Nothing." He shakes his head. "I just hope one day I find a woman like you. Kostas got himself a good one. He better treat you right."

"He more than treats me right," I tell him. "He treats me like his queen."

When I get to Zoe's room, the door is closed and locked. "Mom," I call out.

"Talia! I heard a gunshot! Are you okay?" she says through the door.

"Yes, I'm okay. You can open the door." I want to make sure nobody is in there. I knew something was up with Fowler. Who knows who else is a rat.

When she opens the door, I sigh in relief at the sight of my daughter bouncing up and down in her crib. "Go ahead and lock the door again. Phoenix has Fowler, and Kostas will be on his way shortly. Don't open the door unless it's one of us."

"Okay, be safe, sweetheart." She gives me a kiss on my cheek.

I get back to the room to find Phoenix has Fowler propped up in my reading chair and has used my robe belt to tie his hands. He's awake, but his head is hanging down. I bet he has a massive migraine. The thought makes me laugh. When my husband is done with him, a migraine will be the least of what he feels.

"What the fuck are you laughing at?" Fowler hisses. "You think tying me up is going to stop Aris from getting to you again?" He laughs wickedly, and I take a step back. Gone is the pervy flirt, and present is a ruthless mobster. "That man is on a revenge mission, and he ain't gonna stop until he has everything Kostas cares about. Mark my fucking words."

The room chills several degrees like a cold storm has surged into our bedroom, ready to destroy everything in its path.

"My brother will get to my wife again over my dead fucking body," Kostas says, entering the room. He saunters over to Fowler like he doesn't have a care in the world. But I can see the darkness in his usually light eyes. He's pissed and he's going to make Fowler pay...after he makes him talk.

"We can make this easy or difficult. Are you going to tell me where my brother is, or am I going to beat it out of you?" Kostas cracks his neck to one side and then to the other, the bones popping in an intimidating way.

Fowler laughs. "I'm not saying shit." He spits at Kostas. "I already know my death warrant's been signed. I'm not going down a fucking rat."

Kostas glowers at him as he sheds his jacket and rolls up his sleeves. "The hard way it is." He turns to me, and I give a look that tells him I'm not going anywhere. I'll be damned if I don't get to see this asshole get what's coming to him. Kostas simply shakes his head, not even bothering to argue.

Kostas unbuckles his belt and pulls it through the loops. For a second, I wonder if he's going to whip Fowler with his belt, but instead he wraps it around his neck, tightening it so tight, Fowler's veins in his neck and face bulge. He doesn't stop until Fowler's face is bright red.

"This is for teaming with the wrong side." He tightens it some more, and I worry he's going to kill him before he gets any information out of him.

"And this is for even *thinking* you would try to take my daughter and wife from me." Kostas tightens the belt, and Fowler's survival instincts kick in. He tries to wriggle his body to get free. His head lashes back and forth as his face color turns to a deep crimson.

"Sis, you sure you wanna be here for this?" Phoenix asks, his tone laced with worry.

"She's not going anywhere," Kostas says, answering for me. "Your sweet little sister has quite the dark side in her." While still choking Fowler, he looks back and shoots me a knowing smirk, causing my belly to flutter with butterflies. Jesus, I think I might be as crazy as my husband.

chapter
twenty-five

Kostas

WHEN I'D GOTTEN THE TEXT FROM PHOENIX, I'D seen red. But thankfully, Talia's brother is one of the few people I can trust around here. He'd been onto Fowler's bullshit already and had his eye on him. And when the fucker thought he could hurt *my fucking wife*, she shot him.

Good girl.

Good goddamn girl.

The prick is whining and hissing against the leather belt that has him in a chokehold, but all I can do is admire my wife. She looks borderline angelic in her yellow sundress and sunny hair that hangs down her back in what she calls beach waves. Even the smile on her plump red lips is serene. It's the eyes, though.

Brilliant and blazing.

Wickedly blue.

A monster who teases my own.

If I didn't have this dickhead to torture, I'd bend her over my bed right now and take her bloody cunt. I'd smack her ass in the way bad girls get their reward and use my crimson-soaked dick to push between her cheeks, taking her where she doesn't bleed but sure as fuck will feel like it.

Having a hard-on with a rat in my presence is inconvenient.

"Take him to the garage. This shit is going to get bloody." I nod at Phoenix. "Don't kill him yet."

While Phoenix handles him, I grab Talia's wrist and haul her into our giant closet. I close the door and then pounce on her. My lips crash to hers as I grab her ass.

"I was fucking terrified something happened to you," I growl, nipping at her bottom lip. "And here you are, ruling over your mere mortals like the queen you are. You make me proud, *zoí mou.*"

She kisses me hard and works at my tie. "You can't wear your good tie to cut off limbs, husband."

"And sundresses are meant for the beach, not stabbing rats," I tell her, ripping at the fabric and pulling it down one shoulder so I can kiss her bare skin. "As much as I want to fuck my gorgeous wife, I need to get down there and find answers."

She grumbles as she grips my dick through my slacks. "You can't go down there with this." She squeezes me. "You'll accidentally poke someone's eye out." When she drops to her knees, I groan in pleasure. Her wicked grin is back as she tugs at my zipper and reaches into my boxers to free my cock. She pulls it through the zipper hole and admires it with exaggerated excitement.

Little brat.

Playful and sexy in a time where we need to be ruthless and evil…and yet I want to make them wait for five goddamn minutes so my wife can suck my dick.

Her pink tongue darts out, wetting my tip, and she circles it in a teasing way. I grip a handful of her blond hair and pin her with a fierce stare.

"Wrap your fat lips around my dick," I growl.

She scowls. "Fat?"

Oh, Jesus, fuck.

"Plump. Juicy. Perfect. Your lips were made for sucking dick, Talia. Fucking own it."

This earns me a smile and then she wraps those lovely lips around my thick, veiny cock, ravishing me with her hot mouth. I grunt and flex my hips, slightly fucking her mouth. Her teeth scrape along my flesh and her blue eyes dart up to mine, a warning gleaming in them. I take her challenge and buck again. She gags and purposefully drags her teeth up my shaft to the crown. Her cheeks indent as she sucks on the crown, hard and unyielding, as though she can bleed me dry of cum with such a simple maneuver. It nearly fucking works. A growl rumbles through me and I thrust again. Her throat constricts when my tip slides into its tight, warm depths.

She's so fucking pretty when her blue eyes water when she tries to swallow me whole.

"I'm going to come down your throat and then tonight I'm going to come in your ass," I tell her smugly, daring her to challenge me.

She doesn't because it's hard to argue with a nine-inch dick for a lollipop down your throat. Her slender fingers massage my balls before she twists slightly, reminding me of the fact that just because she's on her knees, it means nothing.

She. Fucking. Owns. Me.

Seeing her so goddamn powerful on her knees with

a monster's balls in her grip has me snarling with my release. She takes me deeper in her throat the moment that first burst of cum hits her throat. I hiss as my dick is swallowed down her needy throat. I flex my ass cheeks as I milk the rest of my cum into her hot mouth and then I pull away abruptly.

Talia rises to her feet and kisses my lips as she tucks my wet cock back into my slacks.

"Good boy," she purrs. "Now let's go torture that motherfucker."

It's true love with this one.

Talia leans against the wall, quietly watching, while Phoenix paces the floor in front of Fowler. Adrian has Fowler's phone and is already tracing numbers to locations. He'll work his tech side to get information while Phoenix and I do it the good old-fashioned way: by brute force.

Fowler's shirt has been removed and someone poured superglue in his gunshot wounds to keep him from bleeding out. That shit has to hurt like a bitch. Exactly what we wanted, too. It's only going to get worse from here.

"Where's Aris?" I ask coolly, fiddling with the tip of my knife.

He spits at Phoenix's feet. "Fuck you."

Phoenix bitch slaps him, making Fowler cry out in surprise. These men can take punches, but a slap to the face like a fucking girl is jarring to them. He gapes at Phoenix incredulously.

"You tell me where my brother is and we'll let you live."

I snort. "Man, I can't even say that with a straight face. How about this? We'll let you die quicker if you tell us where he is."

"I won't tell you shit," Fowler snaps.

"So you don't need your tongue then?" I step forward, loving the way his eyes widen marginally so.

"He didn't get a chance to tell me before your cunt wife—" Fowler starts.

Phoenix bitch slaps him again and snarls at him. "Her name is Talia. Use her name."

Fowler is pissed, but he rethinks his fight because he grits out his words. "Talia interrupted."

"Give us something," I say calmly. "Anything."

"What will you give me?" Fowler attempts to negotiate. "Maybe I'll tell you what I know, but I need something in return."

"You give me the information and I will cut you loose." I smirk at him. "Trust me?"

"I *don't* trust you, though," he says, scowling.

"You don't have many options," Talia reminds him.

Fowler snaps his head her way and glowers at her, but not before raking his eyes boldly down her body. This fucker has a death wish. He thinks he has the upper hand. That if he'll be openly salacious against her, I'll just end him now and put him out of this misery. When he licks his lips suggestively, I consider it, but Phoenix bitch slaps the look right off his face.

"What the fuck man?" Fowler bellows. "Stop fucking slapping me."

Phoenix smirks at me. "This is the most fun I've had… ever, frankly. Every time you open your bitch-ass mouth to spew more bullshit, I'm gonna slap the words right out of it.

Man the fuck up, Fowler. Tell us what you know and you'll die like you have a pair of balls between those legs."

"Agia Fotia. There's a hotel there that the Galanis used to hide out in. You know it?" Fowler asks.

I give him a clipped nod and then cut my eyes over to Talia. She slips from the room, hopefully to pass on the news to Adrian.

"Yeah, I know it. Is he there?" I demand, stepping closer.

"Fuck if I know, but he mentioned a hotel there in our last conversation. Didn't say if he was going there or not because your cunt—"

I press my blade to his lips, glaring down at him. "Careful, rat. We're not done talking and if you keep calling my wife a cunt, I'm going to cut your tongue from your throat. I'll make you learn goddamn sign language to finish this conversation. Don't fucking test me."

Blood trickles down his chin and I pull the blade away.

"We never got to finish our conversation," he gripes, before licking the new cut on his bottom lip.

Talia returns and gives me a nod before mouthing, "Adrian," to me. At least he can be checking our contacts there before this dick sends us on a wild goose chase.

"What's he planning next?" I ask.

"I don't fucking know." Fowler glowers at me.

"What do you know?"

"Nothing else."

Well, I guess our time here is over.

"Look at my wife," I order.

Now the greasy motherfucker tries to disobey me. Phoenix steps behind him and grabs his hair, yanking his head to the side.

"Boss says look," Phoenix growls, "you fucking look."

"And when Boss says keep your eyes to yourself, you keep them to your fucking self." I whistle for Talia. "Come here, woman, and hold my knife."

I sense her hesitation, but she won't undermine me now. She walks over to us and takes the knife from me. Fowler watches her with pure hatred that burns hot through my veins. He thinks I'm going to make her cut him or stab him. She's not fucking touching him.

"Like what you see?" I purr, my voice deceptively calm.

"Looks like a spoiled, used cunt—AHHH!"

I dig my thumbs into his eyes hard, cutting past the inner membrane inside his lower eyelids. His screams are otherworldly as he thrashes in his chair. Phoenix holds him in place as I rip through the flesh beneath his eyeballs. Vomit spews out at me when I pull my thumbs away and blood gushes down his cheeks. I flip my palms up and push three fingers into each hole beneath his eyeballs before curling them up around the back side of his eyeballs. He sputters and gurgles and hisses. With a hard yank, I relieve him of his wandering eyes, leaving two bloody, gaping holes in his head.

Talia has retreated, her back now against the wall. Good. I want her away from this sick fuck. I open my palms to look at the rat's eyes. Beady and fucking useless now. I toss them on the ground and Phoenix stomps them with his combat boot. Fowler has officially been renamed Howler because he's crying out like he's a fucking wolf lost from his pack.

Adrian enters the garage and his dark eyes gleam with approval. He hates this fucker too. When he nods at me, I know the intel is good. We'll need to leave soon.

"Toss me the knife," I say to my wife.

She throws it at me and it clatters at my feet. I pick it up and then begin sawing Howler free. He squawks and carries on like the little bitch he is.

"What now?" Phoenix asks, violence gleaming in his eyes that match Talia's.

"A promise is a promise," I reply, shrugging. "I told the fucker I'd cut him loose if he gave us information." Then, I grin at Phoenix. "But you, man, you didn't promise him a damn thing. He's all yours. I need you here protecting Melody and Zoe. Talia and I are going on a second honeymoon."

After we showered, changed, and packed some weapons, Talia and I headed out to Agia Fotia Beach with Adrian following behind in his new Jeep. Fucking Phoenix corrupted him with that corny-ass Jeep shit. But, since my wife smashed Adrian's car, it was only fair I bought him a new toy. Even if the toy is meant for a man twenty years his junior.

To an outsider, Talia and I in my Maserati look like any other rich couple. Carefree and happy. We're happy, that's for damn sure. And we'll be carefree the moment I have my hands around my brother's throat. Until then, we'll keep hunting his awful ass down.

"We're almost there," she says, yawning. "Are we really going to stay at the beach house?"

"You mean the Cliffside monster stairs home?"

She laughs. "Remember when I made you carry me up all those steps?"

"Remember when I fucked you on four hundred rocks and made you mine?"

We both smile.

"It won't always be like this," I promise her. "The people in Greece know they can't fuck with me. They can try and I'll hunt their asses down. If they're smart, they'll pay their taxes, do my bidding, and be fucking merry."

"Is that all?" she asks dryly. "Want them to suck your dick too?"

"That's your job," I tell her with a smirk.

"You have to admit, you like it when I negotiate using blowjobs."

"Your blowjobs are the true secret behind world peace. Too bad you only give them to a tyrant."

She taps at her lips and feigns a thoughtful look. "Maybe I should spread the love around."

"Maybe I should spread you over my lap and make you fuck me the rest of the way."

"I did not come through all this to die in a ditch because my sex freak husband wanted to have more period sex while driving a million-dollar car."

Three mil, but who's counting.

"There's always the ride home," I tease, gripping her jean-clad thigh.

The rest of the trip we drive in contented silence. I know she's nervous about finding him, but I'm eager as hell. It's long overdue.

Rather than going to the hotel the Galanis always stayed at, I take her straight to the Cliffside home. It's my first destination. We pull into the driveway and I lean over to kiss Talia.

"How long will it take to find out if Aris is at the hotel?" she asks once we park.

"He's not there," I state as I climb out of the car.

She follows me, grabbing my hand. "What? What do you mean?"

"If there's one thing I know about my brother, it's that he likes to play games. He doesn't trust anyone. You think he'd give such an obvious clue to his man?"

Talia stops to frown at me. "No."

I caress her cheek. "No, because if the man was found out, then he'd tell me. And if Aris knows me, he had to know I'd find out because I'm not fucking stupid."

Her plump lips purse, making my dick thicken with need. Not now, but soon, I'll have those lips on me again. "He wanted to lure you to the hotel." She lets out a rush of relieved breath. "So we outsmarted him then?"

"Did we?" I muse aloud, darting my eyes to the house.

Her blue eyes flicker with fear, but I shush her with a kiss. "He knew we'd stay here if we came looking for him at that hotel. He'd attempt to catch us off guard."

She pulls away, whirling around. "Where's Adrian?"

"Don't worry about that," I say with a grin as I lead her over to the front door. "Let's get you inside. I want to fuck you in the hot tub."

Her shoulders are tense, but she trusts me as I guide her into the home. As soon as we walk inside, we see Aris. Gun in hand and evil fucking smile on his face.

And then Adrian tackles him from behind.

Aris's eyes blink open slowly. He looks like shit. I'm not sure he's showered recently and the scruffy beard he's sporting doesn't make him look refined. It makes him look like trash.

That's what he is to me.

Trash.

Ready to be kicked to the goddamn curb. Indefinitely.

"The almighty Demetriou reigns," Aris snarls, finding his venom past the haze of recently being knocked out.

I snort. "Nothing's changed, little brother."

His brown eyes dart to Talia, who's perched in my lap like a fucking goddess waiting to be worshiped. Rather than worshiping his queen, he spits her way. She flinches and I hate that he holds some sort of power over her.

Not for long.

Adrian is still as a statue, leaned against the wall like a fucking gargoyle. All it takes is Aris to move the wrong way and Adrian will pounce on him, gutting him like he gutted Basil. The violence ripples from Adrian in waves like heat from the sun. Powerful, malevolent, unforgiving.

"You didn't think you'd go on terrorizing me and not get caught in my web eventually, did you?" I stroke my fingers through Talia's blond hair, my eyes fixed on him. "You're caught now. Nothing but a useless fucking moth, struggling to get free." I flash him a smug grin. "You, Aris fucking Demetriou, are a victim now. Something to be destroyed and ruined. Forgotten."

"Fuck you," he snarls. "Your theatrics are boring, Kostas. Get the hell on with it."

"Personally," Talia pipes up, her voice wavering slightly. "I find his *theatrics* quite charming."

"You always were a dumb bitch," Aris growls, fighting against his restraints.

"They're mouthy as fuck when they're looking death in the eye," Adrian bellows from across the room, making the three of us look his way. His hateful glare is fixated on Aris. I should let him deal with my brother, but that wouldn't be fair to Talia. She suffered too. This is her vengeance.

"I've been planning your death for a while now," I tell Aris. "I imagined all the ways I'd cut you and drain you of your blood. How I'd make you suffer slowly. But then I realized it's not up to me." I pat Talia's thigh. "It's up to her."

She rises from my lap and I rake my eyes down her perfect jean-clad ass.

"I trusted you," she says, her voice small as she picks up the knife from the table. "I tried to comfort you."

"Aww," Aris taunts, his nostrils flaring. "You thought your magical pussy would make me all better? Sorry, princess, but your cunt is just like every other cunt out there. Although, you squealed like a little pig when I shoved my dick in it."

She freezes and I'm tempted to leap over the table to crush his fucking skull. But I won't. Not unless she asks me to. And my brave wife doesn't ask for help. She slowly approaches him, like a viper ready to strike. The knife in her grip gleams in the light.

"You raped me," she accuses, her voice breaking. "You took advantage of my kindness and then you took advantage of me."

He laughs hatefully. "It didn't feel like rape when you were impaled on my cock. It felt like vindication." He sneers at me. "How does it feel knowing I popped that cherry, big brother? Does it burn you up every night knowing your brother's dick has been inside your wife? Does it—what the fuck?"

Blood runs down his cheek from the slash of the knife. Her body trembles as she stares down at him.

"It was rape and you know it," she seethes. "Admit it and I'll let you keep your cock."

"My cock belongs to you, though, bitch," he taunts. "You

damn near begged for it the whole time I had you holed away from Kostas. If Selene weren't there, you know we would've already made another baby."

She slashes again, this time ripping through his bottom lip. Blood runs thick down his chin. His eyes turn wild as he realizes he's dying in this living room. Tonight. At the hand of the one he brutalized.

Eye for a fucking eye.

Even Howler learned that lesson.

"Say it," she orders. "Say it or I'll cut you a thousand times. Don't fucking test me, Aris. I will. I'll cut you for every time I lied to your face and told you Zoe was your daughter."

His nostrils flare. "I raped you because I could," he sneers. "I haven't deflowered a virgin since I was a fucking teenager. I should have taken your ass instead."

She turns her head to look at me, tears gleaming in her blue eyes. Even had he not admitted, I knew the truth. But this was something she clearly needed to hear. To confirm. For me to know without a shadow of a doubt. This is her vengeance, not mine.

Yes, he took and took from me, but he didn't take that.

He stole her virginity and her freedom. He stole her happiness.

For that, she will make him pay.

I give her a nod of support and a wink.

"You thought you could bring down my husband, but you couldn't," she whispers, turning back to him. "You couldn't because you were always the weak one. The un-loved one. The least favorite. Poor little Aris. Only Mommy loved you, but even still, she loved you equal to your brother."

"Fuck you," he roars. "Don't ever talk about my mother."

"Your mother is rolling in her grave because the man she hated most is the man you turned out to be," Talia continues, her body vibrating with power. "You turned into him. Ezio. You're that spineless bastard, weak and afraid."

"I am not like that motherfucker!" he screams, his face turning purple with rage.

Aww, someone still has daddy issues.

"You always did look more like the gardener," I muse aloud.

Talia laughs. "How does it feel to be powerless? You only had the illusion of power for a short while there. Your brother always wielded it and it drove you fucking crazy. He got the empire, he got the girl, and he got the kid." She slashes again, this time slicing a big gash on the side of his neck. "What do you have, Aris? A mediocre cock in your pants and a burning desire to be him?" She points her knife at me. "Well, you're not him. Not even close."

"Go to hell," Aris slurs, his skin quickly paling with the blood loss that's pouring like rivers down the side of his neck.

She straddles his thighs and presses the tip of the blade against his chest, right over his heart. "You soon will." Her body trembles, but she doesn't make the move.

"Talia?" I ask, rising to my feet.

A sob chokes her. "I want to, but…"

Walking over to her, I stare down at my brother she's singlehandedly ruined with her knife. I could end him right now. Hell, we could leave him and he'd bleed to death within minutes. That won't bring her peace, though. She needs to do this.

I lean forward and wrap my arms around her. My hand grips hers on the hilt of the knife. Nuzzling her hair with my nose, I inhale her sweet and sweaty scent. I kiss her hair and murmur my words against her head.

"Ready, *zoí mou*?"

"Yes," she breathes.

I use my other hand to cover the top of the hilt of the knife and drive it forward. Her hand flexes beneath mine, but she doesn't squirm away. Together, we push the blade past his flesh and into his chest. Together, we pierce his heart. Together, we breathe raggedly as we watch the life quietly drain from the monster in our lives.

Releasing the knife, I hook my arms around her middle and pull her away from him. I walk her outside so Adrian can deal with the body. She turns in my arms, sobbing against my chest. I stroke her hair and kiss her head. The waves crash down below.

"It's over now, *moró mou*. You can be happy."

She pulls away and places her blood-splattered hands on my cheeks. Her blue eyes are watery as she regards me. "I am happy, Kostas. With you, never doubt that."

"I love you," I murmur. "My beautiful, brave, fiery wife."

"I love you more."

"Impossible," I growl, nipping at her juicy lip.

A smile tugs at her lips. "Then prove it."

"Anything."

"Give me a piggyback down to the beach."

All those stairs. All. Those. Fucking Stairs.

"Aww, I'm only teasing," she says, laughing. "You should have seen your face!"

With a growl, I scoop her into my arms.

I carry her down all those goddamn stairs. Every last

one of them. And when I've fucked her in the warm sea and made her scream my name in pleasure, I'll carry her back up all those motherfucking steps. Every grueling one.

I'll carry her anywhere.

To the ends of the earth. Through heaven and hell. And into the next life.

She's fucking mine forever.

epilogue

Talia
One Year Later

"**M**OMMY, WHAT'S THIS?" ZOE ASKS, POINTING at the exquisite fountain in the middle of the courtyard.

With me almost two weeks overdue, we decided to drive over to the Pérasma Hotel with Kostas today to hang out, swim a little, and get some sun while being waited on.

When Zoe asked if we could go for a walk, I figured it would be the perfect opportunity to try to walk my over-ly-pregnant behind into labor. Big mistake. Because now I've plopped myself onto the wicker lounge chair to relax for a minute, and there's a good possibility I may never get back up.

Not wanting to tell her what she's pointing to is Bernini's *Rape of Proserpina*, I go with a more childproof answer. "It's a statue of a man and a woman."

"Not just any man and woman," a masculine voice says, catching my attention. I glance over and spot my sexy hus-band sauntering over. Unlike the first time I saw him in this very spot, dressed casual in khakis and a button-down shirt, today he's sporting his power suit. I would take him either way, but truth be told, my favorite Kostas is the one without any clothes on in our bed.

Kostas picks Zoe up and she squeals in excitement. "This statue is of Pluto and Proserpina," he tells her as if she can understand. He always talks to her like she's an adult. It's oddly adorable.

"Pluto?" she questions. "Like the doggy?"

He gives me a confused look.

"Pluto is the cute puppy on Disney," I explain.

He laughs and shakes his head. "No, this Pluto was a very powerful god." He gives me a knowing look. "He stole Proserpina and brought her into the Underworld. And because he loved her so much, he tricked her into staying by tempting her with delicious food. She, of course, took the bait and was sentenced to remain with him for the rest of eternity."

I grin at his version of the story. It was my version. The safe version. The one that made Pluto out to be the bad guy and kept Proserpina innocent. But as I look at my handsome husband holding our daughter in his arms, I realize my view of the story has changed. That I've changed.

"He didn't trick her," I say out loud.

Kostas's eyes gleam with excitement. "No?"

"No, that would be giving him too much credit and her not enough," I admit. "I think you were right before. If she didn't want to stay, she wouldn't have eaten the seeds. But she did so because she wanted to."

I attempt to stand, but my big belly weighs me down.

"*Moró mou,*" Kostas says. "Let me help you." He sets Zoe down, who runs over to the fountain to dip her hand in the water.

As he helps pull me into a standing position, my stomach tightens, and I cringe slightly at the pain that shoots down my back. "I made Proserpina out to be the damsel in distress," I tell him. "The victim, but maybe she wasn't. Maybe she was just scared and he helped her come to the realization of what she already knew."

"And what's that?" Kostas asks, gripping the curve of my hips and leaning over to kiss my lips.

"That she was always meant to be loved by Pluto and to be the Queen of the Underworld."

I can imagine how she felt. When she met Pluto, there was no turning back. She fell for him the moment she laid eyes on him. He didn't have to drag her there, because she belonged there. She just needed to come home.

Another pain shoots down my back and then it feels as though I've peed myself. I glance down and liquid is dripping down my legs under my bathing suit.

"Talia, are you okay?" Kostas asks, his eyes widening in fear. It's not often I see my husband appear to be scared.

"Yeah." I nod with a smile. "But our baby is finally coming."

Kostas

Fuck. Fuck. Fuck.

Fuck. Fuck. Fuck.

Fuck. Fuck. Fuck.

"Stop saying fuck," Talia seethes, "or I will rip your tongue out of your mouth."

The doctor smirks at me from between her legs and I tense. Clearly I've been chanting the words that have been running inside my head from the moment she was put into this hospital bed. I wonder if she heard the other ones.

She's brave and resilient and strong.

The best mother in the world.

Beautiful beyond reason.

"A real Casanova, that one," the nurse says to Talia, winking.

I look down to find Talia's eyes watering. "I love you," she whimpers.

Leaning down, I kiss her plump lips. "I love you too. You're doing great."

"Oh shit," she whines. "I can't do this."

"You've done it before," I remind her.

"And her head wasn't as big as Nora's either!"

I can't help but grin at her. The moment we found out we were having another little girl, Talia asked if we could name her after my mother. It broke my heart and healed it all at once. Of course I said yes. My mother would be so fucking proud of me. She would've loved those girls with everything she had. Thankfully, we have Melody and she does the job of two grandmas at once.

"I see dark hair," the doctor says, his eyes crinkling with delight. "The baby is coming. Want to watch?"

I dart my eyes to Talia, who nods. I missed Zoe's birth, so seeing Nora's is a gift. Releasing Talia's hand, I shuffle down to the end of the bed.

"Holy shit," I utter, completely transfixed to see the head of my daughter trying to come through the small hole. "Talia, she's almost here."

"Another contraction," the nurse says. "That's it, honey, push and hold."

Talia bears down and the head begins to push out. When she can't push anymore, the dark hair disappears some. Another contraction hits right after the other and my incredible wife pushes harder. I'm awestruck by how strong she is—scrunched face in determination, purple flesh as she uses every ounce of strength she can muster, sweaty hair stuck to her forehead.

"There we go," the doctor says, drawing my attention back to our daughter.

Fuck. Fuck. Fuck.

Fuck. Fuck. Fuck.

"STOP SAYING FUCK!" Talia warns through gritted teeth.

I gape in part horror, part fascination as I stare at the head sticking out of my wife's body. A film of something covers her face and she's as purple as her mother. Birthing a baby is a fucking miraculous thing.

I gently caress Talia's thigh. "I can see her head, *moró mou*. She's so perfect."

Talia sobs but then she's pushing again. And again. And again. Until the baby seems to slide out of her body and into the doctor's waiting arms. Bloody and messy. Screaming at the top of her little lungs.

"Big baby girl," the doctor praises as he shuffles the squirming infant onto Talia's stomach. Blood is everywhere. The good kind of blood. The blood of miracles.

Talia's whole body trembles as she cries and admires our daughter.

"Want to cut the cord?"

I snap my eyes over to the doctor, who offers me a pair of scissors. Sure enough, the thick umbilical cord that's attached to our daughter needs removing. Will it hurt if I cut it? Can Talia feel it?

"Cut the cord, Kostas," Talia urges, her words no longer laced with violence. They're gentle and sweet and encouraging.

Frowning at the doctor, I shakily accept the scissors. "Are they going to feel it?"

"No, son, they're not going to feel it," he says, chuckling.

I've cut off limbs and eyeballs and every other body part imaginable.

So why the fuck do I feel like I'm going to pass out?

It's a cord. A tiny passage of nutrients our daughter no longer needs.

With bile rising in my throat and sweat coating my flesh, I start to snip through the cord. But it doesn't cut smooth and easy. I have to hack through the thick rope.

Fuck. Fuck. Fuck.

Fuck. Fuck. Fuck.

This time, Talia laughs.

"Baby ears are listening," she teases.

I manage to sever the cord, making Nora officially ours to take care of and protect. The weight of the responsibility nearly crushes me. But I've managed to do it with Talia and Zoe. What's one more?

As they continue to deliver the placenta, I abandon the scissors and opt not to watch that part. I may be a fucked-up mobster who's seen some shit, but I haven't seen that, nor do I fucking plan on it. No, I'd rather keep my eyes glued to our perfect daughter and her adoring mother.

"Zoe is going to be so proud," Talia tells me tearfully. "You think she's giving Uncle Fee hell?"

I snort. I hope so. Phoenix is a pussy-magnet player who's corrupted Adrian with his manwhore ways. When they're not working, they tear up the fucking town looking for women. I'm glad one little girl owns his heart. Now he'll have another one soon wrapped around his finger.

"I hope she tells him the names of all her stuffed animals," I say with a chuckle.

She has tons. Too many. Talia and I both have been the victims of her lengthy sessions of telling us the name of each and every one of them. If you interrupt, she starts over. If she forgets a name, she starts over. I've tortured many a men, but Zoe has invented a form of torture all on her own.

I'd say she got it from me, but that has Talia written all over it.

We admire her until they take her away to clean her up a bit and run some tests. Then, they hand our daughter back, bundled in a warm blanket.

"Want to hold her?" Talia asks, her smile serene.

I nod as I pick up the tiny thing. She weighs nothing. So light and fragile. As I pull her to my chest and cradle her, my eyes burn with emotion. I'll protect this little one like I do her sister and her mother. With everything I own until the day I die.

Nora scrunches her face and makes a crabby whining cry that has me chuckling. She's so damn cute. When I glance over at Talia, her bottom lip wobbles as tears streak down her cheeks.

"What's wrong?" I demand, alarmed at her crying.

She shakes her head. "Nothing, Kostas. Everything is right. Better than right. It's perfect."

I let out a relieved sigh and kiss my daughter's forehead. "I love you, *prinkípissa*." *Princess.*

"You're a good man," Talia mutters, reaching her hand out for me.

Taking it, I give it a squeeze. "Only for you."

Our eyes lock and a million emotions pass between us.

Talia and I are the earth, the sun, the stars, and everything in between. We're evil and good, wrapped in one complicated ball of love. She challenges me. I provoke her. Vases get broken and words get said. Sometimes we fight like hellions straight from the bowels of the Underworld.

But we love hardest of all.

Fully. Passionately. Dangerously.

Our love is violent and messy, destructive for those who dare near it. It slaughters and slays. Powerful and intimidating to those around it. Love between a Demetriou king and queen is chaotic like the tropical storms that often ravish our seaside properties. We're a pull of two forces of nature, only working when orbiting the other.

Fate drew us together—victims of a complicated history of our parents.

Love kept us there.

"What are you thinking about?" Talia asks, her blue eyes gleaming with adoration and utter loyalty.

"You. Always you."

The End

*****If you loved this duet, you'll love **Heath** also by K Webster and Nikki Ash!*****

authornikkiash.com/co-written-books-by-k-webster-and-nikki-ash/

playlist

Head Above Water by Avril Lavigne

Complicated by Avril Lavigne

I'm a Mess by Bebe Rexha

Broken-hearted Girl by Beyoncé

Reason to Stay by Brett Young

Never be the Same by Camila Cabello

Consequences by Camila Cabello

The Scientist by Coldplay

Let it Go by James Bay

In Case by Demi Lovato

i hate u, i love u by Gnash

Desire by Meg Myers

Stay by Rihanna

Back to You by Louis Tomlinson

Bad Things by Machine Gun Kelly and Camila Cabello

Love on the Brain by Rihanna

Rock Bottom by Hailee Steinfeld

The Monster by Eminem

So Good by Zara Larsson

Remind Me to Forget by Kygo & Miguel

Him & I by G-Eazy & Halsey

Bad Blood by Taylor Swift

Mad by Ne-Yo

I'm a Mess by Ed Sheeran

acknowledgements from
K WEBSTER

Thank you to my husband! Love you, honey!

Nikki Ash, thank you for creating magic yet again with me! I always have so much fun writing with you!! These characters hold a special place in my heart…right next to you!

A huge thank you to my Krazy for K Webster's Books reader group. You all are insanely supportive and I can't thank you enough.

A gigantic thank you to those who always help me out. Elizabeth Clinton, Ella Stewart, Misty Walker, Holly Sparks, Jillian Ruize, Gina Behrends, Rosa Saucedo, Ker Dukey, and Nikki Ash—you ladies are my rock!

Thank you so much to Misty Walker for being the best friend a girl could ask for! Love you!!

Thank you so much, Wendy Rinebold, for proofing this book! You're a star, lady!!

A big thank you to my author friends who have given me your friendship and your support. You have no idea how much that means to me.

Thank you to all of my blogger friends both big and small

that go above and beyond to always share my stuff. You all rock! #AllBlogsMatter

Emily A. Lawrence, thank you SO much for editing this book. You rock!!

Thank you, Stacey Blake, for being amazing as always when formatting my books and in general. I love you! I love you! I love you!

Lastly but certainly not least of all, thank you to all of the wonderful readers out there who are willing to hear my story and enjoy my characters like I do. It means the world to me!

acknowledgements from

NIKKI ASH

hank you to my children. Your love and support is everything. To Bret, thank you for being the peanut butter to my jelly. Kristi Webster, thank you for believing in me and in this story. You make me a better person and a better writer. Thank you for your friendship. Nikki Ash's Fight Club reader group. In this crazy world, you guys are my safe place. Thank you! Thank you to all of the ladies who have my back. Stacy Garcia, Ashley Cormier, Brittany Ridge, Andrea Hebda, Tabitha Willbanks, Shannon Voyles, Kaylee Ryan, Lisa McKay, and Kristi Webster. I can't imagine doing any of this without you. Emily A. Lawrence, thank you for editing this book. Stacy Blake, thank you for making the book so pretty! Ena and Amanda with Enticing Journey, thank you for keeping me sane! I don't know what I would do without you guys! To all of the bloggers who take time out of their day to share their love of books, thank you for everything you do. And a huge thank you to the readers. There are so many books out there for you to read. Thank you for opening your hearts and allowing my words to speak to you. It's because of you, I get to continue to do what I love.

about
K WEBSTER

K Webster is a *USA Today* Bestselling author. Her titles have claimed many bestseller tags in numerous categories, are translated in multiple languages, and have been adapted into audiobooks. She lives in "Tornado Alley" with her husband, two children, and her baby dog named Blue. When she's not writing, she's reading, drinking copious amounts of coffee, and researching aliens.

Keep up with K Webster

Facebook: www.facebook.com/authorkwebster

Blog: authorkwebster.wordpress.com

Twitter: twitter.com/KristiWebster

Email: kristi@authorkwebster.com

Goodreads: www.goodreads.com/user/show/10439773-k-webster

Instagram: instagram.com/kristiwebster

about
NIKKI ASH

Nikki Ash resides in South Florida where she is an English teacher by day and a writer by night. When she's not writing, you can find her with a book in her hand. From the Boxcar Children, to Wuthering Heights, to the latest single parent romance, she has lived and breathed every type of book. While reading and writing are her passions, her two children are her entire world. You can probably find them at a Disney park before you would find them at home on the weekends!

Reading is like breathing in, writing is like breathing out.– Pam Allyn

Contact Nikki Ash

Facebook: facebook.com/authornikkiash

Twitter: twitter.com/authornikkiash

Instagram: instagram.com/authornikkiash

Amazon: amazon.com/author/nikkiash

Website: www.authornikkiash.com

Nikki Ash's reader group:
www.facebook.com/groups/booksbynikkiash

Subscribe to Nikki Ash's newsletter:
bit.ly/NikkiAshNewsletter

books by
K WEBSTER

Psychological Romance Standalones:
My Torin
Whispers and the Roars
Cold Cole Heart
Blue Hill Blood

Romantic Suspense Standalones:
Dirty Ugly Toy
El Malo
Notice
Sweet Jayne
The Road Back to Us
Surviving Harley
Love and Law
Moth to a Flame
Erased

Extremely Forbidden Romance Standalones:
The Wild
Hale
Like Dragonflies

Taboo Treats:

Bad Bad Bad

Coach Long

Ex-Rated Attraction

Mr. Blakely

Easton

Crybaby

Lawn Boys

Malfeasance

Renner's Rules

The Glue

Dane

Enzo

Red Hot Winter

Dr. Dan

KKinky Reads Collection:

Share Me

Choke Me

Daddy Me

Watch Me

Hurt Me

Contemporary Romance Standalones:

Wicked Lies Boys Tell

Conheartists

The Day She Cried

Untimely You

Heath

Sundays are for Hangovers

A Merry Christmas with Judy

Zeke's Eden

Schooled by a Senior
Give Me Yesterday
Sunshine and the Stalker
Bidding for Keeps
B-Sides and Rarities

Paranormal Romance Standalones:
Apartment 2B
Running Free
Mad Sea
Cold Queen

War & Peace Series:
This is War, Baby (Book 1)
This is Love, Baby (Book 2)
This Isn't Over, Baby (Book 3)
This Isn't You, Baby (Book 4)
This is Me, Baby (Book 5)
This Isn't Fair, Baby (Book 6)
This is the End, Baby (Book 7 – a novella)

Lost Planet Series:
The Forgotten Commander (Book 1)
The Vanished Specialist (Book 2)
The Mad Lieutenant (Book 3)
The Uncertain Scientist (Book 4)
The Lonely Orphan (Book 5)

2 Lovers Series:
Text 2 Lovers (Book 1)
Hate 2 Lovers (Book 2)
Thieves 2 Lovers (Book 3)

Pretty Little Dolls Series:
Pretty Stolen Dolls (Book 1)
Pretty Lost Dolls (Book 2)
Pretty New Doll (Book 3)
Pretty Broken Dolls (Book 4)

The V Games Series:
Vlad (Book 1)
Ven (Book 2)
Vas (Book 3)

Four Fathers Books:
Pearson

Four Sons Books:
Camden
Elite Seven Books:
Gluttony
Greed

Not Safe for Zon Books:
The Wild
Hale
Bad Bad Bad
This is War, Baby
Like Dragonflies

books by
NIKKI ASH

All books can be read as standalones

The Fighting Series
Fighting for a Second Chance (Secret baby)
Fighting with Faith (Secret baby)
Fighting for Your Touch
Fighting for Your Love (Single mom)
Fighting 'round the Christmas Tree: A Fighting Series Novel

Fighting Love Series
Tapping Out (Secret baby)
Clinched (Single dad)
Takedown (Single mom)

Imperfect Love Series
The Pickup (Secret baby)
Going Deep (Enemies to Lovers)
On the Surface (Second chance, single dad)

Stand-alone Novels
Bordello (Mob romance)
Knocked Down (Single dad)
Unbroken Promises (Friends to lovers)
Through His Eyes (Single mom, age gap)
Clutch Player

Co-written novels
Heath (Modern telling)
Hidden Truths
Stolen Lies

www.ingramcontent.com/pod-product-compliance
Lightning Source LLC
Chambersburg PA
CBHW060300310726
48976CB00007B/2150